Praise for Maya Linnell a

'Whenever I pick up a Linnell novel, I know a purely blissful read lies ahead. She excels at delivering warm-hearted, escapist stories, all set against a gorgeous country backdrop. If you're looking for some much-needed time to yourself, pick up *Paperbark Hill*, and fall into the world of the McIntyre sisters.' Better Reading

'*Paperbark Hill* has done a wonderful job of providing that final chapter of the McIntyre family story, with all the same warmth and heart and authenticity Maya has written into each of the other three books.' Bookish Bron

'A wonderfully rich, feel-good read. I just loved it and I know you will too.' Jodi Gibson, Books & Bakes blog

'Full of warmth, humour and genuine heart, just like eating scones fresh from the oven.' ABC Wide Bay

Praise for Maya Linnell and *Magpie's Bend*

Shortlisted for Favourite Australian Romance Author, Favourite Australian-set Romance and Favourite Contemporary Romance in the Australian Romance Readers Awards 2021

'Immersing yourself in the country characters and spirit of Bridgefield is a delight. Just the thing to while away some summer hours.' CWA *Ruth* Magazine, Qld

'We need to petition Netflix as I would love to see these books come to life on our screens, beautiful stories that showcase rural life in Australia . . . highly recommend!' Jodie, Beauty and Lace

'So many moments throughout the book that I caught myself smiling, it definitely was a story that had all the feels and left me with a full heart!' @KateTheBookLover

'Linnell's writing is authentic and enticing, you can almost smell the cakes baking, hear the magpies warbling at sunrise and feel the camaraderie of the community's spirit.' Linda B, Goodreads

Praise for Maya Linnell and *Bottlebrush Creek*

New Idea Book of the Month, June 2020
Sunday Age #3 Bestselling Romance, June 2020
Top 10 Aus Fiction Bestseller, June 2020
Weekend Australian #4 Bestselling Romance, July 2020
Shortlisted for Favourite Australian-set Romance in the Australian Romance Readers Association Awards, 2020

'Maya Linnell's new novel *Bottlebrush Creek* is a brilliant follow-up to her debut best-selling *Wildflower Ridge*. I could have stayed within the pages of Angie and Rob's story forever!' Talking Aussie Books Podcast

'Two big thumbs up for an authentic Aussie story.' Mercedes Maguire, *Daily Telegraph*

'Loved this book . . . such a delight from beginning to end.' Emma Babbington, *New Idea*

'Charming and enjoyable . . . fans of Maya's first novel will keenly enjoy this latest outing.' *Canberra Weekly*

Praise for Maya Linnell and *Wildflower Ridge*

Shortlisted for Favourite Australian Romance Author, Favourite Debut Romance Author and Favourite Small Town Romance in the Australian Romance Readers Awards 2019

'My favourite romance of 2019. A masterful and moving tale . . . her writing is flawless and very believable. Can't wait to see what's next!' Michelle Beesley, SHE Society

'*Wildflower Ridge* is a really wonderful place to start your Australian rural romance journey . . . told with plenty of heart and lashings of authenticity.' Mrs B's Book Reviews

'Very authentic rural flavour, a surprise fast-paced ending, shows you can't deny what's in your heart.' Australian Romance Readers Association

'Five stars—a great addition to the rural family fiction with a dash of romance, a sophisticated plot, very convincing characters . . . a book you can't pass up.' Happy Valley Books

MAYA LINNELL

Kookaburra Cottage

ALLEN&UNWIN
SYDNEY·MELBOURNE·AUCKLAND·LONDON

First published in 2023

Copyright © Maya Linnell 2023

All rights reserved. No part of this book may be reproduced or transmitted in any form or by any means, electronic or mechanical, including photocopying, recording or by any information storage and retrieval system, without prior permission in writing from the publisher. The Australian *Copyright Act 1968* (the Act) allows a maximum of one chapter or 10 per cent of this book, whichever is the greater, to be photocopied by any educational institution for its educational purposes provided that the educational institution (or body that administers it) has given a remuneration notice to the Copyright Agency (Australia) under the Act.

Allen & Unwin
Cammeraygal Country
83 Alexander Street
Crows Nest NSW 2065
Australia
Phone: (61 2) 8425 0100
Email: info@allenandunwin.com
Web: www.allenandunwin.com

Allen & Unwin acknowledges the Traditional Owners of the Country on which we live and work. We pay our respects to all Aboriginal and Torres Strait Islander Elders, past and present.

A catalogue record for this book is available from the National Library of Australia

ISBN 978 1 76087 970 9

Set in 12/16.5 pt Sabon LT Pro by Midland Typesetters, Australia
Printed and bound in Australia by the Opus Group

10 9 8 7 6 5 4 3 2 1

The paper in this book is FSC® certified. FSC® promotes environmentally responsible, socially beneficial and economically viable management of the world's forests.

Bestselling rural fiction author Maya Linnell gathers inspiration from her rural upbringing and the small communities she has always lived in and loved. *Kookaburra Cottage* is her fifth novel, following *Paperbark Hill*, *Magpie's Bend*, *Bottlebrush Creek* and *Wildflower Ridge*. A former country journalist and radio host, Maya also blogs for Romance Writers Australia, loves baking up a storm, tending to her rambling garden and raising three bookworms. She writes to a soundtrack of magpies and chickens on a small property in country Victoria, where she lives with her family, their menagerie of farm animals and the odd tiger snake or two. For a regular slice of country living, sign up to Maya's quarterly newsletter at mayalinnell.com or follow her on social media.

@maya.linnell.writes

*Dedicated to Amelia and Elizabeth,
for the title, brainstorming sessions and
insisting on tortoises in the story.
This one's for you*

1

The winery car park was swirling with rubbish when April Lacey pulled up on a blustery summer's day, and she groaned, wondering how many early-morning tourists had driven into Lacewing Estate, taken one look around the tired, litter-strewn entrance and headed straight back out.

Tugging on the handbrake, she jumped down from her Hilux ute and reinstated the fallen sandwich board before chasing after the windblown litter.

A gust of terra rossa soil followed April inside, settling on the polished concrete floor.

'What a gale,' said Fran Lacey, emerging from the barrel room. 'Strong enough to blow the milk from a teacup. Thought you'd be halfway to Adelaide by now.' Fran plucked a navy-and-orange brochure from the pile April had brought in, casting an appraising eye over the gold embossing and thick card.

Even covered in dust, next door's brochures looked expensive.

'I should be,' April said, 'but the builder had a cancellation. By the way, I found the yard plastered with Winklin Wines promotions. I'll send them home with Archie when he comes over next week.'

Fran glanced out the window to the neighbouring vineyard. 'That little boy needs friends his own age, just like a certain someone else I know. A ten-year-old should be surrounded by nose-picking, bug-hunting, trouble-making little boys, not someone almost two decades his senior.'

April shook her head with a grin and kissed her stepmother on the cheek. 'Love you too, Franny.'

'Good luck with the builder,' Fran called, dusting the wine bottles. 'And make sure you lock your doors when you hit Glen Osmond Road. More car jackings on the news last week.'

April waved goodbye and stepped back out into the warm morning. She walked towards the dilapidated stables in the middle of the shiraz and chardonnay vines, just a few hundred metres from her home. A Commodore ute towing a trailer was parked alongside the stone building, and when she got closer, April saw the builder was still sitting in the car, phone to his ear.

Tradesmen were thin on the ground in the rural South Australian town of Penwarra and she was grateful the builder had called her when he'd had a cancellation, even if it meant a later departure for the city.

It'll be well worth it, she told herself, waving off the builder's apologetic 'be there in a minute' gesture.

April checked her own phone, wondering where Justin was. There had been no reply to her message this morning. *Another winemaking dilemma?*

Or maybe he'd assumed this builder would take one look at the old stables before laughing in her face, like the last tradesman she'd requested a quote from.

Shrugging off the memory, she pulled open the double doors. The hinges shuddered under the weight of the aged oak, and April's eyes took a moment to adjust to the dim space.

Although it had been decades since the last tenants lived there, the earthy aromas of the Clydesdales that had carted grapes from the vineyard to the winery still lingered in the air, along with a faint hint of straw and the rich leathery smell of saddlery. These days, the stables were a jumble of stored clutter. *Not for long*, thought April.

Dust from the rough and ready paddock-rock walls rained down on her navy linen dress. Not bothering to brush it off, April reached for the light switch, then turned when a low whistle came from behind her. The builder crossed his arms, his experienced eye assessing the structure.

'You know it'd be cheaper to build something completely new rather than renovating this old hut, right?'

'Have you been talking to my boyfriend?' April laughed, given the small town and the many links between the nearby communities, it wasn't out of the question.

The builder shook his head. 'Just telling it how it is,' he said, before introducing himself as Gordon Whitty. 'A small space like this might seem easy, but working with materials this old . . .' He trailed off, noticing the hopeful look on her face. 'I'm not saying it can't be done, but even if you're keen to help out, it won't be a cheap exercise.'

Not a screaming endorsement, but not a flat-out refusal either. Looking around at the dirt floor, dilapidated roof and cobwebs, April felt a thrill of excitement—despite the challenges, she knew these old stables could be the bed and breakfast she'd always envisaged.

Gordon pulled a metal ruler from his pocket and gently scratched at the mortar holding the stones together. The lime and sand mix yielded easily, sending a sprinkling of grit to the ground.

'Truth be told, I'm surprised the council and heritage team approved it. You'll want a structural report, an energy assessment, a new floor and depending on the quality of those timbers, the whole roof might need replacing. And that's before you can even start working on an ensuite or that loft you mentioned.' He continued to rattle off the jobs one by one until he'd run out of fingers.

'I've already got the plans drawn up and those things taken care of,' said April, unable to keep the enthusiasm from her voice. 'The paperwork side of it was pretty lengthy but I've been saving and planning this for years. I've just got to find someone brave enough to take it on.'

'Or crazy enough,' came a droll laugh from outside. April looked over the builder's shoulder to see Justin Magill in the doorway, his hair like a cockatoo's crest in the wind, dimples flashing and a smile that softened his words. The breeze picked up, and a small cloud of dust seeped through a crumbling mortar line in what April hoped would become the mezzanine bedroom.

'There you are.' She introduced the builder to her boyfriend. 'Hopefully Gordon here sees it as a challenge, not a folly.'

The builder looked between them, perhaps noticing the way she said 'folly', and held up his hands. 'None of my business either way; if you're willing to pay for the work, I think I can shuffle it in between a few other projects.'

April beamed as Gordon quizzed her about the project and discussed the timeline. She had barely let herself hope they'd find a builder willing to give the old building a chance.

Ten minutes later, when Gordon had left, and April had kissed Justin goodbye, she pulled onto the Riddoch Highway and set the cruise control to 110 kilometres per hour. Although it was still early, heat was already shimmering off the asphalt. She'd only just got up to speed when her father's number appeared on the touchscreen display.

'I've already locked my car doors, Dad,' she said, pre-empting a repeat of Fran's warning.

Lloyd Lacey chuckled. From the sound of the wind whistling against the phone, she guessed he was outside, assessing his grapes.

'Righto!' said Lloyd. 'Keep your hair on, we're only looking out for you, you know. Fran said you finally had a builder turn up. No wonder Justin was late. Is the builder any good?'

April let the comment about Justin pass, knowing it wasn't wise to add more fuel to that particular fire—not with vintage looming and the hot summer creating an extra level of stress for the winery staff.

'Gordon seems great, Dad,' April said, checking her rear-view mirror. She cranked the air conditioner a little higher. 'With a bit of luck, we'll have the bed and breakfast ready for the first guests in spring.'

Leafy green vines whizzed past on either side as April drove out of Penwarra and allowed herself the pleasure of imagining her bed and breakfast in its finished state, with striped curtains fluttering in the windows, flowers on the dining table, sumptuous French linen on the bed and glowing reviews from honeymooners whose married lives had started at the converted stables in the vines. It was only when the Adelaide skyline came into view that she wondered why her father had told her that Justin was late. *Wasn't he up to his eyeballs in winery stuff*, with *her dad? Where had he been this morning if not at the winery?* She shook the thought away, blaming the heat and the ad hoc appointment with Gordon for the misunderstanding.

Connor Jamison rummaged around in his suitcase for his sunglasses. They had never seen the light of day in England, but were now an essential frontline defence against the dazzling Australian sunshine.

He smoothed down his white-blond hair in the hotel's bathroom mirror, tucked a paper map into his back pocket and stowed his sunnies inside his suit jacket, right next to his wallet. He was about to shut down his laptop so he could lock it in the safe when the Zoom ringtone sounded.

Connor accepted the call and his sister Heidi appeared on the screen. 'Even with jetlag, you scrub up well.' Her incredulous tone made him grin; she'd seen him decked out in his finest for concerts, weddings and funerals umpteen times before. 'And that sunshine streaming in through your window!' Her breath fogged the air. 'I'd sell a kidney for just a fraction of it.'

'I've barely defrosted,' he replied. 'Though with this Aussie weather, it shouldn't take long,' he said, eyeing the knitted cap pulled low over Heidi's brows, her red fingerless gloves and the bright woollen scarf wrapped around her neck. 'Is it snowing at home yet?'

Heidi shook her head. 'Trying to, but all we've seen so far is sleet. Enough about our miserable British weather though, how was your fancy event? Met your new boss yet?'

Connor shook his head, glancing at the hotel's digital alarm clock. 'It's tonight, I'm just heading off now. The rest of the winemakers are meeting for drinks beforehand—a bit of Dutch courage before we stride into a room full of Australian icons.'

'They're no better than any of you lot,' said Heidi, her eyes flashing. He wasn't sure if it was from sisterly pride, or simply because she was patriotic, but it was touching all the same. 'You might end up teaching *them* a thing or two about vineyards and vintages.'

'That's not quite how this program works,' Connor reminded her. 'We're here to learn from the experts.'

A knock sounded on his door and Connor stood.

'Have a great night, Con, and make sure you call Mam and Dad when you get back tonight, they're itching for updates. They still worry, you know.'

Connor brushed off her concern with a quick farewell. He knew she meant well—all his family did—but ever since the accident their concern had at times felt suffocating.

The knock came again, along with a cheerful hurry up. 'C'mon, lad. Adventure awaits!'

Recognising the Scottish brogue of Fergus, one of the winemakers who'd caught the same flight from Manchester, Connor stowed his laptop in the safe and stepped out to meet him.

The conference venue wasn't far from the hotel, and the sunshine was warm enough that most of the young winemakers, who'd travelled from the northern hemisphere winter just days earlier, carried their suit jackets over their forearms.

'This is when the fun starts,' Fergus said, looking left and right at all the people, as if he were entering a ballroom of royalty instead of a conference room full of the nation's top winemakers.

Anticipation bubbled in Connor's stomach. He'd applied to be part of this international program several times over the years and now that he was finally here, he was both nervous and exhilarated. But would it be the fresh beginning he'd been so desperate for?

When the waiter sashayed past with a tray of champagne flutes, April grabbed two glasses, quickly downing the first as she surveyed the conference room. Yesterday had been a long day, with the four-hour drive to Adelaide blowing out to over five hours thanks to roadworks in Tailem Bend and an accident requiring a detour through Murray Bridge. She'd missed the first workshop, but made up for yesterday's late start by arriving early this morning and sitting up the front of each session, taking notes and photographing the most pertinent presentation slides.

Setting her empty glass down on a wine barrel, April picked up a program, scanning the information about the international winemakers' exchange.

As if on cue, a group of newcomers emerged through the big double doors on the far side of the room.

Even if one of them hadn't been wearing a kilt, she would have known immediately they were the international newbies. They moved as a pack towards the wine bar, and one of them pulled a phone out and snapped a selfie beside the distinctive kangaroo logo on the banners for the DestinationSA Program. The program was synonymous with the food and wine tourism industry, and a key reason April had chosen to attend the city function.

'They look happy to be here, don't they?'

She turned at the sound of an amused voice, surprised to discover that while she'd been watching the new arrivals, someone had been watching her. A lady with an off-the-shoulder gown nodded in the direction of the bar. 'I always like seeing fresh faces in the industry, and this program with the UK winemakers and viticulturalists is a win for everyone, don't you think?'

April recognised the woman instantly.

How's this for good luck? she marvelled, introducing herself to Stephanie Scouller. 'I've just finished your audiobook on winery marketing,' April said, trying not to gush. 'It felt like you were talking directly to me the whole drive to Adelaide yesterday. If I hadn't been running late, I would have pulled over several times to take notes. No wonder it won you so many awards.'

Stephanie inclined her head modestly, though she was clearly pleased, and fixed April with a broad smile. 'Glad you got so much out of it. After all those years in the industry, I wanted to help others wade through the marketing and branding jungle without bankrupting their wineries. It's a tough market for small wineries, every employee wears multiple hats, every dollar counts.'

'You're not wrong, there.' Grateful for the low lighting inside the conference room, April toyed with a loose thread on her pink lace dress—it had looked so elegant on the Penwarra charity shop mannequin, but on closer inspection it had a few faults in the lacework—then added brightly, 'I hope you've brought boxes of books with you, I'm sure there'll be a queue at the signing table after your keynote speech.' She didn't mention that Stephanie's name on the conference program, along with the DestinationSA workshop, had sealed the deal for April's city trip.

'I've booked a one-on-one session with you tonight.' April rummaged in her handbag, grabbed a business card and passed it to Stephanie. Like her dress, the business card was a little tired around the edges. 'Hopefully you can steer me in the right direction for grants and marketing opportunities. I'd love to get involved in the DestinationSA program, but I don't even know where to start.'

Stephanie stowed the business card in her leather purse with a nod. 'That's what I'm here for,' she said. 'That food tourism program has been the making of so many of my clients. Once you're on their books, you'll see a huge upswing in visitors and promotion. If you want to chat leadership opportunities and rebranding, we can look at that too. Loads of potential for keen young winemakers and vitties looking to make their mark on the industry. Tell me, have you applied for the young wine leaders' award?'

April looked up from under her fringe, feeling suddenly shy. On paper, she was probably the perfect fit for the young wine leaders' award: she just scraped into the under thirty age bracket and she was from a winemaking family . . .

April drained her second glass of bubbly, searching for an explanation that didn't sound like a cop-out. 'I'm just a horticulturalist, not a winemaker. My folks run a small winery and I mostly work off-farm, but I'm hoping to open a little B & B on the property and I've got some great ideas in the pipeline . . .'

April trailed off, wishing she hadn't mentioned the DestinationSA program. There was so much to do before they could even think about applying and she didn't have a firm plan in place yet. *Justin's right, I shouldn't try to run before I can even walk.*

April ran a hand over her wavy hair and deflected Stephanie's attention back to the group of newcomers. 'I wonder how many of those international crew are coming down to the Limestone Coast? We're always struggling for workers in our region.'

Stephanie picked up her glass of wine and gestured towards the bar. 'Let's go find out.'

The buzzing room, the enthusiasm of his fellow ex-pats and the free-flowing wine were the perfect ingredients for a good night. The minute the formalities were over, Connor's new friends grabbed their jackets and handbags.

'We've paid our dues for the evening; waddled onto that

stage like a bunch of penguins and made small talk with the hobnobs sponsoring the program,' said Fergus, rising from his chair so fast his kilt nearly flicked up. 'Let's cut loose.'

Connor looked around the function room, then back at the program. 'According to last week's email, I think we're supposed to stay and network.'

Fergus grinned, tucking his scruffy ginger hair behind his ears. 'You're off to Rossvale in a few days, I'm heading to a winery four hours south of here and the rest of the group will be scattered across the state. We'll have more fun making our own after-party, don't you think? Hindley Street beckons.'

Connor laughed. He'd read enough TripAdvisor reviews to know Hindley Street was where you went if you were looking for trouble. 'I think I'll stick around,' he said, scanning the room. 'Apparently there's a marketing and tourism team here, offering free mini-consultations after the event.'

'Suit yourself,' Fergus shrugged. 'I'm off the clock for the night. Catch us up later, when you're done brown-nosing!' He jogged off to join the rest of the group, leaving Connor alone at the table. Connor pulled out the conference timetable, reread the spiel that had caught his eye earlier, and went in search of the team from DestinationSA. If their collaborations between small wineries, catering teams and corporate clients were as successful as their website promised, he wanted to find out more.

He headed towards a group of people carrying clipboards and pens. Connor couldn't see a formal line, but a petite, dark-haired woman in a pink dress was deep in discussion with the clipboard-wielding officials, so he hung back, letting the Australian accents in the room wash over him.

Connor's ears pricked up as he eavesdropped on her conversation. He gathered she was keen on boutique accommodation; *Smart*, he thought. The Kiwi winery he'd worked for had diversified with luxury guesthouses and glamping tents to great success.

A waitress walked past slowly, her eyes darting down at her tray as if she were holding a live grenade. Connor wasn't sure if it was her braids or her frown of concentration, but she reminded him of his littlest sister, Pippin, and even though he wasn't particularly thirsty, Connor held up his hand.

'I'll grab a water please,' he said.

She looked at him gratefully. 'The quicker I get rid of this load the better. It's only dumb luck I haven't dropped a tray already.'

'First night waitressing?'

She nodded, then gasped as the glasses wobbled.

'It gets easier,' Connor said, giving her an encouraging smile. 'Just make sure you keep the tray balanced.'

Connor turned to see the conversation wrapping up in front of him.

'That's great, I really appreciate your help,' the pretty brunette said, shaking their hands. Connor caught his breath when she turned her sunny smile on him. Her eyes were almost hidden beneath a dark, heavy fringe, but he could see they were sparkling with excitement.

'Sorry to hold up the queue, my appointment evaporated into thin air. So many good ideas!'

Connor smiled back at her, noticing how her rose-coloured lipstick matched her dress. 'Don't rush off on my behalf.'

'They'll probably start charging me if I stay any longer,' she whispered with a grin. 'And I've studied their website enough to know they're well out of my budget. Mind you, I'm not above loitering and eavesdropping on the other conversations. Too cheeky, do you think?'

He admired her pluck. 'May as well make the most of the opportunity.'

Connor was just stepping across to introduce himself when an unmistakable tinkling of glass and then a string of swear words came from behind them. He turned to see a tumble of glasses smashing on impact, the young waitress looking ashen, and a red-faced bloke with wine dripping down his trouser leg.

Connor started towards them, followed by the brunette he'd been speaking with.

'What a mess,' Connor said. 'That poor waitress.'

'Of course it had to be Dan. He's got two left feet and the worst butterfingers in the district,' the woman said.

'You know him?'

She nodded. 'My neighbour. Daniel Winklin.'

Connor took his jacket off and, averting his eyes, handed it to the panicked waitress. 'You might need this,' he said gently. The young lady looked down, shocked to see her white shirt was drenched. She clutched his jacket to her chest.

'He knocked the tray, I swear it wasn't my fault,' she said, tears carrying the mascara down her cheeks in murky black streaks.

Connor shook his head. 'You won't be the last person to drop a tray of glasses, trust me.' A steady stream of business cards fluttered from his jacket pocket, landing in the puddle of wine.

'Oh look, now I've gone and wrecked your things too,' the waitress sobbed, fishing out a soggy business card. 'I can't get anything right.'

'It's fine.' Connor kneeled down and began collecting the largest shards of glass. 'They're out of date anyway; my UK phone number won't work out here. I'd forgotten they were in there.'

'You teach music?'

Connor looked up to see the brunette in the pink dress examining a dripping card. With the cute dress, broad accent and dark eyes that crinkled with happiness, she was a sight to behold.

'I teach piano, but only when I'm not making wine,' he said, glancing away. If all Australian women were this attractive, he was going to be in deep trouble.

2

April had always known Dan Winklin was clumsy—growing up together, their teachers had kept boxes of Bandaids in their top drawers especially for him—but after his outburst drew the attention of everyone in the room, she could tell he'd had a little too much to drink.

As far as she could see, the pair of them were the only Limestone Coast representatives there, and while Winklin Wines might have enough money to weather a bit of bad press, Lacewing Estate didn't have that luxury. After the worst of the broken glass had been cleared up, she gently pulled her friend and neighbour aside.

'Can't take you anywhere, Winklin,' she said, looking over her shoulder. The British chap was reassuring the young waitress, and other staff had arrived with buckets and mops. 'What's going on?'

Daniel wasn't much taller than April's five foot three inches, and he was only a month or so older, but his shoulders sank at her question, making him seem even shorter and more world-weary than his twenty-nine years.

'Andre dumped me.' Even though Daniel's head was lowered, April noticed he was fighting back tears. She rubbed his arm awkwardly, not sure where to start. While Daniel had doted on the French winemaker from the moment he arrived in town, she'd never warmed to Andre's haughty arrogance.

'I thought you guys were patching things up?'

'I thought so too,' Daniel sighed. 'But apparently our versions of fidelity are quite different. He was packing his bags to leave when I woke up this morning. Starting a new life in Tassie with his new lover, apparently.'

April winced, ready to suggest taking the conversation to a quiet corner when he straightened up and hailed a passing waiter. 'Which is the perfect reason to get rollicking drunk, I say! Better than sitting at home crying into my teacup.' He scooped two glasses from the waiter, keeping hold of them both. 'What about you? Tell me about your accommodation project. Any progress?'

April updated him on her meeting with the builder. 'I've had a couple of great sessions on marketing pillars and wine tourism today too,' she added. 'So with a bit of luck, the bulk of the building work will be finished by late winter, our marketing plan will be firmed up in the next few months and we'll be taking bookings for late spring, early summer.'

Daniel raised an eyebrow. 'And does the charming Justin still think it's a folly? Tell me you're not going to be the one baking fresh bread and making picnic baskets for your guests?'

Unlike Justin, cooking wasn't April's strong suit and Daniel knew it. 'I don't want to give anyone food poisoning. Of course he's on board; I'll do the gardens, and once he's finished with vintage, he'll magic up a menu of hampers using local produce. It'll be great.'

April remembered the Winklin Wines brochures cartwheeling through the car park. 'Which reminds me, I rescued a bunch of your new flyers from the wind yesterday. They look great, really sharp.'

'Oh, those,' said Daniel, dabbing at a cabernet-coloured stain on his shirt. 'There's a typo on the second page, just toss them straight in the bin. Dad nearly had a coronary when he heard I'd signed off on the proofs with a single 's' in dessert wine.' Daniel gave a sheepish shrug. 'What's a few grand in the scheme of things, right?'

A few grand . . .? April wished she had that type of money to burn.

The handsome Brit stepped in beside her, and when she caught his eye, she sensed he was also holding his tongue. Even converted to Euros, the printing slip-up would probably fund a cross-hemisphere airfare.

'Dan Winklin, Winklin Wines.' Daniel stretched out a hand to introduce himself.

'Connor Jamison.'

April introduced herself too, warming to his quiet confidence and enthusiasm to learn from Australian wineries.

'I've heard of Penwarra. Best shiraz in the state, yeah?' Connor said.

Daniel visibly pulled himself together, his maudlin musings about his break-up forgotten as he bombarded Connor with facts and figures about the grape varieties they grew, ageing periods and workforce issues.

Connor stood between them, quietly sipping his wine and nodding at the right moments while Daniel rabbited on.

April heard one of Fran's sayings in her ears, unbidden. *Handsome is as handsome does.* An apricot gown drifted through her peripheral vision, prompting April to remember why she was there and stop her imagination from wandering.

'I've just got to catch someone,' she said, shooting Daniel and Connor an apologetic look. Even though she'd already suspected Andre the French winemaker was a cheating scoundrel, she'd be able to give Daniel her full attention and sympathy when they were home. She turned and headed in pursuit of Stephanie Scouller. There hadn't been time to chat for long after Stephanie's keynote speech, not with so many fans also queuing to get their books signed, but this wine tourism and marketing conference only came around once a year and she needed to make the most of this opportunity, for Lacewing Estate as well as her new bed and breakfast.

April picked up her pace.

Connor pocketed the Winklin Wines business card, wished Daniel all the best and made his way through the crowd and outside. He saw April sitting on a bench by the entrance and made his way over.

He wasn't sure what she'd hoped to glean from the conference, but he found himself hoping it had been worthwhile for her.

'Did you catch the person you were after?'

April lifted a shoulder in a shrug. 'She had checked out for the night, I should have made my move earlier. Then, to add insult to injury, the team offering free wine-related marketing advice waltzed out with their clipboards and banners. Just when I'd thought up a dozen more marketing questions.'

She sighed, leaning her elbows on her knees, then resting her chin on her hands.

'I don't think they were planning on doing overtime tonight,' Connor said gently, taking a seat beside her. 'The minute the clock struck 11, they capped their pens and headed for the hills.'

She twisted to meet his gaze, and along with a 'I know you're trying to cheer me up' look, there was something else too.

'Can I buy you a drink? I'm no expert on B & Bs, but I can share what I've seen in the UK, New Zealand and French wineries I've worked at.'

'I've just ordered a taxi,' she said, straightening up again. As much as she tried to hide it, the flash of reluctance in her eyes indicated she was momentarily torn between calling it a night and changing tack in pursuit of marketing titbits.

'Nightclubbing? I hear Adelaide's pumping on a Friday night.'

'You're welcome to it,' she said with a smirk. 'I'd rather drink a case of cheap white wine than set foot in one of those sleazy sweat factories.'

'What?' Connor acted shocked. 'How can you not love bad music, body odour and cheesy pick up lines? Though it does depend on the wine, I suppose. How cheap are we talking?'

Their conversation moved from the worst wine they'd tasted, to the sleaziest night clubs they'd visited, and Connor found himself laughing as she described a dive from her uni days. It was the first time he'd felt a spark since Phoebe.

Connor pushed away the thought, not wanting the past to cloud the present. He snuck another look at April, trying to get a better read on her, when the phone lit up in her hand, and just like that, a mask fell over her face. 'Anyway, I've got an early start tomorrow morning.'

Dozens of people milled around, waiting for Ubers and taxis. 'You might be waiting a while,' he said. 'Which direction's your hotel in? It's a nice night for walking.'

April quickly shook her head, her gaze darting down the well-lit street. 'Have you read the front page of the

Advertiser recently? Walking around the city at night is not for the fainthearted.'

He laughed. What would she make of the London crime stats? The stories his sister Heidi shared from her shifts on the beat were full of opportunistic crimes.

'Don't let me hold you up, though,' April added. 'I'm happy to wait, the taxi shouldn't be too far away.'

As she lifted her phone, he spotted a photo of a shaggy golden retriever grinning at the camera.

Connor uncrossed his legs and leaned across to get a better look at the phone screen. 'I'm in no hurry. Nice dog. Retriever?'

She turned, her hair tickling his cheek and her warm eyes crinkling at the sides as she nodded. 'Mishka's our winery mascot and chief troublemaker.' April enlarged a photo of the dog lounging on a timber deck beside a fire pit, with fairy lights and fruit-laden vines dangling from a pergola. 'Thinks she's the lady of the manor.'

'We had a retriever when I was a kid,' Connor said, smiling as he remembered the placid pooch. 'Duke was soft as butter but he was gentle and loyal, and didn't mind when my sisters dressed him up in ridiculous Halloween outfits.'

'Duke? As in Marmaduke?'

'As in Duke Ellington,' he clarified. 'The—'

'Jazz player,' April finished, giving him an appraising look. 'That's right, you're a piano guy.'

He sensed he'd just jumped a few bars in her estimation, and although he couldn't take credit for his musical family, he was happy to see her guard drop a little.

'I'm more of a Nina Simone and Billie Holiday fan myself, but I don't mind a little Duke. Louis Armstrong and Charlie Parker are on my playlists every now and then, too.'

'So which region are you destined for? Barossa, Clare, McLaren Vale?'

Connor gave her the name of the Rossvale winery, one of the most prestigious in the state.

'I've heard stories about their chief winemaker. Wait till you see this,' she said, rifling through her phone's photo library. 'Now, where did I save it?'

April held up her phone for both of them to see as she scrolled and he caught a whiff of sweet, musky perfume.

Between the screenshots of website pages, close-ups of grapes and panoramic vineyard shots, there were dozens of photos of her dog and more than a few of vegetables.

A market gardener, perhaps? He wanted to ask her about her vegetables, to see if they were a profession or a passion, but the moment disappeared when he saw a photo of her hanging off another bloke's arm. Although there was no ring on her finger, the photo explained her reluctance to go out for drinks.

She found the image she was after and enlarged it.

'One of my uni mates snapped this photo last vintage. The winemaker, Johann Riverton, rolls out a swag in the middle of the vineyards and sleeps there when they're waiting on ripening,' April said, chuckling. 'He sets his alarm hourly so he knows the moment the grapes are ready to harvest.'

'I'd heard he was a hard task-master but . . .' Connor gave a low whistle. Still, if camping out in the vineyard was what it took to make award-winning wines, he was prepared to give it a go. 'Well, I guess I didn't come all the way to Australia to twiddle my thumbs.'

April put her phone away as a convoy of taxis pulled up outside the conference centre. He looked at his watch, surprised to see it was past midnight already. It had been a long time since he'd lost an hour talking about dogs and wineries and jazz, and even though he now suspected she was off limits, he was still disappointed.

'I think that's mine,' April said, pointing as a taxi with distinctive branding pulled in. 'Thanks for keeping me company; it was nice getting to know you, Connor Jamison.'

Connor opened the cab door and bade her farewell, but before he could close it, he heard his and April's name being called.

Spinning on his heel, Connor saw Daniel Winklin, the drunk chap from earlier, waving from the top of the stairs.

'Dan?' April scrambled out of the cab. 'Hold the taxi a minute, please.'

They made it to the bottom of the stairs just as Daniel lost his balance and pitched forwards, stumbling down a few steps before finally catching the metal handrail. They let out a collective breath, but from Daniel's moan, it was clear he'd hurt something on his way down.

Connor's left leg had been aching all night and he discreetly flexed his foot to ward off cramping before crouching by Daniel's side.

'All right, cobber?'

'No wonder Andre left me, I can't even get down a flight of stairs without making a scene,' Daniel spluttered.

'He's sozzled,' April said, shaking her head and patting down her neighbour's pockets until she found a wallet. Connor couldn't help noticing the yellow banknotes in the wallet, confirming his initial thoughts. *Dan Winklin wasn't short of coin.* April pulled out a hotel key card and with a bit of prompting, confirmed the hotel Daniel was booked into.

It took a few attempts, but eventually they managed to hoist him down the stairs and into the waiting taxi.

'Will you be right getting him into the hotel room?' Connor asked after he'd plugged Daniel's seatbelt in for him.

April cast a hopeful glance at the taxi driver.

'You can keep talking as long as you like while the meter's ticking, but I'm not hauling nobody to their hotel room,' the driver said with a shrug.

'I can help if you need,' Connor offered. 'No offence, but you're only tiny and he's kind of heavy-set.'

He could see her hesitation, but when Daniel's head sagged against the leather seats and something between a moan and a snore erupted from his lips, she relented.

'You're right,' she said. 'I'm going to need a hand.'

They got in and buckled up.

'You come to Adelaide often?' called the taxi driver from the front seat.

April and Connor both shook their heads. Daniel snored.

'I flew in a few days ago,' Connor said. 'Hopefully, I'll spend more time here, though.'

'Beautiful city,' said the driver, a laconic pride in his tone as he changed lanes and navigated the streets. 'Safe as houses. Cleaner than Melbourne. Like a big country town really.'

April chuckled. 'I'm not so sure about that. Dan left his wallet in his car in Penwarra last week; keys in the ignition, in the main street. Both were still there when he came out of the supermarket, but I don't think you'd have the same luck here.'

While April's view of the city seemed to be tainted by potential dangers, Connor couldn't help appreciating the anonymity the city afforded him. Since getting on the plane in Manchester, nobody had looked at him with pity, or rubbed his arm and asked how he was holding up.

Mind you, he thought as they roused Daniel and helped him to his hotel room, *I've never had a neighbour pulling off my shoes and ushering me into bed when I was completely rat-faced either.*

'Can you fetch him a glass of water?' April asked, pulling a packet of painkillers from her handbag and sitting them on the bedside table. By the time Connor had returned with the water, she'd written a note on the hotel-issue stationery and placed it beside Daniel's bedside table.

'He *is* a lucky guy to have such a nice neighbour,' Connor said, grinning at the note, which said exactly that and was signed with a smiley face.

Once Daniel was settled, they headed off, both reaching for the elevator button at the same time.

'Sorry—'

Connor laughed, feeling a warmth where her hand brushed his. From the way she jumped backwards, she'd felt it too.

'You go,' he said.

They stood on opposite sides of the lift and he waited for her to exit first.

'Do you want me to walk you out or find you a taxi?'

Smothering a yawn, April shook her head. 'I'm good, thanks, my hotel's just two doors down.'

Connor said goodbye and headed towards the CBD. He looked back when he reached the traffic lights, but April was nowhere to be seen.

He pulled his new phone from his back pocket and dialled his Scottish friend's phone number. 'Where's the party at, man?'

Despite the loud music in the background, he could hear Fergus cheering. *You're here for a good time, not a long time,* Connor reminded himself.

April slathered her olive skin with a generous handful of sunscreen, trying to remember the last time the heat had continued so far beyond harvest. The vines at Lacewing Estate had handled the warm weather pretty well, and the grapes had come off without a hitch, but the hot summer had knocked her extensive veggie plot and frazzled the fussiest flowers in the private garden she managed in Mount Gambier.

It hadn't been the most memorable summer on a personal level, either, and she felt a little like the plants, not yet back to full strength after a rough January and February.

Leafy greens brushed April's legs as she walked between the raised garden beds, filling a bucket with sun-warmed tomatoes. She'd been relying on the drip irrigation system to keep her crop hydrated but as the all-important Penwarra Show raced closer, it was clear the garden needed an extra boost.

She dragged a sprinkler around the side of house. Mishka dashed across the yard and April couldn't help smiling at the fluffy golden dog frolicking in the arc of water, snapping at the droplets.

The only downside of having a trophy-winning garden, she mused, *is the hot afternoons spent shifting sprinklers and shade cloth instead of swimming.* Still, she had a reputation to uphold, and short of a blistering drought, there was no way she'd enter wilted, sub-standard veggies in the show's produce competition. Once Mishka was soaking wet and suitably sated, they headed towards the winery.

Her father, Lloyd, emerged from the shiraz plot in a wide-brimmed hat that had seen the full gamut of Limestone Coast seasons. Tanned legs peeked out from under his baggy drill shorts and white chest hairs sprouted from the collar of his faded chambray shirt. Lloyd shaded his eyes and pointed to the stables.

'Your renovations are rocketing along,' he said, pulling a dog treat out from his pocket for Mishka. 'New roof was an instant upgrade.'

April agreed. True to his word, the builder, Gordon, had worked tirelessly to get the major works done over the last few months, replacing the rafters and riding the local plumbers like a jockey until they finished re-sheeting the tin.

'The place was in surprisingly good structural condition for something built over a century ago. Now it's watertight, we can keep working throughout the worst of the weather.' A blowfly buzzed past, and although the sun was now nipping at their skin, April knew the blustery winds and lashing rain would be relentless once winter set in. 'Who would have thought, getting this far on such a fool's folly?'

The term had been Justin's parting shot, a final sprinkle of salt over her bruised heart.

'I never doubted you,' Lloyd replied, his wry smile reflecting hers. He reached out and squeezed her shoulder. 'Only a fool would underestimate you, my girl. And that lying, cheating idiot was the fool in this situation, just remember that.'

It felt like yesterday that she'd returned from the Adelaide conference to discover Daniel's partner, Andre, wasn't the only winemaker playing around. April wasn't sure what was more humiliating: finding out Justin had left her for his ex-girlfriend or her complete obliviousness to his infidelity.

Once the initial heartache had eased, she'd thrown herself into the renovations. Converting the old stables, with its crumbling walls and unlimited potential, had proved the perfect project to channel her anger into productivity.

April swallowed the lump in her throat and showed her father the new steelwork they'd installed around the entryway, adding strength and security to the original oak doors.

Mishka sniffed around the piles of recycled timber flooring for mice and spiders, both of which continued to frequent the building. When April switched on the lights, the room brightened, chasing away the dull ache that came when she thought about Justin.

Lloyd gestured to the heavy beams straddling the ceiling. 'You going to paint those?'

April was horrified by the suggestion. 'Not a chance, they're one of my favourite things about the stables. People booking a B & B in the middle of a winery are going for rustic, Dad, not shiny chic.'

'I'll take your word for it,' he said, nodding as she stepped him through the floor plan.

It was stuffy inside the stone building and a sheen of sweat glistened on their foreheads when they returned outside.

'Can't say I'll be sorry to see the cooler days arrive,' Lloyd said, watching as she locked the double doors before pocketing the key. 'Hopefully it eases before the show. If it's this hot, they'll definitely be down on gate numbers and entries. Now, Fran mentioned the cooking section, didn't she?'

April blinked. Why would her stepmother mention cooking when she knew April had nothing to contribute? 'You mean veggies?'

Lloyd shook his head as they walked side by side between the vines. 'There's been a stoush in the cooking department. Audrey and Eileen are at war, apparently.'

April couldn't help laughing. The trestle tables in the cooking pavilion always groaned under the weight of Audrey Cartwright's and Eileen Mawson's baking, and there was little doubt the two ladies could singlehandedly feed Penwarra's entire population for morning tea if they pooled their show-day entries.

'Haven't they been threatening to pull out for years? I'll believe it when I see it.'

'Don't laugh,' said Lloyd, snipping off a few spent bunches of grapes the pickers had missed. 'I think it's serious this time. Fran said they're boycotting the event if the show society doesn't appoint a new judge.' He gave a guilty laugh. 'And she may have nominated us to cook a few things, to help fill the tables.'

Of all the things April had imagined for the week ahead, cooking was so far off the list of priorities that she found herself chuckling.

'You're hilarious, Dad,' she said, calling Mishka back to her side. 'But thanks for the laugh, I needed that.' She grinned as she turned to him, and it was only when she met his eye that she realised he was half serious.

'Given we can't really help with donations this year, I've said we'll help out this way instead . . .' He paused, looking sheepish now.

April shook her head, clipping the lead back on Mishka, who was intently eyeing off a little blue wren. 'No, no, no,' she said. 'You've got the wrong person for the job. I'd try putting together a posy or entering the flowers if the garden section was desperate, and you know I'll fill the produce tables with whatever veggies survive this heatwave, but I'm the wrong gal for baking. You know it, Fran knows it, even Mishka knows it.' The dog barked as the blue wren flitted away to safety.

'You didn't know anything about renovating either, but I've seen you helping out with this project. Every time I walk past you're leaning over the sawhorse or learning how to use a new power tool.'

April rolled her eyes. 'Only because I have to, Dad. Justin was meant to be the hands-on helper, I was just supposed to take care of marketing the darn thing. But it's not brain surgery. It would be like you jumping from the winemaking to designing labels and doing all the bottling. You'd do it if you had to, but that doesn't mean you'd voluntarily put yourself in front of the firing squad.' She wasn't sure if it was the heat or the complete ridiculousness of his suggestion that had her mixing up her metaphors, but April felt pressured. Her dad and stepmother had never asked her to cook anything.

They must be light on.

She cast her gaze across to the large mudbrick house on the eastern side of the vineyard, and in the distance saw Fran waving back at them from the clothesline.

Lloyd raised his hand, but instead of waving, he gave the thumbs-up signal. April grabbed his arm, pulling it down.

'You've already registered me, haven't you?' She groaned theatrically.

'It's just to get plates on the table, love. You know how the committee gets about these things.'

April *did* know. In between winery commitments, her stepmother spent endless hours chasing, cajoling, plotting and planning ways to keep the show relevant and vibrant in the face of changing community interests.

'Maybe if they can't fill the tables,' she said gently, 'it's time they threw in the towel?'

Lloyd baulked. 'Don't say that in front of Fran. It's the ninety-eighth show and they're determined to make it to the centenary. I can burn water as well as the next person, and Fran's put my name down for a chocolate cake in the bloke's section. It's just to make up numbers, and nobody will know they're our entries—anything's better than nothing.'

Connor woke to a persistent noise somewhere outside the house. He prised his eyes open, squinting against the light filtering through the thin curtains, and struggling to work out who might be rapping on the door at the crack of dawn on a Friday.

'I'm coming,' he grumbled, pulling on a pair of jeans. It wasn't until he was halfway through the lounge room that he realised the noise was coming from his housemate's bedroom across the hallway, not the front door.

Connor was no stranger to the dynamics of sharehouse living. Awkward flatsharing experiences in London and backpacker hostels in Europe were par for the course, but his tolerance of his loved-up housemates had worn thin over the last three months.

He cleared his throat, hoping it might remind them how easily the sound carried through the flimsy walls. The banging stopped, followed by a giggle. Connor finished dressing quickly and slipped his toothbrush and toothpaste into his backpack, then grabbed a banana from the kitchen counter.

Strictly speaking, the fruit was his housemate's, but Connor reasoned it was a fair trade for the awkward early-morning wake-up. He shut the front door firmly behind him, unlocking the Camry he'd bought on Gumtree. The car had blown a tyre on its maiden voyage from Adelaide, and coughed out more smoke than a Newcastle coal mine, but it had been cheap. Which, given the volatility of his boss, Johann, had proved a smart decision.

Although his working day didn't start until 8 am, Connor had been leaving the house earlier and earlier to avoid the flushed faces of his housemates. The vibe at the sharehouse was the polar opposite of his new workplace, where the tension and camaraderie made it feel as cold as a snowy Christmas.

Connor pulled into the winery car park, unsurprised to see Johann's Audi already there, and tried to guess what mood the boss was in today.

He finished the banana, wishing he'd detoured past the shops for a proper breakfast, then leaned out of the car, using his water bottle to moisten his toothbrush and wash his face. Connor waited until the piano-heavy jazz track finished before locking the Camry, pocketing the keys and making his way inside.

'Morning, Johann,' he said, stowing his backpack in the staff lockers. 'What's on the agenda today?'

The winemaker ignored him, taking a sample from one of the oak barrels. It was only after he'd swirled and sniffed and scowled at the red wine that he acknowledged Connor.

Another one of those days then. Connor made a small plunger of coffee and took his laptop to the timber table outside the barrel room. The week seemed warm for early autumn, with the soft golden light spreading across the vineyards and not a whisper of breeze.

Connor skimmed his inbox, pleased to spot Fergus Abernathy's name. He eagerly read the reply, hoping he hadn't sounded like a whinger in his email last night. From all accounts, his Scottish friend was having a great time in the Limestone Coast and sounded delighted to weigh in on the matter. Connor looked at his watch, then dialled Fergus, who answered on the first ring.

'Alright, pal? Sounds like Rossvale isn't treating you so well.'

Connor glanced through the window where Johann was making his way along the tanks, checking the fermentation. 'The winery's nice, but the mosquitoes are friendlier than the guy running the place.'

'Well, there're plenty of class wineries down this way. If you don't like the one you're at, join me. You heard from the rest of the crew? A few have already jumped ship for other wineries,' Fergus said. 'Ye wouldna be the first.'

Connor hadn't kept in touch with many of the ex-pats who had flown into Adelaide with him in January, and the news made him feel better about the decision.

He ended the call and quietly packed his laptop away, still uncertain about calling time at Rossvale. But by the end of the day, after Johann had sacked a cellar hand and made the viticulturalist cry, Connor handed in his notice. He passed dozens of vineyards on his way out of town, knowing he could have approached other local wineries, but the lure of Penwarra wasn't just about the grapes or his Scottish mate. Not for the first time, he thought of April Lacey and the marketing tips she'd been so keen to learn at the conference. Had she put them into action since January? Was the guy in her phone photographs still in the picture? Would she be happy to see him or had she barely spared a thought for him since?

He set the Camry's cruise control and sat back in his seat. *Only one way to find out.*

3

'He did what?' Lauren Bickford looked up from the pot she was stirring and turned in April's direction, her mouth agape.

With the bubbling saucepans of tomatoes on the stove, the little winemaker's cottage was like a sauna—a tomato-scented sauna. April unwound the windows to their limit, hoping for a hint of a breeze.

After flicking the ceiling fan up to high, April updated her housemate on the show baking scenario.

'Tell me you're not actually going through with it?' Lauren's face was creased with a mix of disbelief and amusement. 'I've seen you baking and it ain't pretty.'

'I know, but fortunately entries only have names displayed if they're winners, so only the steward and I will know it's my disaster.'

Even as she said it, April felt unease skittering through her stomach. Her natural instinct was steering clear of things unless she was sure she could do them well.

Lauren scooped up a spoonful of relish, blew on it and sampled it before handing the spoon to April. 'More salt?'

April let the hot mixture tingle on her tongue. 'It tastes like relish to me.' She shrugged apologetically. Her father Lloyd had been able to taste the difference in grape varieties from a young age, and as much as she'd tried to follow in his footsteps and discern the taste, smell and texture of their wines throughout the fermenting and winemaking process, she'd never mastered the skill. It was part of the reason she avoided cooking too.

'It's good though,' she added quickly. 'Is this for the show?'

'Yep.' Lauren nodded, adding a pinch of salt anyway. 'You can't be the only trophy-winner in the household. Even if your cake is raw in the middle, you'll be the queen of the produce section like every other year.'

April stood on tiptoe and lifted the perpetual trophy from the overhead shelving. It still gave her a thrill to see her name engraved on the plaque multiple times, and as she buffed the small cup, she caught sight of her father's name from two decades ago, and, a little further down, her grandmother's name.

'We'll see,' April said, returning it to the shelf between a finicky maidenhair fern and a trailing hoya that needed trimming. 'Brian Treloar said his veggie garden is in tiptop shape this year, and young Archie Winklin from next door will be giving me a run for his money at this rate. I mightn't win a thing.'

Lauren tasted the relish again and, seemingly pleased with the flavour, turned the stovetop down and stacked the glass jars inside the warm oven for sterilising. 'I'll believe it when I see it. Archie's lucky to be learning from the best, he'll scoop the juniors pool in the produce section, surely? And what does Daniel say about it all? Shouldn't that be something a brother could teach him, instead of a neighbour?'

'Daniel's got two black thumbs, and their dad Rupert doesn't have the patience for it. I don't mind, Archie's a good kid.' April moved around the kitchen, pulling out a cookbook from Lauren's extensive collection. 'Hopefully, he'll win something. Archie's worked hard on his corner of the veggie garden, a ribbon or two will be just the encouragement he needs to keep at it.'

Leafing through the glossy book with its photos of brimming mixing bowls, precisely floured benchtops and artfully messy drips of batter was disheartening but the thought of Fran fretting about empty tables on show day outweighed April's doubts. *It's just a stupid cake to help Fran. Get over yourself!*

April shoved a slip of paper into the most basic butter cake recipe, one with ingredients she could pronounce, then helped Lauren spoon the hot relish into the jars.

'If you've got enough tomatoes in the patch for sauce and chutney, I'll make those on the weekend too.'

April baulked. 'Don't we already have enough to sink a ship?'

'Pfft!' Lauren twisted the lid on the final jar. 'No such thing. A little tweak here and a new flavour there ... I'll be taking as many varieties to the show as possible.'

After washing up, they headed outside to assess the tomato crops.

'I think I'll get a few more kilos from the Roma tomatoes and the Black Russians, but the cherry toms are about done and the last of the Beefcakes are on the bush,' April said, studying the plot.

For all her faults in the kitchen, the garden was a place April had always excelled. The raised beds were lush with greenery, and all manner of autumn vegetables were nestled in the soil and gleaming in the afternoon sun.

April followed the concrete path around to the shaded side of the house and switched off the sprinkler before returning to the tomatoes. She eased a yellow grape tomato from the vine, relishing the moment the sun-warmed fruit exploded in her mouth.

'I don't want to leave you short for show weekend, though,' Lauren said, cradling a cluster of heirloom miniatures. 'Worst-case scenario, I could buy a carton of tomatoes.'

'Just take my heart and rip it in two,' said April, feigning offence before pitching an overripe cherry tomato at her friend. Mishka pranced between them, amped up by their laughter. The tomato narrowly missed Lauren and splattered against the path, just missing the cream-and-ochre walls.

'You're cleaning that up,' Lauren said. 'And while you're at it, you might want to tidy yourself up too, we've got plans tonight.'

April groaned, fanning her face. 'I've got mountains of work to do, Loz. The building site isn't going to clean itself and I'd rather Gordon spend his time labouring, not carrying wood scraps to the skip bin or sweeping sawdust. Not to mention my paid work—I've got plants to order and need to write a winter fertilising and pruning schedule to send to my client before the end of the weekend.' She hosed the tomato pulp off the path. 'And did I mention I need to start thinking about the website for the bed and breakfast, so customers can actually book accommodation?'

Lauren crossed her arms and raised an eyebrow, unperturbed by April's protests.

'You can't spend every spare minute renovating, and it's too warm to work tonight, you said so yourself. There's no way you're backing out now, we've got a booking in Beachport.' Lauren gave her another grin, then retreated inside.

'Tell me it's not Zumba again,' April called after her, still unsure whether she should be grateful or insulted by Lauren's regular attempts to liven up her social life.

The tomato smell lingered inside the house and April had to admit that after such a stinking hot day, the beach seemed like the perfect destination. But when she emerged from the shower, the sight of Lauren rifling through her wardrobe told her it mightn't be quite as straightforward as she'd hoped.

'What, we need more than bathers, sunglasses and a stubby holder?'

Lauren thrust a floaty floral sundress and a pair of pink sandals at her.

'Swim first, then I've booked a table for four at Bompas.'

A table for four?

April sighed. 'Does Jean Dellacourte have anything to do with this?'

Jean prided herself on being the town cupid, making it her business to set up all the young people in town. Both April and Lauren had suffered through several of Jean Dellacourte's match-ups over the years.

Lauren ignored the question. A sinking feeling settled in April's stomach as her housemate strode to the door.

The little rental property at the Penwarra Golf Course wasn't big, Connor soon discovered, but what it lacked in size and style, it more than made up for in company and location.

Surrounded by well-watered and carefully manicured greens, the house was nestled among gum trees and only a short drive from town.

'The best bit is that little club house over yonder,' said Fergus, pointing out the large building in the distance. 'The Nineteenth Hole, it's called. Amazing tucker, cheap beers and good kin. You'll be happy here, Con, I've no doubt. We'll find you a job in no time.'

With Fergus's help—and a running commentary about the town's attractions and highlights—Connor was soon unpacked.

'Shall I rustle us up something to eat or do you fancy hitting the town?' Fergus asked.

Connor didn't have to look at his watch to know that bed was calling him. An early start, a full day's work and then a five-hour drive south had taken its toll.

'A bag of crisps is about the extent of my enthusiasm tonight,' Connor said, watching his Scottish mate rummage around in the pantry.

'Nah, it's no bother,' said Fergus, heaping the benchtop with rice, eggs, spices and tinned tomatoes.

'Don't go to any trouble on my part, really,' said Connor. 'I'll just have a shower, call my folks and crawl into bed, I'm zonked.'

Fergus emptied the random ingredients into a frypan and switched on the gas hob. While he didn't know much about cooking, Connor was pretty sure those items didn't all belong in the pan together at the same time.

'Call it a housewarming present,' said Fergus, cracking open a beer. 'By the time you get out of the shower, this glorious concoction should be cooked.'

Although the water pressure was underwhelming and the shower was one of those over-the-bath contraptions that required his full attention on exiting, Connor felt like a new man when he donned fresh shorts and a T-shirt.

A haze of smoke and persistent beeping greeted him in the hallway and it took a huge effort not to laugh at Fergus standing under the smoke alarm, waving a tea towel like a surrender flag.

'Now you're just making me homesick,' chuckled Connor, quickly opening the kitchen windows. The frypan with their supper—or what had been intended as such—was now smouldering outside the front door. 'I thought charcoal-de-jour was only my specialty.'

Fergus groaned. 'I barely left it for five minutes. Sorry, mate, not much of a welcome.'

'I'm not a cook's elbow either, trust me, but it was awfully nice of you to offer.' Connor took a beer from the fridge and held open the back door. 'An ale under the stars sounds like a top alternative.'

Fergus pulled out two chairs and they caught up under the moonlit sky. As Connor listened to the sounds of animals and birds calling in the distance and the wind rustling through the gum leaves, he got the feeling he was going to like it in Penwarra.

They tossed their empties into the recycling drum afterwards. 'I'd better call home,' he said, thanking Fergus again for his hospitality and heading into the spare bedroom where they'd unpacked his things.

He opened his laptop and within moments, the lounge room of his family home in Derbyshire, England came into view.

'Ey up, here's our boy!' Jock Jamison loomed so close to the screen Connor could see the individual bristles of his beard and an alarmingly close-range view of his nose hair.

'Oh, you look tired, love, are you getting enough sleep?' His mum, Sharyn, chimed in, swinging the computer screen around and nestling in cheek to cheek with her husband. She long believed sleep and tea to be the cures to all ailments, no matter how old you were.

'All good, Mam, just a big day. Hey Nell, hiya Pippin.'

The video screen lurched sideways as his little sisters moved the laptop and crammed onto the couch beside their parents.

'When are you coming home, Con?' Pippin hugged a colourful ukulele to her chest.

Connor chuckled. 'Same answer as last week, Pipsqueak, it's still a two-year visa. Anyone would think you're missing me.'

Nell leaned in close, the light of the computer screen glinting off her braces. 'We do. There's this super annoying kid in class, he thinks he's the king of Year eight. I've already told him to stop being such a complete knob, but if you were home, I could at least tell them my big brother's ready and willing to go a few rounds. He'd take one look at how tall and strong you are and pee his pants.'

'Nelly Jamison.' Their mother swatted her on the arm. Connor chuckled. There was no debating his height, but he'd always thought of himself as fit rather than strong. If he'd had to choose between music and muscles, he'd pick Beethoven, Nat King Cole and The Beatles in a heartbeat.

'How's your new housemate, lad?' Jock asked. 'And have you found a new job yet, then? They'd better treat you better than that joker in Rossvale.'

Connor hooked an arm behind his head and leaned against the wrought-iron bedhead. 'Given I've only been here a few hours, I'm still currently unemployed, but my housemate Fergus is a good bloke and he'll put in a good word at a few of the wineries.'

'Good to hear. Right then you lot, we'd better let our Con get some shut eye,' said Jock. 'You look like you're spent, lad, off you go then.'

'And send us some photos of your new place,' said Pippin, strumming a tune as the others waved goodbye. 'It's probably not as nice as your old flat, not without Phoebe there to make it all pretty.'

Sharyn chimed in with a reprimand before Connor had even thought up an appropriate response.

'They're only kids, they don't mean anything by it,' Jock apologised.

Connor waved it away. 'No bother.' Just because he'd tried to remove all traces of Phoebe Lawson from his life, it didn't mean everyone in his orbit had to do the same.

'What? What did I say?' said Pippin, still bewildered as Jock signed off for the night.

Connor was about to shut his laptop when an email popped up on the screen. A tired smile crept across his face as he opened it: he'd been offered an interview for the head winemaker's gig at an award-winning Herefordshire winery.

Mam and Dad will like this. He took a screen shot of the email and forwarded it to his dad, who'd pushed him to apply for the role. It was the type of opportunity he would have accepted in a heartbeat five years ago.

He wouldn't be accepting it, not with his Aussie adventure underway, but the offer was validating anyway. If a winery of that calibre was reaching out now, similar opportunities would arise when he returned after his stint in Australia. Two years Down Under was just the fresh start he needed. Connor took one last look out the window at the twinkling Australian stars, searching out the brightest one through the stretch of glass before rolling over and closing his eyes.

April flung open the curtains in her bedroom and studied the sky. It was a glorious day with barely a cloud to be seen, and she could already feel the warmth of the sun through the windowpane. Like everyone in the district, she was looking forward to more bearable temperatures.

Maybe it'll give me more patience when dealing with morons, she thought, recalling the stunned silence the night before when she had told her blind date exactly what he could do with his octopus hands.

Mishka tore down the hallway and dropped a tatty tennis ball at April's feet. 'A beautiful dog, the prettiest home in the district, a great job and good friends. Who needs men, hey Mish?'

The dog barked, as if that arrangement was fine by her too. April picked up her phone and saw a message from the builder, Gordon.

She quickly replaced her pyjamas with a sleeveless work shirt and denim shorts. If he was coming in to work on the weekend, she wanted to be ready to lend a hand the moment he arrived.

April kicked the dog's tennis ball across the room, then laughed when Mishka emerged from under the bed with dust-bunnies stuck to her whiskers and the ball between her teeth.

'You heading to the stables? I thought you were gardening and baking this morning?'

Lauren leaned against the bedroom doorframe, a pen and shopping list in one hand and a recipe book in the other. April ducked past her down the hall and into the kitchen.

'Yeah, I was planning on it, but Gordon's available, so I'll be his lackey. Maybe he'll let me near the nail gun today,' she said, slotting two thick slices of sourdough into the toaster. 'Coffee?'

'I think I should be making you coffee after last night,' Lauren cringed, setting the recipe book down by the espresso machine. 'Rowan sounded much better in Jean's phone call than in the flesh, I promise.'

April waved away Lauren's apology. 'It's not your fault he was a creep, but there was a silver lining at least.'

'That you didn't toss a glass of water over him or storm out halfway through dessert?'

April grinned at her housemate and shook her head. 'Don't try telling me he didn't deserve it. Nope, the good news is that

Mr McOctopus won't be breaking this heart anytime soon. In fact, after I tell Jean Dellacourte about last night, she'll probably scratch him off her list of eligible bachelors.'

The kitchen buzzed with the sound of grinding beans, and soon the room was filled with the glorious aroma of coffee and warm bread. 'If that's the quality of the guys Jean's rounding up, I'd hate to see the ones she knocks back,' said Lauren, frothing the milk and handing April a steaming cup.

'I'd rather do Zumba or gardening on a forty-degree day than go on any more blind dates,' April said. 'Please promise you'll give me more than forty minutes notice before you pull a stunt like that again.'

'Would you have come?' Lauren pulled the butter towards her, slathering an extra thick wedge onto her sourdough before holding up a finger. 'As much as I adore you, April, I don't want to be sitting here in twenty years sharing coffee and toast in matching dressing gowns, wondering why I'm still single. We have to take opportunities as they arise.'

'Don't let me stand in the way of your dating schemes; I'd just personally rather sweat it out in the gym or distributing a few cubic metres of mulch.'

'That Justin . . .' Lauren rolled her eyes. 'He's got a lot to answer for.'

April had never been more grateful for her friend than in the month after Justin left. As well as keeping up the supply of chocolate, tissues and wine, Lauren had happily removed all the Justin-related photographs and mementos from their house, so that when April emerged from the post-break up fog, there was barely a trace of his presence in the winemaker's cottage.

'I'm in no hurry to repeat that mistake, especially not with a loser who thinks he's entitled to cop a feel just because he bought me dinner.'

'True, true,' Lauren conceded. 'Before you head off, do you have any special requests for the next batch of sauce? I've already got chilli jam, fruity tomato chutney, tomato and capsicum relish, regular sauce and sauce from the CWA recipe book, but I'm keen to make a few more varieties. Cover all bases, you know?'

'You're mad. It's even hotter today than yesterday.'

'I'm on a mission,' Lauren announced, flicking through the cookbook. 'If you'd just let me teach you, you'd see there's nothing to this cooking business.'

April smiled and shook her head. Lauren was a brilliant friend, but April knew from experience that she wasn't a natural-born cooking instructor.

Gulping down her coffee, she strode over to the stables with Mishka. Grass had started growing around the wheels of Gordon's tradie trailer, which had been parked there since he'd taken the job on. Knowing he wouldn't be far away, she opened the trailer box and pulled out the portable radio. Half an hour passed quickly as she cleared the dust and debris from the job site, listening to the radio station's gardening show.

April's mind skipped ahead as she cleaned. Soon, the bulk of the building work would be done and she'd be able to start landscaping. She had already earmarked some reliable standards like box hedge, lavender and rosemary for the garden base, with a few flowers and annuals to add colour and form.

And a small veggie garden, of course, she thought, imagining guests picking their own herbs if they fancied fresh basil or parsley on their omelettes, or sun-kissed tomatoes on the side.

Omelettes weren't something she'd ever cooked for herself, but researching the bed and breakfast market, it seemed hosts who value-added, providing goods like locally-sourced eggs and warm loaves of homemade bread, scored high on the customer experience 'feel good' scale.

She was so busy daydreaming about happy customers with higher culinary skills than her own that April didn't realise Gordon had arrived until he walked through the oak doors.

'Howdy!' She set aside the broom, eager to see what task they'd be tackling today.

'Hey,' he replied flatly, his gaze flitting around the room. April waited for him to mention the tidy workspace, or at least rattle off the day's tasks, and was surprised when he instead turned to their supplies, carefully measuring the timber and making a lot of 'hmmm-ing' noises.

'You've measured that length three times now,' she said. 'Everything okay?'

Gordon pulled out his pocketknife and sharpened his pencil with careful, considered movements.

'This job might take a little longer than we expected,' he admitted finally. 'We'll run up against the edge of your budget before long, so we're either going to need more volunteers or an increase in the budget to get it done on time, I'm afraid.'

'I thought we were on track,' April said quickly, 'and I've factored in a buffer, but I really wanted to be open for spring, so we can iron out any kinks before the serious tourist season starts. How much more money are we talking?'

Gordon looked apologetic as he explained the additional expenses and handed over an invoice from the timber supplier. 'They've had a price hike too, to cover the extra delivery costs. I'm sorry,' he said. 'I know it's not what you want to hear, but I wanted to give you a heads-up now.'

He gave her a ballpark figure of the extras they'd need to consider. The details sat like a rock in the bottom of her stomach as they worked, and they finished a little later than usual, both of them intent on getting the maximum value from each length of timber.

'We haven't got this far into it to give up now,' April said finally, locking the double doors behind them and waving Gordon off.

There has to be a way to make it work, April thought, striding across to the winery. *I just need to find it.*

She closed the door of Lacewing Estate behind her, forcing her lips into a tight smile when she spotted Fran. But the grimace didn't fool her stepmother, who took one look at her and realised something was amiss.

'You're the spitting image of your mother when you frown like that, pet. Is it the cooking? You haven't burned the cottage down, have you?' Fran went back into the tea room and emerged shortly after with a tray. Setting it on the cluttered wine-tasting bar, she peered out the window in the direction of April's house. 'I'm pleased you're helping with the show baking, but only if it's not too much trouble.'

April took a Monte Carlo from the biscuit barrel. 'The cooking's the least of my troubles,' she said. 'Maybe this stables project was doomed from the start ... First Justin hotfooted out of here, now the costs and the timeline are blowing out ... Am I the only one who thinks it's not completely mad?'

Fran removed her glasses and rubbed the bridge of her nose. 'It's not straightforward, I'll give you that, but we're behind you, April. Your dad was saying just last night how proud he was of all the work you've done so far. Of course, he'd rather you were in the winery with him every day ...'

April took a bite of her biscuit. 'We all know how well that'd go.'

With their contrasting views on technology and operational matters, and her rusty winemaking skills, April found it easier working for someone else. She helped as was needed at the vineyard, especially during harvest and pruning, but she liked the independence her fulltime horticulture job at Laughton Gardens offered.

'We've loved seeing you pour your heart and soul into this project. If a B & B keeps you connected to Lacewing Estate, then that's pretty special to us. What can we do to help?'

April didn't need to look far to confirm Lacewing Estate wasn't in a position to shell out extra funds for this project. Her eyes lingered on the paintwork puckered by salt damp and the bottle labels that had barely changed since Lloyd took over.

'This is supposed to be a project to help boost the winery, not suck extra funds from the coffers,' April insisted. 'I'll think of something.'

As she walked back to the winemaker's cottage she'd called home for almost ten years, she fervently hoped she was right.

Archie Winklin sat on the front step of April's verandah, a wheelbarrow at the ready.

'You're late!' the young boy called, jumping to his feet and jamming a straw hat onto his head.

Mishka strained at the end of her leash, eager for his attention.

'Oh, Arch.' She'd forgotten he was coming today. April let go of the leash. 'Can we take a raincheck?'

His face fell. Archie buried his head in Mishka's shaggy coat and began to sing. As April got nearer, her own problems receded as she heard his mournful song, not quite muffled by the dog hair.

'Nobody likes me, everybody hates me, I think I'll go and eat worms.'

A giggle escaped her, surprising them both. 'Now there's a blast from the past, I didn't realise anyone still sang that song,' she said, sinking onto the step beside him. 'How does it go again?'

Archie looked up, eyes narrowed and bottom lip jutting out, as if trying to establish whether she was pulling his leg or not.

'Go on, I could do with a good song today.'

'Nobody likes me, everybody hates me, I think I'll go and eat worms.' He sang the first line again, his petulant tone perfectly complementing the playground ditty.

She nodded encouragingly.

'Short ones, tall ones?'

Archie shook his head. 'Nope, that's not right.' He leaned his head against Mishka's golden back and began the second verse.

'Long ones, short ones, fat ones, skinny ones, worms that squiggle—'

'And squirm,' April finished, assessing Archie's face, and his choice of song. *I'm not the only one having a rough day.* 'What's up, short stuff? Surely you've got something better to do on a Saturday than gardening with me? What about your brother?'

'Half-brother.' Archie's clarification was automatic. 'Daniel's gone to Victoria, Dad's busy with the wine like always, Mum's working and all my friends are away for the school holidays. Nobody wants to hang out with me, not even Marty and Barbara. Ever since Dad shifted them to the big paddock with the older sheep, they don't want a bar of me.'

April tickled him under the chin. 'You're telling me Baaaarbara and Maaaaar-ty don't want a baaaaaa-r of you?'

That got him laughing.

'Maybe if you'd called them Hamburger and Chops, like Dan suggested, they'd be better behaved.'

'Maybe.' Archie turned to study her, still clinging to the dog. 'Why did you say you needed a song?'

He doesn't miss a beat.

'Just boring money stuff,' she said, scanning the rows of vines surrounding her little cottage. *Boring, expensive, potentially project-ending stuff.* 'And nobody hates you, buddy, you know that, right?'

His nod was so small she wouldn't have seen it if she hadn't been looking directly at his freckled, sun-bronzed cheeks.

'If you don't want me here, then I'll probably go home and die of boredom,' he said, using his hat to fan himself.

Dwelling on her renovation budget worries wouldn't help right now, but perhaps a few hours in the garden would.

'Well, we can't have that then, can we? You may as well help me.'

He jumped to his feet and headed for the garden shed, Mishka hot on his heels. 'Can we work on my veggie patch first? Pretty please? We can have it weeded in no time.'

She nodded, watching him shift gears with the ease of a rally driver and wishing she could do the same. Archie emerged from the shed with gardening gloves, spades and buckets looped over his gangly arms, beaming from ear to ear.

Crisis of confidence over.

Archie carried the tools to the raised garden bed he'd helped build during the summer holidays. It was half the size of April's veggie patch, but he'd helped her cut, cart and arrange the old railway sleepers, and he'd spent hours lining it with plastic and filling it with soil—one small shovel after another. With her guidance, he'd planted it out with seeds purchased from his pocket money.

Only a smattering of veggies from Archie's inaugural crop would be ready in time for the upcoming show, but he had grand plans to ensure it was brimming with produce the following March.

April pulled her gloves on. 'Right then. You know which ones are the weeds and which ones are the seedlings?'

Archie nodded, quickly identifying them before tackling the task. Soon his small plot was weed-free, watered and covered with a layer of mulch. As he worked, Archie told April about his lambs and ideas for the upcoming show.

'Do you think I could enter Mishka in the best-dressed pet competition? Dad said my lambs are too much trouble to take to the show, but Mishka's good on a lead,' he said hopefully, looking up from his plot.

'I'm not sure you can enter someone else's pet,' she hedged, not wanting another responsibility on show day. It was enough that she'd agreed to bake, as well as helping Archie with his veggies and her own. 'Let me think about it over afternoon smoko.'

Leading him beneath the shady gum, April wiped her gloves on her denim shorts and handed Archie a water bottle.

'Do you think I'll get a championship show trophy like you one year, April?'

She took a big mouthful from her own bottle, relishing the cool water, then opened a packet of Twisties. 'Anyone can grow stuff in this dirt, Arch. It's some of the best soil in the country and the reward's in the growing, not the showing.'

Archie groaned, before taking a handful of Twisties. 'You only say that because you always win.'

'Not always. But the more you grow and the more you enter, the better your chance of winning something. We've got twelve months until the next show, plenty of time for you to get a few crops under your belt and whip your veggie garden into shape . . .'

There was a spring in Archie's step as he headed for home. He paused at the end of her lawn and turned head-over-heels in a cartwheel, barely breaking stride.

'Show off!' April laughed.

The young boy did another for good measure, [gave a] cheerful farewell, and then disappeared between t[he trees].

April leaned against the gum tree, trying to rec[all the] last time she'd cartwheeled and sang playground ditties. *Nepal, perhaps?* Closing her eyes, she thought of the month she'd spent living at the foot of the Himalayas after her parents' divorce. Her mum, Polly, had been swept up in the excitement of their overseas adventure, relishing her new classrooms and colleagues, the foreign languages and fresh friendships.

It was the afternoons that April found the hardest. She missed the routine and familiarity of the vineyard; a simple yearning for the after-school winery tasks quickly gave way to a desperate longing for home that Polly struggled to understand. There had been teary nights with maps spread across the table, suggestions made for countries April might like better, promises of more pocket money and unlimited long-distance phone calls to hopefully ease her homesickness.

But when the plane touched down in Adelaide, seven months after they'd left, and the flight attendant had asked if they were visiting or returning home, April's relieved answer had sealed the deal.

Lloyd was ecstatic. Polly continued teaching in far flung places, sending her love via postcards, parcels and phone calls to the winery. Fran's arrival helped fill the void, and after a while, April stopped minding her mum's absence.

Mishka ambled over, dropping a well-chewed builder's pencil at her feet.

'No use dwelling on the past when the future needs our attention, right Mish?'

April fetched her laptop and returned to the outdoor setting. She was pulling up the B & B spreadsheet when a kookaburra called in the distance.

She listened to the bird's laughter, and the subsequent replies that echoed from the neighbouring trees.

That's it! Her fingers flew across the keyboard. There was only so long she could keep calling the bed and breakfast 'The Stables' and there was plenty of local birdlife in the gum trees dotted throughout the winery.

Kookaburra Cabin?

Kookaburra Shack? April paused, then quickly hammered on the 'delete' key.

Nope, too informal.

She paused, absent-mindedly nibbling a hangnail and tossing around a few more names in her head before committing them to the spreadsheet.

Kookaburra Lodge?

Kookaburra Inn?

April glanced at her winemaker's cottage, then back to the small stone building that was steadily taking up a big part of her heart, then deleted all the previous ideas.

How could it be anything other than Kookaburra Cottage?

With a smile, April renamed the spreadsheet, hit 'save' and hoped prospective guests would be just as charmed by Kookaburra Cottage. Now she just had to find a way to finish the renovations.

4

Connor looked around the Penwarra clubhouse a week after arriving in the district, feeling slightly out of place in a room full of people he'd never met.

He ordered two pints and checked his phone to find an update from Fergus, who was running late.

Connor paid for the dirt-cheap drinks and perched on a cushioned stool beside a display case of trophies. The club was brimming with golfers, who looked to be the same vintage as his parents.

'Were you one of the Kalangadoo players? I don't remember seeing a strapping young lad like you on the course today?'

Connor turned to look at the woman waiting at the bar beside him. *Kalanga-whatzit? Is she talking to me?* 'Not me, I'm afraid,' he said. 'I've just moved into the little rental over the hill with Fergus.'

The short lady beamed, patting his arm, and introduced herself as Jean Dellacourte. 'Oh Fergus, he's a pet. We've asked him to give a talk at Probus next month. Perhaps you can come along too and we can hear what brings you to our beautiful district. If I were a gambling lady, I'd wager you're either in winemaking or teaching. Or,' she rubbed her hands together, 'please tell me you're the new doctor we've been waiting for.'

Although Jean hadn't ordered, the barman arrived before them with a glass of house wine and took her money. *A regular then, obviously.*

'Winemaker,' Connor sipped his beer. 'Though it sounds like you need doctors more than winemakers at the moment?'

'Crying out for 'em,' she confirmed. 'But for some reason, we can't seem to get them here, and when we do, we have trouble convincing them to stay longer than a year or so. It's a lovely town, take my word for it, but the distance from the city scares some people off. Are you a city boy yourself?'

It had been a while since anyone called me a boy, Connor thought with a smile.

'I've mostly lived in villages or cities, so this is quite new to me.' Noticing her raised eyebrows, he hurried on, 'But I can already tell it's a brilliant spot here, with all the fresh air and space.'

From the expression on her face, it was clear he'd said the right thing. She waved her hand at the bartender again and a packet of crisps appeared in a cane basket. Jean climbed onto the bar stool beside him.

Despite Connor's protests, she heaped a handful of potato chips onto a napkin and sat it in front of him. 'Go on then,' she said, waiting until he'd taken one before continuing her potted history of the town.

'And you'll just love the community,' Jean paused for a sip of wine. 'We look after our own around here. Bob Nellestein over there was really sick a few years back.' She pointed to a man with a green golf cap and high socks. 'We all jumped in to help with lawn mowing and the footy club ran a firewood raffle to help with petrol while he travelled to the city for treatment.' She cast another glance around the room, warming to her topic.

'A funeral's always a good excuse for a community cook up too,' Jean continued. 'Dot over there was bedridden with shock when her Ronald died, even though he'd had a good innings. Seventy-nine, he was, but still, the poor love was heartbroken. The pennant girls and I set up a roster so she had hot meals for a week or two. Pasties, casseroles, soups and stir-fries. You name it, we cooked it.'

Connor was impressed. They knew their immediate neighbours in Derbyshire, and his parents had many musical friends, but as far as he knew, nobody had ever dropped a casserole at their front door. Jean was delighted when he told her as much.

'That's the country charm,' she said, heaping a few more crisps onto his napkin. 'We've got lots of committees and the like. You'll feel like a local in no time if you're happy lending a hand here and there.'

'Thanks Jean, I'll keep it in mind,' Connor promised, finishing his beer and looking at the one he'd ordered for Fergus. If his housemate was much longer, the beer would be at British pub temperature instead of the icy cold brew he knew his friend favoured. As if on cue, the main door opened and Fergus lumbered through, greeting half the people in the club as if they were old friends and the rest like they were new friends waiting to happen.

'Over here, Fergus,' Jean called, waving at him from across the room. 'I've got to know him quite well over a few baskets of chips,' she confided. 'If my granddaughter still lived locally, I'd have no hesitation setting the two of them up. Still, there are plenty of lovely young ladies in the district; I'm sure I'll come up with the perfect match.' Her eyes shone and he guessed it wasn't the first time she'd played matchmaker.

'Jean, I see you've met Connor already,' Fergus looked like a giant beside the wren-like lady.

She nodded, patting Connor's arm. 'I have indeed,' she said, offering the last of the chips to Fergus. The Scotsman had no hesitation in accepting and he listened attentively as Jean updated him on a hedge Fergus had apparently helped her prune.

Connor ordered a fresh pint for himself and a wine for Jean before ducking to the bathroom. When he returned, Fergus was deep in conversation with another local. It wasn't hard to see why his Scottish friend had integrated so easily into the new town. He remembered people's names and went out of his way to talk to them.

'Is it normally this packed?' Connor asked Fergus once he'd finished his conversation, gesturing to the crowd and watching the wait staff drag extra tables across the room, laying out more napkins, cutlery and wine glasses.

'There's a fair crowd most Friday nights, but this one's a little bigger—they hosted a tournament today. Safe to say, they'll be putting on the best tucker for their visitors,' said Fergus, rubbing his hands in anticipation.

Connor's phone buzzed in his pocket and he opened a message from his little sister, Pippin.

> Those kangaroos are BRILLIANT!!! Can you FaceTime me tomorrow if they're still around so I can see them hopping?

Connor checked with Fergus before replying.

'Oh, they'll be here all right,' Fergus confirmed. 'The greenskeeper said they're worse than vermin. You know they've got kangaroo on the menu tonight, if you're keen to sink your choppers in?'

Connor shuddered, not quite ready to reconcile the Aussie icon with a menu item or imagine them being considered pests. He wouldn't mention *that* to Pippin or Nell tomorrow.

A man with a microphone encouraged patrons to find their seats. Weaving through the families and friends, Connor followed Fergus to the far corner of the room, just between the bar and the bathrooms.

'Best spot in the house when they're doing these formal nights,' Fergus said with a wink. Their table was beside a wall covered in photographs of club champions, taken on a night just like this, and next to a familiar, cloth-covered shape. Connor lifted the linen sheet, a quick glimpse confirming it was indeed a piano.

His fingers were itching to dance across the ivories and he realised how much he'd missed playing music in the past three months.

The upright piano wasn't as tall as the one he'd grown up with, but he'd taught many young students on models just like this. *Who had banished it to the corner and hidden it under a sheet?*

'Nice,' Connor murmured.

'You're looking at that piano like it's the best thing you've seen all week,' said Fergus, nudging him with an elbow. 'You play?'

Connor nodded, then replaced the sheet and turned slowly, his mind skipping ahead. Johann had insisted his staff kept their weeknights free so they were available for whatever winemaking tasks he saw fit to ask of them, which had ruled out the opportunity to start teaching piano lessons. But perhaps if he couldn't find a winery job, he could cover his rent with lessons here? It wouldn't hurt to ask.

April's week was a rush of cooking failures, budget revisions and much head scratching, so by the time Friday rolled around, the last thing she felt like doing was presenting a trophy at the golf tournament.

But she took one look at her father, hunched over a spreadsheet, and knew he was dreading it more. April's budget concerns had prompted Lloyd to look at the winery's figures, revealing things were even tighter than usual at Lacewing Estate.

Lucky I didn't accept his offer of financial help, after all.

'Can you go, love?' asked Lloyd. 'They'll feel me out for another year of sponsorship and at this stage, I'm not sure we'll be able to deliver. They won't ask you, and Fran's elbow-deep in show stuff.'

'Righto,' said April. 'I'll pop in, present the trophy, give vague replies to any queries about future sponsorship and get out of there the moment the presentations are done.' If they hadn't been the major sponsors for the night, she'd be on the couch with ice cream, chocolate and wine, but they were, and so she went.

Parked vehicles spilled out onto the quiet country lane when April arrived at the golf club.

Her earlier bravado had disappeared somewhere between her blow-dry and her shonky reverse park beside a sedan with a 'Golf is Life' bumper sticker.

She stared at her grim reflection in the rear-view mirror. *Get in, get it done and get home.* Using her pinkie to smudge her hastily applied eyeliner, April applied a fresh coat of lipstick and reached for the trophy she'd be presenting on stage in under an hour.

Another thought struck her as she joined the stream of golfers heading towards the club rooms.

Have we already paid this year's sponsorship dues, or are they still to come? Not once had she considered whether such donations came out of their account at the start of the financial year or the calendar year, but as April walked towards the clubhouse, she hoped it was the latter. Their ability to support the community would be limited if they couldn't even fund their next team of pruners or pickers, not to mention their next shipment of bottles or printing run of labels.

'Need a hand?' Daniel Winklin emerged from a silver Prado, his crisp shirt and ivory moleskins as impeccable as his car.

'It's not heavy,' she replied, lifting the trophy a little higher and scanning the driveway for slippery stray pebbles. Falling on her bum, right at the entrance, would be the icing on the cake after the week she'd had.

'You just don't want Winklin Wines to steal it off Lacewing Estate, right?' Daniel's joke fell flat when he saw her face.

April had no doubt the Winklins would happily take over the sponsorship gig—there was barely a sporting club in Penwarra without their navy-and-orange branding plastered across some part of their website—but the good-natured jibe was a little too close to the bone tonight.

'Where're your folks?' Daniel looked behind him, as if he'd somehow missed Lloyd's tall stature or Fran's silver pixie hairdo amongst the crowd.

'Show week,' April said. 'I'm glad I caught you, though, I wanted to run something past you about Archie's veggie garden.'

Daniel grimaced. They paused for a trickle of cars merging into the car park. 'My little brother's worse than those sheep of his, never stays where we want him to. I hope he's not too much of a pain in the butt, always coming over to yours?'

April rushed to reassure him. 'He's welcome anytime, Dan, really. I just wanted to check if there's space to make a small bed in your dad's garden, too, just so Arch doesn't have all his eggs in one basket? He wants to grow a giant pumpkin for next year's show and I'm not sure I've got the room.'

'Between Dad's obsession with lawn and Felicity's aversion to dirt, they're looking at ripping out what little garden there is and replacing it with turf. They want less garden, not more. Last I heard they were talking about a rosebush bonfire.'

April couldn't help but gasp. 'Not the roses on the side of the conservatory?' Although April wasn't a regular visitor to the Winklin's grand home, she'd been there for Archie's birthday party in January. Burning the delicately-cupped heritage roses would be criminal.

Daniel shrugged. 'I guess, they're the only flowers on the property. And you know what my stepmother's like. Once she gets something in her mind, she's a hard woman to convince otherwise.'

April nodded. It was what made Felicity so good at her job as the winery's business manager. 'Well, that answers my question about Archie's extra veggie patch, we'll sort something out.' She looked around the car park. 'Are they here or did Archie manage to drag your dad to the movies tonight?'

'Beats me. The babysitter arrived as I was leaving. Dad and Felicity looked dressed for a cocktail party, not a kids' movie, but I could be wrong.'

April's heart went out for little Archie. He'd called in after school yesterday, telling her in intricate detail about the movie snacks he'd already picked, the Ninjago T-shirt he'd chosen to match the film, and the session times he'd been poring over all week.

A ute pulled up beside them, and April continued inside, leaving Daniel comparing golf handicaps with the newcomer.

Archie's disappointment and the budget worries at Lacewing Estate weighed on her mind as she approached the club rooms. Shifting the trophy onto her hip, April tried to twist the door handle, but whether it was from sweat or the moisturiser she'd lathered on earlier, the door wouldn't budge.

'Bugger,' she said, as the trophy toppled to the ground.

Tell me I haven't just dented the club championship trophy. April closed her eyes and bit her lip as she swooped down to pluck the cup off the path. *Phew, no major damage.*

Breathing a sigh of relief that they wouldn't need to buy a replacement trophy, she brushed off the limestone dust and headed inside.

April scanned the room, mentally placing townsfolk, past colleagues and parents of school friends before landing on a set of sky-blue eyes and white-blond hair she'd been thinking about since January.

Even though she'd last seen Connor Jamison in Adelaide, she'd thought of him often. And here he was, sitting in the golf club rooms at Penwarra, like he was one of the locals.

*

The chap on the microphone was settling into another long-winded joke, and Connor was about to make a wager with Fergus about the length of the speeches when the door opened and the piano became the second-best thing he'd seen all week. There in the doorway, wearing a daffodil-yellow dress with an enormous trophy in her arms, was April Lacey. She was even prettier than he remembered and from the look of it, she was coming their way.

'Connor, what are you doing here?' she whispered breathlessly as she sat the trophy down with a clunk on the table beside him, almost starting a domino of tumbling trophies.

They both reached for it at the same time, electricity sparking between them as their hands met. It felt like all the eyes in the room swivelled towards them.

A loud 'shhhhh!' came from the front.

Connor had many questions too but from the frown on the club president's face and the elbow in the ribs from Fergus, he didn't dare breathe another word until the speech had finished.

He recognised a hint of black cherry—the same scent he looked for in a full-bodied shiraz—when April leaned towards him.

'Are you visiting? It's quite the day trip from Rossvale.'

He shook his head, speaking quickly as a new speaker stepped up to the stage, adjusting the microphone height and slowly unfolding a page of handwritten notes. 'No, I've just moved here, the Rossvale job didn't work out.'

April's eyes lit up, a slow smile building. 'Really? That's great news.'

The speaker cleared her throat and launched into a spiel about the turf rejuvenation program.

Connor caught April's eye and thought to himself, *Moving to Penwarra was definitely a step in the right direction.*

Ten minutes later, the audience had evidently reached the limit of their interest in turf irrigation issues. Chairs scraped against the floor as people fidgeted, a troupe of teenagers in white shirts and black pants hovered at the kitchen door, arms laden with entrees, and Connor spotted a few golfers yawning. The speaker eventually gave up her microphone, looking confused about the enthusiastic applause. A surge of people headed for the bar.

'It's great to see you,' said April. 'Where are you staying?'

Connor introduced Fergus, who was gathering up their glasses.

'Oh, you're working at Beesley Brothers, right? I heard they had one of the international vitties there. Are you settling in well?'

Fergus stepped aside as a waitress arrived with prawns and bruschetta. 'Aye, they're a great bunch of people.' He gestured to the bar. 'I'll just top us up before the next round of presentations start. Can I get you a bevvy?'

April requested a sparkling red, then turned back to Connor, who felt warm just being in her presence again.

'I tried to Insta-stalk you,' April said, 'but you're not on social media. What type of person isn't on socials?'

He laughed. 'Nah, I got sick of being heckled by my little sisters for my poor attempts at photography. If my finger wasn't half over the camera, then the lens was filthy, and if the lens wasn't filthy, then the photos were totally rubbish. Sisters, right?'

Just then a man made a beeline towards them, plonking himself down in Fergus's chair.

'You're a sight for sore eyes, April, and not just because I need your help at the show,' he said, waving to Connor and rushing ahead, barely drawing breath. 'Fran said you're making a cake, right?'

April nodded. 'It mightn't be pretty, and it mightn't even be cooked all the way through, but I'll give it a shot.'

'Bless you, child, I knew you wouldn't let us down. And you?' The man turned his frenetic energy towards Connor. 'You're an unfamiliar face. Where do you fit in?'

Connor held out his hand. 'I'm Connor Jamison. I've just arrived in town.'

'Wonderful, brilliant.' The man's handshake was as hurried as his words. 'I'm Harris O'Brien, head vigneron at Costin and Jankowski Wines. Also one of the chief stewards at the local show. You should come. Always a highlight of the year and plenty of room for newcomers. Feel free to enter too, we could do with some more entries, especially in the baking department.'

From the corner of his eye, Connor could see April stifling her amusement. Before he could answer, the man sprang out of his chair, waving a hand in the air. 'Hold that thought, I've just spotted Brian.' He left as quickly as he'd arrived, determined to garner more bakers between the speeches. But from this brief conversation, plus the warmth of April's greeting and the shared chips with Jean at the bar, Connor felt something that had been sorely lacking at his Rossvale posting.

He felt welcome.

5

The entrees were soon cleared and April was surprised to find the first hour of the night was over.

That went quickly, she thought, sneaking another look at Connor. His head was thrown back in laughter and from the sound of the carefree banter between the two housemates, they seemed to get along well.

Connor caught her watching them and leaned an elbow on the table, cupping his chin in his palm. His pale skin had acquired a slight tan in the months since she'd last seen him, making his light hair look even fairer. Scandinavian genetics, perhaps? With his almost-white hair and blue eyes, he looked positively Nordic.

'You having a good night?'

April smiled. 'Good wine, good food, good company. I've had plenty of worse Friday nights.'

Next it was time for the juniors to receive their trophies, a lengthy process as proud parents snapped endless photos of their golfers with the sponsors and the club president. She'd have to trek up there for her official sponsorship duties soon, too.

'I've never won anything like that in my life, but I can imagine if I did my parents would take even more happy snaps than they are,' Fergus said between announcements.

A familiar face strode towards their table and April's intention of giving Jean a stern talking-to about the disastrous double date vanished in light of their company.

'Hi Jean,' said Fergus, pulling out a chair. *Did they know one another? Had Fergus already been added into the local matchmaker's black book?*

'We're just talking about those snazzy trophies,' said Fergus. 'Do you have a houseful, yourself, Jean?'

'Trophies? Gosh, not me, but April here regularly scoops the pool at the Penwarra Show. Best in class for how many years running?' Jean thrummed her hands on the table in a mock drum-roll. 'Three years? Five?'

April shifted in her seat, mumbling an answer.

'Sorry?' Fergus cupped his ear, leaning in closer.

'Seven,' April repeated, taking a large sip of wine. She wanted to tell them the produce convenor begged her to enter every year, and she grew the veggies because she loved them, not because she wanted accolades. But if she was completely honest, a small part of her liked the thrill of show day and visiting the produce hall after judging was complete to see if she'd won anything. She couldn't cook to save herself or sew a single button, but she could grow things.

Connor caught her eye, as if sensing her reluctance to be in the spotlight.

'Well, I feel better now,' he said. 'I'm from a family of musicians, and my parents considered a month without a concert or a performance trophy a tragedy. Once my little sister Pippin cooked up a plan to hock the trophies to buy a new Lego set,' he laughed, then launched into a story about a piano recital, his littlest sisters and a family road trip to Cornwall, which had them all in hysterics.

He's a concert-level musician? April was impressed.

The wait staff circulated with the mains. 'I'll come back later, I don't want to miss my roo burger,' Jean said, wiggling her fingers and returning to her seat.

'Fergus told me the food is great here,' said Connor, leaning back as the waitress delivered their meals.

'You both chose the lamb roast?' said Fergus, picking up his cutlery to halve his kangaroo burger. 'I hate to say it, but you're missing the best meal of the night.'

Connor grimaced. 'I'm not sure I'll ever get my head around the concept of eating Skippy.'

'You might change your mind after a few months dodging them on the roads,' offered Fergus between chews. 'And it's incredibly delicious too.'

Connor cast a doubtful look at Fergus's burger, then tucked into his roast.

'Man, this food is something else,' said Connor. 'You weren't exaggerating.'

'It gets better,' Fergus said, staring wistfully at his empty plate, as if he wanted to lick it clean. 'The chef, Geraldine Corcoran, is our neighbour and lives on the far side of the golf course. On a good day you'll smell the food coming out of her kitchen from the ninth hole. I've been entering her raffle for her cooking classes ever since I arrived. They'll send the raffle bucket around the tables after dessert.'

April's ears pricked up. Her mum, Polly, had given her a voucher for cooking classes last Christmas, but with the rush of summer, the shock of Justin's departure and the chaos of vintage, none of the classes had lined up with her schedule. *You're about to open a bed and breakfast, you should probably shake off this ridiculous phobia of cooking.*

'Which one's Geraldine?' She followed Fergus's gesture to the kitchen, spotting a brightly dressed woman beyond the servery window.

'Her main business is catering with ready-made meals, but she does Friday nights and functions at the golf club, plus the cooking lessons.'

Although the district was small, April had trouble keeping up with the comings and goings of new residents. It felt like each time she went to the supermarket there were more unfamiliar faces in the aisles. She turned back to find Connor's eyes on her charm bracelet.

He reached for the silver charms, his long fingers dwarfing the miniature music notes and instruments.

'What do you play?'

'Not sure I'd officially call myself a musician, but I pull out the guitar every now and then,' April said, turning as the microphone at the front crackled. 'I'll strum anything, but my playlists are chock-a-block full of old tunes. What's your weapon of choice?' If she had to guess, she'd peg him as a lead guitarist or maybe a trumpeter. There was something about his presence that deserved centre stage.

A memory stirred from the Adelaide conference, but before she could grasp it, or Connor could answer, a voice came over the microphone, asking guests to take their seats. Only a few trophies remained on the table behind them, including the award Lacewing Estate had sponsored for almost two decades.

April jumped up from her chair. She'd need to move quickly if she wanted to make it to the bathroom and back before the final round of formalities. She applied a fresh coat of lippy, smacked her lips together and dashed into the loo.

The bathroom door opened, letting in a wave of chatter from the club rooms, along with a conversation that continued as two women entered the stalls. First they bemoaned the lengthy speeches, then the conversation turned to the wine Lacewing had supplied for the event.

April smiled to herself. It was always nice to hear people say good things about Lacewing Estate and she didn't often have the chance to eavesdrop on a conversation about her father's most recent vintage. But after listening for a moment, her stomach soon sank.

'I'm not sure how many years Lloyd Lacey's been at the helm, but perhaps it's a few years too many,' said the first lady. 'It's a nice winery, but they've been putting out the same old varieties for thirty years, they haven't changed with the times. It's just a little . . .'

April waited silently to find out what the woman was about to say.

Dated? Behind the times? Fusty?

None of the words were especially nasty, nor were they officially incorrect, but it still hurt to hear her father's pride and joy being discussed so flippantly.

'Stale! That's the word,' said the first woman finally. 'Not bad, not ridiculously expensive or pretentious—just plain old stale.'

The other lady agreed. 'It's so sad when the smaller wineries die a slow death. They can't compete with fresh young businesses, but there's so much history going down the gurgler. Still, you've got to move with the times, right? Maybe if they grew a few more varieties or made a bit more of an effort with their presentation.'

An indignant heat rushed into April's face. *Who was this lady, and how was she in any position to comment?* Had she spent years nurturing new vines, risen in the wee hours to register pickers before the sun was scorching and packed last-minute orders at midnight like Lloyd? April wanted to march out of the cubicle and demand to know if this armchair critic had ever worked a day in a vineyard, but instead she stayed in the cubicle, frozen to the spot.

The second lady raised her voice over the sound of flushing cisterns. 'Street appeal's half the battle with new customers, isn't it? I mean, the wine's fine, but people probably write it off without tasting it.'

Fine? Fine!

Both ladies stepped out of their stalls, continuing their critique as they washed their hands. 'A little va-va-voom would go a long way to improving foot traffic. I see the daughter's working on a little accommodation venture, but will it be enough to bring them into the twenty-first century? What was the name of the winery that folded a few years back?'

April gulped, her brain finding the answer as the ladies left the bathroom. Millie May Wines had gone into receivership several years ago, and everyone in the district had seen their demise coming from a mile away.

The couple who had owned the Millie May winery had subscribed to the same ideals as her father, intent on making wine the same way their forebears had, relishing the challenge of working the land rather than crunching numbers, with no interest in drastic modernisations or following trends and technical advances. They'd bowed out of the industry with grapes still hanging and unfulfilled sponsorship promises. The vines were eventually ripped out and replaced by the new investors. Was that where Lacewing Estate was heading?

Connor savoured every morsel of his Black Forest cake and from the rapid rate Fergus gobbled down the lemon tart, it was obviously a winner too.

'I'd better buy myself some raffle tickets,' Connor said, noticing the chef emerging from the kitchen with a bright-yellow bucket. Wallets were opened and bank notes were exchanged for raffle tickets. When it came around to their table, Connor and Fergus bought five each.

'Geraldine, meet your new neighbour,' Fergus said, introducing them both. 'Connor here just moved into my spare room—he's looking for a job at one of the wineries.'

Geraldine beamed as she handed them their tickets. 'Pleasure meeting you. Do call in if you need anything, my place is the next best thing to a supermarket. Save you driving into town.'

The kind offer was unexpected. 'I'm even more useless in the kitchen than Fergus; at least he can manage eggs without burning the house down. My specialty is toast, but if I run out of bread, I'll keep it in mind, thanks.'

Geraldine's face twisted, like the concept caused her physical pain. 'Well then, as a welcome to the neighbourhood, I'll toss in a few extra entries for the raffle,' she said, ripping off two more tickets and handing them over. 'It sounds like you need the cooking classes more than most. And I'll keep an ear to the ground about any winery jobs.'

Connor thanked her, and as Geraldine left, he scanned the room for April. He should be asking *her* about potential job vacancies and yet another question was on the tip of his tongue . . . She'd come to the event alone, did that mean she was single? And if so, would she now agree to that drink they'd talked about in Adelaide?

He flexed his ankle one way, then the other, the twinge in his leg jolting his thoughts back to the UK and the heartache he was determined to put behind him.

Connor checked his smart watch, relieved there were no new emails or missed calls from international numbers. His ex-fiancée Phoebe hadn't understood the ebb and flow of a winery, and she hadn't liked jazz much either, but she'd been a constant in his life for so many years. He'd lost count of their break-ups and make-ups, but this time it was different ... This time he'd been the one to end things.

The club president stepped up to the microphone.

'This should be the last gong,' Fergus said, mistaking Connor's restlessness for impatience. 'But everyone usually kicks on for a few hours afterwards. Nobody knows how to party like a bunch of boomers at a sports function,' he chuckled.

The bathroom door clanged and he watched April conferring with the club president before striding to the trophy table and collecting the trophy.

With her bright dress and smooth legs, she didn't need a microphone or trophy to grab the room's attention, but now, watching April studying her shoes as she was introduced, Connor thought her smile seemed a little forced.

He fought the urge to step up beside her and take her hand. *You barely know her*, he reminded himself.

'Excuse me, coming through,' said a familiar voice, and he twisted in his seat to see Jean squeezing between the chairs towards them. She took April's chair.

'Like a deer in the headlights, isn't she?' Jean whispered, nodding to the stage. 'Much prefers her vines and her veggie patch to the spotlight, but she's a smart cookie and a hard worker. Single too, in case you were wondering.'

Single. Connor reined in his reaction to this news, keenly aware of the older lady's watchful gaze.

On stage, April was fumbling in the pocket of her yellow dress, and time slowed as she tried to open a folded sheet of paper while juggling the trophy.

She's going to drop it!

'I think somebody should give her a hand up there,' Connor said, sliding out of his chair and skirting around the now-empty trophy table. As he stepped onto the stage, April gave him a grateful look, relinquishing the trophy. Her hands trembled as she unfolded the paper.

'Thanks,' she whispered, sitting her typed speech on the lectern and angling the mike to better suit her short stature. Once she had everything under control, Connor handed the trophy back and retreated to his seat.

'A gentleman too,' Connor heard the old lady murmur to Fergus as he paused by their table before continuing to the bar. He had a feeling it would be safer than sitting beside Jean . . .

April's voice was shaky with nerves as she began her speech. *Why did I let myself get roped into this?* Fran was the pro at schmoozing and sponsorship gigs, and while her dad wasn't exactly charming on stage, he at least had the advantage of experience.

Butterflies swooped around in April's stomach. The wine hadn't helped—if anything, it had made her feel more scatty, especially combined with the surprise of seeing Connor and the knowledge there were rumours flying around town about Lacewing Estate.

All the more reason to nail this, she told herself. 'Tonight I'm proud to be handing over the major award at the Penwarra Golf Club. I heard the Kalangadoo golfers put up a great fight in the pennant championship today, so commiserations to them and congratulations to our players from Penwarra.'

She wiped a sweaty hand on her dress before continuing. 'For those who don't know me, I'm April Lacey, standing here on behalf of Lacewing Estate. In fact, the wine many of you are enjoying tonight is from my father's 2020 vintage, and we hope you like it as much as we do.'

April caught sight of dozens of golfers, including Dan at the back of the room, raising their glasses in her direction. There was a lot of love in the town for Lacewing Estate. That wasn't something anyone—not even the knockers—could take away from them.

'We might not be the fanciest winery in the district,' she continued, her voice getting stronger and her confidence building. 'Our cellar door and tasting room were built by my father and grandfather forty years ago and they've poured their hearts into the wines and the vines over the years. We have a proud history and our customers are like family to us. Without this passion, we wouldn't be here tonight, and perhaps we mightn't have been able to sponsor quite so many trophies like this whopper.'

There was a round of applause as she presented the trophy to the winning team, and as she looked around the room, April knew she needed to help her father keep their doors open.

'Thank God that's over,' she said, barely breaking stride as she collected her handbag from the table and sat down beside Connor at the bar. 'Are you hiding from Jean too?'

He nodded vigorously. 'Absolutely. I can't believe Fergus didn't warn me, she's a force to be reckoned with. Is she always—'

'So nosy?' she offered. 'Meddlesome?'

Connor smothered a grin. 'I was going to say *intense*. Great speech, by the way. Another sparkling? I hear it's from an outstanding winery. In fact, I've just had the full run-down of your strengths from Jean.'

April groaned. 'Jean has no shame. You should see her in the lead up to Valentine's Day. Or even better, if you *do* see her, quickly turn around and run in the other direction or you'll find yourself dating one of her many nieces, nephews, grandchildren or neighbours. My housemate, Lauren, has been sucked into her matchmaking schemes half a dozen times, but I'm steering well clear from now on.'

As much as she had enjoyed Connor's company tonight, she felt the weight of responsibility resting on her shoulders and wanted to get back to the winery. The women in the bathroom were correct. If Lacewing Estate was going to have any chance of thriving, they needed to change things.

'I have to head off, but I'll see you again soon, yeah? I'd love to pick your brain about marketing.'

'Count me in,' he said with an easy grin.

It might have been the adrenaline or just plain instinct, but without thinking it through, April leaned over and kissed his cheek before making for the door.

God, why did I do that? It's like taking out one of those stupid billboards and telling all of Penwarra that I've got a thing for the new winemaker in town. She felt more eyes on her on the way out than she had on the way in, which was saying something. Mortified by her faux pas, she nearly collided with Daniel, who was pulling his phone from his pocket outside the golf club entrance.

'Jean will have a field day with that,' said Dan nodding back into the club rooms. 'You know she doesn't need any encouragement, especially with a hottie like Connor.'

April waved away Daniel's teasing tone. She liked Connor, and he was certainly a better match than Jean's blind double date, but was she really ready to get back on the horse?

That would be a conversation for another day; right now, she had more pressing things on her mind, like helping her father bring Lacewing Estate into the new century without wounding his pride.

Her ute beeped as she pressed the keyfob. 'I've got to run, have a good one.'

'I'll try,' Daniel glanced at his phone with a grin, probably in the middle of digital matchmaking. 'I'll see you at the show next weekend, right?'

'It'll be hard to miss me, just look for the lady wheelbarrowing veggies into the produce hall. I'm hoping your little brother gets a few ribbons too.'

'Surely they'll give all the primary school kids a participation ribbon? He'll be crying into his fairy floss if not.'

※

Connor watched April leave, then quickly pulled Google Maps up on his phone, checking Lacewing Estate's location in relation to his new digs.

According to the app, it was a five-minute drive or an hour's walk from the golf club, which sounded like a pretty easy stroll compared to the distance between wineries in England. Although the wine industry was one of the fastest-growing agricultural sectors in the UK, the British weather rarely lent itself to leisurely strolls between vineyards.

He returned to the table with two fresh pints, finding Fergus with a smug look on his face.

'Wait till you see the magic trick I've just pulled for you.' Fergus winked, then confirmed that April was gone before hoeing into her untouched lemon tart.

Magic trick? Fergus wouldn't elaborate and it wasn't until the speeches resumed that Connor understood what on earth he was talking about.

'We're almost done here,' said Barney Anderson, the golf club president, from the front of the room. 'I just want to draw your attention to a few newcomers tonight.'

The club president gestured to Fergus and Connor. 'Raise your hand, lads, so everyone can get eyeballs on you.'

They dutifully lifted their arms as they were introduced.

'We all know our local winemakers are our biggest supporters, so on behalf of the town, let's give them a warm welcome. I've also heard on the grapevine—' Barney paused, a smile on his face as he listened to the groans and cheap laughs ripple through the room, '—that young Connor here is a qualified piano teacher, with a background in performance, and that he'll be taking bookings for lessons. He's also after a job in one of the local wineries, so spread the word, folks, and if we're extra lucky, maybe we can convince him to tickle the ivories for us sometime.'

Connor whipped around to see the smug look still on Fergus's face.

'You can thank me later,' Fergus said through his mouthful of dessert.

'I don't even have a piano,' Connor said, uncomfortable that the information had been shared when he'd barely unpacked his suitcase or arranged a job, let alone printed new business cards. And then there was the small matter of performing. Or, more to the point, his lack of performing since the accident. He'd only shared the information to take the attention off April, who'd faltered under Jean's laser focus.

'Ah, minor details,' said Fergus, nudging him with an elbow. 'I was chatting with the lovely lass at the bar and she reckons they'd be happy to see this one back in use. Bit of a tune up and you'll be sorted.'

The volume of conversations ramped up the moment the president stepped down from the microphone. Connor rose quickly, keen to catch Barney and check that it was officially okay to use the Yamaha piano hiding under the linen sheet.

The last thing he wanted was the town thinking he was taking liberties with their musical instrument.

April's yellow dress appeared in his mind.

Or taking liberties with the local women.

6

April shook two Berocca tablets from the canister the next morning and placed them on a tray with a glass of water.

Lauren's bedroom smelled like the bottom of a wine vat, and the precautionary bucket by her bedside table didn't bode well either.

'Why didn't somebody stop me drinking a whole bottle of champagne?' Lauren groaned, tossing an arm over her eyes.

'Ah, the perils of youth. Old enough to know better but young enough to do it again. And unless you were buying the fancy French stuff, I think you mean sparkling white.'

Lauren started shaking her head before realising it made the hangover worse and settling on grimacing.

'Same same. But even the alcohol wasn't enough to salvage my Tinder date. It was terrible. From now on,' Lauren said, tossing the Beroccas into the water and watching them fizz, 'I'm only dating younger blokes who aren't as likely to mention their brood of children halfway through dessert. It was going great until then, but I'm not old enough to be a stepmum.'

'Well, if he was prepared to leave that level of detail out of his profile, you wouldn't want to touch him with a ten-foot bargepole anyway.'

'True,' Lauren said, sipping the drink cautiously. 'Or maybe I need to resort to Jean's match-making services again, or just give up on finding a single bloke who's in his thirties without a bucketload of baggage or a gaggle of kids.' She shuddered theatrically, then groaned again. 'Ugh, my brain feels like it's in a blender when I do that.'

'I'll let Jean know, she'll be here in a jiffy,' April grinned, pulling her short dark hair into a stumpy ponytail.

'Don't you dare, at least not until I've recovered from last night. I'm never drinking again,' said Lauren, giving her a sharp side-eye. 'Was the trophy presentation as bad as you expected?'

April shook her head. 'I'll explain over brekky. Can you stomach toast?'

She returned to the kitchen and whisked two thick slices of sourdough from the toaster before slathering them with butter and jam, then perched on the edge of her friend's bed with a plate of her own and explained about the renovation's budget blow-out, Connor's surprise arrival and the conversation she'd overheard in the toilets.

'Dad loves it, he really does, but if they want something to retire on, they'll need to shake things up a bit. My little B & B will be good for tourism, but I get the feeling we need a few more irons in the fire.'

'And you're the one breaking that news to Lloyd?' Lauren nibbled her toast doubtfully.

'Softly, softly.' April thought of Connor and the idea that had been brewing in her mind overnight. 'Dad's not brilliant with change, but if I can bake a cake for Fran's show tables, the least he can do is consider a few new options.'

She'd been both disappointed and relieved that the lights had been out at Lloyd and Fran's mudbrick house when she'd arrived home last night, but in fact, it had worked out well.

After spending the evening poring over Stephanie Scouller's bestselling marketing books, April felt better prepared for the conversation they needed to have.

'It might be madness, but I can't *not* say anything,' April said. 'I've gone over my notes from the Adelaide conference, I'm totally across the food tourism program and the opportunities with DestinationSA and I'll convince Dad to give Lacewing Estate a freshen up, even if I have to die trying.'

'Good luck!' Lauren said, stretching out in her bed.

April gathered her phone and notebook, determination fuelling her stride.

'I hope your dad's had a coffee before you march in there,' Lauren added. 'Last I heard, Lloyd thought marketing and makeovers were wanky, airy-fairy nonsense. His words, not mine.'

April laughed. She'd heard him use the same terms more than once. 'He doesn't have much choice. He mightn't like it, but what else are we going to do?'

Halfway down the laneway to the winery, she stopped to admire the beauty of their vineyard in the morning light: the dew glinting off the grassy rows and the vines still majestic as the last of the foliage embraced the rich tones of autumn.

Could she pull it off? Anything had felt possible when she stood on the stage last night, with the golfers raising a toast to Lacewing Estate, but now in the bright light of morning, doubt nipped at her heels. April looked at the stables to her left. She'd poured her money and heart into the B & B, but it was just part of her plan for the winery, not the linchpin.

A kookaburra swooped down from the gum tree, intent on the long grass by Gordon's trailer and emerged with a wriggling lizard. In the blink of an eye, the bird returned to its nest in the hollow and the lizard disappeared, likely a meal for hungry chicks.

Mishka nuzzled her hand, as if unsure why they'd paused. April continued walking. Small, flagging wineries couldn't afford to rest on their laurels. If she didn't encourage her dad to act now, it might be too late.

Connor tossed a load of laundry into the washing machine and set out for the town centre, keen to explore his new surrounds.

While he'd been unprepared for Barney's announcement at last night's function, Connor had left the golf club with more than five potential bookings. One of the trophy winners, who was also a local principal, had assured him there'd be a flurry of interest when she put a note in the primary school newsletter. So that was his side hustle sorted—now he just needed to find a day job.

He took the main street slowly, parking at the far end and exploring on foot. Awnings overhung the footpath and Connor peered into shop windows, getting a sense of the rural town and the local businesses servicing the small population.

The scent of pastry and warm bread lured him to the bakery at the end of the street, and as he waited for the steady stream of customers to breeze in and out of the doors, he spotted a community noticeboard. Connor photographed two promising notices, then headed inside, his mouth watering at the display.

'How does anyone choose?' he asked with a smile.

The bemused bakery worker glanced from the sultana-studded, sugar-coated cream buns to the wedges of assorted slices and savory scrolls. 'One of each,' she quipped with a laugh. 'But if you're into moderation, you can't go wrong with a snot block.'

'A snot block?' What type of food did the establishment stock out the back, and why would anyone choose something so indelicately named when they could have a cinnamon scroll, jelly cake or bee-sting slice?

She pointed to the tray underneath the cash register. 'The snobs call it vanilla slice, but either way, it's the most popular item on the menu. You a tourist?'

Connor nodded, then shook his head. 'Not for long, I hope. I've just moved here,' he offered, pulling out his wallet. 'A black coffee please. And I've not yet tried vanilla slice, but when in Rome, right?'

She nodded, pleased with his decision, and pulled not one but two slices from the glass-fronted cabinet. 'How about two-for-one as a "welcome to town" deal? And next time you're in, I want to hear whether you prefer traditional or French vanilla.'

Connor promised to report back. Taking a seat at the outdoor table, he studied the generous slices, which looked to be custard sandwiched between layers of flaky pastry and topped with a glossy icing. One filling was butter yellow, while the other was a delicate creamy colour. His phone rang as he deliberated on which he liked best.

April's voice on the other end caught him by surprise. But what she said surprised him even more.

'An assistant winemaker? Yep, I'd love to come for a look,' he said, brushing crumbs from his polo shirt and jotting down the address. 'Rivoli Lane? This sounds random, but I don't suppose you have a little brother called Archie? I'm already heading your way at 2 pm.'

'He's my neighbour,' she explained. 'Remember Dan, who you met in Adelaide? It's his half-brother.'

'Cool,' said Connor. 'That works out perfectly, I'll see you afterwards.'

Connor paused outside Lacewing Estate as he drove to meet his first prospective student, Archie. There was a stark difference between the two neighbouring properties; Winklin

Wines boasted imposing stone gates, a tree-lined entrance and a glass-fronted winery. In contrast, Lacewing looked distinctly down at heel, with a humble cellar door, dusty parking area and tired landscaping. He could imagine which winery received the most foot traffic and, with a stab of guilt, knew which one he would have chosen if he was judging strictly on appearance.

He continued down the lane to the Winklins' home, and a few moments later, was sitting in a magnificent glass conservatory with Rupert Winklin.

'I've never met a winemaking piano teacher before. What do you teach?'

'It's not the most common career combination,' Connor agreed. 'Mostly primary students, but I've taught adults too. Classical, modern, jazz, I love it all. What's your son interested in?'

'Depends what day of the week you ask him,' Rupert said, smoothing his silver hair. 'Archie's a gifted child. He took a shine to the piano but he's barely touched it since his last teacher moved interstate. I've tried, but—' He lifted his hands in the air and shook his head. 'Archie always responds better to someone else pulling him into line. I don't want him throwing away his talent.'

'I can't promise anything but I'd certainly like to meet him and see what he's capable of. Is he here?' Connor was pretty sure he would have noticed a ten-year-old child by now, but he glanced around the room anyway.

A loud crash echoed through the house followed by the sound of footsteps on the terrazzo tiles. 'Dad, you should have come to the movies. It was awesome, you need to come next time, even Mum liked—'

A gangly-limbed, freckle-faced boy skidded to a halt at the sight of them. 'Who are you?'

Connor stifled a grin. 'You must be Archie? I'm Connor, and from what your dad's told me, I might be your new piano teacher.'

Archie's little mouth twitched as he mulled over the information. 'But you're not old enough to be a teacher. Mrs Damhuis was as old as the hills, even older than Dad.'

Rupert coughed, his heavy grey eyebrows furrowing. Connor guessed that Rupert was probably half a century older than his son. A lady closer to Connor's age than Rupert's joined them. *Rupert's second wife,* Connor suspected.

'Manners, Archie!' she said, introducing herself as Archie's mother, Felicity Winklin. She stayed only a moment before disappearing into the cavernous house. Rupert ushered him and Archie into the piano room.

'Library' was a more accurate description, thought Connor, looking at the floor-to-ceiling bookshelves and the sliding ladder with wheels on the bottom. A glossy piano took centre stage in the middle of the floor.

What a home.

It only took a few moments to establish that Archie had a keen ear for music. Connor suspected he'd make steady progress with the right guidance.

'I'm happy to go ahead if you both are?'

Rupert pulled out his phone and checked his calendar for the best afternoon to begin the lessons, while Archie looked a little less certain.

'Do you smack people's fingers with a ruler?'

''Course not,' replied Connor.

'Will you make me practise all the boring exercises every single lesson?'

'Depends what they are. Possibly.'

'Do you give out lollies for extra-good kids?'

Leaning against the piano, Connor considered this for a moment. 'Occasionally. If they've worked hard and made a solid improvement. Certainly not each lesson, though.'

'Okay. This is the most important question and if you get it wrong, I'm not gonna be happy.'

Connor smothered a laugh. *Archie would get on famously with Nell and Pippin,* he thought, bracing himself for the deciding question.

※

April strode into the winery after lunch, hoping her father hadn't done a backflip on everything they'd discussed this morning.

'The position's still vacant,' she reminded him. 'And you said it would be a perfect opportunity for the right person.'

Lloyd grumbled and fussed with the wine order he was packing. April lifted an eyebrow. He'd used the early harvest as the excuse for not hiring someone the moment Justin left, but now she got the feeling her father wasn't being entirely honest.

'You weren't thinking *I'd* step into the role?'

He taped the box, giving a noncommittal shrug. 'You arrived home from that Adelaide conference more jazzed about Lacewing Estate than I'd seen you in a long time. I wanted to leave space in case—' Lloyd paused. 'Would it be such a bad thing? You're invaluable during harvest and one day this will all be yours.'

'Dad,' she said gently. 'We tried that and it worked for all of about two months. I love Lacewing, but I'm a mighty fine horticulturalist. This is your winery, and you can run it however you like.'

'It's *our* winery,' he said, leaning in. 'Always has been.'

She smiled and slotted the invoice into the packing label before passing it to her father. 'Even so, I'll stick with lending a hand when and where I can. You need someone who can tell a shiraz from a cabernet at a hundred paces and know exactly what's missing from a blend. I just don't have the winemaker genes, not like you. Connor seemed to know what he was talking about.'

'I'll see what he's like in person but I'm not making any promises,' said Lloyd. 'I'm not interested in someone barging their way in here and telling me how to run things. He might be a dill like that Justin fella, and if that's the case, we're better off ambling along the way we are.'

Ambling was the right word, thought April, looking at the dark timber trim and the terracotta tiles. It was in dire need of an overhaul.

Lloyd cleared his throat. 'And I've thought on your suggestions about using your long-service leave to spruce the place up.'

April's ears pricked up at those words. 'And?' She tried not to sound too eager.

'You don't want to waste your time off on something like that,' Lloyd said, shooting her a smile as he packed more wine bottles into a second box. 'You should be sunning yourself in Bali or skiing in New Zealand, not fussing about filling in potholes or whatever else you think needs doing around here. Our customers don't worry about little things like that.'

April thought otherwise, and she'd told him as much when they'd spoken this morning, but she knew better than to push. Ensuring the meeting with Connor went smoothly was the first hurdle, then she'd begin drawing up a list of improvements and presenting Lloyd with a water-tight marketing plan.

Softly, softly.

'I'm just thinking a freshen-up, not a drastic refurbishment,' she said, running her finger through the dust that had settled on a bottle. 'I'll be working on bright, clean lines in the B & B, so why not factor in a little extra paint to give this place a lift? And I've made up my mind about my long-service leave. I'm already looking forward to eight glorious weeks here in Penwarra, helping Gordon finish off the stable,' April beamed. 'Who needs to be a jet-setter when you can be a go-getter, right?'

Lloyd sighed but she could tell his heart wasn't in it. 'You know I don't like it when you use my sayings against me.'

'I should start writing them down,' she teased, heading out through the tasting room as her stepmother came through the door.

'Hey Franny, how's it going with the show entries?'

With a groan, Fran unloaded an armful of paperwork onto the long timber bar that was meant for wine tastings but spent half the time being used as a desk.

April added another thing to her mental list of winery upgrades. Creating a designated workspace for Fran's admin duties would free up the far end of the bar for its official purpose.

'I've had a trickle of new registrations over the weekend, but it's slow going. I wonder if this Connor is much of a cook? It'd be a tragedy to have only one or two entries in the blokes cooking section.'

'A tragedy,' repeated April, trying to keep a straight face. 'He'll be here shortly, how about we quiz him then?'

'I've got a spare show program here somewhere.' Fran rummaged through her paperwork, then opened and shut drawers on the other side of the bench, becoming more flustered by the minute.

Fran had been bothered by the golf ladies' gossiping. But, April reasoned, surely it was better they knew the town was speculating on Lacewing's future?

She put a hand on Fran's arm. 'I've got one at my place,' she offered. 'And I've got a few errands to do at the stables before Gordon leaves. I'll bring the program back with me.'

Connor wasn't sure what type of question Archie was about to lob his way, but from the earnest look on the young boy's face, it was evidently important. Archie's father had been keen for twice-weekly lessons, but it wasn't just the regular income that made Connor want to answer it correctly. He'd worked with hundreds of young pianists over the years, and he knew Archie's natural gift for music would make him a joy to work with.

'Go on then,' Connor said. 'Hit me with it.'

Archie folded his arms across his chest. 'What's better? Cats or dogs or sheep?'

Connor considered this carefully, suspecting his answer would be a deal-breaker. There hadn't been signs of any animals in the immaculate household—no half-chewed shoes or scratching posts—and he'd been so busy admiring the grand home and extensive vineyards that he'd failed to look at the paddocks beyond the house.

No clues there.

Connor looked at Rupert, who was intent on his phone, and then back at Archie just in time to see him glance in the direction of Lacewing Estate. He recalled the golden retriever April had spoken about in Adelaide.

'Dogs first,' Connor said firmly. 'Then sheep and then cats.'

Archie's face lit up, confirming he'd passed the all-important test. And although he'd only come to introduce himself and discuss lesson timetables, Connor soon found himself leaning against a fence post as Archie rattled off the names of his pet lambs.

'That ram lamb is AJ, the small ewe lamb is Spice and there's her twin, Sugar.' Connor followed the boy's outstretched arm, observing the livestock. He'd only dealt with the end result—when it was roasted or presented as a herb-crusted rack at a restaurant—and couldn't differentiate the ewes from the rams.

'Are they friendly?'

Archie shielded his eyes with a hand, squinting. 'Sometimes. If you have a bucket of lamb pellets, they're extra friendly, but most of the time they're more interested in grazing than patting. Can you see two more lambs?'

Connor scanned the grassy paddock. 'They could be sleeping, or hiding behind the big trees,' he suggested.

But the boy frowned and looked over his shoulder at the main house. His father, Rupert, had his back turned, making a phone call.

'How good are you at catching sheep?' Archie asked in an undertone.

Connor spluttered. 'Me?'

Archie nodded sagely. 'Yep, we need to get Barbara and Marty back in the paddock before Dad notices they're out again.' He tipped his head to Lacewing Estate. 'And before they eat April's grapes. Or worse, the veggie garden.'

Without waiting for a response, the boy jogged across the narrow limestone road that divided the two properties. Connor wasn't sure about the intricacies of sheep herding either, but he acknowledged it would be easier with two people. 'I'm not sure I'll be much help,' he said, quickly catching up to Archie.

'Last time I went near a sheep, it was a petting zoo at a school fair and the thing bit me.'

Archie giggled, shaking his head. 'Just help me sneak up on them and then when you get close enough, grab one and toss it over your shoulder like a sack of wheat.'

Connor didn't have the heart to tell Archie that although he'd lugged plenty of wine barrels and musical instrument cases, his experience with sacks of wheat were on par with his shepherding skills.

They found the two lambs gorging themselves on the fresh grass between the gold- and red-leafed vines. But despite their fuzzy, innocent faces and contented grazing, the sheep moved like greyhounds when they spotted Archie and Connor. After five minutes of zipping between vines and getting no closer than an arm's length, Archie reconsidered his plan.

'You can't go straight behind them, Connor, you have to kind of sneak up on them; fool them into thinking you're going one way and then grab them from the side. Like a footy tackle, you know? Only gentler, we don't want to hurt them.'

'I was never much good at rugby,' Connor admitted. Wiping a trickle of sweat off his forehead, Connor wondered how long it would be before Rupert realised they were missing. 'We might be better off asking your dad for help.'

'No!' Archie's vehemence was clear and Connor sensed the boy would rather spend all day trying to catch the lambs himself than involve his father. Was it smart getting between the two Winklins before the first piano lesson had even started? Probably not, but looking at the scowl on Archie's face, he figured the boy must have his reasons.

'This is April's winery, right?' Connor asked. 'Does she know how to catch sheep?'

Archie nodded, relief crossing his face. 'She's much better than you,' Archie assured him, turning on his heel and loping away.

A quaint cottage was nestled on a grassy plot amongst the vineyards. With its simple peaked roof and freestone paddock-rock walls, it looked like it had been built by convict settlers. Archie knocked on the door and April emerged, followed closely by a shaggy golden retriever.

'Mishka!' Archie called, then explained the problem to April as he fawned over the dog.

'Connor?' said April, stepping onto the verandah decking. 'We're not expecting you yet? And how on earth did you get roped into sheep wrangling?'

Connor grinned. She looked just as good in cut-off denim shorts, a polo shirt and with messy hair as she did dolled up in a dress and heels.

'Right place, right time, I guess,' he said with a shrug.

'Oh boy, Baaaaarbara will be going on the baaar-be-cue at this rate. I'll grab my boots,' she said, pulling a baseball cap over her hair. Mishka rushed over from Archie to greet Connor, blithely ignoring April's whistle. 'Can you grab her, Connor?' said April. 'Mishka's not much help when it comes to rounding up sheep.'

'I know how you feel, old girl.' He kneeled down to greet the friendly dog while April hurried over with the lead. With Mishka tied to the verandah post, they went in search of the lambs. Connor was surprised how easy they were to capture with an extra set of hands.

'Man, they've been pigging out big time,' said Archie, grimacing as he lifted one of the lambs.

Connor looked between April and Archie. They'd each slung a sheep over their shoulders with practised ease, but the animals couldn't be especially light with those bulging bellies.

'Want a hand?'

'I'm fine,' said April.

'Me too,' Archie panted.

Connor offered his assistance again when Archie stopped for a breather a hundred metres later.

'They're heavier than they look,' the boy admitted, handing Connor the woolly escape artist. Connor tensed as the animal quivered, struggling against him, but it settled once he'd tucked it over his shoulder as April had. The sheep even rested its head against the back of Connor's head, as if finally resigned to being ferried home.

'I thought their hair would be wiry,' he said, stroking Marty's coat.

'Wool,' Archie corrected.

'You should snuggle them when they're a few weeks old,' said April, opening the gate to the Winklins' paddock. 'Softer than a brand-new pair of Ugg boots.'

Just like putting kangaroo on the menu, Connor wasn't sure how he felt about the living, breathing creature he was holding being turned into footwear. 'But you've named them? Aren't they pets?'

'Let's just say they're multi-purpose,' April said, noticing his conflicted expression. 'You're in the country now, Connor, and we grow some of the best food and fibres here in the Limestone Coast. You'll get used to it.'

Connor and April set the lambs down, watching them hurtle across the paddock to rejoin their mates.

Archie piped up, 'Are you letting Connor start a veggie patch too, April?'

'I've got enough trouble with you in my veggie patch,' she said, ruffling Archie's hair. 'Connor might help my dad with some winery stuff.' She caught Connor's eye, and he could see her hesitate. 'And if you're still happy to hand over a few of your marketing tips, I'll happily soak up all your hints? It doesn't have to be now,' she hurried to add.

But from the look on her face, Connor could tell she hoped it would be sooner rather than later. 'I think we're done here, right Archie?'

The boy opened his mouth to protest as Rupert Winklin rounded the corner. 'I was wondering where in the blazes everyone went to,' Rupert said, then pointed at Archie. 'You've got two minutes to change into something smarter before we leave for Robe.'

Connor wasn't sure where Robe was, but from the look on Archie's face, it wasn't as much fun as the prospect of an afternoon at April's place. He looked completely glum as Rupert led him back inside.

'Now that the sheep-herding's done for the day, I'm wide open until 2 pm,' Connor said to April with a laugh. 'Does now work?'

She nodded eagerly.

7

Wiping his feet on the doormat, Connor instinctively ducked as he walked inside April's home.

'This isn't one of those English buildings with the hobbit-height doorways, you know,' she quipped.

He returned her grin. 'Thank God for that, I have a constant crick in my neck from ducking under doorways back home.'

April's place was cosy but bright. Unlike his golf course digs, which was full of functional but mismatched furniture, April's soft green couch was covered with cushions that matched the fabric of the curtains and there were houseplants in nearly every corner of the timber-floored living room.

'Nice place,' he said, setting his keys and phone on a scrubbed oak dining table and turning his attention to the boisterous retriever prancing around at his feet. 'And you're a friendly pooch, aren't you,' he said, laughing as Mishka flipped onto her back and offered her belly up for a rub.

'Thanks, it's not huge but I love it. And Mishka's completely shameless when it comes to visitors,' said April. She hooked her finger towards the arched doorway beside the kitchen. 'Bathroom's in there if you want to wash up.'

The pot plants continued along the hallway to the bathroom, where a huge maidenhair fern dangled from the ceiling above a corner spa bath and the tiles looked like something from his grandmother's house, with tiny bunches of grapes on every third tile. Connor washed his hands with citrus-scented handsoap, then walked back out to the kitchen.

'So this is part of your family's estate?' he asked, leaning against the bench.

April nodded, pulling glasses from a cupboard. 'This was the original winemaker's residency, back when the first vines were planted. It's been a guest house, a storage shed and back in the forties it housed an Italian prisoner of war.'

April sounded so proud of these historical facts that Connor didn't mention that the stone walls in Derbyshire dated back centuries.

'Really?' A wet nose nudged his leg, and even though he'd just washed his hands, Connor found himself stroking the dog's velvety ears again.

April carried a jug of iced water over to the dining table and placed it between a notepad, laptop and vase of eucalyptus leaves.

Connor sat across from her and listened as she outlined her ideas for the winery. April had been keen to soak up information at the city conference, but it felt like something more was driving her now. She pressed him for feedback, welcoming his suggestions and quickly noting down the websites and blogs he recommended.

'If I'd known you were a marketing boffin, I would have made an appointment with you at the Adelaide conference instead of spending my money on the whiz-bang consultation,' April said.

He laughed. 'I'm not a guru, but I like putting this part of my uni degree to good use,' he replied. 'Most of the winemakers followed straight science and agriculture modules, but I sneaked into as many tourism and sales tutorials as I could. So far, it's proved pretty helpful. The Kiwi winery was happy to let me work with their marketing person, and they were in the middle of cost-conscious rebranding, so it was all about making the most of local opportunities and using a shoestring budget to improve what they had.'

'That's music to my ears,' she said, scribbling down a few more of his suggestions. 'I wish I could plug you into my laptop and download all your tips right now, but Dad's expecting us.'

'I don't mind coming back afterwards,' Connor offered, holding her gaze. She looked away to clip the lead on Mishka, then fixed him with a grin.

'Are you flirting with me, Connor Jamison?'

He raised an eyebrow, so his expression mirrored hers. 'I'm not sure that'd be the smartest idea, given I'm about to walk into a job interview with your father and I really *do* need a job. Unless of course, you thought it might work in my favour?' Connor spread his hands and shrugged, feigning nonchalance. 'In which case, I could certainly rise to the challenge.'

He couldn't interpret the fleeting expression that crossed April's face. *Too forward, perhaps?*

'Trust me,' she chuckled, giving a shake of her head. 'It probably wouldn't be the most strategic move right now.'

But there was something about the way she said it, and the wistful glance his way, that contradicted her words. *Right now . . .*

They strolled across to the winery, pausing at the building April was renovating for her bed and breakfast.

'It's a beauty,' said Connor. 'Made from the same paddock rock as your home?'

'Yep,' April said proudly. 'It's got a long way to go before it's ready for guests, but I'm thrilled with how it's come up so far.'

And while the cellar door and tasting room weren't in the same state as the old stables, Connor immediately saw why April was pushing for an overhaul. The facilities were tidy and the equipment looked well maintained, but the front-of-house areas had a tiredness that suggested first impressions weren't a priority.

April's father strode over from the tasting room. 'Lloyd Lacey, nice to meet you.'

Connor shook his hand, quickly discovering Lloyd was extremely proud of his daughter and his wines. Fran Lacey rushed in half an hour later, greeting Connor with an unusual and completely unexpected request.

'Nobody's ever asked me to bake a cake before,' Connor laughed, 'and if you could see me trying to cook, you'd probably understand why.'

Fran wasn't deterred. 'I don't care if it's got lumps in the batter or the odd bit of browning on the sides, I just need plates on tables,' she insisted. '*Please.*'

Sensing this was almost as much of a deal breaker as Archie's earlier question about dogs versus cats, Connor found himself agreeing. *What's the worst that could happen?*

He left with a show program, an entry form and a job at Lacewing Estate.

'You made a good impression on Dad,' April said, pointing out the different vines as they walked back to her place. 'He's a bit stuck in his ways but he loves his wine and treats both his customers and his staff like family.'

'Sounds way better than my last boss in Rossvale. There's something to be said for predictability. Though this cooking business might be a bit of a clanger. I really can't cook to save myself.'

'Me neither,' said April. 'In fact, it's a sign of exactly how desperate they are that Fran even asked me to enter. Whatever you cook would have to be completely black and inedible to beat the mess I'll be plating up.'

'I take my hat off to anyone who can pull off a proper dish,' said Connor. 'All my mates think they're the next Jamie Oliver or Heston Blumenthal but I'd rather teach piano chords to a six-year-old than attempt a roast dinner. I mean, the timing, for starters! How does anyone get the peas done at the same time as the potatoes, not to mention the gravy?'

April lifted her face to the sky. She seemed delighted to find another non-cook. 'Finally, someone who speaks my language. And I don't know about the UK, but a leg of lamb is too pricey to risk in the hands of an amateur. I'd rather sink thirty dollars into a cheese board than risk burning a roast, or worse, giving myself food poisoning because it isn't cooked enough. My mum, Polly, actually bought me a voucher for cooking classes for Christmas after I had a little cooking mishap involving a frypan and a fire extinguisher.'

They arrived at April's house and Connor leaned against the verandah post, studying her. 'And how were they?'

'The classes or the frypan?' April grinned. 'The pan went in the bin, and I haven't taken the classes yet. I'm sure it'll be a room full of tragic widowers and bachelors, old guys who are only just learning to cook because their wife or mum died, right? And bored housewives who want to be the next Donna Hay.'

'I've never been called tragic before, but I purchased tickets in the raffle for the cooking classes with Geraldine. It's being drawn at the show and I'm terribly tempted to buy extra tickets between now and then.'

'Stop it,' she said, raising an eyebrow cheekily. 'Piano playing, cake-baking, sheep wrangling and now raffles. You're a dark horse, Connor Jamison.'

And as he followed her inside, Connor found he was already trying to think up new ways to make her smile like that again.

April pulled a bottle of chardonnay from the fridge, poured two generous glasses and found a packet of white chocolate Tim Tams in the freezer.

She set them on the table on the verandah in front of Connor. It was the least she could do after picking his brains about marketing. Plus, she liked that things hadn't gotten awkward after she'd put the kibosh on them dating. She wasn't ready for romance again, not after Justin. There was nothing unprofessional about talking marketing strategies with the new winemaker over a glass of wine, not when she was in her daggy weekend clothes, smelling like lanolin and without a hint of make-up, was there?

'Now, this isn't a traditional pairing,' she said, gesturing at the table, 'but I'm ready for a sugar hit and these two go perfectly together.'

'You're right,' he said after sampling the combination. 'They go well together. Okay, show me your list again.'

She spun her notebook around so he could see the list of jobs that needed doing around Lacewing Estate, and the loose costs she'd allocated for the tasks and the timeframes.

'I bet I could help you jazz up the cellar door for less than that.' He tapped his finger on the figures that she'd allocated for the venue make-over.

'You're just saying that to make me feel better,' she said, nibbling the chocolate coating off the edge of her Tim Tam. It was already an ambitiously low figure, yet given their current financial restrictions, it was still more than they could afford to spend. 'I plan on doing a bunch of landscaping and tidying up myself, but a new fence, signage and website will gobble up a huge chunk of that sum.'

'You'd be surprised how much you can do yourself.'

His optimism was infectious, and it would have been easy to get swept up with Connor's suggestions and enthusiasm, but April had done her research. She knew shortcuts and unrealistic expectations led to either a shoddy job or disappointment, quite often both.

His phone had lit up multiple times throughout the afternoon and it did so again as she carefully folded the A3 sheet of paper they'd covered with their brainstorming ideas.

'I've taken enough of your time for one day,' she said, offering him another biscuit. 'Thanks so much for your help, I've got some great ideas to follow up with.'

Now that she had her long-service leave approved, plus a loose budget, a timeline, an action list and a vague plan, she felt better about the scale of work that needed to be completed.

'I don't mind, really,' said Connor. 'I'd rather that than spend my whole Australian trip working inside a winery or on the couch in my rental.' He stretched and a flash of toned stomach appeared below the hem of his T-shirt.

April found her eyes lingering a little longer than necessary and startled when Mishka brushed past her in search of crumbs.

She'd noticed he was a blusher—his face and neck flushing red when he got animated or embarrassed—but right now April felt like she was the one with a hot, splotchy face.

Remember what happened with Justin . . .

She shuffled into the shade, welcoming the slight breeze.

'Can't complain about this weather, either,' he said, turning his face up to the sun streaming onto the verandah. 'How far's the beach from here?'

'Beachport's my favourite and it's only fifty minutes away, but they're all good,' she said, giving him a rundown of the three nearest swimming spots. 'There's Southend, if you're after somewhere quiet, and the Winklins have holidayed at Robe as long as I've known them. Plenty of surf breaks too.'

'Surfing?' He considered her question with amusement. 'I've never imagined myself on a board, but—' He shrugged. 'Maybe I'll have a shot?'

The funny thing was, despite her earlier emphasis on professionalism, April had no trouble picturing him in bathers, a surfboard under one arm and a striped towel slung around his neck. Waxing his board, jogging into the swell, paddling after a wave. If his strong arms were any indication, it would be quite the sight.

'We really, *really* need to get out more,' she told Mishka after she waved Connor off.

Connor's first week at Lacewing Estate was a stark contrast to his inaugural week in Rossvale. While Johann was happy to throw new employees into the barrel room and assess their work with alternating bouts of buoyant praise and scathing criticism, Lloyd was adamant that Connor mosey around the vineyard to get a feel for the grapevines first, then take his time acquainting himself with the vats, presses and processes.

'It feels like I'm slacking off,' Connor admitted at the end of his third day, outside the cellar. 'I'm used to hitting the ground running, not easing my way into a new job.'

Lloyd seemed completely bemused by Connor's proactive attitude. 'No sense rushing headfirst into mistakes, I always say. There'll be plenty of time for working; first you need to understand what we do, how we do it, and—most importantly—why we do it.'

Nodding, Connor followed Lloyd into the underground cellar, where the air was always cool, the atmosphere serene. The radio was set to a classical music channel and Chopin's Sonata No. 3 in B Minor rippled from the speakers.

It was a piece Connor had learned in his teenage years and even as he stood in the musty cellar with an empty box in his arms, his mind took him straight back to the Birmingham Music Hall, where he'd sat at a baby grand piano wearing a suit that was a little too snug. He could vividly remember the polite applause of the crowd as he'd accepted a cash prize at the end of the event.

'April teases me about wasting power on this little radio,' Lloyd said, bringing him back to the present. He took a bottle of red from the bottom rack and held it up to the light, his movements unhurried. 'But I like to think the wine is alive, and the music calms it down as it matures.' Dust floated through the air as he wiped the label with his sleeve. With a silent nod, Lloyd put the bottle into the box Connor was holding and looked for another.

'My grandfather was all about hands-on simplicity, hand-pruning vines, using a pair of Clydesdales to plough up the soil and transform the flat country into vineyards,' Lloyd went on. 'My dad replaced the horses with tractors and added chardonnay and riesling to the collection, and I've tried to keep the ball rolling by making the same great wine, removing the vines that aren't performing well and keeping the flavours consistent.'

'Makes a lot of sense,' said Connor. 'And how about the future?' It was clear Lloyd lived and breathed the winery, and although he seemed averse to risk and expansion, surely he had a vision for Lacewing Estate's future?

The silence stretched out as Lloyd filled the box with six dusty bottles.

Too deep a question for the first week, perhaps?

'I'm not quite sure where the future takes us,' Lloyd said eventually. 'As you've seen, my daughter lives on the property but makes her income elsewhere. She's taken a different path to the one I expected, but that's her prerogative, I guess.' His tone was stilted and Connor sensed he was explaining it to himself, as much as to Connor. He gestured for Connor to follow him out of the cellar and put the box on the long timber bar in the tasting room. 'Hopefully, one day she'll change her mind and make this her main focus, but until then, I'll keep on doing what I love and making good wine. The stables is a good project though, I think.'

They both turned to the broad window that overlooked that aspect of the vineyard, complete with April's home, Kookaburra Cottage, and a smattering of ancient gum trees.

Not for the first time, Connor wondered what it would be like to live onsite at a vineyard, waking up every morning surrounded by the vines that had been planted, pruned and nurtured by your ancestors.

If it were me, I'd be lining up to take the reins and put my stamp on the business.

'Anyway, enough of all that for now. I've chosen six of my favourite vintages here, ones that encapsulate what we're all about at Lacewing Estate so you can get a feel for the place. Shall we?'

Connor looked at the small clock beside the shelf of wine glasses. It was 2 pm.

'Sorry Lloyd, I've got piano lessons booked for later in the afternoon. Tomorrow?'

Lloyd nodded agreeably. 'Sure, tomorrow or the next day. Whenever suits you. I don't need much of an excuse to knock off early and enjoy a good drop.'

And although Lloyd Lacey seemed relaxed about the winery, Connor suspected he wouldn't be too thrilled about someone messing with his daughter's feelings. What was it he'd said about rushing headfirst into mistakes?

Fergus was shuffling around the kitchen when Connor finished work, the fixings for a fry-up spread across the bench.

'You know where the fire extinguisher is, right?' Connor joked, admiring his housemate's determination and persistence in the face of repeated cooking failures.

'Don't laugh, at least I dinna sign up to bake a bloody cake,' Fergus called out cheerfully from the depths of the fridge.

Ergh, the cake. Connor closed his eyes. He needed to put a bit of brainpower towards that, but it'd have to wait until after his piano lessons. He changed and headed to the golf club.

Three hours later, after six piano lessons, Connor was in dire need of a drink and something to eat. The smell of scorched eggs still lingered when he returned home.

'I can whip you up a batch of eggs,' said Fergus, removing the frypan from the sink where it was soaking, and tackling the engrained black grit with a steel-wool scourer. 'And I've been thinking about this cake-making malarky. Are they really that desperate for entries?'

Recalling Fran's plea, Connor slid the show program across the benchtop. 'From the sounds of it, they need all the cakes they can get. And there's a cash prize as incentive.'

Fergus set aside the scourer. 'Well, that's that, then. I'll bake a cake too. Now, how about those eggs?'

'This'll be fine, thanks mate,' said Connor, peeling the plastic lid off a frozen curry. He slid it into the microwave and opened his laptop at the dining table, knowing he was cutting it fine if he wanted to catch his little sisters before they went to school.

'Happy birthday, Pipsqueak,' he said, smiling at the sight of their neat braids and the crisp white shirts under their school blazers.

'Aren't you going to sing me happy birthday, then?' Pippin put on a mock stern look and cupped her ear until he started singing. Nell joined in with an imaginary conductor's baton.

'I got the best presents, Con. You should see the new school bag Mam and Dad got me, so much better than the Godawful St Mary's bags, and Nelly got me the whole series of *Wolf Girl* books. They're Australian, you know. Heidi gave me the Harry Potter novels too.'

She chattered on, with his parents chiming in for a brief hello between packing lunches.

'And where are you off to tonight, Pip? Nightclubs, high tea at the Shangri La?'

She stuck out her tongue. 'Ha ha. Mam and Dad are taking me to Pino's Pizza. And you'll never guess who's coming.'

Pippin sounded breathless, and with the lag in the computer conversation Connor couldn't tell if the flash in her eyes was mischief or glee.

'King Charles? Um, you've got a boyfriend? No, no! I've got it,' he deadpanned. 'You've invited Harry Styles and he's bringing all his mates with him?'

Pippin gave him a withering look, just as Sharyn clapped her hands and reminded them they'd miss the school bus if they dillydallied too long.

'Nope, it's your Phoebe. She called around last night and I invited her.'

It took all of Connor's acting skills to seem nonchalant. She certainly wasn't 'his' Phoebe. Not any more. A million questions popped into his head, but instead he exhaled slowly.

'Is that right?'

His ex-fiancée hadn't been in touch with him for months and now she was tagging along to his family's birthday celebrations? Without him? What the hell?

Sideshow alley was adorned with colourful show rides, from the clowns with their expressions of perpetual astonishment to the swinging chairs that fanned out at speed.

It's amazing what can be achieved in show week, thought April, surveying the showgrounds. They'd been bare just a few days earlier. Now marquees and stalls were in various stages of being erected, and a small army of volunteers in yellow high-vis vests were marching across the lawn, looking harried even though the show gates didn't officially open for another two hours.

April pulled the Hilux up between the poultry pavilion and the produce hall, enjoying the familiar pre-event excitement.

'Another magnificent haul there, April?' called Jean, who was attaching an awning to the front of her coffee van.

'I hope so, Jean,' said April, stepping out from the ute. 'Are you set up for coffee yet?'

'For you?' The older lady gave her a grin. 'Give me five minutes, pet.'

With its polished floorboards and cloth-covered trestles, the weatherboard hall was a space April knew well and even without a single entry or place card to tell her what went where, she set about adorning the empty tables with the first load of her homegrown fare.

Tomatoes over here, root vegetables on this one, mixed basket in this corner. She'd always preferred arriving early and setting out her entries before the 9.45 am rush.

Soon the numbered cards were neatly propped beside each of her entries and all that was left on the backseat of her ute was a red Tupperware container that she'd borrowed from Fran.

Not that anyone will know whose container it is, April thought, running her finger over the strip of electrical tape she'd used to cover Fran's name.

She collected two coffees from Jean, inhaling the fresh, earthy scent.

'Come by after you've given Fran her latte, I've found a great fella for you,' Jean said, putting the finishing touches on her set-up. 'He's a pig farmer from Tarpeena, a real lovely lad.'

Balancing the coffees on top of the Tupperware, April waved a non-committal hand, hoping Jean would be flat out with customers when she returned. Jean meant well, and although April didn't want to be roped into another of her matchmaking schemes, she also didn't want to hurt the older lady's feelings.

She strode through the hall before pausing at the arched doorway that divided the produce and baking sections. The only reason April had ever previously entered this side of the hall was to admire the sky-high sponges and perfectly paired yo-yo biscuits, or to scan the bottled preserves for Lauren's handiwork or deliver lunch to Fran, who always started show day in a flap and finished ready to collapse into a heap.

April looked down at the red container, taking a breath to compose herself before walking beneath the arch. Last night's baking efforts had yielded a bench full of dirty dishes and a cake that still wobbled in the middle when she liberated it from the baking tin. She had a newfound respect for her stepmother's dedication and culinary skills.

'I bought you this,' April said, setting a takeaway coffee cup on the table beside Fran's clipboard, 'and this.' She set down the cake with an apologetic wince.

'You're an angel,' said Fran, pulling out an entry ticket and sliding her ruler down the entry chart. 'First and only entry in the beginners' cake category.' While her smile was quick, April knew that tight voice.

'What type is it?' Fran lifted the lid, squinting at the cake. 'Chocolate?'

April shook her head with another wince. 'It's vanilla.'

Fran took a gulp of her coffee and gave a pained nod. 'Vanilla it is then. Thanks love, just leave it there and I'll pop it on the table for you.'

April rubbed her stepmother's shoulder. 'How's everything going? Did Audrey and Eileen bury the hatchet or are they still boycotting the event?'

With a glance at her watch and then at the sparse entries studded across the tables, Fran shook her head. 'No sign of them yet, but they've got an hour until entries close. I'll even let a few late entries slip through if that's what it takes to get more plates on those tables. We'll be the laughing stock of the show circuit if we have to cancel the cookery display for next year's celebrations or the centenary the year after that.'

April wasn't sure how to erase the deep lines between Fran's eyebrows, and wished once again that she shared her knack for cooking. She supposed it was normal for most people to persevere when they failed, until they were able to cook enough to feed themselves at least a few square meals a day. In all her years of adulthood, she'd never aspired to fill her fridge and pantry with home-cooked food, nor compete against the region's best bakers in the annual show extravaganza. But looking at Fran, and then the near-empty tables in front of them, she realised it wasn't just Fran fretting, that the show could actually crumble if they didn't get more support.

'You won't have to cancel,' April promised. 'I'm going to take those cooking classes and by this time next year, I'll have more than a burnt cake to contribute. Well,' she laughed, adding a caveat, 'they might be bone-dry muffins, crumbling biscuits *and* burnt cake, but it'll be a good effort. And I'll rope in some more contributions too, yeah? Archie will be an easy recruit, Dan too, and I'm sure I can bully Lauren into it.'

She saw Fran blinking furiously. 'Oh April, I can't ask you to do that.'

Footsteps sounded on the floorboards behind them and April turned to see Connor and Fergus both carrying plates with plastic bags over them.

'Two more entries!' April was impressed that in a single week, Connor had grasped how much the event meant to Fran.

'I know Lloyd said you'd be happy with anything,' Connor started, a familiar flush creeping across his cheeks, 'but the cake was so bad, I thought I'd warn you first. Fergus's was marginally better than mine, the show-off, but we won't be offended if you'd rather they went into the bin.'

April bit her lip to stop the grin spreading across her face. While Connor's sank in the middle like a crater, Fergus's was distinctly volcano-shaped, with a peak on the top that was only accentuated by the lumpy icing.

In terms of baking precision, they were on par with April's singed offering, but Fran brushed away tears and opened her arms to accept the entries. 'Thank you both,' she sniffed.

April caught Connor's eye.

How is it possible that his quite-likely inedible cake just amplified his hotness level tenfold?

'That was tense,' Fergus said the moment they emerged from the hall. 'Normally people make jokes about smoke alarms and fire extinguishers and food poisoning when they see my cooking, but I thought Fran was going to kiss me.'

April laughed, surveying the extra stalls that had popped up in her absence. 'It's been a big week, she'll be so glad when this weekend's over.'

The entry into the showgrounds was even more congested when they exited the hall and she hoped some of them were making a beeline for Fran's registration table. April thought of the cooking classes voucher Polly had given her for Christmas. It was time to get comfortable with being uncomfortable.

Walking into the show hall that afternoon to find his horrendous excuse for a cake had been sliced in half, with the raw middle oozing out onto the plate, was a bit like opening the message from his little sister last night and seeing a photo of Pippin in a birthday hat, blowing out the candles with one arm around his ex-fiancée, Phoebe.

Connor still hadn't responded to the message, nor had he acknowledged the photo his eldest sister Heidi had sent the next day of Pippin and Nell beside a small terrarium, holding two tiny tortoises. Normally he replied immediately, but with the wine tasting, baking and show hoopla, it had been easy to nurse the hurt a little longer.

A snicker and a giggle from the young couple in front of him brought Connor back to the present. Lingering by the motley array of entries in the blokes' section, they singled out his flop. He couldn't really blame them—his cake *was* comically bad.

'Yeesh,' said the girl, quivering with laughter. 'I bet that guy's a bachelor.'

Harsh!

Connor ducked his head, not quite hearing the man's comeback. There had been something about the Lacey women that had made him enter. April, with her reluctant acceptance that she was bad at baking but would do it anyway, and Fran, whose stress levels had risen as the week progressed.

It's just a cake, he told himself, glad to see Lloyd's effort had won second place, despite looking a little mushy in the middle. He continued to the beginners' section, browsing the entries in the cake category.

'Could've been worse.'

He turned to see April standing across the table. 'At least there were three entries in my category, otherwise that sad excuse for a vanilla cake would have a card next to it with my name on it.'

Connor tried not to grin at the square slab of coffee-coloured cake. The chunk missing from the side suggested it had put up a fight coming out of the tin.

'If you want to feel better, just have a look at my oozing mess over yonder. If anything, I think we've helped all these other contestants feel a bit better about themselves,' he said. 'How'd you go in the veggies?'

'Not bad, but the showstopper was little Archie. His bunch of herbs won a prize and he was runner-up in the cherry tomatoes.'

Connor followed her to the produce section. 'Not bad? Come on! You've got your name plastered on prize cards up and down this aisle. In fact, if I didn't know better, I'd think you raided the veggie aisle at Foodland for these.'

He picked up a bunch of bright-orange carrots, the featherlike greenery tufting out the top. 'Peter Rabbit would risk his fluffy tail for these,' he marvelled, liking the way she glowed with humble pride. 'And these aubergines? I've no idea what you'd cook them in, nor would I know a thing about growing them, but seriously. Mind. Blown.' Although he wasn't a gardener, he could appreciate vibrant, fresh and perfectly formed produce when he saw it. 'I thought Jean was exaggerating at the presentation night, but there's hardly a category that you haven't got a guernsey in.'

There was no doubt she could grow things, so why on earth was she spending her days digging, planting and mowing for private customers instead of growing grapes with her father? A memory of the photograph from Pippin's birthday party flashed in his mind and he swallowed the question. *Who was he to make judgements on what someone else should and shouldn't do with their life?*

'Want to see my favourite part of the entire show?' April smiled, lifting an eyebrow in question. 'Follow me.'

Connor dragged his attention from April's entries and followed her out the door, wondering what could top winning an entire room of prizes.

A cacophony of noise and smells and colour greeted them as they walked out into the bright sunlight. Children bounced gleefully on an inflatable castle, horses cantered around a grassy oval, families queued for the sizzling onion-scented sausages and the air was thick with a carnival atmosphere.

'That's normally the footy ground,' April said, following his gaze to the horse events. 'And cricket in summer.' But today it was a whir of ponies with plaited tails, elaborate jumps and sharply dressed riders. They continued past the oval, April greeting most of the people she passed with a wave or quick hello, before they arrived at a small tin shed.

Inside, to Connor's surprise, were a mishmash of homemade scarecrows. From the traditional straw-stuffed shirt and hat combinations to the quirky and artistic entries, it was a sight that would chase away the most maudlin of moods.

'These are gold,' he said, stooping down to read the names pinned to the entries. Sparkling wine baskets and corks dangled from the hat of Mary POPpins, and a green bucket-hat, blood-spattered shovel and black suit made sense when he realised that Frankenfarmer was a riff on Frankenstein. But it was the smallest scarecrow that captured his heart. Wearing a red, yellow and navy jumper, and a knitted scarf and beanie, the scarecrow held a red football under one arm, with matching red, yellow and navy socks pulled up to his straw-stuffed, stockinged knees and a goofy grin on his hand-painted face. In his opposite hand—a stuffed washing up glove painted with stripes to match the rest of the uniform—the scarecrow clasped a fan flag for the Adelaide Crows.

'Oh, I get it,' he chuckled. 'The epitome of a scare *crow*!'

'It's the biggest footy team in the state, and the kid who made it must have known it would be the perfect ploy to win votes.'

A lady handed them slips of paper so they could cast their vote in the people's choice award. Connor recognised her as the mother of one of his newest piano students, Selina.

'Hey, Fiona. Tough gig choosing between these brilliant entries,' he said. 'They're all super. People go to a lot of effort, don't they?'

Even though he'd only been there an hour or so, it was clear the show was a much-loved celebration.

'They certainly do,' she said. 'Maybe you'll enter next year?'

Connor looked at April, then nodded at Fiona. 'I suppose I could try, though I'm not sure I'm creative enough to top those entries.'

Fiona shook her head. 'You're worse than Selina! It's about participating, not winning,' she laughed. 'Enjoy your day. And April, I hear you're doing great things with those renovations.

I've held a few items aside at the shop that I think you'll like. Call past when you're in a shopping mood.'

'Will do, thanks Fiona,' said April, waving goodbye.

'A shopping mood?' asked Connor curiously.

April explained that Fiona ran a second-hand shop in town. 'She has a great eye; half my furniture came from there and I've already bought a few things for Kookaburra Cottage. Dining table, linen tablecloths, crockery. You name it, they sell it,' she said.

They detoured past the petting nursery, which resembled a pram parking lot with excited children, wary animals and even warier parents. Between the kids and the lambs, ducklings, goats and piglets, the stall was the noisiest they'd passed so far.

'Dad, can we buy a puppy?'

'Charlie, say cheese for Mummy!'

'No, *don't* bite the kitten's tail, Lizzie.'

Connor watched as a tiny white-and-grey kitten leaped from a little girl's arms. Barely breaking stride, April scooped up the runaway feline and passed it back to the distracted stall supervisor.

'I bet they draw straws to see who gets that volunteering gig,' Connor said, enjoying their unhurried stroll around the grounds. 'Potato spirals, pulled pork burgers or dippy dogs?' He turned to April. 'My shout, I still haven't thanked you for getting me a job.'

They'd just finished their lunch when they spotted Archie emerging from the weatherboard hall, his face almost split in two with an ear-to-ear grin. 'I won something!' he called, jogging across to them with a ribbon in his hand. 'And did you see my scarecrow? It's the footy one!'

Connor whooped. 'That's what I voted for and I didn't even know it was yours.' He felt the warm glow of Archie's unadulterated joy and wondered if the boy would respond the same way when he nailed his piano pieces. He hoped so.

Archie and April left him in the line for hot jam donuts and headed back into the hall for another look at the produce display. Connor was two people from the front when he heard his name being called.

'Ah, Connor Jamison. Just the man I was looking for.'

The other people in the queue turned to watch as Geraldine Corcoran clapped Connor on the shoulder.

'I've just this morning drawn your name from the raffle bucket, if you're still keen on those cooking classes?'

'Is this a pity prize?' he laughed. 'Did you see my entry in the cookery section and then fossick around in the bucket for my sorry name?'

She shook her head, the large painted wooden beads around her neck clunking. 'I'm insulted,' Geraldine said. 'I haven't seen your cooking but now I'll make a point to suss it out. That way,' she said with a wink, 'I can get an idea of what we need to work on.'

'Oh, there's a whole lot to work on,' Connor replied, feeling his face grow pink as he listened to her outlining the lessons and the food they'd learn to cook by the end of it. *She doesn't know what she's getting herself into.*

8

There was a tang of salt in the air when April pulled into Beachport the following weekend. Just the sight of the mighty Southern Ocean and a lungful of brackish air had the tension in April's shoulders loosening, though she was still thinking about the renovation as she approached the Beachport jetty.

She and Mishka had skipped last Sunday's beach walk due to a post-show hangover, but the rest of the week had been productive, with the B & B's battered walls transformed by smooth grey sheets of gyprock. She'd worked alongside the tradies, mixing glue, passing tools and admiring the way the plasterboard instantly made the space feel more like a guesthouse than a horse shed.

April stopped several times as she walked the length of the jetty, chatting with keen fishermen along the way. She found herself pausing to watch a girl and her father catch a small pinkie on a hand reel. Mishka was equally fascinated by a fisherwoman's bait bucket and tackle box, so April moved on before the retriever nosed her way into trouble.

Shrieks of laughter came from the shore and she looked up to see a group of swimmers wading into the water, laughing and squirming as their bodies adjusted to the cold temperature.

'Mad as a bunch of cut snakes,' said another jetty stroller as she fell into step beside April. 'Wouldn't catch me doing that for quids.'

'Not sure I'd be brave enough either,' April agreed, shivering. The temperature was one thing, plus the sharks, stingrays and seaweed, but the distance... She couldn't imagine making it out to the pontoon, let alone the end of the jetty.

By the time April was back at the shore, the swimmers were on the home stretch, and when she emerged from the coffee shop, a latte warming her hands, the swimmers were peeling off wetsuits, swimming caps and goggles, and rinsing off under the outdoor shower.

April threw a tennis ball into the shallows and Mishka bounded after it, flying into the water. As she waited for Mishka to return, a colourful beach towel caught her eye. Even with dripping wet hair, she recognised the swimmer as the chef from the golf club presentation the previous month.

'Beautiful morning, isn't it?'

'Sure is! Though I'm not sure it's warm enough for bathers,' April admitted.

The lady wrung the water from her curls and chuckled. 'That's why most of us wear wetsuits. It's fine once you get moving around and makes for a great start to the day. You never regret a swim.'

'You're Geraldine from the cooking school, right?' April rushed to change the subject, suspecting the start of a swimming group sales pitch ahead. 'I signed up for your beginner classes yesterday. I wasn't sure the voucher would still be valid, eighteen months later.'

'I'll always honour vouchers, even if they're curling around the edges and speckled with fly poop. Wonderful, we've got enough for a full class now,' Geraldine said, reaching into a tote bag and donning a fleecy jumper. She fished a business card from her bag and handed it to April. Her fingers were icy but her smile was warm. 'What made you finally sign up for the classes, then?'

April told her about the show baking and her bed and breakfast. 'Might be a bit of a stretch but I'm hoping to have warm muffins on arrival and maybe, if I can get the hang of this cooking thing, I'd love to throw together a hamper of freshly baked goodies for vineyard picnics. And I've promised my stepmum I'll enter a bunch of things in next year's show.'

'Ah, the all-important Penwarra Show, right? Sounds like two fabulous reasons to arm yourself with new skills. We'll get along just fine, I can already tell,' Geraldine said, bidding farewell.

After another hour with her toes in the sand, watching Mishka paddle in the shallows as she mentally sorted the to-do list for her week ahead, April headed back to Penwarra.

Lloyd was in the vineyard when she turned into the limestone laneway. She parked at her house and walked across to see what had caught his attention in the shiraz vines.

He pointed to a mound of tiny brown balls in the grass. Wishful thinking hadn't hindered the roaming tendencies of Archie Winklin's poddy lambs, and although she'd ushered them down the laneway and back into their paddock before they'd done any damage to the vineyard last week, they'd left their own unique trail of incriminating evidence.

April tried to look surprised. 'More rabbits?' she asked innocently, trying to cover for her young friend's pets.

'Big woolly ones, I reckon,' Lloyd said. 'I'll have another word to Rupert about fixing those fences. New boundary fencing isn't in our budget right now, but we don't want those sheep thinking our vines are theirs for the taking.

They can't get into the freezer quick enough, that pair of troublemakers.'

'Dad!' She swatted him with the back of her hand. 'Speaking of fences, I've had an idea for the pile of paddock rocks behind the tractor shed.' The mound was mostly limestone that they'd painstakingly, back-breakingly picked from the far paddocks before planting the latest grapes, ranging from football-sized stones to boulders that could only be moved with the tractor.

Lloyd straightened up and dusted his hands on his navy trousers. 'You're going to dig a big hole and put them back underground?'

She pointed to the winery. 'Nope, I'm going to build a new entryway for the winery.'

'You? Or a team of expensive stonemasons we can't afford?'

'Well, I'm going to look into it,' she said. *How hard can it be balancing a few rocks on top of one another*? She'd watched a few YouTube tutorials on dry stone wall building and while it didn't look easy, she suspected it would be more forgiving than a hot oven and expensive ingredients. At least the rocks and her time didn't come with a price tag.

Lloyd shielded his eyes against the sun, frowning at the current entrance. 'What's wrong with the gates we've already got?'

They both knew that wasn't a flat out 'no', and April felt a little ping of glee as she shrugged. 'For starters, the "L" started flaking off the sign last summer and as much as I love the idea of working for *Acewing* Estate, I feel it's one of the easy things to check off the list.'

'Easy?' He snorted. 'Have you tried constructing a rock wall before? Building that mud-brick house was the beginning of the end for your mother and me, and I only continued on with the cellar door out of sheer bloody-mindedness. And because hard labour felt like a better option than drinking my way through the divorce proceedings. Ask your mother if you don't believe me,' he said.

'Maybe next time she calls,' April replied, knowing they would have long forgotten the conversation by the time that happened. For the second time that day she hurried to change the subject.

A conversation about her nomadic mum, who'd happily relinquished parenting responsibilities in favour of travelling, was a one-way path to a grumpy Lloyd.

'I heard from Connor yesterday,' she went on. 'He was impressed with the chardonnay, reckons it tastes great, even at this early stage.'

Lloyd's frown eased a little, as she'd known it would, and she hooked a thumb towards Kookaburra Cottage. 'He had a good idea for the bed and breakfast too, want to come see?'

In no time, she had the front door unlocked. 'I was explaining how I planned to replace the fireplace when Connor spotted the beams we'd removed to make way for the mezzanine. Instead of scouting around for an antique fireplace surround or buying a new one and making it look old, he suggested a floating mantle. They do it all the time in the UK, and when I told Gordon, he said it was pretty common in the rustic American craftsman houses too. What do you think?'

Lloyd studied the chunky piece of timber dubiously. 'You reckon that'll make a good display feature? Looks like it's come off the underside of the Beachport jetty.'

April rolled her eyes. Since Connor had mentioned it, and Gordon had agreed that he could make it work structurally, she'd created a Pinterest board with similar fireplaces and floating mantles. She knew they could do it.

'I don't suppose you can spare Connor for an hour or so a day?' She picked up a broom and began pushing a pile of timber offcuts towards the wall, not wanting her dad to see quite how keen she was to have an extra set of arms. 'Or maybe one afternoon a week. Just while I'm on long-service leave?'

Lloyd looked over from the freshly plastered walls to the portable scaffolding Gordon had set up for painting. She hadn't accepted his suggestion that she take a real holiday, and from the chalkboard full of jobs she'd propped in the corner, it was clear she wouldn't be spending the next seven weeks on the couch.

'I'll think about it,' Lloyd said eventually, throwing her a wry look that usually preceded a 'yes'. April hugged her arms around herself, trying to contain a fist pump. *We'll have Kookaburra Cottage up and running in no time.*

'Cooking classes?' Sharyn Jamison snorted with laughter on the computer screen, her amusement clear even with the slight lag of the internet. 'Good luck to your teacher!'

Connor and his father, Jock exchanged a look. Sharyn *had* attempted to impart her limited culinary skills to her children, but it hadn't been smooth sailing for anyone involved, let alone the kitchenware.

Connor's bedroom window was open, and the sounds of nature floated in on the breeze. Birds, cicadas and livestock from the paddock across the road were a stark contrast to the pigeons, bustling traffic and bin lorries from home.

'Oh, listen to those magpies,' said Sharyn, her face brightening for a moment, then dimming again. 'Now, love, I was telling Phoebe about some of your Aussie plans and she says you haven't even touched base since you've been away. Would it be so hard to reach out, just let her know you're okay?'

Sharyn's face settled into that worried look he knew so well. 'Mam,' he said softly. 'You said yourself it was the right decision, coming to Australia.'

She nodded emphatically, looking to Jock for support, before nodding some more. 'I did, I did. Of course it was, Con. You know we support you no matter what you do. But she's a bit hurt, that's all.'

'Heidi said the young 'uns call it "ghosting",' Jock offered helpfully.

'I know what ghosting is, Dad. And I'm not ghosting Phoebe, I'm just doing my own thing and focusing on the future, not the past.'

'You could still win her back, Con, before someone else snaps her up and takes her ring shopping.' The hint of hope in Sharyn's voice was clear, even as she hurried to get her words out.

Connor shook his head, a small headache forming at the base of his skull and the niggling ache in his leg making itself known. He stood up and carried the laptop outside. Surely, in the unfaltering Australian sunshine, his folks would see the ridiculousness of their suggestion.

'I'm here for two years, Mam. Trying to sustain a relationship that was floundering when we were in the same flat was difficult enough. An overseas relationship needs a hell of a lot of ticks in the right column, and we all know that's not the case with Phoebe and me. I've no idea why you'd invite her for a birthday dinner.'

He felt better once he'd got that off his chest, although one look at his mother's crestfallen face, and her attempt to shake off the comment, made him feel a little guilty.

'She's just such a lovely girl, Con. You should have seen the message she wrote in our Pippin's birthday card. Said Pip was like the kid sister she never had.'

Connor looked away, too easily able to picture the perfectly linked cursive and the careful way Phoebe would have held a ruler under her pen to ensure her handwriting followed a straight line. He changed the subject. 'How's Heidi?'

Jock jumped in to reply, perhaps sensing his son had reached the edge of his tolerance for Phoebe-talk, and updated him on their second-eldest child. Heidi's passion for social issues and justice had made her a shoo-in with the police force and there was never a shortage of conversation when the topic turned to her line of work.

'She's dead keen to join you for a quick jaunt, said something about flying across to meet you in Sydney,' Sharyn added.

'You know I'm twelve-hundred odd kilometres from Sydney, right? That's more than the length of England.'

'You won't stay in the one tiny region for your entire trip though, will you Con?'

After assuring them he had plans to travel, and would happily show Heidi around if she ever saved enough for the airfare, Connor signed off with a promise to call again soon. He headed into the kitchen, prepared a plate of toast and cup of tea, then took his breakfast back outside.

The phone rang out twice before Heidi finally answered the video call. Her fair hair was scraped back into a bun, her high-vis jacket zipped up to her chin and her cheeks were flushed from the cold.

'Busy night on the beat?'

'Enough drama to keep the night flowing. I just nicked a geezer for trying to rob his local curry restaurant, and the idiot not only called the staff by their names, proving he was a local, he also used his football scarf as a mask,' Heidi said with a sigh, adjusting the angle of her phone camera. 'Dead giveaway. I'd hate to think how dull Fridays would be round here without the hardworking drug dealers and halfwits holding up their end of the bargain. Tell me something new from your neck of the woods. Got a pet kangaroo yet?'

'Kangaroos are so passé, Heids. Emus are the next big thing.'

'Unless you're eleven and thirteen, then it's all about the tortoises,' Heidi said, her voice wry. 'Made the books I'd bought Pippin look like chopped liver. It's Turty this and Myrtle that. I don't think Harry Potter stands a chance in comparison to two tiny reptiles. Phoebe's lucky I didn't claim it as my own idea.'

Connor groaned. 'I've just spoken with Mam, who was singing Phoebe's praises. Not you too?'

Heidi held up a hand and he could see she was wearing gloves. When she stepped out of her vehicle, her breath came out in clouds. 'Okay, okay,' she said, striding past brick-walled buildings, with a familiar mess of external power cords he was yet to see in Australia. It was evidently rubbish day in the small city of Derby, with blue and black bins cluttering the background. It felt like the polar opposite of the vast greenery and open countryside of Penwarra.

'Don't shoot the messenger, but she asked after you,' Heidi added.

Connor tipped his head to the sky. Did he have a sign on his forehead that said, 'Advice wanted, bring your five bob here'?

'Alright, I won't say another word,' she said, although it was clear she wanted to. The kitchen door opened, and Connor waved as Fergus walked outside in only a pair of boardshorts, his hair wet and a towel around his neck.

Heidi peered into the camera. 'Why hello, buff Aussie in the background. Connor,' she scolded, 'you didn't tell me your flatmate was a babe.'

'Sorry to break it to you,' Fergus called out, 'but I'm a Scotsman through and through.'

She shrugged and peered into the screen. 'Either way, now I'm even keener to visit Down Under.'

Connor rolled his eyes at his sister. 'Fergus would make a terrible boyfriend. He's just as clueless with a frypan as me and from what I hear, he's already charmed half the ladies in town. He'll be married by the time you get out here.'

'Oh, leave off,' called Fergus cheerfully, returning inside and swigging directly from an orange juice bottle.

Heidi made one more dogged attempt to steer the conversation back to Phoebe, but Connor deftly sidestepped the subject with a story about Archie Winklin's Houdini-like lambs and then an update on his new job at Lacewing Estate.

'It's a tiny family winery, smallest I've worked at yet, but it's not half bad. The wines taste amazing, the people are nice, they just need a revamp to bring the property into the 21st century.'

'Sounds like a job for my big brother,' Heidi said. 'If anyone knows how to make a silk purse out of a sow's ear, it's you.'

Her confidence was heartening and in an instant, he forgave her for pressing him about Phoebe. Connor finished the call and went inside.

'I've lost count of how many sisters you have,' said Fergus. 'Two? Three?'

'Three—Heidi, Nell and Pippin. You?'

'All brothers. I'm the youngest and apparently all I'm good for is free babysitting and odd jobs. I couldn't get out of the UK fast enough, you know what I mean?'

Connor nodded, but the truth was, he already missed his family, even when they thought they knew what he wanted better than he did. He'd spent months away from England at a time, living and working in Europe, plus a six-month stint in New Zealand, but two years in Australia would be the longest he'd been away from home. Unlike Fergus, who sounded happy enough to put down roots in the district if things went well with his work, Connor wasn't entirely sure how he felt about living oceans away from his family long term.

Connor followed the golf course fairways until he arrived at a short, winding driveway. A two-storey homestead emerged from the line of trees, adorned with beautiful stonework, high gables and a balcony that wrapped around the second floor. The gardens weren't to be sniffed at either. One look at the manicured hedges and the array of flowers and clusters of herbs made it obvious that Geraldine dedicated much of her week to weeding, pruning and planting.

I didn't expect this at the bottom of the drive, Connor thought, admiring the home. It wasn't ancient like the manors back in England, but it was the oldest he'd seen since he'd arrived in the country. And from the cheerful chalkboard out the front welcoming the students, it promised to be a warm and friendly space to tackle one of his weaknesses.

A memory of Sharyn's scorched saucepans ran through Connor's mind. Wiping his clammy hands on his T-shirt, he glanced back at the golf course, feeling less confident by the second. Fergus had left half an hour earlier, his four-wheel drive jam-packed with camping and fishing equipment, pumped about his trek across the sandhills to the ten-mile beach.

As far as Connor knew, the Scotsman had never been beach camping or shark fishing before, but he wasn't letting that stand in the way of him and a good weekend.

Connor tried to shake off the burgeoning ambivalence. He couldn't fathom cancelling on Geraldine at the last minute, especially when she was gifting him the lessons, but what would it say about him if he was terrible at cooking even after a suite of lessons?

What if he made an idiot of himself in front of April? And when had he started caring so much about what other people thought of his culinary skills?

9

April pulled into Geraldine's driveway and saw Connor standing at the edge of the yard with his hands in his pockets, looking like he was about to do a runner.

'You really don't like cooking, do you?'

He perked up at the sight of her, the apprehensive look replaced with a smile.

'I'm a bit nervous,' he admitted, closing the ute door for her. 'And it's not helped by wondering why on earth I'm devoting my weekend to cooking when I could have been camping and beach fishing with Fergus and his mates.'

April listened as he described his housemate's weekend plans. 'Ah, the ten mile, right? Trust me, it'll go one of two ways. They'll either get bogged to the hilt and spend all day in the hot sun digging themselves out, or they'll glide over the dunes, catch a few fish and drag you along next weekend. Either way, you'll be pleased you let them do the first run solo.'

'Spoken from experience?'

'I've heard enough four-wheel driving stories from Dad's friends.'

Connor gestured towards the path. 'Ladies first.'

The smell of rosemary and flowers greeted them as April admired the vine-covered pergola. Unlike Lacewing vineyard, the vines here were still covered in ripe fruit. *Table grapes,* April deduced, popping one into her mouth.

They followed a little chalkboard sign to the side of the house, where Geraldine greeted them at the door.

'Come in, come in,' she said, her curls secured with a bright pink headband and an apron that wouldn't be out of place in a paintball skirmish. A chef, green thumb and an artist too, perhaps?

'Your gardens are amazing,' April said, pausing to admire the landscaping again. There was a cheerful mix of annuals, perennials and ornamentals, interspersed with natives.

'The garden was Merv's domain, rest his weary soul. I try my best, but he'd turn in his grave if he saw my shoddy attempts to keep it neat.'

April looked a little closer, noticing the grass creeping over the pavers and weeds dotted in amongst the annuals. Without attention, they'd soon set seed and prove twice as troublesome next season.

'It looks in tiptop shape to me,' Connor said politely.

Geraldine shot him a shrewd look. 'Don't look too hard. That hedge is a flashback to my son's pudding bowl haircuts from the 80s. Not to be repeated.'

Connor's lips twitched and April spotted the hack marks at the top of the hedge. Battery-powered hedgers and petrol engine edgers weren't exactly light, especially for someone of their cooking teacher's stature.

Geraldine led them into the most well-equipped kitchen April had ever entered. There were three ovens, each with its own workstation of pots, pans and bakeware, and a ginormous farmhouse sink in the middle of the island bench.

You could bath a baby in there.

As well as the impressive facilities, light flooded into the room through French doors and wide windows. The kitchen overlooked a park-like backyard, which echoed the well-watered golf greens next door. The class was bigger than April had expected, with eight students ranging from a twelve-year-old girl called Maddie to a bloke older than Lloyd. The other students were all gathered around the massive island bench in the equally large kitchen. 'Connor, could you be a gem and hand out name tags, please?'

Here a month and he's already on a first-name basis with locals I've only just met? Definitely not a wallflower.

April rolled up the sleeves of her striped shirt, looped an apron over her head and stuck a sticky name label on the front. She looked the part, but as she glanced at the matching oven mitts and utensils, she wasn't sure she *felt* the part. A buffet of burnt roasts, undercooked chicken and over-salty soups ran through her mind and she glanced back at the door. *Was it too late to make a hasty exit?*

And then she remembered her father's delight when she had told him about the cooking class this morning. She'd never hear the end of it if she bailed now. April stole a look at Connor as Geraldine ran through the items on their menu today. She was glad he was doing the lessons too, and that he was evidently as nervous as she felt.

When she looked up, Geraldine's eyes were on her. 'Showing up is half the battle, so you've all taken the biggest step. It will be fun, I promise.'

April smiled to herself, wondering if the teacher knew quite what she was in for, and resolved to give it her best shot.

Connor cracked an egg on the side of the bench, sneaking a quick look around the class to see if everyone else was fishing slippery shards of shell from their bowls too.

'Now this is the most basic version of a quiche,' said Geraldine, who was much more at ease in the kitchen than his mum had ever been.

'Basic? It's got more than one ingredient and requires both a mixing bowl *and* a frypan. In my books, that's pretty close to the "too-hard" basket,' harrumphed the older gentleman beside him.

Connor smiled in agreement.

As if sensing discord, Geraldine slipped in between the students, giving suggestions and correcting techniques without making anybody feel thick.

'See how if you crack the egg on the side of the bench, or the side of the bowl, you'll get more shell in the bowl? Try cracking it on the flat of the benchtop, see if that works better,' she said, demonstrating the difference for Brian, a winemaker and widower who was flummoxed by the prospect of feeding himself after forty-five years of married, three-square-meals-a-day bliss.

Little by little, the eggs cracked more easily, with less shell and more egg filling each bowl.

'We add mustard? I thought that was just for roast beef,' said Brian, eyeing the recipe dubiously.

'Trust me on this one, folks,' said Geraldine, 'the right combination of little flavours can make a big impact.'

Connor did as he was told, and while the sloppy mix in front of him didn't exactly scream 'gourmet' in its uncooked state, it was the most elaborate thing he'd attempted in all his thirty-two years.

After putting his quiche in the oven, he ventured to April's workstation just in time to catch an egg rolling towards the edge of the bench.

'Missing something?'

'I thought I'd put all the eggs in already?' With a frown, April counted up the cracked shells in front of her. 'Hmm, obviously not. This isn't as easy as it looks, is it?'

The perplexed expression on her face reminded him of his young students struggling with a new piano piece.

'Nope,' said Connor, taking a cloth from the sink and swiping up some of the Jackson Pollock-esque splatters from the bench. 'But at least you've still got all your fingers. And you were right about the four-wheel driving.'

He pulled out his phone and opened the message he'd received while Geraldine had been showing them how to fry up the onion for the filling.

April's lips twitched at the sight of Fergus's car sitting low in the sand. A pair of ladies were laughing in the background, while a bunch of men were equally amused, watching with beers in hand. A trio of utes were pulled up beside them, fishing rods strapped to their bullbars.

Connor read Fergus's caption aloud.

Not going anywhere fast! A new way to make friends though.

'Ha! I bet he's filing that one away for the grandkids.' She put on a gruff voice, smiling as she tried impersonating his Scottish accent. 'And then, after getting bogged for the fourth time, and not even complaining when we arrived at the ten-mile beach too sunburned and tired to bother with the fishing, I knew she was the lady I wanted to spend the rest of my life with.'

Connor was impressed with her imitation, but April's smile faltered as she studied the pie dish in front of her. 'I can barely believe this will be edible in an hour's time. Did yours look like this?'

Even though she was laughing, he could sense the vulnerability beneath her words, and he got the impression she was an all or nothing person. Either she did something well, or she didn't do it at all.

But how did the stables fit into the equation? And the value-adding ideas she had told him she wanted to implement?

'Mine looked identical, honest to God. And so did Geraldine's.' He hooked a thumb towards Brian, who was still faffing about, trying to whisk mustard into his egg mix. 'And Brian's too.'

She wrinkled up her nose, as if she still didn't believe him. Connor shrugged. 'I'm no chef, but I've tasted enough of Geraldine's food at the golf club to trust she knows what she's doing.'

At that, his neighbour appeared by their side. 'You'll see, in a couple of hours you'll be heading home with a lovely quiche. Enjoy it tonight with a loaf of crusty bread, green salad and glass of wine.'

Geraldine murmured a few words of encouragement, and as she walked over to the next student, April turned to Connor.

'Or, you could come around to mine tonight and we can do a comparison, see if there's any difference between the two?'

The suggestion caught Connor by surprise. Since accepting the job at Lacewing Estate, he'd kept things strictly professional between them. But when he looked up to ask if she'd changed her mind, or whether she was inviting the cooking class as a whole, not just him, her face fell.

'Oh, bugger. I forgot, I'm going out for dinner.'

'Hot date?'

He rinsed the cloth then set about cleaning his workstation, and as he waited for April's reply, Connor found himself unreasonably curious to hear her answer.

April shook her head, feeling her cheeks heating up. 'Nope, just dinner with my housemate, Lauren. She starts a new job tomorrow at the radio station, so we're celebrating.'

She felt like a dill for throwing out the invitation, then retracting it in the same breath, and even though Connor accepted her explanation with an understanding nod, April wondered what he would have said if she'd answered differently.

Should she explain that she had sworn off dating for the foreseeable future, thanks to their last winemaker? Or was it better to let him hear it on the bush telegraph? *At least,* she conceded, *that way I won't have to see the look of pity on his face.*

Geraldine clapped her hands, getting the class's attention as she explained how to check the oven temperature by flicking the dial backwards until the little light went out. April looked around, glad to see most of the class listening as if they didn't know about that either.

She whisked the eggy mix. Despite her best efforts to pay attention, April's thoughts soon drifted to the family business. Just like following a recipe, she knew the right combination of sunshine, rain and fertiliser were crucial to a successful vineyard yield, and although she didn't have the same skill for winemaking as her father, she had the horticultural side of things under her belt and understood balancing flavours was crucial to creating delicious, big-hearted wines.

But if you can't master a bloody quiche, you'll never have the instincts to eventually run the winery. April felt an invisible band tighten across her chest, squeezing her insides.

'Remember,' Geraldine said, 'cooking is different for everyone. Some people cook because they love the process—'

Maddie, the twelve-year-old whose apron matched her headband, nodded eagerly, while Brian, who April knew as a fellow show produce competitor, snorted. 'Others,' continued Geraldine, 'cook because they want to nourish their bodies, or show their love through food. All equally valid reasons.'

April followed Geraldine's instructions to tuck the puff pastry in the base of a rectangular baking dish.

'Brian might like mustard, ham and tomato in his quiche, and April here might master this one and then branch out with asparagus and salmon when she makes it next.'

'I'll do well to remember this recipe,' muttered April, then pushed away the negative self-talk with a determination to master this 'basic' dish. Even if she had to make it every day for the next week, she would darn well nail it.

While the quiches were in the oven, Geraldine guided them through making the fluffiest pancakes April had ever tasted. Granted, some were a little brown on one side, and they didn't look perfectly symmetrical like the ones half the class had made, but at least she hadn't set off the smoke alarm like Connor.

'These look fabulous,' said Geraldine, leaning over April's shoulder as she heaped strawberries and whipped cream onto her pancake stack.

'Better than the Shake-and-Bake mixes,' admitted April. 'Not sure I'll have room to try the quiche though.'

'That's why you'll be taking it home with you, and the savoury muffins we'll make next,' said Geraldine. 'Perfect food for any time of the day. Brekky, lunch and even dinner if you pair them with a salad or veggies. Good hot or cold.'

Sure enough, when the oven timers dinged, like an auditory Mexican wave around the kitchen, April's belly was fit to burst. The corn and cheese muffins and her quiche would make it home in one piece, and with a celebratory pub meal planned for tonight, the baked goods would probably feed her for most of the week.

But as she watched Connor easing his quiche onto a large plate, she admitted it would have been nice to spend the night in his company, taste-testing their wares.

She washed away the idea with a glass of water. Even if Connor wasn't working for Lacewing Estate, she wasn't sure she was ready to trust someone again, not after Justin had let her down so badly. *It's easier to be on my own.*

Geraldine wrapped up the class with a preview of the menu for the next lesson—a variety of lunch dishes more daunting than today's effort. She handed out copies of the recipes they'd made today and encouraged them to try to recreate at least one of the dishes in their own kitchen.

'Didn't know we'd have homework,' said Brian, stacking his odd-shaped muffins into one of the containers they'd been asked to bring with them. Unlike April's brand-new plastic containers, Brian had brought well-worn Tupperware with him. One had a pink lid, the other a blue one, with his surname written in cursive in the top corner of both items. She wondered whether his late wife had imagined he'd take up baking in his sixties.

'Look forward to seeing you next week,' called Geraldine as they filtered out of the kitchen, goodies under their arms.

Connor held the door open for April. 'Fran will be right impressed when you tell her about that lot.'

April couldn't smother a triumphant grin. Even though she wouldn't have attended the classes if it weren't for her mother's gift voucher or her stepmother Fran's encouragement, she had to admit she was pleased with how it had gone. And it had been fun cooking alongside Connor.

'It's a long way from cooking three-course meals, but this is a step up from the frozen aisle.'

She loaded her containers into the backseat of her ute and turned back to Connor. 'Need a lift home?'

He waved away the offer. 'It's only a few hundred metres, I can manage. See you around,' he said, loping off with arms full looking much happier than when he'd arrived.

April said goodbye to the other cooking students and drove along the hawthorn-lined driveway, slowing to a snail's pace as she passed Connor. She didn't want another boyfriend, but there was nothing stopping them from being friends. And friends did lunches and brunches, didn't they? She wasn't sure what his Sundays were normally like, but maybe he could squeeze in a taste-testing session tomorrow instead?

After a lesson with a thirteen-year-old student who made it clear she'd rather be sleeping than practising piano scales on a Sunday morning, Connor followed the highway through Penwarra towards Lacewing Estate.

Wineries, cellar doors and vineyards flashed past the car window and he turned down Rivoli Lane, dust billowing in the rear-view mirror as he drove between the vineyards. There was no sign of young Archie Winklin outside his family's grand home, but as Connor looked to the west, he spotted the paddocks with Archie's sheep and hoped they'd been sticking to their side of the fence this week.

Connor parked beside April's ute, loaded his arms with yesterday's baking and followed a paved path to her house. Her text message had been a welcome distraction from the trip down memory lane he'd been torturing himself with for most of the night, and he hadn't hesitated to agree to a Sunday tasting session.

A folded newspaper flapped on the wire outdoor table beside the arched front door, as if April had been sitting there in the morning sun just moments earlier, with a coffee and crossword.

He knocked, noticing the petunia-filled wine barrels by the door were now brimming with new seedlings and fresh mulch. The door opened, and he braced himself for a whirlwind greeting of barking, slobbery kisses and excited 360s.

'Mishka, come here. Sorry, Connor!' April appeared, her dark hair in a messy bun atop her head, and reached for the wriggling dog's collar as Connor held the food out of the dog's reach.

'You'd barely believe it, but she's already done a lap of the winery and tagged along beside me on a five-kilometre bike ride.'

He could believe it. Over the last few weeks, he'd become very fond of the golden retriever and could see why Archie stole across the laneway whenever he had a free moment to spend time with the dog.

And time with April.

April handed him a knife, and Connor sliced their quiches in half while April cut up two muffins. 'Reckon we should heat them up before eating?'

It was Connor's turn to shrug. 'Don't ask me. Geraldine said we could eat them warm or cold.' He liked that April knew as little about cooking as he did and didn't pretend otherwise. And despite their lacklustre culinary skills, both quiches passed the taste test.

'Better than I expected,' April admitted, after they'd cleared their plates and done the dishes.

'I've eaten worse,' Connor agreed, laughing at the low bar they'd set for themselves. 'My dad's cooking was fine when he stuck to the script, but when he started substituting ingredients, it was a slippery slope between experimental and inedible.'

'One of my earliest memories in the kitchen,' April said, 'was watching my mum scrape a layer of mould off cream, then pouring the rest into a potato bake.' April's dramatic shudder made him laugh.

'Does she live locally?'

April shook her head and peered out the kitchen window at the swathe of vines in every direction. 'Last time I checked, she was teaching in the Tiwi Islands.' Spotting his blank look, she elaborated. 'They're in the Top End, not far from Darwin. I grew up here, just like my dad and my grandfather, but Mum, Polly, was from up north. She never quite got used to the climate or the intensity of winery work. They're better off apart,' she said, and although her comment was flippant—practised, even— he sensed there was something she wasn't saying.

'My boss back in the UK always said it takes a winemaker to marry a winemaker,' he offered with a light shrug.

He watched as she considered before agreeing. 'Maybe,' she said, moving to the door and pulling on her boots. 'How's your veggie supply? Need a top-up yet?'

April had given him fresh produce several times since he'd started working at Lacewing Estate and their strong flavours and size left the supermarket veggies for dead. He followed her outside, with Mishka hot on their heels. April stopped at the small garden shed and grabbed a pair of secateurs, a calico carry bag and a handful of dried dog snacks. She handed him the bag and half the dog treats. 'Nothing quite like cupboard love. Whoever holds the food is her new best friend.'

Sure enough, when April raised a piece of dried dog food in the air, Mishka promptly lowered to a sit and quivered in anticipation, waiting for the treat. Watching the dog brought back a rush of memories for the scatterbrained but loveable dog he'd grown up with.

'It's been a long time since I've had a pet in my life,' he said. Mishka turned to him to see if he had any similar treats on offer.

An image of rescue shelter leaflets came to mind and Connor remembered the day he'd suggested it to Phoebe as a distraction—an unofficial therapy dog, in the dark days directly after their accident. She hadn't answered yes or no, but the leaflets in the recycling bin had sent a clear message. In retrospect, it was better they hadn't had an animal tethering them together. *Just a bucketload of shared history and a whole heap of sadness.*

He grimaced and turned his attention back to Mishka, who was looking at him with molten eyes and a trail of drool. He tossed her the tidbit and they moved to the raised garden beds, April pointing out varieties as she went.

'You have to try these mini cucumbers,' she said, slipping them into his bag. 'Perfect with olives, feta cheese and the last of the Black Russian tomatoes,' she said, adding three of the luscious, dark-skinned tomatoes to his bag.

She caught sight of his smile as he admired the overflowing vegetable patches. 'I bet you thought your Aussie adventure would be full of crocodiles, kangaroos and pub crawls, not show baking, renovations and cooking classes?'

Connor leaned against the post-and-rail fence beside her. 'It's not exactly what I'd imagined when I booked my trip Down Under.' *But*, he thought, as he watched the blue sky stretching out beyond the vines, his stomach full from their Sunday lunch, *that certainly wasn't a bad thing.*

10

The sinking sun cast deep shadows over the vineyards as April unpegged her washing from the line and cast her mind back to the pleasant time she'd spent in Connor's company. He was easy to be around, and between the stories about their cooking fails, her childhood growing up in a winery and the countries they had both travelled to, their Sunday lunch had extended until late afternoon.

He hadn't seemed to mind.

The guitar hanging in the study caught April's eye, and she abandoned her laundry in favour of the instrument. It had been too long since she'd lost herself in music, and the tips of her fingers tingled as she pressed the frets and plucked the strings.

She looked over the vineyards to the gnarled gum trees, with the golden light kissing the horizon goodnight, and strummed a Cat Stevens song.

'Hello?'

April startled, messing up the chorus of 'Wild World'.

'I didn't even hear you pull up,' she said, walking out of her study with the guitar still around her neck.

'Don't let me interrupt,' Lauren said. 'No matter how many times I hear you playing, it puts a lump in my throat every bloody time.'

April laughed. 'You're just a big softie. You cry during Kleenex adverts. Was your first day a breeze? Did you spot any platypuses?'

Lauren shook her head. 'Nope, just a mountain of hikers all heading out with their cameras. Busier than Rundle Mall in some parts. But we filmed some good footage for the social media channels, and our brekky presenter got a few good grabs for tomorrow morning's show.' April set her guitar down and helped Lauren with her bags, keen to learn more about Lauren's new role at the radio station.

'Helping with the outside broadcast was an eye opener. I have no idea how I'll manage when I'm supposed to be responsible for producing the whole kit and kaboodle.'

April made a 'pfft' noise. 'You'll be running the show with your eyes closed after a week or two, tops,' she said.

'Not sure about that,' Lauren replied. 'And how was your lunch?' She opened the fridge, pulled out a bottle of wine and eyed the Tupperware container on the second shelf.

'I've never seen you make anything as impressive as a quiche, we should have stayed in last night instead of going out. Did it taste as good as it looked?'

April basked in Lauren's compliment. It was probably the first time she'd been praised for her cooking and she was going to soak it up. 'Connor's was pretty good too. And neither of us have come down with food poisoning, so that's a win.'

Raising an eyebrow, Lauren poured them both a glass of wine and sat down on the couch. 'I'm looking forward to meeting this guy,' she said, as April sat beside her. 'Especially if he's as clueless in the kitchen as you. Poor Geraldine.'

Grinning, April nodded. 'I know, isn't it great? And he seems to have fitted in well at Lacewing too. Dad hasn't moaned about him once, and he's been there a few weeks now. And next week, I'll get to steal him for a few hours a week to speed up the stables reno and knock a few jobs off the list to spruce up the winery.'

She looked up from her wine to see Lauren smiling back at her.

'What?'

'Noth-ing.' Lauren drew out the word with a smirk.

'Get over yourself. He's just easy to be around. And after the dropkicks I've dated in the last few years, it's refreshing to meet someone who thinks before speaking. He listens to Beethoven not the Beastie Boys, and even if he's as useless in the kitchen as me, at least he's doing something about it.'

'It's the accent, isn't it?' said Lauren. 'You always did have a thing for those David Attenborough documentaries, now that I think about it.'

April picked up the closest cushion and tossed it across the room, narrowly missing Lauren's wine glass.

'I'm arranging drinks,' Lauren announced, snatching up April's phone and tapping out a message. 'You, me, him, his crazy Scottish housemate.'

'I didn't say Fergus was crazy,' April protested. 'Just that he isn't afraid to wear a kilt, entertain a conversation with Jean bloody Dellacourte and risk his life on a four-wheel drive beach fishing trip.'

'Yep, pure crazy. Still, it'll make it less obvious I'm scoping Connor out as prospective boyfriend material for my bestie if there's someone else there. I promise not to take my notepad and score him as he goes,' she said with a smile, hitting send.

'You know I'm sworn off men for good. He's just a friend.'

'For good? I thought it was just until your poor heart was healed?'

April rolled her eyes as she read the message Lauren had sent. Tomorrow she'd have to explain to Connor why there were starry-eyed emojis, plus eggplants and love hearts at the bottom of the text.

As in his previous international posts, the familiar rhythm of the cellar helped Connor settle into the town, which was so different from the one he'd grown up in. While he'd endured snow at the winery in Scotland and aloof locals at the cellar in Auckland, his first month in the Limestone Coast was marked by a warmth not just from the sunshine, but the people in the town.

A conversation at the post office helped him acquire another piano student, and by the end of autumn he had people greeting him by name at the bakery and supermarket.

The sun was still high in the blue sky one Friday, with not a cloud to be seen, when Connor and the golf club president, Barney, finished a round of golf.

'We were robbed,' said Barney, slipping off his golf glove and shaking Connor's hand, before tossing his score card into the bin by the Nineteenth Hole.

'I told you I was better on the piano than the fairway,' laughed Connor, stashing his borrowed golf bag back in the storeroom. 'But it wasn't a bad day for a stroll.'

Barney had taken to dropping into their rental occasionally, officially to check they were keeping the place in good shape, but unofficially, Connor suspected, to have a glass of wine or a stubby with him and Fergus.

'You must be a darn sight sharper on the ivories than the putting green, all those piano students you've got.'

Barney opened the door to the clubhouse and nodded to the piano.

'My Emma would have loved hearing you play,' Barney said. 'It was her mother's piano, and she asked me to look after it when she went into a nursing home, but we didn't have room in our little house.'

There was something about Barney's wistfulness that made Connor lift the lid on the keys and check inside the stool for sheet music.

Bingo. Propping the yellowed paper on the stand, he launched into Debussy's 'Clair de Lune'. He played a few bars and turned to see Barney with his hands on his hips, chin almost to his chest as if he were struggling to hold back his emotions. A pair of golfers had arrived as he'd been playing and they launched into a round of applause.

'It could probably do with a good tune,' Connor said stiffly, shuffling the stool back and returning the music to the spot under the cushioned seat. Three golfers and a bar or two didn't make an audience but still, Connor felt uncomfortable in the spotlight.

'For an average golfer, you make a bloody good piano player,' said the chap by the door, who had whipped Connor and Barney in today's round.

Connor whistled as he walked back to the rental. Fergus was home, and judging from the music blaring out of the speakers, he was either cleaning or trying to recreate another of the intricate dishes from the recipe book he'd borrowed from the library.

He'd been a good sport about Connor winning the cooking classes, but during Friday night drinks with April and Lauren the week before, halfway through a bottle of wine, Fergus had announced he was planning his own kitchen skills improvement regime.

Connor was pretty sure he was just trying to impress Lauren, but to his credit, Fergus had been binge-watching

SBS Food shows and seemed dedicated to keep up with April and Connor.

The scent of onions and garlic greeted Connor when he opened the door and he spotted a mop bucket by the shoe shelf.

'Cooking and cleaning? You've really got it bad, haven't you?'

Even before Fergus spun around, Connor could see he'd had a haircut too.

Blimey. When was the last time Connor himself had made such an effort? Not since he was at uni, when dinner anywhere other than the chippie plus a clean shirt were the main prerequisites for impressing a girl.

'That lass we saw for drinks last week, it's her birthday,' Fergus said, tapping the portable speaker's volume down. 'I'm attempting to make her dinner—wine her and dine her, you know? You staying for supper? There'll be enough to serve an army.'

Connor shook his head, saying a mental farewell to his plans for a quiet evening in. The ingredients he'd bought for a second attempt at the quiche would keep until tomorrow, and although Fergus sounded optimistic about his cooking, he didn't want to be a third wheel.

'Nah, I'll sort myself out.' Connor dashed through the gleaming shower, admitting it looked a million times better without the black spots on the grout, and with a fresh set of clothes and spritz of deodorant, carried his laptop and a beer outside to the wooden table and chairs.

Birds carolled in the trees, and a wallaby bounded out of the scrub behind their house, making a beeline for the fairway. Connor tried his parents and sipped his beer as the Zoom call connected.

'Ey up, how's our lad?'

'Good, Dad, good.' His mam shuffled into view, delight on her sleep-creased face as she pulled her dressing gown up higher.

'Hello, love, we were just lying here arguing about who was getting up to stoke the fire. I feel warmer just looking at your sunshine though. Is it as hot as it looks there?'

He nodded. 'A balmy 21 degrees, as still as you like, and we're in for even nicer weather on the weekend. Not bad for late autumn.'

Sharyn closed her eyes, marvelling at the thought of it, as Jock yawned and looped an arm around her shoulders. 'The weatherman's tipping a frost, can you believe it? You're not missing much here, son. Tell us what you've been up to, then.'

They spoke for another ten minutes before Nell and Pippin wandered in, rugged up in matching dressing gowns and fleecy pyjamas.

'You should see how much Turty has grown, Con,' said Pippin, disappearing and then moments later reappearing and shoving a tortoise in front of the laptop camera.

'Amazing,' he said, trying to muster up a little more enthusiasm for the creature climbing over his littlest sister's palm. Just because Phoebe had bought it for her, didn't mean the tortoise—or his sisters—were to blame for his conflicted feelings.

'You should see the spider living in our bathroom,' Connor said. 'It's almost as big as that tortoise.'

A cherry-red SUV pulled up and Lauren climbed out. Like Fergus, she'd dressed up for the occasion, in a flowery dress with her blonde hair loose around her shoulders. She waved as she walked across the front yard.

'Ohhh, do you have a new girlfriend, Con?'

'Can we see her? Puh-leeease,' added Pippin.

Connor shook his head. 'No you can't, you nosy buggers.'

Lauren, who had overheard the conversation, backtracked and came to stand beside him.

'G'day guys,' she said, smiling at the four faces crammed into the laptop screen. 'You look nice and cosy there.'

'It's not long until summer but you wouldn't know it. Dad says it's colder than a witches tit,' said Pippin mischievously.

'Pippin Delores Jamison, I'll wash your mouth out with soap. She's a right horror, our Pippin,' Sharyn said, flushing with embarrassment. 'Don't mind her.'

Lauren hooted with laughter as she headed for the front door.

'She's way too pretty to be one of your girlfriends, Con,' said Nelly matter-of-factly.

'Are you saying Phoebe isn't pretty?' Pippin glared at her younger sister, her voice loud with outrage.

Lauren paused.

Had she overheard? Connor swallowed hard. Phoebe, and the accident that had upended not just one but three lives, belonged in the past, not here in Australia.

'Oh, we saw Phoebe in the supermarket with her sister,' said Jock. 'Your mam and I didn't know she had a little one on the way.'

The news rendered Connor speechless. *Phoebe's pregnant?* Instinctively, his hand went to his bad leg, massaging the scar tissue that had formed over the wasted muscles.

Sharyn elbowed Jock in the ribs. 'Your dad made a dog's breakfast of that. It's her sister who's pregnant. Natalia, not Phoebe. Are you okay, Con?'

Connor made his farewells, assuring them he was fine, then closed the laptop and grabbed his keys.

It would take more than a long drive to chase away the tiny ache in his heart. He sped down the highway, his eyes on the rugged roadside, his mind back in the UK. How would Phoebe be coping with that news? Maybe it was finally time to call her.

Connor's phone worked its way through the Nina Simone playlist he'd chosen for the afternoon's work in the stables, and when he ascended the ladder to the mezzanine floor, he found April singing along to a moody jazz number.

The loud music, hum of power tools and April's upbeat mood were almost enough to distract him from his worries back home.

Almost but not quite.

He'd tossed and turned all night, unable to decide whether or not it was wise to call Phoebe. He'd eventually relented, leaving a message at 4 am. Coffee and a sense of purpose had helped, but Connor knew he wasn't firing on all cylinders today.

'Man, my knees weren't made for this type of caper,' April said, rocking back on her heels and taking the lengths of jarrah Connor had passed her. She looked at Gordon, the builder, kneeling beside her. 'Dunno how you do it, Gordo.'

Gordon lifted the nail gun and gestured to his earplugs with the other hand.

'Your knees!' April shouted, pointing to hers. She'd arrived at the cottage this morning wearing a set of builders pants with seven million pockets and slim foam pads over the knees.

'I found these at the op shop last week,' she told Connor, gesturing to the utilitarian trousers. 'But they're made for a giant, so the knee pads are excellent at cushioning my shins but not so useful in the knee department.'

Connor blinked, the breath catching in his chest as April yanked her T-shirt up, showing him how she'd cinched in the too-big waist with a belt.

'Still, they're pretty good for three dollars, right?' She laughed, not seeming to notice that his eyes were taking in the expanse of olive skin and the tiniest hint of pale-blue underwear instead of the leather belt looped almost twice around her waist.

'Three dollars? Cheaper than a vanilla slice,' he said, moving his attention to the floorboards they'd laid. There was only a small section of joists visible now, and at the rate they were working, they'd have that gap closed by knock-off. 'This looks super, I love the dark wood.'

April passed him a length of flooring, and when their hands brushed, he felt his stomach flip. Connor grabbed the exposed joist with one hand, steadying himself. What the hell was that? He hadn't been a monk since breaking off his engagement, but even in his distracted state, he couldn't remember the last time he'd reacted like that to an innocent touch.

'Does this floorboard need another pass?' He cleared his throat, looking at the piece that evidently needed trimming.

'Yep, only a whisper though,' she said, holding her thumb and pointer finger close together to indicate a few millimetres. A cheeky grin formed on her lips and she looked across to Gordon, who was reloading the nail gun. 'Or as our mate Gordo would say, only a bee's dick.'

Connor bit his lip, descending the ladder before Gordon looked up and saw them both laughing at him.

Soon the pile of floorboards in the living room was almost gone and April's voice was triumphant as she called out the last measurements.

'One more floorboard at 635 millimetres and then we're officially done for the day.'

He scribbled down the number, then took the tape measure out to the lengths of jarrah. It was only once he'd cut the timber that he saw his phone light up on the windowsill.

Fergus with a fishing meme? Another new piano student or perhaps news of a sick child that would leave a gap in his lessons tomorrow night?

But when he looked at the phone screen, he saw a name that hadn't appeared on his phone screen for months.

Phoebe.
Connor swallowed, reading her message.

Can we talk? Please x

He calculated the time difference—early morning in England—and unplugged the phone, preparing to take the call outside.

'Come and see this, Connor,' called April. He glanced up from his phone to see her standing, slowly backing away to better admire Gordon's work. 'We're nearly finished.'

'Mind the drop,' he yelled, the warning coming out sharper than he'd planned. April looked over her shoulder, then gasped when she realised how close she was to the edge of the mezzanine. She quickly stepped forward, tumbling onto the freshly laid floor. Connor heard her squeak, then a thud.

'Bugger!'

The moment was over in mere seconds, but Connor hadn't counted on the feeling of hopelessness that followed or the way his mind surged from Phoebe to April, the baby they'd lost years before and his panic at April almost plummeting backwards, some four metres to the ground floor.

He shimmied up the ladder as quickly as he could. On the mezzanine floor, he found April sprawled on the red jarrah, groaning. Gordon set down his tools.

'You right there?' Gordon grimaced as April let out another groan. 'You went down like a sack of potatoes.' Seeing that Connor was going to her aid, Gordon returned to tapping the jarrah boards into place.

'Ouch,' April said, gingerly pushing herself up into a sitting position. She seemed more embarrassed than injured.

'That sounded like it would've hurt,' Connor said gently, scanning her from head to toe.

No blood, no protruding bones. It was a good outcome, though from the way she was rubbing her hip, he suspected she'd have a corker of a bruise in a few days' time.

Double-checking he wasn't anywhere near the edge, Connor held out both hands and helped April to her feet, then instinctively pulled her towards him.

'You going to be okay?' He rubbed her back, giving her the type of hug he'd have given his sisters or his mam if they'd tripped on the way into Tesco, and the same soothing tone he used with shy new piano students.

Her dark hair tickled his chin as she nodded. 'I tripped over my own feet. What an idiot.'

'You're not an idiot, but you've really got to stop throwing yourself at Gordon like that.'

She chuckled, and the gesture went from comforting to charged as he felt the heat of her torso against his. He pulled away, walked across the new mezzanine floorboards, and let out a shaky breath before descending the ladder.

You can't protect her either, he reminded himself as he reached the ground. And even though Connor knew it wasn't his lifelong burden to stop bad things happening to people who meant something to him, the reaction confirmed something he hadn't yet admitted to himself.

Like it or not, he cared about April Lacey.

Connor jammed his hands into his pockets, his thoughts in a whirl.

'I've got to head off,' he mumbled, tugging on the door and stumbling into the late-afternoon sun.

He heard April calling after him but he didn't turn back until he reached the white Camry, turned over the ignition and tore out of Lacewing Estate in a cloud of limestone dust.

11

April walked slowly back to her house after Gordon left that afternoon, still confused about Connor's rapid departure. Like Gordon, he didn't always stay for a knock-off beer, but she'd thought he'd stay to watch them put the finishing touches on the upstairs flooring.

Not that she expected him to be as invested as she was—after all, the bed and breakfast had been her dream for years and he'd only arrived in the country several months ago—but from the last few weeks of working together, she'd got the sense he was enjoying seeing it take shape too.

Mishka barked, her ears pricking up as she noticed a white blur in the distance. It wasn't until the dog tugged at her lead, and a woolly intruder bolted behind the winemaker's cottage, that April realised Archie's lambs had squeezed through the fence again.

She tied Mishka to her kennel and set off for the Winklin house. The lambs would be halfway to Millicent by the time Mishka ran out of steam, if she was off leash. Piano music floated through the windows and she followed the mesmerising sound around the side of the house. Archie was perched at the grand piano, his skinny arms sticking out from a sleeveless footy vest. She listened a little longer, watching his frown come and go as he worked through a difficult section. It was beautiful to hear him play and she thought of Connor again, wondering what it would be like to have him playing just for her.

Had he forgotten an appointment this afternoon? Was that why he rushed out?

She resolved to message him after she'd helped Archie with the lambs. Catching the young boy's attention with a gentle tap on the window, she looked around as she waited for him.

A wheelbarrow was parked on the lawn, not far from the conservatory entrance, and she remembered the chat she'd had with Daniel about Felicity ripping out the roses.

Had he been serious about his stepmother instructing their gardener to pile them into a heap and burn them? The prospect worried her almost as much as Marty and Barbara nibbling on her veggie patch.

'Whatcha up to?' Archie said, coming through the glass doors. 'Mum's putting a new lawn in there,' he offered, hooking his thumb towards a small bobcat parked under the trees. 'I asked if we could put veggies in but she just wants grass. Bor-ing!'

As if summonsed, Felicity Winklin's sleek Jaguar rolled down the driveway and she emerged with a briefcase, laptop bag and armload of dry-cleaning.

'We've got a situation with you-know-what,' April whispered quickly, as Felicity headed in their direction.

Archie looked at her blankly. 'Huh?'

'Lambs on the loose!'

Archie's eyes widened and he nodded quietly, retreating inside and emerging with work boots instead of thongs.

'You off to the footy or the farm, Arch?' asked Felicity, smiling at her son's unusual ensemble. 'How are you, April?

Brilliant effort at the Penwarra Show, by the way. This young guy slept with his first-place ribbon under his pillow for a week afterwards.'

Archie bristled, the tips of his ears going red. 'Did not,' he mumbled. 'Anyway, we've got some important gardening stuff to do, don't we, April?'

'We sure have,' she said, turning with a wave. 'Oh, and those roses . . .?' April paused a moment. 'If you don't want them, I'd happily take them off your hands. Only if you're not planning on replanting them elsewhere.'

Felicity looked up from her phone, sparing a brief glance for the burgundy standard roses, and nodded. 'Go for your life. I'm sick of my clothes catching on the thorns every time I walk outside. Dig them up and they're all yours.'

April couldn't believe her luck. She wasn't sure whether she'd plant them out the front of Lacewing Estate or lining the path that led to the bed and breakfast but anything was better than burning them.

'I thought you only liked veggies and grapes, not fussy flowers,' said Archie, studying her as they ducked through the fence.

'Equal opportunity, mate,' she said with a grin. 'I'm all for things you can eat, but a splash of colour and beauty never goes astray. Especially if the alternative is that they go to waste.'

They found the lambs in April's veggie garden, and a quick look showed they'd had quite a feast on the carrots and snow peas.

'Naughty buggers,' she said, herding the biggest lamb, Barbara, between the garden shed and the garage, where Archie was waiting. With one secured, she hunted Marty in the same direction.

'These guys are wearing out their welcome,' she said, lugging the lamb over her shoulder and ignoring the ache in her hip from where she'd landed on the hardwood floor. 'We won't be able to carry them like this in a few months' time.'

Archie panted beneath Barbara's load, his freckled face red with the exertion. 'Tell me about it,' he grunted. 'Dad said we're lamb marking this month. Maybe they won't be so naughty when they've all got a rubber ring around their tails and the boys have got one on their knackers?'

April cringed at the thought. It would be enough to kerb anyone's roaming tendencies, surely? *Maybe,* she grinned to herself, *Justin could have done with one?* With the lambs safely back in their paddock, April left Archie to his piano practice and ran a much-needed bath. Every pore of her body felt like it was full of either sawdust, sweat or lanolin from the sheep's wool.

Adding a dollop of bubble bath, she found the bath caddy in the cupboard and set it up with her favourite bathing supplies—something to eat, something to read and something to drink—before stripping off.

A patch of red marked the top of her thigh. *It'll be black and blue by tomorrow,* she thought, sinking into the warm, frothy water.

When Lauren arrived home, April was on the couch, feeling relaxed after her hour-long soak. Switching her radio station uniform for shorts and an old Cold Chisel T-shirt, Lauren helped herself to April's bowl of Twisties and announced she was going fishing with Fergus.

'Wine bars one week, fishing the next,' April waggled her eyebrows. 'You guys are really getting cosy, aren't you? Do I need to start looking for a new housemate?'

Lauren shook her head, but the smile on her face remained. 'He's a sweetheart, for sure, but we've only had a few dates, we're not setting up house just yet. Especially while his cooking skills are so dire. He tries, but—' she shuddered, shaking her head. 'How about you and Connor?'

April thought of the warmth of Connor's body against hers when he'd hugged her on the mezzanine, the way he'd so instinctively scaled the ladder to check on her, even though there'd clearly been something else weighing on his mind all day. Gordon, on the other hand, had given her a visual once-over to ensure she hadn't split her skull open, then returned to work.

'Even when you're trying not to smile, adamant that you're not ready to date again, I can still see your eyes crinkling up and the twitch of your lips.' Lauren was watching her closely, smirking. 'Aren't you the least bit interested? Just the teensiest, eensiest bit?'

'I'm not sure,' April admitted. 'There're a million reasons why I shouldn't even consider it. For starters, I don't think he plans on staying in Australia long term.'

'If that's your biggest barrier, then maybe you should cross that bridge when you come to it.' Lauren munched on a Twistie and then fell silent. 'Hey, do you know anything about a girl called Phoebe?'

April shook her head, trying to follow Lauren's conversation leap. 'I'm going to need a little more info. From the radio station? Penwarra? The winemaking crew?'

'Nah, the Phoebe from Connor's neck of the woods. He was speaking to his family the other day and it was Phoebe this, Phoebe that. One of his sisters maybe?'

April tossed a Twistie to Mishka, then popped another one in her mouth and shook her head. 'Beats me.'

Connor's phone trilled again shortly after he left Lacewing Estate.

It was his sister, Heidi, this time.

It was a struggle to keep his mind on the road and not the incoming call. Connor almost drove straight past Fergus's ute in the main street of Penwarra, not noticing the fishing rods lashed from the bullbar to the roof racks, until Fergus tooted and waved enthusiastically out the window.

A note on the kitchen bench confirmed Fergus was indeed off fishing for the evening, with an offer for Connor to help himself to the leftovers from last night's dinner. His stomach curdled at the thought. Despite his cast-iron constitution, Fergus's stir-fry hadn't sat well the first time around.

But he was glad the house was empty. Connor dialled Heidi's number, trying and failing to remember the last time he'd missed a call from Phoebe.

Heidi answered on the second ring. 'You'll be calling about Phoebe, then?'

Connor felt his shoulders bunch together. Heidi and Phoebe had been friends for years, of course she'd know Phoebe was trying to get in touch with him. 'Have you seen her recently?'

'She's pretty upset, Natalia's pregnancy came as a big shock for her.'

'I didn't even know she was in a relationship, did you?' As he asked the question, Connor realised how pointless it sounded. He'd called things off with Phoebe, so why would he have known? 'I'm not sure what I can do for Phoebe from the other side of the world, though.'

Heidi let out a soft breath. 'Maybe not, but you could still call her back; check she's okay. I think it'd mean a lot.'

Connor moved to the sink, the words Heidi didn't say were running through his head.

It'd mean a lot, after what you went through together.

It'd mean a lot, given the promise you made.

We both know it's the least you can do.

'You're right,' he said, opening the pantry. The conversation would require tea or wine. Possibly both. 'I'll call her.'

But when he hung up from Heidi, Connor found himself procrasti-cleaning. Only after the bins were emptied, the toaster shaken until every last crumb was on the lawn, and the gunky bits of food were pushed down the sink plughole, did he feel ready to make the call.

Wine. Definitely need wine.

He put the laptop aside and was pouring himself a generous glass of red when Geraldine knocked on the front door. Connor slid it open, welcoming the distraction.

'I've been working on a new flatbread dough recipe and need a professional opinion,' Geraldine said, passing him a basket covered by a checked tea towel.

'Mmm.' Connor lifted the tea towel, inhaling the steamy, yeasty warmth. 'If this bread tastes half as good as it smells, then it's a gold star from me.' A wave of tiredness kicked in from the weight of the phone call he hadn't yet made combined with the post-adrenaline slump from April's near-accident. He leaned against the doorframe, resting his eyes a moment, and taking a second, deeper whiff of the flatbread.

'You look knackered, love. Come sit down a minute,' Geraldine said, steering him to the couch. His laptop was open, the Zoom interface on the screen, the wine he'd not yet touched sitting beside it.

'I'm fine, really,' he protested, but he sat nonetheless.

She fossicked in his cupboards for a plate and a serviette, unloading them onto the coffee table and then adding a glass of water. 'I hope you know my door's always open, Connor. If you're low on supplies, or you need a chat, just knock.'

He promised to keep it in mind. 'Thanks again for the flatbread,' he said, gesturing at the thick wedges she'd put on the plate before him.

'Tell me which one you fancy tomorrow,' she said. And with a wave, she was off.

Connor ate the first piece, his tastebuds picking up garlic and olives, then moved onto the herb-studded alternative. He washed the warm, salty carbs down with a mouthful of cabernet and called Phoebe on Zoom.

It was early morning in the UK, but she'd been an early bird as long as he'd known her. In spite of the message and the missed call, Phoebe was surprisingly calm when she answered. He eased out the breath he'd been holding.

'Are you okay? You had me worried.'

Phoebe sat in the living room of the semi-detached flat they'd once shared in Derby, blowing cigarette smoke out the open window. 'I know I probably shouldn't be upset, Con, but it's been a tough week.' The screen jiggled as she stubbed out her cigarette. He could almost feel the nip of the damp air and the minty menthol of her Dunhills as she collected the phone and moved around the house. It worried him that she was rattled enough to start smoking again.

'I think you've got fair grounds, Phoebe. Even if you're happy for Natalia, it's still going to stir up a lot of memories,' he said quietly. 'I'm sorry I didn't get back to you straight away, I needed a little time to digest.'

There was mess on most of the surfaces and when she propped her phone on the bookshelf and flicked the lounge room lamp on, he could see dark circles under her eyes. There was none of the shine or vitality that he'd seen in the photos from Pippin's birthday.

'Work made me take leave,' she said, her voice breaking, and when she lifted her left hand to swipe away her tears, he saw the ring he'd given her a decade ago.

'Hey,' he said. 'Hey, it's okay, Phoebe. Have you thought about booking an appointment with the counsellor again? Are you taking the meds?'

A strand of blonde hair fell over her face as she admitted she hadn't had the energy to leave the house when her script for anti-anxiety tablets ran out. Connor ran through a mental checklist of options, wishing it didn't hurt to see her upset like this.

'I'm sorry for calling, babe. I know it's been a long time but you're the only one who understands what we went through.'

Connor reached for his wine, taking a deep swig and trying to gather his thoughts. He closed his eyes for a moment, the grinding of metal on metal and the squeal of tyres ringing in his ears. The flashback disappeared when he opened them again, but the pain on Phoebe's face reminded him it wasn't easy for her to forget either. She'd been the one behind the wheel, but it may as well have been him.

It should have been him. He should've been driving.

And while he'd regained his strength and taught himself to walk again, one painstaking PT session at a time, Phoebe's mental scars hadn't healed quite so successfully. It was something he was acutely aware of when he looked at her face on the laptop screen, a lump of guilt and responsibility in his throat.

'I hear you're quite the tortoise whisperer.' It was the first light-hearted thing he could think of and he was relieved to see it break the tension.

She laughed, and while it was more of a sob-laugh, it was better than the silent, shoulder-shaking sobbing. 'I knew the girls would like them, but I wasn't sure what your mam would say.'

Connor smiled. 'I've heard only good things,' he said. 'And stuff work, you never normally take sick leave, so it's about time they paid you to take a break.'

She curled her knees underneath herself on the couch.

And as much as he had planned to end the phone call the moment he'd ascertained she wasn't about to plunge into a pit of deep despair, Connor stayed on the line and let her vent.

'I've taken up enough of your time,' Phoebe said a little later, when the sun had set on the golf course and the sky had turned a deep navy. 'Thanks for listening.' She smiled then, looking more like herself. 'And for cheering me up with your Aussie adventures.' Her voice was wistful then, and he wondered if her sister's pregnancy would have been easier to bear if she'd been with him in Australia when she got the news.

He waved at the screen then signed off, leaving his computer and makeshift dinner dishes where they were and crawling into bed. Parts of the conversation replayed in his mind as he lay his head on the pillow: the stories he'd shared about Archie's wayward lambs and Fergus's fishing escapades, the glorious sunshine and the sunburnt landscape, and Phoebe's updates from their friendship group.

And while he hadn't specifically avoided mentioning April, Phoebe hadn't asked. It would have been churlish to raise such a detail when the aim of the call was to cheer her up, surely? It was only as he was drifting off to sleep that he realised Phoebe was a part of his life he hadn't yet shared with April.

Would April look at him the same way when he revealed that side of his life, a chapter he'd worked so hard to move on from? He nestled into the blankets, hoping like hell that she'd understand.

※

April's mind was on Connor as she left for cooking class the next morning. He'd been on her mind as she'd slept too, in a saucy dream where they'd been alone in the stables, christening the new jarrah floor before anyone else could claim the honour.

The intimate scene ran through her mind again as she drove past the B & B, which was looking less like a horse shed and more like a romantic accommodation option with every passing week. She paused at the bakery on her way through town, collecting fresh sourdough and coffee, and trying to avoid the temptation of a French vanilla slice.

'I hear good things are happening at Lacewing, April. When's your love nest open to the public?'

She turned to see the endlessly energetic winemaker Harris O'Brien, at the counter with a keep cup, his eyes shining with mischief.

Love nest? Ick! 'That makes it sound so tawdry, Harris,' she scolded, not missing the snort of amusement from the lady behind the counter. 'I assume you mean "Kookaburra Cottage"?'

Winking and handing his keep cup to the bakery worker, Harris gently nudged April with an elbow. 'You're an easy mark,' he said cheerfully. 'But seriously, when will you be finished? My wife's birthday is just around the corner. Even if I can just get a voucher, then we can book an actual date once you're open for business.'

She beamed, forgiving his teasing as she promised to whip something up on the computer. 'I haven't got the website sorted yet, and I'm not sure exactly what the rates will be, but I can email you a ballpark figure and if you're happy with that, I'll print up a voucher.'

'Deal,' Harris said, paying for his coffee and holding the door for her. Harris had a big mouth, but also a big heart and wide-reaching networks, and Fran had been grateful for his help promoting the Penwarra Show.

Imagine if he starts spreading the word about Kookaburra Cottage? The bookings will start flooding in! April smiled the whole way to Geraldine's.

'You look pleased about something,' said Brian, pulling in beside her. April told him about Harris's interest, and at Brian's prompting, gave him a full update on the project, from the jarrah flooring upstairs to the polished concrete benchtops she was planning for the quaint kitchen and the potager garden.

'Kind of like Geraldine's gardens?' Brian asked, skimming his hands along the rosemary hedge on their way in. Fragrance filled the air.

'It'll take a few years before they look this gorgeous,' April said with a smile, 'but it's definitely the cottage vibe I'm aiming for. As long as Archie Winklin's lambs don't treat it like their own personal smorgasbord. They were in my patch again yesterday.'

'Must have been a full moon,' Brian said, opening Geraldine's gate. 'My calves were right royal pains in the you-know-what yesterday too. It's like they know I've got plans and push through the electric fence on purpose.'

She grimaced, picturing him protecting his heirloom varieties from a convoy of skittish calves.

'Lucky it's calves, not goats I s'pose,' he said. 'They would have eaten the patch then started on the wooden stakes. Just glad I didn't waste my time building a twig fence with my vineyard prunings. Might be useful against sheep, though?'

April had seen the hand-woven barriers on gardening websites, and while she wasn't sure the whimsical idea would be much use against the insistent lambs, the decorative element tickled her fancy.

'That's a great idea,' she said. 'How about your cooking? The last few weeks have flown past. Did you do your homework?'

As Brian nodded she noticed he'd taken a little more effort with his appearance. Gone was the wrinkled jumper, and in its place was a check shirt. His wiry white hair was looking a little less windswept today too.

'Oh, that reminds me!' Brian turned on his heel, trotted back to his car and returned with a bunch of rhubarb, tied with gingham ribbon.

Was he trying to woo Geraldine? There had to be a decade at least between the old bachelor and their cooking teacher, but the ruby-red stalks and crisp shirt were like a flashing neon light. Brian's run-down of his attempts to soft-boil eggs—one that had boiled the saucepan dry and two that had gone to his dog—had her in stitches as they walked through the garden.

The students washed their hands, tied their aprons and settled around the bench for the lesson. Connor came in just as Geraldine was explaining today's feature ingredient—mushrooms.

'Field mushies,' Brian marvelled. 'I haven't had these since I was a kid.'

They were given the choice of store-bought mushrooms—'perfect for those who are on the fence about fungi,' according to Geraldine—and the freshly foraged ones.

'These are safe to eat, I promise,' Geraldine told them, watching as everyone made their choice. 'But it's not something you want to gamble on. The wrong types of mushrooms can make you very ill and can be easily mistaken for edible varieties.'

Despite Geraldine's assurances, April opted for the store-bought mushrooms and, much to her pleasure, the knife seemed to move a little easier in her hand this week. It felt like an achievement that she wasn't the last to finish dicing the mushrooms and onions. Connor's onion went sliding across the bench and tumbled to the floor at one stage, and Brian had to ask for a Bandaid after nicking his fingertip.

'I think this could almost be categorised as fun,' said Brian, his deep baritone tinged with disbelief as he helped Geraldine with the dishes. April listened into the conversation as she tidied her space, ready for the third and final item on the agenda—rhubarb and cinnamon muffins. 'My dear wife would turn in her grave if she knew I was prancing around in an apron, laughing and joking as I sautéed onions and deglazed frypans.'

'She'd probably wish you'd done it while she was around to enjoy it,' countered Geraldine.

'She came from a long line of outstanding cooks. I wouldn't have dared.'

April heard the fondness in Brian's words but also regret. Geraldine laid a hand on his arm, gently, and murmured something April couldn't catch. Whatever it was, it seemed to perk Brian up.

'And how are you getting on?' April crossed the room to Connor's workstation. Normally they set up their workstations side by side, but he seemed distant today.

His phone beeped with an incoming message.

'Someone from home?' April asked.

'Yeah,' Connor replied, glancing at the screen.

'Isn't it the middle of the night over there?' She noticed a cloud cross his face fleetingly.

'Definitely too late for messaging,' he agreed, jamming the phone in his pocket and reaching for the laminated recipe Geraldine had handed out.

April had to park her curiosity to concentrate on the measurements and mixing, as Geraldine walked the class through a new variation on the muffins they had made in their previous lesson. Much to April's delight, the quick-mix muffins proved true to their name and before long, the batter was thick and relatively lump-free.

'I don't think there're any eggshells in this batch either,' April said proudly.

'See, you're getting the hang of this,' said Geraldine in a voice that indicated it was only a matter of time, rather than an unscalable mountain.

April heaped the batter into her muffin tin, liking the way it slopped off the spoon in a luscious dollop.

'It's quite relaxing, really,' Maddie said, giggling as her batter-coated rhubarb cubes landed with a satisfying plop.

With Geraldine's gentle encouragement and Maddie's easy tween chatter, the kitchen was an enjoyable place to spend an afternoon, but April couldn't help wondering what had made Connor so jittery.

'Did he just put his muffins in the fridge, not the oven?'

April followed Maddie's gaze and chuckled as the twelve-year-old ribbed him about the mistake. By the time they'd packed up, the muffins were ready to come out of the oven.

'Not bad,' April said, admiring the baked goods as they tumbled out of the tins and onto the cooling rack.

It felt like sacrilege to take a perfectly formed, oven-warmed muffin and crack it in two—and the height of decadence to add butter to something that already contained more calories than sin—but Geraldine was right, April concluded, melted butter running down her chin as she bit into one. They truly were heaven on a plate.

Unlike the rest of the students, Connor didn't linger, saying a quick goodbye before making a hasty exit.

'Something's not quite right,' she said, intercepting Geraldine's worried look at the door.

'No,' Geraldine agreed, mopping up the pool of melted butter on her plate with the last morsel of muffin. 'But I'm sure you'll have a better chance of getting to the bottom of it than me.'

12

When April carried her baked goods inside, she discovered a shredded roll of toilet paper scattered across the living room, an upended Ficus tree and a boisterous golden retriever who showed absolutely no signs of remorse.

'Cabin fever, huh? You're a deadset terror,' April said, stashing the cinnamon and rhubarb muffins in the pantry.

As she cleared away the mess, trimmed the gnawed branches and repotted the Ficus, April reconsidered her afternoon plans. There was no question of lounging on the couch to work on the stables' website and she had a feeling Mishka would dig holes in the garden if she wasn't exercised soon. April pulled on her sandals, threw a few supplies into the back of the ute and lowered the tail gate.

'Come on then.' Mishka bounded up without any further instruction and kept her eyes on the road ahead the entire drive to the coast.

When the Norfolk Pines came into view on the outskirts of Beachport, Mishka howled from the ute tray.

'Steady on, you crazy mutt,' April called out the window,

chuckling at the sight of those golden ears flapping in the wind like Dumbo.

The breeze that swept off the water, drifting inland and cooling the vines, was better than any air conditioner, and April took a moment to appreciate the salty air when she parked at the surf beach.

She tugged on a baseball cap, grabbed the lead and stashed her wallet in her jeans pocket. There were only a handful of people on the beach, but plenty of seaweed, so she let Mishka off the lead. Together they set out for the small fishing village. It was good to feel sand between her toes, and there was plenty of room for Mishka to zigzag from the shore to the sand dunes. By the time they reached the boardwalk, April's head felt a whole lot clearer.

'Nice arvo for it,' said a man being tugged along by a boisterous border collie.

'Sure is,' replied April, clipping the lead on Mishka. He paused beside her, letting his dog introduce itself to Mishka.

'American or Canadian?' she asked, trying to pinpoint his accent.

'I'm Californian born and bred,' he said. 'But I've been living Down Under for a decade or so. Too many crazies with guns back home.'

April agreed with him. 'I've always wanted to visit Napa Valley,' she said. 'It'd be neat to see the contrast in the winemaking; I bet it's different to how we do things in Penwarra.'

His eyes lit up. 'Really? I take my wine drinking very seriously, I've got a whole cellar of the stuff. I love the local wines. Which label are you with?'

She told him and then had to reassure him she wasn't offended that he hadn't heard of Lacewing Estate. 'It's only a small family winery,' she insisted. 'Really, don't feel bad.'

'Give me your details and I'll make sure I call in when I'm passing through next.'

April handed across a business card that was in dire need of a makeover. It had been on her to-do list since the Adelaide conference. 'We're just about to open a boutique B & B too,' she said, explaining about Kookaburra Cottage.

He left with a promise to call in when he was next in Penwarra. April thought about his blank look when she'd told him their winery name. The fact that he was a local wine buff, and he'd never heard of them, made her even more worried that the winery would shrink into insignificance if they didn't do something to increase its profile soon.

Her mind was so deep in marketing, events and tourism rabbitholes that her arm was nearly wrenched from its socket as Mishka took off down the beach towards someone. Her frown softened when she saw who it was.

Connor.

'I thought you must have had to go and dig Fergus out of a sand bog, the way you bolted out of cooking classes,' she joked, unclipping Mishka before her shoulder was dislocated. The clouds parted, and in the sudden sunlight, she saw a haunted look on his face.

What had happened? Where was the upbeat, happy-go-lucky Brit she'd come to know so well?

'Connor, is everything alright?'

Connor looked down to see a well-chewed tennis ball dropped at his feet. Mishka wagged her tail and looked at him with wide, pleading eyes.

'Go fetch it, girl.' He tossed the ball back into the waves and took a deep breath. He hadn't expected to find April on the beach too.

'She'd fetch it all day long, if you had the patience, then hobble around tomorrow like a geriatric. In her mind she's still a pup,' April said, wrapping her arms around herself as the wind whipped up. 'Are you okay?'

'There's a bit of a situation back home in Derby.' The words tumbled out before he could stop them, a rash decision he regretted the moment he saw April's concerned expression.

'That's no good. Anything I can do to help?' She lifted her shoulders. 'Not that you have to tell me.'

He liked that she didn't drill him for the nitty gritty. The old Phoebe would have been pulling out popcorn, eager to get the inside scoop on someone else's drama. Post-accident Phoebe wouldn't have wanted the burden of someone else's trauma. Current-day Phoebe ... He wasn't quite sure. He hadn't seen her in person for over a year, but yesterday on the Zoom call, she'd been shattered. Almost numb.

Connor threw the ball again, trying to find the right words.

'My friend, Phoebe,' he said eventually. 'She's going through a tough time. Family dramas bringing up sad memories.'

'I'm sure she's glad to have a good mate to talk with. Is she a school buddy? Ex-girlfriend?' April's voice was mixed with compassion for both him and Phoebe. Compassion he felt he didn't deserve.

'Ex-fiancée.' He looked out to watch a large fishing boat cutting through the water, choosing a careful path between the other moored vessels, and decided he had nothing to lose by telling April about the loss that had bonded them forever and the cycle of making up and breaking up that had pockmarked their relationship ever since.

'It wasn't a long engagement really,' he added quietly. In that moment, the sound of the ocean melted away, replaced by the memory of an ambulance siren and the sheets on the ambulance gurney turning from white to red. The weight of their loss hit him like a punch to the stomach, despite the years since. Connor blew out a long, carefully measured breath and looked out at the waves as he recalled the day they'd lost Xavier.

'Her sister's having a baby, you see. She's taken it really hard. It's hard to know how to support someone from so far away,' he said. 'We went through a lot together. We lost a baby of our own.'

He looked at her again, trying to work out why he'd told her about Phoebe's and his miscarriage, when it wasn't something he'd mentioned to anyone else on his travels.

'That's so sad,' April said softly, brushing sand and wet dog hair from her jeans. 'When you say "a lot", I'm guessing there's more. Do you want to tell me the rest?'

He jammed his hands in his pockets. 'It's not exactly a heart-warming weekend conversation to raise anyone's spirits. You don't want to—' He was glad when Mishka emerged from the surf and shook her wet coat all over them.

But who else can I debrief with? Deep and meaningful conversations didn't fit in with the easy banter between him and Fergus. And Heidi, his usual sounding board, felt a million miles away.

'It's not a good story,' he said finally.

Understatement of the year.

'I'm all ears if you want to share,' April said, throwing the ball back into the water for Mishka. 'Don't feel you have to, but sometimes it's the stories we don't tell that weigh the heaviest.'

❦

April wasn't sure what surprised her the most, the details Connor had just shared, or the fact that he had trusted her enough to share them with her.

'We weren't planning to have a baby,' he continued, his eyes on a cray boat that had pulled up alongside the jetty to refuel. 'Mid-twenties, we were more about mini-breaks, music festivals and earning our stripes at work. Me as a winery cellar rat and Phoebe on the graveyard shifts at the hospital. She picked up a stomach bug at Glastonbury and couldn't keep a thing down, including her pill, we later found out.'

April glanced across at Connor. Up until now, she'd thought of him as an adventurous guy racking up a few stamps on his passport, who shared her love of jazz and ineptitude at cooking.

You never really know what someone's been through.

Connor continued, watching the commercial fishermen unload their catch. 'We weren't sure what to do about the whole baby situation, to be honest. We still thought it was the height of sophistication to host a dinner party that didn't involve drinking games, so a pregnancy was like being handed a live grenade. There was a time limit and no end of repercussions, whichever way we handled it. Phoebe and I went to the clinic, but . . .' Connor trailed off. 'There was a picket line outside, a heap of pro-life activists. I mean, what are the chances?'

April felt a wave of sympathy for them. *Such an enormous decision.* Her worries about the bed and breakfast and tasting room makeover felt ridiculous in comparison.

'It just felt like a sign, you know? A sign that our decision was the wrong one.' Mixed emotions flitted across his face. 'And I was the prat who convinced her that we should make a go of it.'

The dog bounded into the waves again, emerging from the water a little slower this time. She was finally tuckered out and nestled her way between April and Connor. Connor's hand went to Mishka's damp muzzle, gently tracing the outline of her eyes and nose as he considered which part of the story to tell next.

April picked up a clump of sargassum seaweed, pulling the rubbery round balls from the leaves. Connor seemed lost in thought again, his gaze fixed on the fishing trawler laden with plastic tubs, his mind far from the southern rock lobster catch on board.

'And it didn't work out?' she asked gently.

Connor shook his head, his Adam's apple bobbing. 'We started looking at all the baby gear, talked about putting a teddy-bear frieze on the nursery wall. Then we were driving home from a concert. I'd been performing in London. Phoebe wasn't a confident night driver, but I'd had a few whiskies to celebrate.'

A lump welled in April's throat.

'Wet road, ambulance, jaws of life to cut us out of the car, specialists, the whole box and dice. The stress and trauma sent Phoebe into premature labour. The doctors warned us it was too early, and the minute they placed the baby in her arms, I thought they were wrong. I *wished* they'd been wrong. He was tiny, but otherwise perfectly formed.' Connor shook his head, pinching the bridge of his nose. 'But he was far too young. Xavier didn't survive the first night.'

As the silence stretched between them, April wondered if it ever got easier to tell, or if he never spoke about Xavier because of how hard it was. And how to respond?

'I'm so, so sorry, Connor.' She looked at him through eyes that prickled, then shuffled a little closer, so Mishka was wedged between them, and laid a head on his shoulder. April's only brush with death was her grandparents when she was in primary school, young enough that she hadn't registered the toll of their loss. But a baby . . .

She couldn't guess at the harrowing pain, the grief and conflict, and her heart went out to Connor, for all that he'd been through.

With one arm looped around his knees, Connor ran his fingertips back and forth over Mishka's velvety face. It wasn't the same as letting his hands find the right piano keys, eliciting the gentle notes that diluted the guilt and emotions that arose every time Xavier ran through his mind, but it was comforting nonetheless.

The sand was damp underneath his legs, and he heard the words the counsellor had told him, almost as if he were perched in her grey office on a wet, drizzly British day, instead of sitting in the sunshine on an Australian beach. *Connect with the earth to ground those feelings. Tap your feet against the grass, run your hands through the soil. Remember this too shall pass.*

The advice sounded like codswallop at the time, but when a piano was out of reach and he couldn't play until the emotions were gone, he sometimes opted for the grounding technique he'd angrily scoffed at.

'Connor,' April's quiet words were close to his ear, 'it must have been so hard.'

Connor dug his feet into the golden sand until his ankles were only just visible.

He hadn't planned to burden her with this information today. Hell, it wasn't the type of story you shared on a beach, with the salty air settling on your lips and grains of sand clinging to your skin. Surely, if there was a movie standard for this type of conversation, it included raging storms, dark middle-of-the-night musings or at the very least, a half-empty bottle of gin in a dimly lit pub.

But he'd started, and the least he could do now that he'd brought the mood down to ground zero was finish it. At least then she'd understand why he still felt like he owed Phoebe, no matter how odd that must seem to an outsider.

Tourists ambled down the jetty, their laughter and chummy conversation carrying over the waves. Seagulls hovered above the water. A tinnie spluttered its way to the boat ramp. Connor resumed his story.

'Saying goodbye was the hardest thing I've ever done. Once the funeral was over, the guilt amped up. If I'd just ignored the protesters and ushered Phoebe into the clinic that day, or accepted that bloody concert trophy with a little humility instead of downing celebratory whiskies, then we would never have had Xavier, or lost him. We would have avoided the pit of despair.'

'Maybe,' April said, her voice gentle. 'I guess it's a bit like those sliding doors moments, not knowing what would have happened one way or the other.'

Connor turned to study her, hoping she wasn't going to out herself as a closet 'what's meant to be' kind of person or peddle a line like 'everything happens for a reason.' She gestured for him to go on. 'And you cancelled the wedding afterwards?'

'Ah, yes,' he said, clasping both his hands in front of his folded knees. 'The wedding. As it turns out, proposing to someone in the depths of despair is totally overrated.' He put a dramatic air in his voice, hoping by taking the mickey out of his ignorance and blind obliviousness, that he could break the sombre mood. 'As I found out the hard way, declarations of love and suggestions of doing things over, getting married and then trying properly for a baby, aren't always what a grieving mother or girlfriend wants to hear.'

April grimaced. 'Ouch. But I can see why you would've suggested it. A new focus, a bright future together.'

Connor nodded wearily. 'Yep, that's what I thought too . . . stupid, right?'

He had got Phoebe into that situation, so he simply needed to step up and do what was right. That's what he'd told himself.

'I'd promised we could start afresh, that we'd heal together. In comparison to losing Xavier and Phoebe's wellbeing, my injuries seemed like the least of our problems.'

He rolled his shorts up. A soft gasp slipped from April's lips, and he tried to see the injury from her perspective, studying the mass of lumpy scar tissue where his femur had shattered and pierced his thigh.

'My God, you didn't escape unscathed either, Connor.'

Did her surprise at his scars mean she hadn't noticed the limp he worked so hard to minimise? It was only a small thing, but he was glad for it.

'That was after the power pole concertinaed the glove box into my leg,' he said, dismissing the injury with a wave of his hand. 'If that were the only collateral damage, it'd be fine.'

'You can't blame yourself,' she said.

He didn't bother contradicting her. He pushed himself up, holding out a hand to April. 'I think I owe you a strong coffee after listening to all that,' he said, the gritty sand crunching between their palms as he hauled her to her feet.

April dusted herself off.

'I had the easy end of the stick, Connor. I really am sorry for everything you went through; I'm blown away, honestly. Something like that really puts things in perspective, doesn't it?'

She gave him another of those warm, gentle smiles and he noticed a strand of seaweed clinging to her pink polo shirt, right next to a stain that looked like she'd slopped her last coffee down her front. The sight boosted his spirits. Of all the places in the world to make a fresh start, he'd also been lucky enough to find someone like April—who had found him a job, shared a fondness for music and made him feel like he had better days ahead.

'What will you do about Phoebe, though?' April asked as they crossed the road to the small cafe. 'It sounds complicated.'

'She's still pretty close to my family. Heidi was in her year at school,' he explained. 'They're keeping an eye on her, and I'll try to check in on Zoom a bit more often.'

April looped Mishka's lead around her fingers, listening but not judging. Or, if she was, she was doing a darn good job of keeping her judgements to herself.

'Nobody likes seeing someone they care about in pain,' said April. He met her eyes, relieved to see kindness, rather than pity, compassion or judgement. 'You're a good man, Connor Jamison.'

The sun had gone down by the time April returned to Penwarra. She parked beside Lauren's red car, which had its boot popped open, as Lauren emerged from the cottage.

'I was just about to call the coast guard,' April joked, letting Mishka out of the Hilux. 'How was the four-wheel driving? Bet you're pleased you made it out alive.'

'The sand dunes were epic,' said Lauren. April helped her lug an esky towards the cottage. 'Fergus almost got bogged on the way home, and I thought we'd never get back. My chief of staff would have had a fit if I called in sick for tomorrow's show at this late notice.'

'I'll be tuning in expecting to hear a segment on beach fishing. Or, could the brekky presenter ask listeners to share their favourite "can't make it to work" stories? Bogged in the sand dunes would have to be a pretty good excuse.'

'Worth it for all this shark,' said Lauren, flipping the esky open to reveal several long lengths of freshly filleted fish on ice.

'What are you going to do with that?' April had never seen so much fish, and although she'd never bought it at the supermarket either, she suspected it would command a fair price.

'We moved onto mushrooms and muffins in cooking class today, but I'm not sure I'm ready for the challenge of sashimi or fish curry.'

Her housemate laughed, pulling out a handful of freezer bags and packaging the shark into meal-sized portions. 'I'll take care of cooking this, don't worry. Fergus said it tastes better after it's been frozen, so we don't have to do anything with it tonight.'

April nodded, relieved. 'A bowl of reheated risotto on the couch with a glass of wine is all I've got the energy for,' she said, heading to the bathroom.

The ache in her hip from yesterday's tumble in the stables had escalated during the afternoon and as April peeled off her clothes and eased into the steamy shower, she saw the red mark was now a whopping, inky black bruise.

Nothing like Connor's injuries would have been, mind you.

'Ouch,' said Lauren later, when April gingerly lowered the waist of her pyjama pants to show her.

'Tell me about it,' April said. 'I'll be sleeping on my left side for a week.'

'Ah, the perils of falling head over heels for the second sexiest foreign winemaker in the district,' teased Lauren. 'Fergus said he's a genuinely nice guy. No bullshit, no masculinity complex. He's close to his family, he's even friends with his ex still, and that's not something you see every day.'

April flinched at the terminology. To be fair, there weren't many ways to refer to someone's former partner or fiancée, but ever since Justin had reunited with his ex-girlfriend, who he had always referred to as his 'ex' instead of her first name, April had taken an intense dislike to the term.

Connor's in a different stratosphere to Justin. The little voice inside April's head caught her by surprise. Comparing Connor to Justin . . . *Am I really ready for that?*

'I heard a little more about the mysterious Phoebe today,' April blurted.

'Go on then, spill the beans,' Lauren prompted, setting out the cutlery.

April chided herself as she served up risotto, trying to work out how to deflect the conversation. The news Connor had shared with her that afternoon at Beachport felt too raw, too personal, to pass on second-hand. Maybe once she'd had time to digest it, but not today.

'Just that they were engaged and she's going through a rough time at the moment.' April pulled both bowls from the microwave. 'Now try this risotto and tell me what you think. It tasted amazing at cooking class, but you're the food guru, and anything more than Lean Cuisine is a win in my books. You can be the official judge.'

She pushed the steaming bowl into Lauren's hands, hoping the topic change and the taste test would be smooth. Lauren tucked into the dish.

'This is divine,' Lauren said, going back for another large spoonful.

'Not sure they'll be inviting me onto "My Kitchen Rules" just yet,' April said modestly, 'but I'm definitely improving.'

'Too right,' Lauren yawned. 'Gosh, all that sea air and sunshine have worn me out.' Lauren said with a wink, making April suspect they'd managed more than a little romance between baiting hooks and reeling in fish.

With the dishes done and Mishka fed, April fixed them both a hot Milo and carried it to the couch with her laptop bag.

After watching a few tutorials on the accommodation booking software, she started drafting up a new page for Kookaburra Cottage on the Lacewing Estate website. There wasn't much she could do until the renovations were complete and she had a suite of stylish photographs to attract customers, but with a little more assistance from YouTube, she eventually designed a new set of business cards and created a 'coming soon' webpage.

'Hey, that looks amazing,' said Lauren, setting down the television remote and leaning across to look over her shoulder. 'You're good at that.'

Pleased, April hit 'publish' and Lauren cheered when the fresh web page loaded showing the site was officially live.

'It's not as hard as it looks,' April said with a shrug. 'I've wanted to update the Lacewing Estate website for ages, and while it was tricky at first, once I understood the basics, I realised the templates are pretty user-friendly. It's this next bit I'm nervous about.'

She opened a new browser window and showed Lauren the DestinationSA website.

'I've been thinking about this food tourism program for months,' April said. 'It seemed like a "pie in the sky" idea for so long, but I think Lacewing Estate's almost ready to start hosting events.'

'Events? Like weddings and birthday parties?'

Lauren commandeered the laptop trackpad and scrolled through the website, reading testimonial after testimonial from wineries and event venues that had been accepted into the exclusive program.

'More like silver service dinners, lavish long lunches and opulent events,' April said, shaking her head. 'After I've given the tasting room and cellar a makeover, I want to tap into the high-end events market. This company—DestinationSA—have a niche in foodie tourism, training operators and creating package deals.'

'Can't you just whack a few adverts in the trade magazines and pop a note on the website, saying your venue's for hire?'

April laughed. 'Not quite. A place in this program will open so many doors for us. If we're accepted, we'd receive access to resources, support, promo opportunities and exposure. Here, this endorsement says it all.'

April cleared her throat and read aloud from the testimonials page. '"Best decision ever. DestinationSA helped put us on the map for foodie tourism. Couldn't have done it without their up-to-date knowledge, support and networks".'

'Is it expensive?' Lauren's tone was sympathetic, aware the winery had a limited budget.

'Very,' April conceded, 'but they have a scholarship program. With DestinationSA's backing, Lacewing Estate would soon be packaged up and presented on a platter for event specialists. I learned all about it at the Adelaide conference.'

Lauren covered her mouth as another yawn escaped. 'Well, you'd better get your skates on. Says here their scholarship applications are closing soon.'

'I know,' said April, 'and it's only offered once a year.'

Easing herself off the couch, Lauren collected the mugs. 'I'll leave it with you, then.'

April stared at the laptop. She had a tentative opening date for the bed and breakfast, and a cellar door makeover in the pipeline, but did she have the confidence to take the next step? Could their tasting room really become a coveted, income-generating function space?

Connor popped into mind.

If he can pull himself together after losing a baby and nearly losing his leg, then I can go out on a limb and help our little winery.

April scrolled to the bottom of the page and slowly, carefully, filled in the application form. The application went off into cyberspace with a quiet 'whoosh'.

God, what have I done . . .?

She closed the laptop, channelling Connor's steely determination. It was too late to rescind the application now. The only thing left to do was sit and wait for it to be accepted or denied.

13

The piano keys felt like they were rising up to meet his fingers, the sheet music in front of him redundant as Connor played from memory. Then the slamming of the front door and footsteps across the parquetry floor shook him out of the zone and he finished the piece abruptly.

'Shh, Mum,' came a hiss from beside Connor, as Archie Winklin wriggled on the end of the piano stool. 'Connor's playing.'

Connor blinked a few times, his mind adjusting back to the real world. He turned to his young student.

'It's okay, buddy. This is your house, remember?'

Felicity Winklin walked across the room, a cape of raindrops on the shoulders of her business suit.

'It sounded like we were in a concert hall,' she said. 'You'll play like that if you keep practising, Arch.'

'He'll play much better than that,' said Connor, confident the small boy possessed greater discipline and talent than he'd ever shown at the same age. It was a little indulgent to play for Archie during the lessons, but Connor hoped showing him what it was like to immerse yourself in the music, to really live and breathe it, would embed his love of music even further. And, he admitted only to himself, he missed having such a fine instrument to play whenever his heart desired. The Winklins' glossy black grand piano was a pleasure to play and he'd since discovered they had an electric one gathering dust in a spare bedroom too.

'How about you show your mam the new piece, mate?'

Connor shuffled across, making room for Archie on the stool.

'Oh, don't fuss on my behalf,' Felicity said with a wave. 'I'll catch my death if I stand around in these damp clothes any longer. I'll keep the ensuite door open so I can hear it while I shower,' she said.

Connor didn't look up, not because he thought Felicity was trying to be suggestive—if anything she probably didn't realise the picture she'd painted with her words—but because he knew the hurt written across Archie's face would cut right through him. He found the score and urged Archie to start while she padded upstairs, hoping that maybe Felicity might throw a small morsel of praise in her son's direction, and was disappointed for him when she didn't.

'You're a pro at this,' Connor said, pumping up the lad's tyres after his first stilted rendition. 'Perhaps we'll run through that middle section again. Try it like this.'

After two more attempts, the piece still wasn't gelling. He could feel the boy's frustration grow with each error and his hopes of turning the mood around took a further nosedive when Archie's father, Rupert, strode through the glass atrium, tailored jacket over his arm and laptop bag dangling from his fingers. Archie wilted beside him.

They'd never nail it now.

'What's the problem? Even from the garage, I could hear the timing was off. Start from the start.'

Connor murmured encouragement, so only his student could hear. 'Feel the music, Arch. Block everything else out.'

The boy took a deep breath and plunged into the opening, faltering on the spots that he'd flowed past before and pulling out halfway through the tricky part.

Rupert's heavy sigh came from behind them. He walked across to the piano, picking the sheet music up off the stand. 'It's not even that complex, Archie. If you just tried harder . . .'

Connor looked away. Not getting caught in the middle of his students and employers was one of the first lessons his mum had instilled in him when he began to teach. Sharyn Jamison's sage words rose to the forefront of his memory.

'If you're in this business long enough, Connor, you'll see every kind of parent, every kind of student and walk into a whole range of homes. Always remember you're only there for one hour, maybe two, a week. Your job is to teach the music, infect them with a love of the piano so deep that it stays with them their whole life, not pass judgement on the students, the parents, or their home life.'

Rupert cleared his throat, set the music back down and folded his arms as he waited for Archie to try again, then groaned as Archie missed a note and butchered the melody.

'If you'd just put in a bit more effort, Archie, you wouldn't have this trouble. That looks like a simple tune.' With a shake of his head, Rupert collected his briefcase and headed down the hallway in the direction of his office, muttering as he went.

'I hate this music,' Archie wailed, pounding the keys so a chaotic noise echoed through the living room. It was the musical equivalent of slamming a door and although there was no doubt who it was aimed at, Connor's ears still ached from the racket.

'Hey, let's just try it again,' he said gently, picking up the sheet music Archie had thrown on the terrazzo floor.

'This sucks, I'll never be good at piano,' Archie cried, folding his arms and tucking his quivering chin into his chest.

Connor's eyes moved around the large house, searching for inspiration among the abstract paintings, tapestry wall hangings and collections of pottery that looked like they belonged in a museum, or at best a *Vogue Living* magazine, instead of the home of a small child. There was nothing in the clean lines and bespoke artwork that spoke of fun, adventure or openness to failure.

No wonder he slips through the fence and seeks out April and Mishka on a regular basis, Connor thought.

'Learning an instrument takes time, mate, and not every piece of music is an overnight success,' he said. 'I made so many mistakes when I was learning, it must have driven my mam crazy.'

'Did she yell at you too?' Archie asked glumly.

Connor deliberated a moment before answering truthfully. 'She isn't much into yelling,' he admitted. 'Only raises her voice if there's a mouse inside.'

'What about your dad?'

Connor shook his head again. 'It's not their style, but every family has their different ways, it's what makes all of us different. My folks wouldn't know what to do with a grapevine if it bit them on the bum. Nor would they let me have pet sheep, especially one as cheeky as your Marty. But they love me and they're proud of me, just like your parents.'

Archie gave a huff. 'Proud? I'll never make Dad proud if I keep messing up the simplest music. And Mum's always at work. And when she isn't at work, she's got her head in winery magazines, reading about work stuff. The only one who ever seems happy to see me is Mishka and she licks her own butt and eats sheep poo, so that's not saying much.'

Connor laughed despite himself. 'When I'm sad, music makes me happy. Listening to it, playing, letting my fingers march up and down the keyboard.'

He lay his fingers on the keys and tried to recall the song April had told him about. Archie's lips twitched as he recognised the playground ditty about worms.

'See?' Connor played another few bars. 'I think I'll go and eat worms . . .'

'Do that line again,' Archie said, his scowl losing a hint of its ferocity as he watched Connor's fingers and then tried to recreate it.

While the lesson didn't end on the high Connor usually aimed for, they managed to claw it back to an even keel after Rupert's interruption.

'Are you heading to April's next, Connor? Want me to show you my veggies?'

Connor found it hard to refuse the young boy's optimistic request. 'Give me five minutes and we'll go after I've updated your dad.'

Archie scampered off to change into gardening clothes and Connor headed to Rupert's study for the brief post-lesson update.

Go on, say it.

Even though he was unsure it was the right thing to do, Connor voiced his opinion in the spotless office. 'I know you're keen for Archie to do well,' he said gingerly, 'but I find a carrot works better than a stick with some kids.'

'A stick?' Rupert barked with laughter. 'Connor, a few stern words isn't a stick. I know it's old fashioned, but when I was a boy, my old man used to take his buckle off and give us a flogging when he didn't like what we were doing, or thought we could try harder at something. The finest winemakers are artists, and just like the vines, you have to be prepared to suffer to make fine wine. If we watered the vineyard all the time, the roots would never dig deep and then there'd be trouble. Just like I want those roots to go down five or six metres, I want Archie to dig deep and reap the rewards,' Rupert said, raising a glass of wine with one hand as he studied Connor. 'Anything worth doing is worth doing well, don't you think?'

Connor grimaced. 'He's ten, though. I don't want to tell you how to suck eggs, but from what I can see, Archie's the type of kid who responds to encouragement and praise rather than being made aware of his every mistake.'

Rupert lifted an eyebrow and sipped his wine. 'I'm not looking for life advice, Jamison, and even if I was, I wouldn't take it from someone half my age. Your biggest concern is the next passport stamp, and how many wears you can get out of a clean shirt.' He held up his wine glass as Connor protested. 'I get that, I was young once too. But you wouldn't have the foggiest what it's like parenting in your sixties or running a multi-million-dollar business, nor the hopes and dreams a parent has for a child.'

The combination of condescension and forced manners landed exactly where it was intended, and Connor felt his cheeks burn brightly. And although he knew he was entering dangerous territory now, the type of quicksand Sharyn had expressly advised him to avoid, he couldn't shake the feeling that he owed Archie this much at least.

'Maybe not,' Connor said carefully, 'I don't have your breadth of knowledge or experience, but I guarantee we'll get further with Archie if you take a different tack. Tell him he's doing a super job and leave me to try to iron out the slip-ups.'

Rupert stood and walked to the door, signalling their conversation was over.

'How about we leave it at that today? I'll pretend you didn't try and tell me how to parent and you'll do the job I'm paying you to do,' Rupert said, with a hint of steel in his voice. 'And when you've got children of your own, plus business investments and a thirty-strong workforce, you might understand where I'm coming from.'

Connor retreated down the corridor with his pay, feeling like he'd let Archie down. The home might have been on the front cover of *Wine Connoisseurs Australia*, but for all its pomp and prestige, the house seemed to be lacking love, laugher, affection and support. Things that had been given to him freely in his childhood, and the four cornerstones of the home he wanted to provide for his own family one day.

Connor paused at the entrance, taking in the glass, stone and soaring ceilings, and then looked over at the kid in torn jeans and gumboots waiting at the edge of the sealed driveway, knowing which parenting style he'd be aiming for when the time came.

Later that week, April looped an apron around her neck, tied the strings in a bow behind her back and gave Mishka a nod that was more confident than she felt.

'Okay then, let's do this,' she said, propping the laminated sheet up against the mini monstera plant that lived in the middle of the kitchen bench. And while the pot plant and the golden retriever had no means of talking back, or correcting her before she made a slip up, April talked through the steps as she went.

'Measure one and a half cups of flour and add to the bowl,' she said, reaching for the bag of flour. 'So far so good, Mish,' April said. She carefully checked each quantity before adding the next items to the mix and before long, she was using her fingers to gently fold the rhubarb through the dry ingredients.

'Geraldine said this stops the fruit sinking to the bottom,' she told Mishka, feigning a blasé tone when what she really wanted to do was hang a banner from the gum tree outside that told everyone she could cook.

Like one of those 'baby on board signs' favoured by proud first-time parents.

Her grin froze. Insensitive, much? How did her brain even come out with that, especially after Connor's story of losing Xavier? April rinsed her hands and started on the eggs and vegetable oil.

It wasn't until she'd spooned the batter into the brand-spanking new muffin tin that she discovered she'd forgotten to switch the oven on. 'Not quite second nature yet,' she told Mishka wryly.

Lauren jogged inside a little while later, just as April was arranging the best of the batch onto a paper plate. 'Look at you go! A few cooking lessons and you're off.'

April smacked away Lauren's fingers, which were inching towards the plate intended for Felicity Winklin and redirected her friend to the other cooling tray. 'We get to eat the ones that stuck to the tin, they're not as pretty as this lot but they're still tasty.'

After Lauren had declared the rhubarb muffins a success, April slipped out of her apron, pulled on her work boots and carried the plate over the laneway.

Felicity answered the door in tan chinos, a white linen shirt and more gold jewellery on one arm than in April's entire collection.

'I won't keep you,' April said, handing over the plate. 'It looks like you're on your way out.'

Felicity looked surprised. 'Not out, exactly, but I've got a few Zoom calls to make this afternoon. And you didn't have to do this. Are they for Archie?'

'They're actually for you,' April told Felicity. 'As a thank you for the roses. But I figured Archie would help you polish them off.' The sound of hurried footsteps echoed down the hallway behind Felicity. She waved at her young friend. 'Hey buddy, how're the lambs?'

'Very sore and sorry for themselves today.' He grimaced, empathy creasing his little face.

April made a face back in solidarity.

'Lamb marking's just part of the process,' Felicity said. 'They'll be fine tomorrow. And you didn't need to bring me anything, honestly April. You'll be doing me a favour by getting rid of those roses and with all the time you've spent minding this little devil, it's the least I can do.'

Archie folded his skinny arms across his chest and April puzzled over his mum's choice of words. Felicity made it sound like a babysitting service, rather than a friendship.

'He's my number one helper,' April said. 'In fact, I was hoping Archie might be keen to earn some pocket money this afternoon.'

'Digging out the roses?' It was Felicity's turn to look puzzled and April almost felt like agreeing, just so Archie knew that at least one person in the conversation thought he was capable of something.

'No, we'll leave the roses for another few weeks if that's okay, until they're dormant, but I'm in need of a keen worker with strong muscles, like Archie here.'

She could almost see his chest puffing up as she flashed him a smile.

'Yeah, that's me,' he said, his eagerness setting off a pang in April's heart. 'What are we doing?'

After hearing about the rocks that needed shifting, Archie happily agreed to ten dollars an hour and loped away to replace his footy shorts with work clothes.

Felicity frowned apologetically. 'He's going through a funny stage at the moment. Doesn't have many friends his own age. I hope he's not bugging you.'

'Not at all,' April assured her. 'Archie's such a good kid, he's welcome any time.'

After promising Felicity that Archie would more than earn his pocket money, they set out for Lacewing Estate.

'That's a big pile of rocks,' said Archie, scratching his head as he looked back at the winery. The cellar door was about half a kilometre from the rock pile.

'Yep, but you and I just need to load them into the tractor bucket, we're not carrying each and every rock to the highway ourselves.'

His relief was palpable, and by the time they'd shifted the pile from the paddock to the main entrance, one tractor load at a time, April knew it was money well spent.

Archie headed home and April ducked through the shower, then fired up her laptop as she dried her hair. Her breath caught in her chest at the sight of an email from the DestinationSA team.

That was quick! Are we in or out?

She left the email unopened, eyeing it as she made coffee, then tossed her dusty work clothes into the washing machine and stacked away the remaining muffins. April leaned against the counter, tapping the edge of the coffee cup with a dirty fingernail, and stewed on what the email might say.

Being involved in the food tourism program would give Lacewing Estate amazing exposure and ensure she knew what she was doing before she opened the doors for functions. And because paying for the program wasn't an option, she prayed they could scrape in with the scholarship.

Erghh, I can't look!

It was only when she'd done the dishes, cut three juicy stems off the monstera plant and set them in the windowsill for maximum propagation conditions, texted a photo of the shifted rocks to Connor, and hung out the load of laundry that April allowed herself to open the email.

'Yes,' she whispered. Mishka whimpered. 'YES!' April jumped up in the air, fist-pumping the sky.

They'd won the scholarship.

Opening her notepad, she flicked back through the ideas she'd brainstormed and jotted down the key dates for the course materials and webinars. If Lacewing Estate was going to host long lunches, degustation dinners and high teas at their winery, they'd definitely need to fancy it up a little first. She looked out the window to the winery and then across to the mudbrick house where her father and Fran lived. There was also the small matter of breaking the news to them.

How could they be anything but happy about it? Surely they'll also see it as a step in the right direction?

April glanced at the calendar. She didn't have much pencilled in for the days ahead, apart from working on the stables with Gordon, but her folks had an anniversary getaway scheduled later in the week. She made up her mind. *I'll tell them Saturday. They'll be in a good mood after a romantic night away.*

Their absence would also be a good chance to make a start on the cellar door's mini-makeover. With Lloyd and Fran away, it would be just her and Connor in the winery.

Even though she tried to stop it, April's imagination jumped ahead, and she caught sight of her smile in the window's glassy reflection. It was as appealing as it was impossible.

But *is it* impossible, though? Or was it time to trust again?

🍇

Connor had wondered if things would be awkward between him and April after their conversation at the beach, feared she'd look at him differently now she knew he'd been to blame for the death of his son, but to his immense relief, the week had passed without a hitch.

She'd seemed happy to see him when he bumped into her around the winery, and if anything, she sought him out more throughout the week, not just the afternoon they worked together at the cottage.

He arrived at work on Thursday morning, locked his car and strolled into Lacewing Estate with a plastic container of slightly overcooked muffins.

'How good do they look,' April said, appearing from the tea room with an armful of painting supplies. 'I'd call you a teacher's pet if I hadn't done the exact same thing this week too. Oddly satisfying, isn't it?'

'Pulling something like this out of the oven, without any smoke or spillage, is hard to beat,' he agreed. He set down the container, noticing the paint brushes and masking tape. 'Are we painting the stables already? I thought you were still waiting on the cornice, arcs and skirting boards? And where's Fran? I was planning to bowl her over with these muffins, reassure her that I'll have something better to offer for next year's show.'

April bit into his muffin, giving him an approving thumbs up. 'Dad and Fran are off to the Barossa for the night, it's their wedding anniversary.'

That's right, Connor thought, remembering Lloyd had mentioned it earlier in the week. 'Right you are. Do you think I can freeze these muffins, then?'

April was just as clueless as him, but a quick call to Geraldine confirmed they'd freeze perfectly. He loaded them into the staffroom freezer as April updated him on her success with the DestinationSA scholarship.

'That's awesome,' he said, shutting the freezer and holding up his hand for a high five. 'Your folks must be thrilled.'

April nibbled on her bottom lip, sheepish as her warm palm connected with his.

'I haven't exactly shared the good news yet—' She swept the fringe from her eyes. 'But a guerrilla makeover for the tasting room and cellar should soften the blow when they get back. How are you with a paintbrush?'

Connor waved a hand to indicate he knew the basics. 'So the paint's for here, not Kookaburra Cottage, then?'

She nodded. 'You find the drop sheets and I'll start masking up,' she said, directing him to the storage shed nestled at the back of the winery. 'And bring the ladder if you can manage it, too.'

He found the supplies easily enough and helped April prep for painting. 'Are you sure about this?' Connor asked, after the carpet was covered with drop cloths and the first wall was taped to perfection.

'Not really,' April beamed, with a cheerful laugh, 'but I bought the biggest tin of Lexicon White I could, and between the stables and the cellar door, I plan on using every last drop. What's the worst Dad can do? Say it looks too fresh, too crisp?'

The conversation danced from music and their new-found baking skills to deliberation on whether or not Brian was making a play for Geraldine and plans for improvements they could make to the cellar on a modest budget.

April's painting technique was prone to drips and Connor's cutting-in was a bit hit and miss, but by the time they'd finished undercoating the long wall parallel to the tasting bar, the room already looked bigger.

'Removing some of the knick-knacks didn't hurt either,' added April, pleased with Connor's suggestion. 'We've looked at that clutter for so long, we don't even notice it anymore. And wait until I find some fresh light shades for that bar. Anything would be better than those daggy old ones,' she said, mopping up a paint drip with the corner of her drop sheet. 'Fiona put aside a trio of glass shades at the second-hand shop—I haven't seen them yet but she knows my taste, so they should be good.'

Remembering the last pre-loved purchase she'd told him about, Connor lifted a wary eyebrow. 'Is she the one who sold you those pants?'

April laughed, hoisting up the khaki builder's pants that were not only too large, but were now also covered in splotches of white undercoat. 'Nope, these were all my own fault. You should see the colour of that bruise.'

And before he could avert his eyes, April had unbuckled her belt and revealed a blossom of indigo and shiraz on her hip, the sight accentuated by the green underwear she was holding aside with her thumb.

'Jesus, Mary and Joseph.' Connor blinked, looking away before his face, neck and the tips of his ears flushed bright red, hoping his comment had sounded more like sympathy than what it really was; appreciation. The gentle curve of her hip, even though it was marred with a florid bruise, took his mind places that didn't belong in her father's winery. The loft of the stables perhaps, but definitely not in Lloyd's domain and Connor's own workplace.

'You should've put some ice on that,' he said, meeting her gaze after she'd reinstated her waistband and re-buckled the belt. 'Is it still sore?'

She wrinkled her nose and shook her head. 'Only when I bang into something or sleep on that side.'

He squeezed past her to open the door. Was it stuffy in here? 'I see you've got the rocks all ready to start the entryway.'

She followed him outside and disappeared around the back, returning with Mishka, a tennis ball and a tin of line-marking paint. 'Yep, Archie helped, the little legend. If you're not too busy this arvo, I was hoping you'd help me mark out the new fence too?'

'Sure,' he said. *Tell her you like her*, ordered a voice in his head. *Tell her you like being with her at work, on weekends, that you'd like to spend a whole lot more time together instead of just a few hours here and there.*

'Please don't feel you have to, though,' she said, looking uncertain. 'The fence can wait until next week, I totally understand if you've got better things to do.'

Better than hanging out with her? He smiled and shook his head, following her outside. 'Nothing pressing.'

'I was thinking we'd use the hose to mark the outline of the stone fences and then spraypaint the lines on the ground once we're happy with it?'

He liked the way she looked to him for assurance. 'My stone-wall building skills are a bit like my cooking skills,' he confessed, 'but I'll give it a shot. I'm willing to look like an idiot if it means it might earn me a snippet of approval.'

Connor wasn't sure exactly where the comment came from, but it made April laugh. He gestured with the hose, which promptly spluttered a trickle of water down his legs.

'I like you, April, and even though I look like I've just wet myself now—' he grinned, and she grinned back, so he set the hose down and stepped in closer '—I've been meaning to check in about something.'

'Oh, yeah?' She looked up at him from under her fringe. 'And what's that?'

Just ask her.

'Before I interviewed for the winemaker's job, hot as Hades and smelling like sheep, we talked about flirting and professionalism. Is that—' he lifted a shoulder in what he hoped was a nonchalant shrug. 'Do you still think that's a terrible move?'

'Flirting with our winemaker? I know it's a bad move. Disastrous even. Certifiably crazy.'

Connor chuckled wistfully, bowing his head to hide his disappointment. He'd clearly misread the situation. *Well, now you know for sure.* He suspected Jean Dellacourte would happily step in with a few suggestions, if he asked.

From now on, he'd be the consummate professional.

April was still shaking her head when he looked up again, but there was a broad smile too. 'It probably *would* be crazy, given how badly I've misjudged things in the past—' She paused, then held his gaze and stepped closer.

Her fingers were gentle as she reached out and touched his cheek. She held the finger out to show him a smear of Lexicon White paint. 'But I think I trust you, Connor Jamison. Despite the wet trousers and paint freckles.'

Connor let out a slow breath. 'So maybe when we're not marking out fences or renovating the stables, we could grab a drink sometime?'

'You know what?' Her eyes crinkled at the sides as a slow smile built. 'I think we should.'

14

'What are you doing with those?' Lloyd jogged across the winery car park the following afternoon, eyebrows skyrocketing as April tossed three dusty rattan light shades into the skip bin. They landed with a clatter at the bottom and were soon followed by Connor's arm load.

'We're doing some spring cleaning,' April replied cheerfully, draping an arm around her father's shoulders and turning him back to the winery. 'Come inside, we've got a surprise for you,' she said, opening the door to their new and improved tasting room.

Lloyd stood in the foyer, his arms crossed so tightly April was worried the stitching along his shoulders might burst. He glanced around the room, taking in the fresh paint job, the new fittings, the spotless, clutterfree surfaces, then shook his head and stormed off.

Music floated through the barrel room as Lloyd disappeared into the cellar.

'That went well.' April pulled a face that was a cross between a grin and a grimace.

'I'll see if I can smooth things over,' said Connor, following her father into the bowels of the building.

Fran's snort of amusement lingered in the air and from the corner of her eye, April noticed her stepmum was wearing a pretty pair of pearl earrings. An anniversary gift, perhaps?

'What did you think was going to happen when you went behind Lloyd's back like that? You know he doesn't like surprises, and he might be a little set in his ways—' Fran rolled her eyes at April's protest. 'Okay, perhaps he's *quite* set in his ways, but he probably spent weeks choosing those light fittings and that beige paint.'

'But this looks so good, Fran, how could anyone argue with snowy-white walls and modern glass pendant lights? They were brand new, in the boxes, at the op shop.'

Fran cast an appreciative eye over the updated space, before giving April a rueful look. 'I'm not saying they're bad decisions, just that new things scare your father. You can't put the juice back in the grapes, so give him time to get used to it.'

April swallowed. Probably not a good moment to mention their acceptance into the DestinationSA program.

'Connor brought you muffins,' she said instead.

Fran's face lit up. 'He's a treasure, isn't he? Nothing's too much trouble, he's happy to turn his hand to whatever we ask of him, and I haven't once heard him swearing, which is quite a rarity these days. And now afternoon tea.'

April knew that crisp nod. It was as good as a gold star in Fran's books.

'You and Connor managed okay while we were away?'

The question was casual enough, but April suspected it was only loosely related to the winery.

Mumbling an answer, April headed back to the cottage and busied herself with garden chores for the rest of the afternoon, unable to shake her restlessness. Thinking of Connor made her stomach do a little backflip, but had she done the right thing agreeing to drinks tonight?

Would it be awkward dating Connor, considering his work ties to her family business? Lauren had been thrilled when she'd shared the news with her the previous night, convinced they might finally have a successful double date, and April noticed Geraldine had already been nudging them into pairs during cooking classes. Then there was Fran's praise.

Three endorsements from people she cared for and respected, but she still felt nervous about opening her heart again. She remembered how crushed she'd been when Justin had left; it had taken a long time to stitch herself back together. Upending the wheelbarrow of weeds onto her compost heap and washing her hands, April pulled out her phone.

It had been months since she'd spoken with her mum, weeks since she'd texted her a photo of the new roof on the stables, and while the chances of catching Polly Sanders were as patchy as the mobile coverage, she decided it was worth a shot. Much to her surprise, Polly answered the call.

'Darling, what serendipity! I was just telling my students about your B & B renovations yesterday, you clever girl. We were poring over your website. Tell me everything.'

Half an hour had passed by the time they'd finished catching up and Polly had shared updates from her extensive travels.

'I'm thinking of settling in the Tiwi Islands for a longer spell, actually. They need more teachers and the people are friendly. You could come visit, swing a hammock between some palm trees and sip cocktails. Maybe a little island romp?'

April laughed. Even if she wasn't flat out, she knew her mum's wanderlust would prevail before long and by the time she'd booked tickets to visit, Polly would be on another continent.

'What?' Polly sounded indignant. 'You don't have a man holding you back, do you? Jason, or is it Justin?'

'Justin's old news, Mum,' April assured her. 'But I do have a date tonight. His name is Connor.' She caught sight of her reflection in the cottage windows as she filled her mother in. Why did she turn into a giddy teenager the moment his name rolled off her lips?

'He sounds lovely, but he's still not a reason to forgo adventure. Lloyd and Fran have got you well trained, haven't they? All work and no play. I suppose at least this Connor's a winemaker, so he knows it's not all Sunday lunches. Promise me you'll throw caution to the wind and have at least one or two wild flings before settling down. Live a little, darling.'

April signed off with the same ambivalence she always felt after a conversation with her mum. Polly Sanders was many things—adventurous, enthusiastic and effervescent—but she'd never been especially maternal or practical. Grand romances were well and good for someone who flitted from one corner of the globe to the other, but she suspected strong relationships were centred on compatibility and compromise, more than sparks and fireworks.

April spent longer than usual getting ready for dinner, eventually settling on a patterned skirt and white blouse, with her hair loose and wavy. When Connor picked her up, she had a hard time dragging her eyes away from the Levi's that moulded to his butt.

'You look gorgeous,' he said, smelling all kinds of wonderful when he leaned in to kiss her cheek. After much deliberation, they'd settled on dinner at the golf club, and once they'd arrived April discovered Connor knew almost as many people as she did.

'Jean's eyes are practically out on stalks,' she whispered as they chose a table beside the sheet-covered piano. 'Brace yourself, she's heading our way.'

'Fancy seeing you at the Nineteenth Hole,' said Jean, surprise on her face. 'I would never have picked you two as a couple.'

'Oh, we're not—'

Connor reached across the table and grabbed April's hand, cutting her off. He nodded vigorously at Jean. 'No denying it,' he said quickly, flicking April a 'back me up here' look.

'Yep,' agreed April, feeling Jean's gaze moving between them. 'And we'd better get ordering, it looks like the Millicent golfers are just about to swarm the counter.'

They excused themselves and made it to the cash register just ahead of the visiting players. It wasn't until they went to pay that April realised they were still holding hands.

'Sorry about that,' said Connor, 'Jean's been playing cupid ever since I arrived. I panicked.'

He looked so forlorn that April couldn't help laughing. 'I don't mind being your cover story, but you realise this will get back to Dad and Fran the moment we step outside?'

'Seriously?' Connor glanced around the room, possibly trying to identify the head of the bush telegraph, before shrugging. 'I'm okay with that, if you are.'

This could really blow up if I'm wrong about him . . . April closed her eyes for a moment, willing herself the courage to trust that things would work out.

He squeezed her hand gently, and she realised his heart was every bit as vulnerable as hers. 'Let's do this,' she said, leading the way to their quiet table for two.

As they'd expected, Geraldine's fare was delicious and it felt like no time had passed before Connor was dropping her back to the winemaker's cottage.

Mishka ran rings around them the moment April unclipped her from the kennel.

'We could open a bottle of wine,' she suggested, feeling shy all of a sudden. Connor's eyes dipped to her lips, then moved slowly up to her eyes again, and the sweet flush he got when he was flustered skimmed his cheeks.

'I'm not sure I could stop at one glass and I don't think we should rush this.' His voice was low and though she couldn't quite see the longing in his eyes in the darkness, it was clear in his voice and in the way his hand caught hers.

April stepped in closer. Her lips brushed his and Connor's free hand wrapped around the back of the neck, gently pulling her to him. *Why did I wait weeks—months—to act on this attraction?* she thought, leaning into the kiss.

She was pleased she wasn't the only one a little breathless when they finally broke apart. 'If Jean's going to be spreading the word, we may as well give the town something worth talking about, right?' April tilted her head upwards and kissed him again. 'Slow is good, though,' she agreed. 'I'm not in any hurry.'

April was too wired to sleep when Connor left and after an hour of smiling at the ceiling, she pulled on her work jeans and slipped outside quietly, so as not to wake Mishka, who sounded like she was chasing rabbits in her sleep, or Lauren, who had got home late and collapsed into bed after a hectic day at the radio station.

Apart from a hooting owl and the wind chasing fallen leaves, the jangle of April's keys was the only noise in the vineyard. With her phone torch wedged between her teeth, April let herself into Kookaburra Cottage, breathing in the sawdust and fresh timber, imagining that amongst the new scents she could still detect a hint of hay and dubbin.

The portable floodlight flickered on with the push of a button, and April perched on one of the sawhorses that was the perfect height for both cutting timber and admiring their progress. And as she studied the pile of leftover floorboards that Connor had neatly stacked, and the tin of Lexicon White paint they'd carried back once the final coat was done in the winery, April felt a sense of achievement that she hadn't even realised she'd been striving for.

Calls from magpies, kookaburras and cockatoos filled the air, and it pleased Connor to have the company of their songs on his morning lap of the foggy golf course. Fat droplets of water rolled off the eucalyptus leaves and down the neck of his jacket as he passed Geraldine's driveway.

A cool breeze had arrived at the start of the week, and the rain had become more frequent, but it was the fog that felt like the harbinger of winter. Connor arrived back at the rental to find smoke pouring out of the chimney, which was much better than the windows, but still rather alarming.

'Do I need to call the fire brigade?'

Fergus appeared with an armload of firewood, stomping his damp boots on the wire doormat before following Connor inside and stacking the wood by the hearth. 'Not sure this thing's been lit since last winter, should settle down soon.'

Over breakfast, Fergus reminded him about the fishing trip he'd planned for them the following weekend. 'Are you in, or what? It's loads of fun and this time of year we should have the ten mile all to ourselves.'

'We still have a freezer full of fish from your last expedition,' Connor said. 'And my holidays as a kid were more about music camps and touring orchestras, not tents and hiking, so I'll probably be about as much use at fishing as my Camry will be over the sand dunes. Simply warning you in advance.'

Fergus wasn't deterred and clapped him on the shoulder. 'You'll love it. Lauren's invited April too, in case that makes it more appealing. You two have been going out for a few weeks now, camping will be a good test. Things alright?'

Connor knew his cheeks would betray him if he acted nonchalant. 'Looking that way,' he said with a grin, rinsing the toast crumbs off his plate and returning the toaster to the pantry.

'And how's her dad handling that, then? Lauren said he's a bit of a stick in the mud.' Fergus added wood to the fire, watching flames engulf the log before settling on the couch and flicking open the *Sunday Mail*.

'We're not exactly romping through the winery, unbuttoning our clothes while he blends the shiraz.' If Lloyd had noticed a warmth between the two of them, he hadn't commented on it directly. Neither had Fran. 'But I get the feeling they'll be pleased to see their daughter happy,' he said, leaving Fergus to read his newspaper in peace.

His mobile buzzed on the car seat when he was halfway through town and after a surreptitious look at his phone while waiting at the pedestrian crossing, he was pleased to see April's name on the screen. Noting her morning tea request, he nipped into a parking spot outside the bakery.

'Just the usual then?'

He held two fingers up to the lady behind the counter, who seemed to remember the coffee size, milk preference and baked weaknesses of all the locals. 'Two actually,' he said with a smile.

He returned to the car with two flat whites and two French vanilla slices to find his phone ringing.

'I hope you didn't want the original snot block because I've already bought you the French one,' he said, picking up the phone without looking as he turned the keys in the ignition.

But instead of April's laugh, there was a long silence. 'Umm, it's me. Phoebe. And I've no idea what on earth you're talking about, but I'm intrigued to find out.'

Connor switched the ignition off again. 'Sorry, I didn't realise it was you,' he said, trying to think why she'd be calling. He'd checked in with her a few times since the news of her sister's pregnancy, but usually it was by text. It wasn't either of their birthdays, or Xavier's anniversary. 'Is everything alright?'

'Ye-ah.' The beat of hesitation suggested otherwise and he waited, knowing she'd either open up or change the subject, and if past history proved correct, his probing wouldn't make much difference. 'Same old, same old here,' she said. 'I saw your folks today. Nell had dragged them out on a riverboat trip.'

'She did?' Connor couldn't hide his surprise.

'I was shocked too, but they said it was quite good, actually. Even Pippin said it wasn't half as bougie as she'd expected.' Phoebe laughed. 'In full earshot of the guy who runs the cruises, of course.'

'I can imagine,' groaned Connor, feeling a wave of homesickness wash over him as he pictured his mum and dad trying to shush Pippin, while Heidi rolled her eyes and Nell piped up with something mischievous just to regain a hint of the limelight. 'She'll grow out of it soon, surely?'

Connor took a sip of his coffee, which had lost the tongue-tingling heat he liked. He knew April would be wondering what was keeping him.

'Con?' Phoebe's voice was soft again. 'It's good to hear your voice, you know?'

'Look, I'd better leave you to it,' he said, turning the car keys and flicking on the indicator. A vehicle tooted behind him, obviously keen for the parking spot, and he ended the call before waving an apology to the other driver.

He leaned his head back against the fabric seat as he drove, letting out a measured breath. Being there in times of need was different to staying in touch 'just to chat' and he didn't want anything to jeopardise his budding relationship with April.

Connor turned the radio to ABC Classic, hoping the music would clear his head, and arrived to find April had started building the stone fence without him. Archie popped up from behind the mountain of rocks, looking mighty cheerful for 9 am on a Sunday morning.

'Hey Connor! Check out the wall, it's not even falling over.'

He couldn't help laughing at Archie's incredulous tone.

'Ye of little faith,' April called over her shoulder, striding over to retrieve the coffee cups from Connor. 'You're a sight for sore eyes,' she said, hesitating, then landing a quick kiss on his lips. 'Did you get stuck talking? Tell me Jean isn't on your tail?'

Connor shook his head, holding up the vanilla slices instead of answering her questions. 'I didn't realise Archie would be here. He can have mine.'

'I didn't realise he'd be here either,' she murmured, 'but he's pretty good value. How about we split one piece and he can have the other? As long as you don't mind sharing?'

Connor pushed the phone call to the back of his mind and when Archie was busy fetching another rock, he stole another kiss. 'Don't mind at all,' he said.

※

'New chairs now?' Lloyd looked up as April squeezed through the winery door sideways, a black stool in each hand. 'I still don't know what was wrong with the old light fittings,' he huffed, raising his palms to the sky. 'How much is this costing us, all this makeover business? Because as far as I can see, we've not had an infinite uptake in customers to equal out the expenses.'

April looked to Fran for assistance but her stepmother only raised her eyebrows pointedly and went back to her paperwork.

'Build it and they'll come, Dad,' April said, admiring how the revamped stools gave the bar a whole new look. 'Besides, these are the same old bar stools, I just unbolted the ugly backrest, puttied over the holes, then Connor and I spray-painted them black.' Her father's eyes widened and she had to press her lips together to stop a laugh escaping.

'Well, then . . .' He cast around the room for a response, then—as if realising he couldn't argue the point without sounding completely churlish—gave a curt nod. 'Good. Connor's working out well, isn't he?'

'He's very handy,' she agreed, catching a glimpse of him out the window, at the top of a ladder, removing a sod of grass from the winery gutter. April cleared her throat, banishing the memory of Connor's hands around her waist and the lingering scent of spray paint on his skin as he'd kissed her behind the stables just an hour before.

'Good manners, too,' Lloyd said. 'You don't see that every day, more's the pity. Much better for you than that last bloke.'

It was April's turn to raise her eyebrows. Her father had never weighed in on her love life and she wasn't quite sure how to take it. As he headed to his office, she realised it would be a good time to mention the DestinationSA scholarship. It had been weeks since they'd been accepted into the program and she'd already attended the first online group workshop, meeting business owners who were equally excited and nervous about diversifying into events and food tourism. The guilt at not mentioning it to her father itched like a label on the neckline of a new jumper.

Do it now, while he's in a good mood.

'About that food tourism plan,' she blurted.

Lloyd turned, leaning against the doorway. 'Nah, I'm not sure it's for us,' he said, sweeping the thin strands of salt and pepper hair away from his eyes.

Tell him, just get it over with.

'It's a little late for that,' she said as smoothly as she could manage. 'We've been accepted into a program with DestinationSA and while we don't have any venue bookings yet, I've started learning the ins and outs of attracting new clients through event hosting. With the holiday season ahead, we're sure to have plenty of bookings coming our way soon.'

Hands on hips now, her father groaned. 'You signed Lacewing up? Without telling me?' He crossed his arms, uncrossed them and then threw his hands in the air again. Fran's only contribution was another soft shake of her head.

'But it will pay well,' April rushed ahead, listing off the advantages on her fingers. 'We get the exposure, they drink our wine, they tell their fancy friends all about it. I mean, how often do we use the venue to its full potential?'

It was a rhetorical question, but before she could continue, Connor stuck his head through the door.

'You expecting a group?'

Fran flicked through the booking ledger behind the bar and shook her head. 'Not today. How many?'

'They've got a mini-van. Interstate number plates,' he said.

April craned her neck, did a headcount and then looked back at the wine glasses. They needed another four, pronto.

'A party of ten from the look of things,' said April. She zipped around the other side of the bar and grabbed a second tea towel, taking over the polishing and setting bottles on the bench as her stepmother welcomed the travellers.

'Come in, come in,' Fran said, knotting an apron around her waist and shutting the door behind their guests. 'Where are you from?'

April listened with one ear as Fran gave her usual spiel about the winery's history and offered their Victorian guests the wine menus. From the striking similarities between them, with various shades of strawberry blonde hair, she was pretty sure the women in the group were sisters.

'Look, Diana, this bottle sounds like it was made for you,' said one of the men. 'It's called Lacewing "Dahlia Dreaming" cab sav.'

A lady with a loose, floaty dress laughed and took one of the glasses. 'We'll try that one first then,' she said. 'I'd love to know how you chose the name for that label,' she went on, pulling up a stool. For a split second, April prayed that every nook and cranny of that spray paint was bone dry.

Of course it is, you finished the last coat hours ago, she told herself, listening as the woman elaborated.

'I run a flower farm just a few hours over the border, so I'm a sucker for anything referencing dahlias.'

April chanced a nervous smile at her father's retreating back, hoping he'd heard that, and quickly placed the last of the glasses on the bar for their customers.

'Well, we decided to name all the varieties from last year's vintage after a different flower,' explained Fran. 'April chose the topic that year, and she went with a horticultural theme.'

April looked up from the polishing and waved. The group all waved back with warm, friendly smiles. These were the type of customers they liked best. Not rolling drunk, not rushing in and out as quickly as they could and using them for their freebies or toilets. People who were interested in the stories behind the wines. With a bit of luck, soon they'd have many more groups like this.

'The previous vintage,' Fran continued, 'the wines were named after poets—that was my choice—and the year before that, all the wines were named after blues musicians.'

April thought of the pushback she'd had from her father when she'd first floated the suggestion about jazzing up the titles and renovating the stables. It had taken years for him to warm to either idea, and even then he only did so after Fran pushed the point. It would be the same with the food tourism. He'd grumble about it for months before accepting it was a masterstroke.

'I'm not sure if you're over this way often,' April said. 'But there's a heap of great events in the pipeline if we can lure you back. We're just about to start long lunches and degustation dinners. We've got a little B & B opening in spring, too.' They seemed impressed with the idea, and April was thrilled to see one of the ladies taking a flyer from the counter and putting it inside her purse.

Fran unscrewed a bottle and poured a small measure of the second wine into each of the glasses.

'No more for me,' said a curly-haired lady. 'I'm the driver,' she added, sounding happier about that arrangement than most of the people on self-drive wine tours. 'And breastfeeding,' she went on. It was only then that April noticed a pram in the corner.

'Oh, what a sweetheart,' Fran said, moving around the bar to coo at the baby. April gave the newborn a cursory smile and tracked Lloyd down in the barrel room. She spent the next two hours explaining what the program entailed, walking him through the modules and online workshops she would attend, and the opportunities she hoped would come their way with the backing of DestinationSA.

The Victorian mini-van was gone by the time April strolled out of the winery that afternoon, and though her father's feathers were smoother, they weren't completely ruffle-free.

'When did we get new business cards? Whose winery is this, anyway?' He headed home in a huff, but not before April saw him admiring the start of the new stone entryway.

'Have a good weekend, April,' Fran said when it was time to close up. 'And thanks for your help with the McIntyre family, they were more interested in the long lunches than I'd imagined.'

'Well, if you happen to be talking to Dad about the DestinationSA thing over the weekend, can you put in a vote of confidence? Tell him how keen those customers were.'

Fran locked the cellar door behind her, pocketing the keys. 'I'm not going to be the meat in the sandwich, April. Never was, never will be.' She softened, giving April's arm a quick rub. 'But if he happens to mention it, I'll remind him that you're an adult and quite possibly he should have a little more faith in you.'

April felt lighter as she walked between the rows of vines, past the gnarled trunks her grandfather had planted. Kookaburra Cottage looked nearly complete from the outside and wasn't far off being done on the inside too. When Lauren and Fergus arrived for a pizza night, she and Connor gave them a tour of the worksite.

'Snazzy as,' said Fergus, running his hands along the paddock-rock walls, which glowed in the afternoon sun. 'I could see myself chilling in that bathtub, a lovely lassie soaping my back and feeding me grapes.'

'Steady on,' Lauren laughed, her hand nestled in his jeans pocket as they walked back to the winemaker's cottage.

Despite all the pizza they'd made, by 9 pm there were only crusts and one lonely pizza glad-wrapped for leftovers.

'Told you there was no such thing as too many toppings,' said Lauren, clearing away the last of the dishes later that night.

'What type of monster are you, April, to suggest such a thing?' Fergus carried the bottle of chardonnay to the table and topped up their glasses.

'She's the type of monster that loves spreadsheets and weeding and puts Vegemite on hot cross buns,' giggled Lauren, throwing her a cheeky look. She'd had a glass or two more than her normal quota and was well on her way to tipsy.

Connor shook his head. 'You Aussies and your Vegemite. It definitely doesn't belong anywhere near sweets.'

After a long debate on Vegemite versus Marmite and Milo versus Ovaltine, the talk turned to the following weekend's beach fishing trip.

'There's something magic about sleeping under the stars,' sighed Lauren, curling her legs underneath her and nestling into Fergus. April didn't miss the look that passed between Lauren and her Scottish sweetheart. It was so intimate she had to look away.

'Are you sure we won't be intruding on your romantic getaway?' April teased, getting up from the couch and changing the music playlist.

'The more the merrier,' Fergus insisted. 'We'll have a campfire on the beach, catch a few fish, tear up and down the sand hills. Even if it's raining, it'll be a hoot.'

April smothered a yawn. She cleared the glasses from the coffee table and although one part of her brain was already campaigning for pyjamas and sleep, the other was curious about how the night would end with Connor. Would this be the night he'd sleep over for the first time? She stole a look at him as she stacked the glasses in the sink. Every time she'd thought of Connor these last two months, it had been with an extra layer of respect and compassion, knowing what he'd been through and the way he'd allowed himself to be vulnerable in front of her.

He pulled his keys from his pocket. *Manners, indeed*, she thought, following him outside. Taking it slowly was a novel concept, but if they continued at this pace for much longer, they'd self-combust—she was sure of it. Mishka raced outside after them, intent on the flowering gum at the edge of the yard.

'Nice night,' she said, leaning in to kiss Connor's cheek, feeling the silky smooth 'just shaved' jaw.

'Good pizzas, though not in the same league as your quiche,' he said, turning his head slightly so their lips met, his hands going to her waist. Even the hard ground between the vines was looking appealing.

Legs wobbly, she stepped away. *Taking it slowly. Taking it slowly.* April repeated the phrase like a mantra, hoping it would deliver her the strength she needed to keep her from unbuckling his belt and . . .

Oh Lordy, that type of mental imagery was not helpful. With the very last vestiges of her self-control, she whistled for Mishka.

'See you at cooking classes tomorrow, then,' she said, one hand on the front door handle and the other on Mishka's collar.

'Can't wait,' he laughed, beeping his car unlocked and looking every bit as conflicted about leaving as her.

Connor would never have considered making his own vanilla slice, but with Geraldine at the helm of the cooking class, showing them how easy it was to make custard, and the steps needed to make it firm enough for homemade vanilla slice, he almost imagined that one day he just might attempt it.

'Of course, the team at the local bakery would probably prefer you didn't,' Geraldine said with a wink, lifting her wooden spoon from the saucepan and showing them how the custard had thickened. 'It's hands-down their bestselling product. But like so many of the things we relegate to the "too-hard" basket, there's magic in the making and sometimes when you're sick of staring at a computer screen, or pulling weeds, or blending wines, you might get the urge to cook something intricate. Something that you know—well before you start—will take a good few hours of your attention.'

'I'm just happy if it's edible,' called April, getting a laugh from her fellow students. It was their second last cooking class and Connor could already tell they'd both miss their group, as well as the routine of the regular lessons and the way Geraldine made the steps feel easy and achievable without a hint of condescension or impatience.

'I hope you're planning a refresher class early next year, so we can all brush up for the Penwarra Show,' Brian said, a fondness in his voice. It reminded Connor of the way his dad looked at his mum, like he couldn't believe how lucky he was. There was definitely something going on between the two of them.

'Absolutely,' said Geraldine. 'But just understand, some people take their show baking super seriously.'

'Oh, we already know,' April said, explaining Fran's sleepless nights as she fretted over registrations and vacant tables, boycotts and badly behaved bakers.

'One year, Petra Sidebottom asked my wife for her blue-ribbon apple jelly recipe, then entered it the next year,' Brian paused a beat, glancing at his audience. 'And beat her using her own recipe!'

Connor grinned, then told them about a conversation he'd overheard on show day. 'One lady was adamant the chocolate mud cake was suspiciously identical to the ones from Foodland.'

The baking tales gradually shifted to other show categories, with the youngest student, Maddie revealing a juicy snippet she'd overheard while collecting her prize money from the floral section and Geraldine admitting she'd been given a subtle warning against entering because she made money from cooking and was therefore deemed a 'professional' and not an everyday home baker.

'Did Fran say that?' April gasped, stirring her pot of custard. Geraldine assured them Fran hadn't been involved.

Connor continued measuring out the caster sugar, liking the way their conversations were punctuated by the 'glop, glop, glop' of bubbling saucepans.

After they'd finished the class, April and Connor walked back to the golf club rental. 'Don't suppose you fancy some more rock wall building this arvo?' April said. 'Otherwise, I'll start getting my head around the kitchen cabinetry. Gordo gave me a rough run-through with the linen press, but I don't want to get halfway through building the first kitchen cupboard and realise I'm completely cocking it up.'

Connor leaned against the kitchen bench and opened his arms, liking the way she walked into them, and the feeling of her cheek resting against his chest. He took in a deep breath, noticing how the sugar and custardy cooking aromas melded nicely with April's signature scent of dark plums and cherries, making him think of a fruit crumble with lashings of ice cream.

'I'm easy, though given there's still a mighty big pile of rocks in the winery car park, maybe we should tick that off the list first?'

She nodded against his chest, making no move to leave, and he felt his heart expand a little. Was this what it felt like to fall for someone? It had been a long time, but Connor was pretty sure that was exactly what it was.

15

Connor's knuckles ached from holding on to the strap above his left shoulder, but he wouldn't have traded his seat in the front of April's car for quids.

There was something downright sexy—and terrifying—about watching her behind the wheel of her ute, gunning it up a massive sand dune.

'The Hilux was born for this,' April said, giddy with exhilaration as she drove over the peak of a sand dune. The sea spread out beneath them like a glittering jewel and the sand was soft and constantly shifting under their tyres, even with a little air taken out beforehand. But just like in the cooking classes, he could see her sense of achievement shining through.

'I can't believe I've lived here most of my life, but I waited more than twenty-nine years to attempt four-wheel driving. You can have a go on the way back if you want,' she said, beaming with delight.

Connor declined the offer, unsure her car insurance—or his travel insurance—would think it was such a great idea.

Before long, they were setting up camp in a little bay between Beachport and Robe and prepping for lunch.

'Now here's something you can't stuff up,' announced Fergus, handing over the tongs and stepping away from the portable barbecue perched on the fold-up table, between a salad and a loaf of bread.

Fergus had found a Weber Q on the local buy, swap and sell page and not only had he taken to cooking on it several times a week, but he was also determined to teach Connor how to use it. Mishka weaved between his legs, her tail going ten to the dozen and her nose high in the air, sniffing out the meaty scent.

Connor accepted the tongs from his housemate and opened the tray of sausages.

'I can't promise they'll be edible once I've finished with them,' he warned.

Lauren laughed. 'All those cooking classes, I'm sure you'll manage just fine with a few snags on the barbie. And if you don't, there's a shaggy blonde garbage disposal unit ready and waiting.'

As if she understood their conversation, Mishka flopped at Connor's feet and licked her lips.

He loaded the meat into the funny little barbecue, which looked more like a luggage pod that belonged on top of a family sedan than a cooking tool, and against all common sense, shut the lid.

'But how do we know if they're burning?' Connor asked dubiously. Fergus winked with the confidence of someone whose cooking had never involved spot fires or caused grievous bodily harm.

'Flip them in three minutes, give them another three on the other side and they'll be perfect.'

The ocean lapped at the shore, their fishing lines rising and falling with each wave, and despite the winter solstice marking the longest night of the year, the sun had finally made an appearance. With the sand dunes blocking the gentle north-easterly wind and the heat of the gas barbecue in front of him, Connor was warmer than he'd been all week.

And as they sat in their camping chairs, plastic plates heaped with Lauren's coleslaw and not-even-burnt sausages in bread, Connor admitted his friend was right. 'These bangers are bang on,' he said, a grin on his face as he went back for seconds.

'Poor, Mishka. She was ready and willing to help with charred snags,' said April, slapping at the sand flies buzzing around her.

The fishing rod jiggled, and Fergus nearly dropped his plate as he rushed across the sand to the closest rod holder.

'Seaweed or a shark?'

Connor met April's mischievous smile. The expedition over the sand dunes had been as exhilarating as the afternoon's fishing had been entertaining.

Fergus whistled as he reeled in the slack. 'It's a big one. Won't need the measuring tape for this beauty.'

'No size restrictions on seaweed, eh?' Lauren teased.

Despite their good-natured ribbing, they all watched closely as Fergus wrestled with the fishing rod. He whooped when a fin appeared in the shallows. Suddenly the second fishing rod, twenty metres further along, and the third rod, both started doing a merry jig.

'Ferg! Those ones are going nuts,' Lauren said, shading her eyes against the sun glinting on the water.

'Grab them! It could be a school of sharks, quickly!'

Lauren rushed to the closest rod. April and Connor hurried to the furthest one.

'If it's seaweed, it's doing a darn good impersonation of being alive,' said April, struggling to wind in the line. She handed it to Connor. 'You try.'

She was right: Connor felt like the catch was getting further and further away. Fergus let out another delighted whoop and landed his first shark of the day.

'I knew we were onto a good spot,' he said, buzzing with excitement as he jogged over to offer them assistance. Connor's arms were burning but he kept on reeling.

'We're all right but Lauren seems like she needs a hand,' April said.

Fergus darted back to Lauren's side and Connor felt April sidle a little closer, squinting along the length of the line for a hint of what was on the other end.

'Look at you go,' she said, grinning. 'First sausages, now reeling in a fish.'

'It can't be too far away,' he said. 'You want to do the honours?'

'It's more fun watching you do it,' she said, a glint in her eye as she lifted a hand and squeezed his right bicep. 'Plus, this might be your one and only chance to reel in a clump of authentic Aussie seaweed. I couldn't deprive you of that experience.'

The fishing rod jerked in his hands, forcing his attention back to the water in front of him.

Connor tugged harder on the rod, gaining a little more line as he worked with the waves as Fergus had told him. He saw a small fin pierce the water.

'It's a shark.'

'No shit, Sherlock,' Fergus laughed, jogging back over holding a knife. 'Keep the tension on, don't lose it.'

The water splashed up against April's ankles as she followed Fergus into the ocean. It was warmer than she'd expected for winter.

'Are you sure it won't bite me?'

'It's got a hook through its jaw, biting you is at the bottom of this guy's priority list,' Fergus said. He was pumped up; so animated that it was hard to understand his Scottish brogue. 'He'll be fresh flake before you know it.'

He grabbed the line near where the small shark was thrashing and started tugging it towards the shore.

April whirled around, holding her hands about a metre apart for Connor's benefit. Like Fergus, Connor's face was flushed and she was pretty sure it was from the excitement rather than the exertion of reeling in a fish.

'Woohoo, it's a beauty,' she called. Lauren was taking photos from the shore, prompting April to pull her phone from her pocket to get an action shot.

She was just lining one up of Fergus and Connor with their catch when something brushed past her legs.

April jumped back instinctively. Shark?

With one eye on the creature Fergus was tugging into shore, and the other on her feet, she shied away from the dark swirl in the sandy water below, then tried to tamp down the rising panic.

Of course it's not a shark. That guy came from over the sand bar, not through ankle-high water.

April strode towards the boys, studiously avoiding seaweed swirls, and was almost out of the waves when she felt a sharp nip on her toe. She squealed.

'Arghh.' Hopping on her foot, she lost her balance and tumbled over in the water, her phone soaring through the air.

She watched it splash and scrambled to her feet, cursing the crab that obviously lived nearby, as she rushed to retrieve it.

'Shit, shit, shit.'

April looked up to see Lauren cackling with laughter. Connor dashed in her direction.

'Don't worry about the phone, it'll be ruined now,' Fergus called, trying to prise the hook from the shark's mouth. 'We need to get this gummy shark out of the water before he hitches a ride on the next wave.'

April scanned the sandy sea bed, squealing again as another crab nipped her when she grabbed her sodden phone. 'Bloody hell, these crabs are everywhere.'

'If I'd known you had a crab problem, I mightn't have borrowed your spare sleeping bag,' Connor deadpanned, failing to hide his amusement.

They turned at the sound of swearing from Fergus. April felt the blood drain from her face as she realised the shark was no longer on the sand.

'Where's the shark?'

She and Connor dashed out of the water like there was a school of sharks at their heels, rather than just one pissed-off escapee. When they got to the sand, they each bent double, panting for breath.

Fergus had a chuckle at their terror-stricken dash.

'He was only a gummy, Con. No teeth. Couldn't have eaten you even if he'd wanted to.'

'You might have told me that before I nearly burst an artery,' Connor said, hands on his knees, sucking in lungfuls of air.

'You should see these photos of you two, they're hilarious.'

Lauren twisted her phone towards them. Connor craned his neck to look, and April felt his blond hair tickling her cheek as he shook his head.

'The one that got away,' Connor said wryly.

Lauren's photo of the shark wasn't as good as the angle April had snapped, with both Connor and Fergus in the background. She grimaced at her dripping phone. Was there a limit to how many times you could bring a smartphone back from a drenching? It had made a full recovery after falling into the toilet six months ago, but last time she'd had a zip-lock bag full of rice on hand to help absorb the water. There weren't such conveniences on the ten-mile beach.

'It was only under for a few seconds, tops,' said Connor, wincing sympathetically. 'Maybe it'll be okay?'

'Salt water though, I think it corrodes the electrics,' she sighed.

April tucked the phone into her back pocket, knowing better than to try switching it on until it was bone dry.

Another thought occurred to her as they trudged back to their campsite. If the phone didn't come back to life, she would have lost her photos from the last few months. Random pictures she'd snapped at cooking classes, shots of the baby grape bunches she had planned to use on the website, the renovations, the drunken pictures she and Lauren had snapped on nights out, before their free time revolved around Fergus and Connor. A dead phone meant no photos of their time together either. April shook away the stab of disappointment. They had a whole future to make together—so what if they lost photographic evidence of the earliest stages of their relationship? But as she wrapped the phone in a tea towel and sat it on the dashboard of the car, she hoped it wasn't an omen for her and Connor.

After they'd hauled in two more gummy sharks and the sun was sliding towards the horizon, Lauren surprised them all by stripping to her bathers and racing into the water.

'You realise it's the middle of winter?' Connor called.

'And there are bitey things swimming around in there,' Fergus added.

Lauren squealed as the waves crashed against her, but then she ducked under the next wave, emerging with her hair slicked to her head. 'It's glorious, you'll see,' she said.

Connor turned to see April, who had been wearing shorts all day, pulling off her jumper, a devilish grin on her face.

'Last one in's a rotten egg,' she said, dashing past him in an aqua two piece that perfectly matched the water, with Mishka hot on her heels. A little more shrieking and then she was under too, swimming to where Lauren was floating, just her toes and head above the water.

Fergus secured his rod in the plastic holder he'd fashioned from poly-pipe and all-thread and wandered across, meeting Connor's ambivalent gaze with a cheerful shrug.

'I guess it's on par with most of our summer days,' he said. 'And remember they're gummy sharks—not a tooth between them,' Fergus added, shucking his T-shirt before joining the girls. Connor relented, wading into the brisk water. Once his body adjusted to the temperature, he realised it was warmer in the ocean than out and lingered in the sea with April after Lauren and Fergus had returned to shore.

'You make it look easy,' he said, leaning back and trying to float as effortlessly as April. A mouthful of water made him splutter and he quickly returned to his feet.

'It's more buoyant than a pool,' April said, flipping onto her side like a seal and diving under with a splash. She surfaced just millimetres from him, all thoughts of sharks and vineyards and cooking disappearing as her cold body met his.

Connor lifted her up so her legs straddled his torso and her arms linked around his neck. He'd liked getting to know her body slowly, and after weeks of canoodling and taking things more slowly than any previous relationship, he now had a fair idea of the type of touch that made her breath quicken. He kissed her neck, tasting the salty tang, smiling as a little half-moan, half-sigh escaped her lips.

'I don't know about you,' she said, unwrapping her legs from around his waist and jumping so the approaching wave went under them, instead of over them, 'but I kind of wish we were staying somewhere a little more deluxe tonight.'

He laughed, reaching for her hand. She didn't have to spell out exactly why she wanted a plush bed and he didn't have to nod or verbally agree—his body was quite capable of broadcasting his wholehearted agreement to such a plan—but there was no question of ditching their inaugural beach fishing trip when Fergus had spent weeks arranging it, taking into account the tide, the full moon and their other commitments.

'Mind you,' April said, her hands tracing a tempting path from his ear to his collarbone. 'Those sand dunes have grassy sections and I did pack a towel big enough to wrap an elephant.'

Connor shook his head. 'One more day isn't going to kill us, surely?'

It had seemed like the smart thing to say, something a gentleman would mention, but as Connor shifted in his swag that night, trying to get comfortable, he regretted his chivalry.

It was ridiculous, really. The ocean air, lapping waves and a day in the winter sunshine should have been the perfect recipe for a sound night's sleep, but longing kept Connor wide awake. What's a little sand anyway, and really, what are the chances of bumping into a deadly snake in the throes of passion? He reached for his phone. The bright light lit up the inside of the borrowed swag, and he squinted against the glare.

Just after 2 am.

With a yawn, Connor crawled out of his swag and walked to the edge of the water. He had just located the Southern Cross when April silently appeared beside him.

'Can't sleep either?'

April's voice was a whisper and the way she grinned made his temperature rise despite the freezing night. Putting a finger to her lips, she tiptoed back to the camp and returned with a towel. Hand in hand, they walked until the coals of the campfire were barely visible and climbed the sand dunes until they were hidden by the native grasses. Their lovemaking was gentle, her body warm against his in the cool, cloudless night, and when they returned to their swags an hour later, he fell almost immediately into a deep, sated sleep.

Sea gulls hovered, watching for unwanted food or unattended bait buckets, as they packed up their camp the next morning.

'No chance of scraps with her around, is there?' Lauren said, noticing Mishka sniffing around the campfire before racing up and down the beach when the curious birds got too close.

'Hard to think she'd be hungry with a belly full of bait,' said Fergus, shaking his head as he slotted the fishing rods into the welded bullbar attachment and tied the tips to the ute's roof racks. 'I hope for April's sake that she doesn't bring all that squid back up on the drive home.'

Lauren wrapped her arms around his waist and planted a kiss on his cheek. 'It's not like you had any room in the esky for more fish,' she teased. 'Five sharks will keep us fed for months, and that's after you've given some to your workmates. In fact, Mishka was probably doing you a favour, with the mercury levels and all that.'

Fergus rolled his eyes but gave her a good-natured smile. April was just grateful her dog hadn't eaten the hook, sinker *and* bait.

Whistling for the retriever, who was now rolling in a clump of seaweed, she spotted Connor halfway up a sand dune. He was photographing something and she remembered with a pang that her phone was most likely knackered.

'Sorry,' he said, half jogging, half sliding down the dune. 'I found an echidna in the scrub, they're so cool. Way different to a hedgehog. I got about a hundred photos, wait until my sisters see them.'

His relationship with his little sisters was touching and she could imagine his photo updates were always eagerly received.

'We're almost packed up,' April told him. 'Are you game enough to ride shotgun with me again, or did I put you off on the way here?'

'Takes more than a near-death experience on a razorback sand dune to scare me off,' he said with a smile as April secured Mishka in the back of the Hilux. 'I can't imagine it'll be much smoother in Fergus's car, unless you'd rather Lauren as navigator.'

'Jump in,' April said, doing a final lap around the ute to ensure their swags and eskies were strapped in tight. She slid into the driver's seat and looked at Connor.

'Glad I packed that towel,' she said softly. With a smile, he draped an arm over the back of her seat and she felt like maybe, just maybe, this had been the perfect weekend.

16

'They're about to start,' Connor called over his shoulder. April dashed out from the bathroom, tugging a jumper over her head and combing her fingers through her hair.

'If I'd known I was meeting your family for the first time tonight, I would have made a bit more of an effort.'

'You don't need to stress,' he assured her. 'Honestly, they'll be so busy with their shed party that we'll basically wave hello and then watch the music performance. It'll be the briefest meet and greet, you don't need to go to any effort or dress up. Plus, I love you in this jumper,' he replied with a grin. She only wore it after her shower at night, sans underwear, but the minute he'd told her he was Zooming into the concert in Derby, she'd added a bra and swapped her trackies for jeans.

The laptop screen lit up as the call connected. Nell waved at them from the other side of the world, her new braces flashing under the disco lights Pippin had insisted on buying for the event. He quickly introduced April to his little sisters.

'So nice to meet you,' April said, waving at the laptop camera. 'I've heard heaps about you both.'

The garden was full of conversation and music, making it difficult to hear. The girls had their instruments with them, and their cheekbones sparkled with glittery make-up as they spoke over the top of one another. 'We've only heard a little bit about you,' Pippin said with a grin. 'We're the last to find out all the juicy stuff.'

'Yeah, right,' Connor said. He leaned into April, wondering what the girls would come out with next. They rarely missed an opportunity to score a laugh, especially at his expense, and he hoped they'd be on their best behaviour for April's benefit, if not his.

'Heidi always gets the good goss,' Nell yelled. 'But you must be okay if our Con says so, April. Hope you like the tunes.'

April laughed and wished them good luck. Then Nell re-arranged the computer to face the makeshift stage, and Connor gave her a thumbs-up.

'Perfect! Now go knock their socks off!'

He poured another drink while the girls prepared for their set, but April remained glued to the laptop, curious about all the people moving in and out of shot on the screen. Although it wasn't the same as being there in person for the neighbourhood jazz concert, Connor was impressed by the acoustics coming through the laptop audio on Zoom.

'It's been held on the July long weekend for as long as I can remember, all of Mam and Dad's muso friends trek across town with their instruments and cases. These days their children take to the stage too,' he said. Although they couldn't see it on camera, he knew most of the guests would be sitting just to the left of the laptop, and on the other side of the shed there was a long tool bench that doubled as a bar for parties and gatherings like this.

His toes began tapping to the music the moment Nell started on the tambourine. His knee jiggled as Pippin joined on the drums and by the time Heidi came in on slide trombone, his whole body was swaying to the bluesy track he'd helped them choose for their opening song.

April glanced at him with a smile. 'If you were home, would they rope you into performing too?'

Connor shook his head. 'I was up on that stage the moment I could reach the foot pedal, but I haven't played since . . .' He trailed off. For the last five years, he'd found excuses to either avoid the party or the spotlight. But now that he was watching his sisters put on a show from 10,000 miles away, he could see he'd been missing the point: it was all about the joy and the music and the togetherness, not about the precision of the musician or the quality of the sound.

The girls stopped for a brief break and Connor saw his dad appear in front of the laptop camera. 'How's our boy?' Jock asked, bending down so the laptop was at his eye level. 'What did you make of the first two songs?'

'Fabulous,' Connor said, raising his voice over the background conversation. 'They've been practising.' It wasn't the perfect time to introduce April, but she was sitting beside him, smiling expectantly, so when Jock finally worked out how to change the laptop camera back to him and Sharyn, instead of filming the stage, Connor quickly chimed in, 'Mam, Dad, this is April.'

'Lovely to meet you both,' April said, sitting up straighter.

Sharyn and Jock's heads were jammed together, so close to the screen that Connor could see his mum had pencilled in her eyebrows and was even wearing eye make-up for the occasion. She cupped her ear.

'Sorry, it's so noisy in here!'

April's voice was loud in Connor's ear as she repeated herself.

Lloyd and Sharyn nodded vigorously, their eyes shining with the same type of warmth they'd always extended to their children's friends, colleagues and partners. 'We've been looking forward to meeting you, April,' Sharyn said. 'It sounds like you and Con have loads in common.'

'Sorry to rush off,' Jock apologised. 'But they girls are about to start again. We'd best get this computer pointed back to the stage. Then Freida's up on the hurdy gurdy at 1 pm,' added Jock, swivelling the laptop around again. 'You probably won't want to sit through that, though.'

Connor nestled back on the couch, resting a hand on April's thigh and thinking how neat it was to see two parts of his life intersecting through the marvels of technology.

Connor's family weren't just any old musicians, mused April, settling into the corner of the couch with a cup of tea. *They were brilliant.* And while he'd already told her they played, it was a whole new experience to see them jamming on the laptop screen, their energy and songs carrying across the world and into the little winemaker's cottage.

'You didn't tell me they were this good,' she scolded, leaning in close while his sisters changed instruments. 'I'd pay to watch this level of performance. If they were over here, they'd be playing at the folk festivals in Francis and Port Fairy, they'd have steady bookings in the pubs . . .' She glanced over at her guitar, on which a sheen of dust was visible even from this distance. It was embarrassing to think she'd strummed some songs for Connor the previous week, her notebook of lyrics propped up against a pot plant and her fingers smarting from the steel strings.

'I mean, I knew they'd be alright, but they're almost ready for a record deal!'

Connor pulled her closer to him. 'Don't say that too loud,' he cautioned with a wry grin. 'They'll start charging appearance fees and demanding riders.'

They clapped and whooped as Heidi, Pippin and Nell took a bow. A blur of blonde and denim moved in front of the camera and amongst the cheering of the crowd, April heard someone calling, 'Phoebe!'

Connor stiffened beside her, and April watched as the lady blocking their view turned, clapped a hand over her mouth and shrugged her shoulders in apology.

So that's Phoebe. April felt like time stood still as she watched Connor's ex-fiancée float past the camera. *She's not just pretty, but beautiful.*

They heard Jock's voice over the crowd. 'You were just blocking the camera, pet, but they're finished now, so no bother. We were streaming it for Con, but didn't the girls do well?'

The video went dark for a moment but the audio stayed connected and April could hear Sharyn chatting with Phoebe as Jock fiddled with the laptop, before the call cut out altogether.

'They'll call back,' Connor said, rising from the couch. 'Another tea?'

April looked down, staring into the dregs of her lukewarm tea and then back at the laptop, shaking her head. *Had Connor expected Phoebe to attend?*

Sensing her concern, Connor crouched down beside her and rested a hand on her thigh. 'I didn't realise Phoebe would be there, sorry about that,' he said, his face creased with discomfort.

She quickly waved him away with an indifference she didn't quite feel. 'That's fine, it was nice to put a face to the name.'

Nice? Nice would be a little notice that she was about to meet his folks, a warning that the concert he wanted to watch this evening was in fact a special family occasion, not a generic Netflix offering. April rubbed at an oil spot on her grey hoodie, hoping it hadn't looked quite so obvious on Zoom, then glanced at Connor as he fetched the ice cream. He wasn't dressed up either, but they knew him. And from the sounds of things, he could be wearing a garbage bag and they'd still be delighted to see him.

And the ex-fiancée.

He handed over her dessert with a kiss. As April raised her first spoonful, the video kicked back into gear, but they were no longer looking at a stage with colourful bunting, fairy lights and musicians—they were in a small, cosy kitchen. Instead of watching the musicians, they were face to face with Pippin, her cheekbones highlighted with glitter, and Phoebe.

Oh, lordy.

Nell rushed into the frame and plonked herself on Phoebe's lap. 'Go on then, make yourself at home,' Phoebe laughed.

'We were fabulous, weren't we, Con?' Pippin, who looked almost like she could be Nell's twin with her identical haircut and complexion, beamed at the camera.

'And modest too,' Connor teased. 'April and I thought it was really good.' Clearing his throat, he introduced her to Phoebe.

With the Zoom time lag, April and Phoebe's polite responses cut over one another.

'Sorry,' said Phoebe. 'You go.'

'I was just going to say the girls were amazing,' added April, 'I was telling Connor you'll have record labels chasing you.'

'Or our own YouTube channel,' Nell said, leaning her head against Phoebe's shoulder and toying with a lock of

Phoebe's fair hair. April watched, her stomach in knots at the easy familiarity between the three of them, as if Connor's ex-fiancée were another sister. While Phoebe made gracious conversation, looking completely unperturbed about this chat with her ex-fiancée and his new girlfriend. Nell twirled the lock of her hair, using it like a paintbrush against the back of her wrist, then slotting it above her top lip like a moustache, and finally tickling Pippin under the chin with it.

'Would you stop that?' Giggling, Phoebe reclaimed her hair and swatted Nell away with an indulgent smile. 'She obviously gets her mischievous side from her big brother. How's everything going in Australia then?'

April sat back, eating her ice cream slowly as Connor filled them in, wondering why he had never mentioned that Phoebe Lawson was still well and truly part of the Jamison family.

Would bringing it up seem churlish? April pushed the idea to the back of her mind, where it belonged.

'They're terrors, but I miss them,' Connor said later, when they were preparing for bed. 'Pippin's getting sharper with her comebacks, and I'm sure Nell's grown an inch since I've been gone. She'll be taller than Mam by the time I get back.'

April paused at the bathroom sink, her mouth full of toothpaste foam.

When I get back.

While she knew his visa was only for two years, neither of them had spoken about what would happen after that point. It felt too early in the relationship to look so far into the future, but maybe it was a conversation that needed to happen sooner rather than later?

Live a little, she told herself, determined to cross that bridge when she came to it.

'They seem sweet,' April said, climbing into bed and switching off the light. 'And they're amazing musicians.'

Connor rolled onto his side towards her, draping an arm over her midriff and resting his head in the hollow under her shoulder. 'Sweet? They're terrorists disguised as teenagers, don't let them fool you. They liked you too,' he murmured, yawning. He fell asleep quickly but after an hour of chasing her thoughts around her own head, April gently eased out of bed, grabbed her Ugg boots and dressing gown and crept into the lounge room.

Mishka's tail thumped against the floorboards but she stayed on her bed, watching as April flicked on the lamp and fired up her laptop.

It didn't take long to find an internet trail for Connor's ex-fiancée, and while her social media was set to private, April found a press release on the Royal Derby Hospital website.

There was a photo of Phoebe in the hospital courtyard in her blue nurse scrubs, accepting a BBC Radio 'make a difference' award for her outstanding contributions to healthcare. April read on, finding it hard not to admire someone who, according to the article, 'went above and beyond for her patients, staying late after shifts to ensure patients were okay'. A little further down the search results she found another few articles celebrating the shortlisting, with one headline calling Phoebe 'one in a million', and then an article Phoebe herself had written for her former university newspaper, encouraging students to strive for great heights in their profession.

April rubbed her eyes and closed the search engine. Phoebe, she surmised, was a nurse who saved people's lives, day in, day out, who was already so beloved by the Jamison's that she was buying Nell and Pippin pets that might live more than twenty years. It was a lot to take in.

A small red icon popped up in her emails as she stared at the screen. April clicked on the new item in her inbox, expecting it to be a power bill or coursework from the DestinationSA program and it took a few moments of blinking at the screen before she realised what it was.

Her frown slowly changed to a smile as she re-read it. A booking! Their very first guests for Kookaburra Cottage were booked and paid for, checking in on the 31st of December and out on New Year's Day. April felt a rush of delight wash over her.

Our first booking. Thank you Mr and Mrs Henderson.

The note at the bottom of the booking form made her smile widen. A fortieth wedding anniversary surprise, booked by the husband.

'And who said romance was dead, Mishka?' she said, turning off the computer and lamp before giving the dog a goodnight pat and slipping back into bed.

Geraldine sent a group text message to the cooking class students one Friday, and when Connor's phone pinged in his pocket, he was standing by April's side in the vineyards, guarding a picnic rug from the ants, flies and a golden retriever with a nose for trouble—who had already slipped her collar twice during the carefully styled photoshoot.

'Oh, this angle's much better,' said April, twisting her body so the phone camera was tilted to the left, with a cheeseboard in the foreground, a bottle of wine and half-filled glasses of Lacewing Estate chardonnay just behind it, and the whole scene framed by the grapevines near the cottage. 'Hmm, maybe we'll just shift the wine glasses to the left side of the bottle so they don't cast shadows on the strawberries,' she said, tweaking the props and then retaking the picture.

'Geraldine says we're finishing the classes with a dinner party.' Connor read the text message out loud to April, which wasn't easy with Mishka tugging on her lead, eager to sample the brie that April had drizzled with honey and topped with walnuts.

'A dinner party? Who would've imagined it, us cooking a dinner party? At least we'll be in forgiving company,' she said, shifting the platter. After a couple more shots they carted the makeshift set back into the winemaker's cottage to enjoy the gourmet nibbles and review April's photos.

'Dropping your phone in the ocean was a masterstroke,' Connor said, admiring the sharp, perfectly styled images. He knew they'd be uploaded to the website before the night was through, and if the last fortnight was any indication, April would set up another few tableaus over the weekend too. It wasn't just the high-spec camera on her new phone that made the website shine, it was the attention to detail April had used when fitting out the B & B, and the way she applied that same attention to detail to the styling and photography.

'You'd never know the splashback isn't grouted yet,' he said, admiring the close-up she'd taken of a basket of freshly baked muffins on the kitchen's concrete benchtop, the background strategically blurred and the angle just so, keeping the tell-tale signs of construction out of the scene.

'I know, right?' April snuggled up beside him, clinking her glass against his. 'Here's cheers to a renovation that's almost done, bookings that keep dribbling in even though we're not open for another month, and good friends.'

'Friends?' Raising an eyebrow, Connor placed both of their wine glasses on the coffee table, ran a hand down the curve of her thigh and kissed her. 'Is that what this is, then?'

She smiled against his lips. 'I'm talking about the friends we'll be celebrating with tomorrow, after graduating cooking school with flying colours. And Lauren and Fergus, who have basically moved in together and let me have the run of the place so I can fully acquaint myself with you, lover boy.'

He laughed, amused by April's nickname. Their transition from friends to lovers had been slow, almost cautious, adding a depth to their relationship. They'd steadily developed a comfortable routine: he worked alongside Lloyd for most of the day, and the afternoons he wasn't teaching piano were spent helping April renovate the stables and tidy Lacewing Estate. Their evenings were enjoyed at the winemaker's cottage and much to Connor's surprise, he was settling into the quiet country lifestyle.

Connor reached for his glass again. 'Righto, here's cheers to good friends, bookings *and* lovers. In fact, I'd go as far as to say I'm falling for you, April Lacey.'

Her grin was infectious and chardonnay slopped over the side of the wineglass as she returned the toast.

'I'll drink to that,' she beamed.

*

They arrived at Geraldine's to find the entrance festooned with balloons and streamers for the final cooking lesson. The day was a celebration of everything they'd made during the course, with each person assigned several different dishes and Geraldine keeping her advice to the bare minimum, striding around the kitchen like a proud mother hen, ushering her chicks through the process with praise, encouragement and a hefty dose of pride.

Rupert Winklin could take a leaf from Geraldine's book, Connor thought, watching her sample April's muffin batter and declare it absolutely luscious.

Several months had passed since his awkward conversation with Archie's father, and while the young boy's piano skills had improved greatly, his confidence still took a nosedive whenever Rupert walked into the music room. Connor recalled his nerves at the start of the cooking classes and how much he'd valued Geraldine's gentle guidance through the sessions. *A good teacher focusses on the student, not the distractions.* He resolved to channel his inner Geraldine from there on in, and turned his attention back to the festivities.

The long table was set with a striped tablecloth, decorative placemats, napkins and crockery, with flowers and candles in the middle of the table. In the corner of the room a banner that read 'happy graduation' hung alongside bunches of helium balloons clung to the ceiling.

And as Geraldine launched into a speech about how far they'd come, how pleased she was for each of them, and how delighted she was to have been part of their journey, Connor felt April's hand clasp his under the table. It might have taken them a good decade or two longer than most people to embrace cooking, but it was the very first thing they'd started and finished together.

'Holy heck, how on earth is this thing so heavy?' panted Lloyd. 'Glad it's going downstairs and not in the bedroom.'

'Nearly there, Dad,' April said, hurrying to open the stable's double doors. Fergus, Connor, Lloyd and Daniel lugged the small wood burner inside and manoeuvred it into place.

'Looks like it was made for this cottage,' said Daniel.

'Exactly why I chose it,' said April, admiring the way the wood fire's arched glass door mirrored the shape of the oak entryway. She led them through to the bathroom to wash up, then gave Fergus and Dan a quick tour, soaking up their effusive praise.

'It's come up well,' she said, looping a hand through Connor's. 'But it's been a team effort. Gordo was a whiz, and this guy here played a starring role too.'

Connor lifted his palms. 'I was just the occasional lackey. You've done an amazing job.'

'Too right she has, we couldn't be happier with how it's come up,' Lloyd added, running a hand along the concrete benchtop. 'And as much as I hate to admit it, the cellar door and tasting room don't look half shabby either. They're not a bad pair, these two.'

Lloyd caught April's eye, giving a wink. Unlike the winery makeover and their involvement in the DestinationSA food tourism program, her father hadn't voiced any reservations about her dating Connor. She was grateful for his quiet support, and as the renovation came to a close, she felt her confidence in the winery growing.

The helpers dispersed when the plumber arrived to fit the flue and ensure the chimney drew nicely.

'Now all that's left to do is collect the kindling and enjoy our first fire,' said Connor, putting an arm around her waist.

'Sweet as, sounds like I'm just in time!'

April and Connor turned to see Archie outside the cottage, a packet of marshmallows in his arms. 'I'll get some sticks.'

He returned with an armful of vine canes April had stacked in the tractor shed.

'Oh, that's not kindling,' she said. 'Those are for the little fences in the new gardens.' April steered Archie back outside and showing the knee-high border she'd built around the first garden by weaving the vine cuttings together.

'Wow, it's like knitting with sticks,' Archie said, crouching down for a closer look. 'Can you teach me how to do it?'

There was rain forecast for the afternoon, and as keen as April was to see the new wood fire slowly warming the stables to the cosy nook she'd dreamed of for months, she couldn't resist Archie's enthusiasm. Plus, if she taught him how to help, they'd have the decorative fences built in half the time.

Connor left them to it, and after collecting her tools—a mallet, a pair of secateurs and a bundle of vine canes—April hefted up her builder's pants so the padded knees were in the right spot and knelt on the grass beside the herb garden.

Archie listened carefully, then sorted through the canes. 'So we use the biggest sticks for the uprights, and just weave the smaller sticks through like this?'

'Close, but not quite,' she said, adjusting Archie's technique so the weaving was tighter and the longer lengths alternated with the shorter ones. 'This way's a little sturdier, better at keeping out the rabbits.' She grinned at him. 'Lambs too, I hope.'

Archie's face lit up, his hands weaving the small twigs as he told her about his preparations for the forthcoming lambs. 'We've got the milk powder ready, and Dan's been saving his clear beer bottles so I can see how much milk's left. That way the new babies don't suck as much air,' he said. 'And I've scattered fresh hay all around their shelter so it's warm and snuggly at night.'

'So all you need now is some poor mumma sheep to cark it and you're set?' April deadpanned, watching to see his response. She wasn't sure if he quite understood that for him to have an orphan lamb, something had to go awry in the process.

Archie frowned. 'Well, kind of. But half the time they're orphans because the mum rejected the lamb, or she had triplets or twins, not because she kicked the bucket.'

'Fingers crossed Marty and Barbara don't teach them their Houdini skills.' She smiled. 'That fence looks great, I'll get some more supplies.'

Even though the temperature hadn't risen above twelve degrees all week, and wasn't forecast to increase anytime soon, April soon warmed up as she hammered in the small stakes, handed the canes over to Archie and weeded the burgeoning herb patch. She paused to appreciate the bees buzzing by the rosemary, oregano, chives, coriander and sage.

When Connor returned that afternoon with another wheelbarrow load of canes, straight off the vines, Archie and April had finished the ornate fences around the small veggie gardens and were planning their next move.

'Smashing job,' Connor told Archie, holding his hand out for a high five. When he got to April, he leaned in and kissed the top of her beanie-covered head.

'Ew! Gross!' Archie called, squeezing his eyes shut and sticking out his tongue.

'A load of mulch, one last twig fence around the roses and the B & B garden will be officially done,' April said, standing up to stretch and discreetly steal a kiss from Connor while Archie was patting Mishka.

With the three of them on deck, the rose garden was soon enclosed with its very own handmade, knee-high fence. While the standard roses she'd transplanted from the Winklins' yard were still dormant, they stood tall and proud, ready to bloom their socks off. It wasn't hard to imagine the first flush of fragrant roses with colourful ranunculus gathered at the base.

Thunder rumbled in the distance and the sky turned an ominous grey as they shovelled mulch into the wheelbarrow and then onto the garden. 'You'd better head home before it buckets down,' April told Archie, thanking him for his help.

'But what about the very first fire?' He looked to the oak doors hopefully.

'Tomorrow,' April promised, holding out her little finger. He shook it, pleased that she'd offered him a pinky promise, and started for the laneway, his skipping turning to a jog as the rain started.

'I'll open the shed door,' Connor said, raising his voice above the wind that had arrived with the rain.

April grinned, her hair lashing her face as she shook her head. 'I'm going to finish this mulch and then the garden's officially done!'

There wasn't any particular reason the garden had to be completed that afternoon, given the first guests at Kookaburra Cottage weren't due for another fortnight, but April felt like a horse with the home gate in sight. They were so close to finishing.

'You're mad, you know?' Connor's navy jumper was speckled with rain drops, and the gentle patter gained momentum as April pushed the heavy barrow across the lawn, but he followed anyway.

They shovelled the mulch in tandem, until the rose garden was blanketed with a layer of woodchips and they were both soaked to the bone.

'C'mon,' Connor called, commandeering the wheelbarrow and making for the shed. She swiped at her wet fringe, which just made the rain run more freely into her eyes, and hugged her arms around her sodden midriff, beaming at the stables she'd transformed and the cottage gardens that were now, officially, complete.

'It looks perfect,' Connor said, stretching out his arm and snapping a selfie of them inside the cottage two weeks later, with the dusky spring afternoon light softening the room. April snuggled in against him, making him take a few more pictures, before looking at her watch. The guests would arrive any moment.

She'd been waiting for this day for years, and the last few months had flown past with Gordon finishing up a few weeks earlier and Connor sharing the 'icing on the cake' jobs, like fitting curtains, buying towels and hunting down furnishings that befitted such a dreamy space.

April moved the warm muffins into the centre of the kitchen bench and slipped a coaster under the vase of gum leaves on the French-polished side table.

'Almost perfect,' she said. She glanced around the room again before giving in to temptation and jogging up the iron staircase. April smoothed a hand over the mossy-green quilt cover and fluffed the grey woollen throw rug at the foot of the bed one last time before switching on the lamp.

'There,' she whispered with a nod, appreciating how the tones of the bedding gave warmth to the crisp white paintwork. 'Now it's ready.'

They walked out the front, trying not to look too eager, when an unfamiliar BMW rolled down the laneway and pulled up beside the 'guest parking' sign.

'Welcome, welcome,' April said, handing across the keys and assessing the couple as they surveyed their accommodation. She tried to look at the building impartially, wondering if they could fathom the number of hours that had gone into every fitting and every fixture, from the hand-cut dowels in the window frames to the little garden markers Archie and Connor had surprised her with on the weekend, so guests could easily differentiate the flat-leaf parsley from the coriander.

Connor slipped his arm around her shoulders, listening as she explained where the firewood was stored and encouraged them to help themselves to the herb garden and call if they had any queries.

'I never understood why Mam cried after Nell's first day of school, but it's a big thing, isn't it, handing over those keys and hoping for the best?'

April brushed her eyes with a laugh, pleased that it was a momentous occasion for him too. 'At least we checked the bed doesn't creak,' she said with a sniff and a giggle.

Connor laughed. 'You can never be too careful about quality control, and I'm sure the reviews will make special mention of that.'

And just like the stone entrance wall they'd almost finished, one carefully placed paddock rock at a time, the guest reviews through spring and into summer confirmed that their attention to detail and the personalised touches were worthwhile.

A hidden gem! April's warm welcome made us feel right at home—Amy & Kev, SA

Perfect romantic getaway, freshly baked muffins and wine on arrival were a wonderful surprise—Phil & Craig, Vic

Glorious vineyard setting, little garden was buzzing with bees, blooms and butterflies—Michelle & Paul, Qld

An hour's drive from the beach, in the heart of wine country—winning!—Katie & Tim, Vic

17

Archie was at the door before Connor had even parked, wearing a Santa-Claus T-shirt and matching hat.

'Check this out, Connor.' As he followed the boy inside, Connor saw the pom pom at the end of his hat was lit up with flashing LED lights.

'Ta da!' An enormous Christmas tree stood in the centre of the Winklins' living room, the star on the top almost touching the twenty-foot ceiling. Connor was so busy admiring the size of the tree, it took a few moments to twig that Archie's pom pom was flashing in time with the tree's lights.

'I can turn it off from here too,' said Archie, pulling out his phone and halting both sets of lights with the touch of a button. He then rushed to show him the train that circled the base of the tree, but Connor said gently, 'We'd better get your lesson underway, Arch.'

'It'll only take a minute, wait until you see the caboose,' said Archie, tugging him towards the tree.

After two lazy locomotive laps, three minutes after the lesson was supposed to have started, Connor heard a voice down the corridor. Connor turned to see Rupert on his phone, watching them with a look that said, 'I'm not paying you to play with tank engines'.

Connor finally lured Archie to the piano stool, but he noticed him faltering under his father's scrutiny as he ran up and down the scales.

'Come see me when your hour's up,' Rupert said when he'd finished his call, frowning as Archie stumbled over a simple C-chord. Archie perked up the moment his dad stopped watching and the rest of the hour flew past.

Connor declined Archie's offer to operate the train's controls, knowing the little boy would happily stretch out his visits half an hour each side. 'Sorry old chap, I've got piano lessons with the Morley girls after this. You go to school with them, right?'

'Ali and Grace are in my class.' Archie nodded, leading the way through the kitchen and down to Rupert's office. 'They're heaps nice. They're probably going to the fireworks at Beachport for New Year's Eve too. Dan can't make it, so I'll be the only kid in the district stuck at home.'

Connor was sure that wasn't the case and told Archie so. 'I do love a good fireworks display, though. I might have to check it out.'

Archie tugged on Connor's arm. 'Maybe I could go with you guys?' His whole body wriggled, just like the lambs when they saw him approaching with the milk bottles.

Connor hedged, not wanting to make promises. 'I'll talk to April, but if it's okay with your folks, I'm sure we could arrange it.'

Rupert looked up from his laptop as they walked into his office. 'Arrange what?'

'The New Year's fireworks at Beachport, Dad!'

'Can't think of anything worse. Hundreds of rowdy kids, dogs howling, all the teenagers traipsing down the street with their contraband alcohol.' Rupert shuddered, tapping on the computer. 'Let's get through Christmas first, before we start worrying about New Year's.'

Archie took no notice, gazing up at Connor with shining eyes.

If he had a tail, it'd be wagging, thought Connor. He looked at Rupert, who was still intent on his keyboard. 'You wanted to see me?'

Rupert stood, finally giving Connor his full attention. 'Now, Jamison. The Vignerons association has been thinking about arranging a Jazz in the Shiraz festival. We have an electric piano you can use. Obviously, it's still in the pipeline, but given our arrangement with lessons it would make sense if you played at Winklin Wines.' It was a statement rather than a question.

But before Connor could politely explain that he didn't perform, and that even if he did, he'd play at Lacewing Estate, Archie interrupted.

'We could play together! That would be so cool.'

Rupert sighed, his frown returning. 'Not if you hammer the keys and drift off into la-la land in the middle of practice, you won't be. This is a proper music event, not a primary school concert. We need music people will pay to hear.'

Connor could see Archie deflating with every word and his heart ached as the boy ran out of the room. 'I don't perform,' Connor said stiffly, his eyes following Archie's retreat.

'You don't perform? I checked your credentials before I hired you and you've played all over London.'

'I might have once, but not anymore,' Connor said, ignoring the ache in his leg.

Rupert's eyes narrowed with a mix of sympathy and disappointment. 'Burnout, I guess? Not everyone can handle the pressure at the top.'

Connor ignored the dig, and picked up the framed photo on the desk. In the picture, Rupert clutched a newborn Archie awkwardly, like he didn't know what to do with the tiny, swaddled bundle in his arms. Evidently he still hadn't nailed it, a decade on.

'Archie's a good kid,' Connor said quietly. 'A really good kid who tries his hardest at so many things. The veggie patch at April's is overflowing with produce, the facts he comes up with about toads and frogs blow my mind and you should see him playing the piano when he hits his stride.'

Connor set the photo frame down, preparing to tell Rupert Winklin to pull his bloody head in and appreciate his son, when he heard a shaky breath. He looked up to see Rupert covering his face with his hands.

Oh God, is he crying? Connor gulped, averting his eyes.

'I know he's a good kid.' Rupert's voice had an edge to it that Connor had never heard before and he waited, unsure what to do or say as Rupert leaned on the desk, oblivious to the paperwork falling to the floor.

'He looks up to you,' Connor said gently. 'Daniel too.'

Rupert cleared his throat. 'I didn't know it would be this hard,' the older man said, so softly that Connor had to strain to hear. 'I'm exhausted just watching him tear around the yard, chasing those ruddy lambs, and anytime I suggest a night at the orchestra or film we might both like, he looks at me like I've grown another head. Do you know what I bought him for Christmas?'

Rupert reached into his desk drawer and pulled out a gift bag.

Connor could think of a hundred things that the boisterous ten-year-old would love, but a 2000-piece jigsaw puzzle wasn't among them. Had Rupert not noticed the boy could barely sit still for five minutes? Nell would probably like it, and he could see Fran Lacey perched in front of a card table with something similar, but Archie . . .? He was more likely to enjoy the opera than an intricate jigsaw puzzle.

'My grandmother got something similar for me when I was that age,' said Rupert. 'Took me all year to finish the darn thing, but it was rewarding from what I remember.'

Connor took a closer look. The landscape painting had a vegetable garden in the foreground and rolling hills in the background, with sheep breaking up the vast expanse of green. Connor didn't care for jigsaws, but he could imagine the green backdrop and the blue, mostly cloudless sky would test the patience of even the most accomplished puzzler.

'He'll like the theme,' Connor offered, handing it back. He chanced a subtle look at his watch. He was officially late for the Morley twins now, but five more minutes wouldn't make much difference.

'He'll hate it,' Rupert said. 'The worst thing is, that was the best of a bad lot. Felicity's bought him something, of course, but she's always insisted I buy him a gift myself too.' He sighed then threw a reproachful glance at Connor.

'I suppose I could ask April, she spends plenty of time with him. Or . . . I don't suppose you have . . .' Rupert cleared his throat before finally blurting out the question. 'I don't suppose you have any suggestions?'

Connor was happy to share them and when he left five minutes later, after a quick goodbye and 'Merry Christmas' to Archie, he felt like he understood Rupert a little better. For all his criticisms and frowns, he really did love his son, he was just stuck negotiating the fifty-year age gap.

By Christmas Eve, April was well and truly ready for a holiday. Her long-service leave felt like a distant memory and with the influx of bed and breakfast guests, a pleasing spike in the number of cars pulling into Lacewing Estate, and preparing for their third foodie function with DestinationSA, Christmas had been the last thing on April's radar.

Their first event in early December had gone off without a hitch. As promised, April had painted, landscaped and cleaned Lacewing Estate until it sparkled, ready to host the first clients for their lavish long lunch. The function had been booked through the DestinationSA website, and using the skills she'd learned through the online course, plus networks she'd created within the program, April worked with an event planner and caterers to pull off a stunning event.

On the back of that success, they'd done it all again in mid-December for another corporate client who had also found them through DestinationSA's promotions—a sumptuous seafood feast for an Adelaide brokerage firm this time—and April was hoping their third hosting experience would be just as smooth sailing.

'You're a brave woman, accepting a booking for such a fancy Christmas lunch,' Lauren said, zipping her suitcase shut. 'But at least by this time on Boxing Day, you'll get a sense of whether the extra money was worth the extra stress.'

April rifled through a bag of Christmas decorations. 'It's a bit late to change my mind now,' she joked. Tomorrow's clients were wealthy graziers with a large family and even larger land holdings across the southeast. Stephanie Scouller from DestinationSA had called April personally to break the news that they wanted to book Lacewing Estate for their extended family celebration.

'And they were happy to pay a pretty penny for the use of the barrel room on Christmas Day. If we get a recommendation from just one of the 25 people sitting around the table tomorrow, drinking our wine, enjoying the atmosphere, then it'll be worth it.'

'Are you sure you have the energy to set up the Chrissy tree at this late stage?' asked Lauren, wheeling the suitcase around the mess of plastic branches. 'It looks like a bomb has exploded in the living room.'

April stooped down to retrieve a slobbery Christmas tree branch from Mishka's basket. 'I almost didn't bother, but Archie was horrified at the thought. He was going to help me put it up, but the second he saw the cabbage moths circling his brassicas, he was a goner.'

Lauren grinned, leaning out the window to see Archie running between the veggie patches with a butterfly net, Mishka hot on his heels.

The sunshine was hot and April felt sweat beading on her forehead and back as she helped Lauren carry her luggage to the car. She wrapped her housemate in a big hug. 'You sure you'll need all this for a week in the Maldives?'

Lauren laughed. 'If my mum has anything to do with it, I'll spend most of my time in yoga classes. But it's Club Med, we're not paying, and it'll give Fergus a great preview of life with my crazy family, so at least there won't be any confusion about what he's getting himself into.'

I hope the Bickford family go easy on Fergus, April thought, waving her friend goodbye. Once the resident cabbage moth population was under control, the Christmas tree was complete and Archie was on his way back home, April headed over to the winery. She'd just opened the tasting room door when Luke, the event planner, called.

'April, glad I caught you. I've got the chef and kitchen hands heading your way as we speak, so they can drop off the prepped ingredients for tomorrow, and I'll be there the minute my kids have unwrapped their presents. The venue's all set to go?'

April walked towards the barrel room, nodding. 'Sure is. The barrel room is spotless and we've got the fairy lights and eucalyptus foliage in place, as promised. Now, let's go over the wines you wanted one last time.'

She ran an eye down the chalkboard list she'd written earlier that day, checking off the bottles as Luke confirmed each course. Everything was ready, they were all set, and with a little luck, tomorrow's event would earn them plenty more word-of-mouth recommendations.

'All perfect,' she confirmed, reminding him that she'd be there to let the staff in.

'Excellent, excellent. I look forward to seeing it myself. The last two events were a raging success, there's no reason this Christmas lunch won't run just as smoothly. And between you and me, I've got plenty more clients who are looking for something bespoke. We could make a right go of this, April.'

She signed off with a smile, hoping she didn't sound like too much of an eager beaver, and silently fist-pumped the air. Hosting these events would be the boost Lacewing Estate needed.

🍇

April woke on Christmas morning to find Connor's arm draped over her shoulder, his legs entwined with hers and his lips curved into a smile, even in his sleep. They celebrated the morning together, making the most of the empty house and lack of time constraints, drinking their coffee under the flowering gum. They left the presents under the Christmas tree at the winemaker's cottage and walked to the winery to check everything was set for their impending guests.

The lunch wouldn't start for another two hours, but already there were bread rolls on the tables, festive table arrangements of grey-green eucalyptus and red kangaroo paws, and gleaming wine glasses, polished to a brilliant shine, at the ready.

'It looks amazing,' April said, taking another photo on her new phone, the improved lens capturing the wine barrels, the fancy table arrangements and, of course, the bottles of their finest wines, hand selected for the exclusive guests.

'This Christmas is going to be hard to beat,' she said, leaving the winery with a spring in her step and her arm looped through Connor's. They ambled through the vines, checking all was well at Kookaburra Cottage, before returning to April's for brunch. After finishing their croissants, April set up her laptop and drew her mum's present, which had arrived in the post the day before, onto her lap.

Polly answered the call with a fruity-looking cocktail in one hand and a wrapped gift in the other. From what April could see in the background, it looked like another perfect day in the Tiwi Islands.

'Merry Christmas, Mum,' April said, smiling at the screen and lifting the wrapped box to the camera.

'I'm so glad it arrived in time,' Polly said. 'You open yours first.'

Under the gift wrap, April found a colourful mass of fine string. 'A hammock.'

'If you're not heading my way any time soon, I thought you could do with one of your own. Unfortunately, I can't send you any palm trees, but it'll be perfect under those big gums.'

April smiled, admiring the careful weaving. Had it really been a year since she'd last seen her mum? 'There's also a voucher for art classes in the card,' Polly said, moving her computer aside to sit her own present on the outdoor table.

'Seeing you liked those cooking classes so much, I thought you could be like Claude Monet and do some "'plein air painting" in the vineyards,' she said.

'Thanks, Mum,' April said, and while she was unsure when she'd find the time for painting classes alongside running the bed and breakfast, her horticulture job and Lacewing Estate, she was touched by the gesture.

'I can't believe you've stayed in one spot for so long,' said April. 'It must be good weather.'

'And good company,' said Polly with a wink, opening April's gift and peering into a small drawstring bag. 'Jewellery, my favourite.' Without any hesitation, Polly replaced her earrings with the new ones. 'How do they look?'

April nodded, pleased. 'They're lovely. I got them in Beachport, there's a local lady there who makes them all by hand.'

They spoke for a while longer before Polly was interrupted by a visitor. 'I'd best dash, darling. The town parade is about to start.'

'Hold on, Mum, I want you to say hello to someone.' April beamed and moved the laptop so the camera caught Connor walking back with their drinks.

'Well, hello, this is a nice surprise,' Polly said.

Connor introduced himself and she could have sworn her mum did a double take when she heard the accent. 'A British boy? Well, that's even more unexpected. As long as you don't drag her back to England with you, we'll get along just fine and dandy.'

'Mum!' April shook her head. Whether she was in Penwarra or England probably wouldn't change the regularity of their catch-ups, but the comment reminded her of something else she needed to raise with Connor. She hadn't wanted to jinx things by pressing him on his plans beyond the two-year visa, but they were getting serious now.

'Anyway, I really do have to dash,' Polly said, waving from the laptop screen. 'Big love from me, have a great day and let's not leave it so long between catch-ups, okay, honey?'

'I'm always here, Mum,' April said. 'Love you too. Miss you.'

'She's in the tropics?' Connor asked, checking out the postage label on the box.

'For now, but I won't be surprised if she gets itchy feet soon, she's rarely in one place for long. Her next stop could be anywhere from Alaska to Borneo. Teaching and travelling are her passion, not exactly a good fit for life on a family vineyard.'

He draped an arm around her shoulder, resting his chin on her head. 'Doesn't know what she's missing,' he said.

They set up the hammock outside, and after checking it would take both their weights, they chose a playlist on April's phone and spent the rest of the morning top and tailing in her new hammock, each with a book in hand.

'Why do I get the feeling you're not actually reading?' said Connor, twisting his head to look down the laneway.

'Hard to concentrate when this angle gives me a prime view of the cellar door,' she said with a grin. 'Look at those flash cars pulling up.'

They both watched the well-dressed guests trail into the winery for their fully catered, no-expenses-spared Christmas lunch. A text from Fran came through at midday, checking what time they were coming for lunch.

'We could play hooky, pretend we're both sick,' April suggested, trudging into her bedroom and changing into a green linen sundress.

'It'll be fine,' said Connor. 'If Fergus can manage a whole week away with Lauren's family, I'm sure we can handle a few hours of being sociable.'

April laughed. 'Well, Dad's still sore about losing access to his beloved cellar door for the day, so I'm not sure even I can handle a few hours with them,' she called out as she searched the bathroom cabinet for a bobby pin. April opened the mirrored cabinet above the sink, smiling at the sight of Connor's bamboo toothbrush.

Just like the space she'd cleared for him in her home, her heart and her life were slowly filling with Connor-shaped moments and memories, and it was getting harder to ignore the ramifications of falling for him. How would she handle it if he returned to the UK when his visa expired? And what would he say if she asked him to stay?

April closed the mirror, pinned back one side of her fringe with a bobby pin, and stared at her reflection. Until she knew the answer for sure, it was better not knowing whether she was enough to keep Connor in Australia.

He appeared in the doorway, the sleeves of his blue shirt rolled up to his elbows, and gave an appreciative whistle.

'All set?'

April thought of her mum's advice. *Live in the moment.*

She nodded and reached for his hand. 'All set.'

Lloyd led them through the kitchen to the formal dining room. The sliding glass doors opened out to the rows of grapevines, offering a view of the winery, the bed and breakfast and the roof of April's little cottage.

'Make yourselves comfortable,' said Lloyd, gesturing to the cheese platter by the sofa and a decanter of red wine. Connor spent most of his days at Lacewing Estate, but he'd never been inside Lloyd and Fran's home before. He complimented the house as April poured them all a glass of wine.

'Your home's made from the same bricks as the winery, right?'

The rustic bricks were exposed along one wall of the lounge room, and he stepped closer to examine the photo frames hanging at regular intervals.

'Yep, mudbricks, made with the dirt from our property, each one hand pressed, just like our grapes. It'd be nice if all the buildings were paddock stone, like the winemaker's cottage and April's stables but the bricks in this old joint have held up well,' Lloyd said.

While the bricks *were* impressive, it was the photos that had caught Connor's eye, documenting April through the ages; sprawled on a rug with a dummy and wooden toys while workers graded fruit; as a toddler standing in the vineyards with a set of pruning shears; as a teenager driving the tractor between the vines, and one of her carrying a tray of wine with a too-large Lacewing Estate apron tied around her scrawny waist, a mess of braces, pimples and a high ponytail with an oversized scrunchie.

He reached out, automatically straightening one of April in her university graduation gown when the frame fell off—hook and all—taking a section of wall with it.

Connor just caught it in time. 'I'm so sorry,' he said, wincing at the small hole it had left in the brick.

'Happens all the time,' said April, getting a brush and pan. 'The mudbrick walls really need plastering over, but someone has trouble letting go of the past.'

They cleared up the mess while Fran and Lloyd tinkered with the meal in the kitchen. 'Dad helped my pop make the winery bricks when he was a teenager,' April explained. 'He and Mum made these ones, and no matter how often we remind him that his hard work will still be visible on the outside if we plaster the internal walls, he won't budge on rendering or covering the insides.' She lowered her voice. 'It's on my to-do list for the cellar door too, but I'm not ready to fight that battle just yet.'

Lloyd returned to the room with several salads, noticing the frame in Connor's hand.

'Like a little shadow, she was,' Lloyd said with a nod to the photo wall. 'Always watching, learning, giving the workers advice on how to pack the wine boxes and ripping into them when they picked too many bunches with rot.'

The image of April as a bossy tween made Connor chuckle, but when he looked up, his boss was a million miles away. 'Had her heart set on taking over the winery at that age,' Lloyd continued, his voice light. 'But that's neither here nor there. Top of her class at uni,' he said, holding a hand out for the frame. Connor passed it to him as Fran walked in with plates and cutlery.

'Look at you, getting all nostalgic,' she said, placing the plates on the table, then rubbing her husband's arm. 'I don't know about you lot, but I'm starving.'

Connor was about to sit down when his mobile buzzed. 'Excuse me,' he said, pulling the phone from his pocket and preparing to switch it to silent.

That's odd.

'It's Barney from the golf club,' he said, looking up to find everyone watching him. Why would Barney be calling him during Christmas lunch? Surely not to wish him season's greetings?

'You didn't leave the oven on or anything, did you?' Fran asked. 'The grass might be well watered, but the scrub around the golf course's tinder dry.'

Unease sat in Connor's chest as he looked back at the missed call on his phone. The oven was fine, but had Fergus turned the barbecue gas bottle off properly before he'd left for Club Med?

'I might just call him quickly, if you don't mind.' All the media coverage of bushfires had Connor nervy about the idea of a fire. Thankfully, when the golf club president answered, he quickly quashed Connor's worries.

'A fire, no, not at all. I think this is good news. You've got a surprise visitor,' Barney laughed. 'She's fresh off the bus from the airport and trying to track you down. You didn't mention you had a fiancée.'

18

The Christmas lunch Fran had prepared looked tasty enough, but April could barely think of anything other than Phoebe's arrival as they sat down to eat.

The mental image she'd built of Phoebe was of a pensive woman who was sporadically hit by bouts of debilitating depression. Even after she'd seen Phoebe briefly on Zoom at the Jamison's annual jam session, and then read about her on the hospital website, she hadn't pictured Connor's ex-fiancée as an international traveller with a penchant for surprises. Was Phoebe trying to rekindle things with Connor? Or did she just want the support only he could give?

Whatever the case, April wasn't sure it had been the right thing to send him back to the golf course house alone. She felt uneasy and guilty that her mind hopped, skipped and jumped to negative conclusions. Connor had given her no reason not to trust him, or his intentions, so why did she feel so anxious?

She eyed the clock discreetly, wondering how early was too early to leave Christmas lunch. It was times like this she wished she were one of six children, with brothers and sisters, nieces and nephews, and a swag of partners or in-laws to add extra numbers and conversations to the event.

Her father hacked a slice of ham off the bone, slathering it with cranberry sauce and wedging it between two slices of bread. If the non-stop grazing and winery-angled window gazing was any indication, he was definitely comfort-eating his way through the day. Mishka looked up hopefully from his feet and was rewarded with a generous sliver of ham rind.

'Remember the time we had my cousins Ted and Saoirse across from Ireland for Christmas? Those were the days,' Fran said.

'That was one of the best Christmases,' Lloyd agreed. 'They couldn't believe how beautiful our winery was, and how perfect a venue it is for a Christmas lunch.'

'The best Christmas? Dad, you nearly sent one of them into anaphylactic shock,' April said, surprised that her father had forgotten. 'We would've had to call an ambulance if she hadn't had an epi-pen in her luggage.'

April also remembered the moment when one of Fran's brothers, who had travelled across from Darwin, had nearly come to blows with a cousin in a heated conversation about the suggested rescheduling of Australia Day.

'From my recollections,' she added with a frown, 'we all breathed a sigh of relief when everyone went home.'

'But the venue, April, the venue. Sunshine pouring in through the winery's clerestory windows, barrels in the background, white tablecloths . . .' Lloyd said wistfully. 'I'm really not thrilled about hiring the place out on Christmas Day.'

'Do you think we should go across and check on the guests?' Fran craned her neck, looking across the vines.

April shook her head. 'Luke makes a living out of event planning, he doesn't want or need us hovering. They've got everything they need there. With a bit of luck the guests will be drinking bucketloads of wine and asking to come back for New Year's, Valentine's and Easter.'

'I thought you already had a New Year's booking?'

April nodded. They were hosting a fancy lunch at Lacewing on New Year's Day and visitors at Kookaburra Cottage, too. It felt like an eon since that very first B & B booking had come through, and although plenty of couples had stayed at the cottage before them, April always smiled when she thought of Mr and Mrs Henderson, their upcoming New Year's Eve guests. Her smile wasn't as quick today, though. April glanced at her watch.

'Time for dessert?' asked Fran, desperate to lighten the mood.

April pushed her portion of Christmas trifle around her plate, then said her goodbyes and clipped the lead on Mishka.

The sun still had some bite in it as she walked from the main house to her little cottage with a gift hamper tucked under her arm, thinking of the glorious morning she and Connor had spent in the hammock, relaxed in the way only sated lovers can be.

Once she got inside, April cranked open the windows and was just deliberating on whether to retire to the new hammock with a drink or call Connor, when a text message arrived from Geraldine.

> Merry Christmas, cooking students. Just a reminder that you're more than welcome to call in for drinks and nibbles this afternoon. I may have gotten a little carried away x G

April opened Geraldine's photo, swooning at the spread their cooking teacher had made. Cream puffs, petit fours, macaroons, mini cheesecakes . . . It was what she imagined high tea at the Ritz would look like.

Another photo came through, this time of Geraldine with a Santa hat on and a glass of champagne raised in the air as if she were doing a 'cheers' through the phone.

Sensing a hint of loneliness behind Geraldine's festive red lipstick and smile, April grabbed two of the small gift bags by the mini tree in the living room. Just because Connor was indisposed, didn't mean she had to sit around moping and stewing.

All the way home from Lacewing Estate, Connor racked his brain for the conversation in which he'd mentioned to Phoebe that he was living at the Penwarra Golf Club, but he was none the wiser by the time he arrived at the rental.

Mam and Dad must have told her.

Phoebe stepped out from under the verandah in a floppy sunhat and oversized sunglasses, an enormous grin on her face.

Even in his surprised state, Connor couldn't deny she was looking as fit as ever, with her long hair falling over her shoulders in gentle waves and a denim dress that set off her pale complexion.

He gulped, hating that he'd even registered such a thing, and switched off the ignition. Phoebe wrapped her arms around him the moment he stepped out of the Camry.

'Surprise!' She squeezed his shoulders, and his manners eventually kicked in. Connor patted her back awkwardly, the questions tumbling out.

'What are you doing here? How did you get to Penwarra? And how did you get Barney here on Christmas Day?'

Phoebe laughed, grabbing his hand and pulling him to the door. 'Ah, so many questions and so many answers. But first, do you mind if I steal a shower? I've been wearing these clothes for days and I feel like death warmed up.'

Connor nodded and unlocked the house, relieved the place was tidy and there wasn't a Scotsman and April's best friend there to pepper him with questions he couldn't yet answer.

At a loss for what to do while Phoebe showered, Connor changed the sheets on his bed. Most of his things were in the back of his car or at April's, but making room in the wardrobe and changing the linen was better than sitting with the knot in his stomach, pondering Phoebe's arrival.

'Miracle of miracles, I'm semi-human again.' Phoebe grinned, emerging from the shower with pink cheeks, wet hair and a towel wrapped almost twice around her body. 'Though it was quite difficult rinsing out shampoo in that shower. I've had better water pressure strolling past the car wash,' she said, combing the knots from her flaxen hair.

'It's the rainwater,' he said quietly. 'Took me ages to get used to the low pressure in the shower too, but the whole house is on rainwater, so water conservation's a big thing here.'

He averted his eyes, trying not to notice the new ink work on her arms.

'Was I supposed to know you were coming?' he asked, busying himself in the kitchen. There were milk and eggs in the fridge, a selection of limp veggies and a quick check of the freezer confirmed there was also bread and a range of frosted takeaway containers. It wouldn't be a festive feast but she wouldn't starve.

'Nope,' she said, grabbing her suitcase as he led her down the hallway to his bedroom before making a beeline for the kitchen.

'I wasn't sure Pippin could keep a secret, but she obviously did well,' Phoebe called from his bedroom. 'Your voice when Barney called was priceless.' Her laugh tinkled down the hall. 'He had you on speaker phone—I may have fibbed about the fiancée bit, but I felt bad for calling him out on Christmas Day. His number *was* on the clubhouse doors, mind you.'

Phoebe breezed back into the lounge, wearing a light-purple dress. 'You don't mind, do you?'

'If I'd known you were coming, I'd have suggested a hotel.' He cleared his throat, trying to clear his thoughts in the process. 'I was just sitting down to Christmas lunch with my girlfriend. Phoebe—you can't just spring something like this on me.'

'You would've tried talking me out of it,' she said, lifting a shoulder. 'I needed a change of scenery and some sunshine.'

Connor waved a hand towards his bedroom. 'You can stay in my room for a few nights. I'm still paying rent so it may as well not go to waste. But I haven't been sitting around waiting for you, Phoebe. Honest to God, I've got a girlfriend and a good job, and I'll be staying at April's cottage, not here.'

Nodding, Phoebe held up a hand. 'I know, I know, I'm not here to upset the apple cart. I wanted to see for myself, that's all. And if you're going to fly all the way across the world, then you may as well make a holiday of it, right?'

Connor poured himself a glass of cold water from the fridge and sagged against the bench. April's folks had been understanding enough, and April hadn't hesitated to offer up her spare bed, but he hated the situation Phoebe had put him in.

He couldn't just turn her away when she knew no one. Connor tapped out a quick message to April.

> I'll get Phoebe settled then I'll come meet you. Are you still at your dad's?

April's reply came back almost immediately, as if she'd been sitting by her phone.

On my way to Geraldine's—meet you there.

Connor smiled wearily, wanting to rewind back to their carefree morning. He replied with a thumbs-up text.

Phoebe joined him at the sink, filling a glass with water.

'I'll be careful, Connor,' she promised, and he couldn't tell if she was talking about the rainwater or the fragility of his new relationship with April. 'And I brought you a present,' she added, pulling a gift from her handbag. 'Go on, take it,' she said. 'Consider it payment for the precious rainwater and fresh bed linen.'

Connor relented, unsure what she could have for him that warranted hand-delivering all the way from the UK. He wasn't prepared for the framed black-and-white close-up of two tiny hands cupped in his own hands.

Xavier.

His eyes burned as he remembered the momentous weight of such a tiny, cold hand in his. Phoebe had taken a series of these photos, but he'd long since packed the tiny leather-bound photo album in the storage boxes in his parents' attic, the contents too raw and upsetting to have close by.

'He had long fingers like you,' she whispered. 'Do you remember?'

'Of course I remember.'

She stepped in closer, resting a hand over his. 'I wish I'd come to Australia with you, Connor. I shouldn't have let you leave.'

Connor slid his hand out from under hers and ran it through his hair. He'd wanted to hear those words eighteen months ago, not now. He turned abruptly, collecting his phone and a light jumper, the small gift he'd bought for Geraldine and a bottle of wine. He hesitated at the door, then ducked back and grabbed a second bottle.

'I'm not even sure what to say to that,' he said. 'There's food in the pantry and freezer, I'm going out.'

'Where are you going?'

Her thin voice cracked on the final word and it took all of Connor's strength to keep walking out the door.

※

April stood up when Connor entered, the haunted look on his face reminding her of their conversation at Beachport, when he'd spoken about the accident. And was it her imagination, or was his limp slightly more pronounced?

'Here he is,' cried Brian, clapping Connor on the shoulder and draping a paper crown over his blond hair.

Geraldine pulled him into a hug, clearly oblivious about the reason Connor was late.

'I didn't think it was my place to say anything,' April said in a hushed voice, handing him a glass of wine while Geraldine pulled another platter from the fridge. 'How's Phoebe?'

He shrugged. 'Complicated. Let's talk about it later, yeah?'

She threaded her fingers through his, pleased to have him close again.

Brian rifled through Geraldine's record collection and selected a Cat Stevens album. They set up a feast beneath the pergola, toasting the occasion and listening to Brian's latest update on his veggie patch.

'I've spent half the week on the end of a grubber,' Brian said, finishing off another fruit mince pie.

'A grubber?'

April and Connor both grinned, trying to picture whether it was a machine or tool.

Brian rolled his eyes, looking to Geraldine for backup, but she was none the wiser.

'One of those hoe thingamabobs, flat blade on one side, point on the other?'

'I haven't got the foggiest,' Geraldine said. 'It must be a Victorian term.'

Brian eased himself out of his wicker chair and wandered across to the small garden shed at the bottom of the yard, rummaging around like he'd been there before. He emerged with a garden tool and gave them a quick demonstration on how to easily remove a section of cape weed.

'Now I've got a hole in the lawn, thanks to your grubby grubber,' scolded Geraldine with a chuckle. 'You'd best fill that in.'

'But at least it saves your back when you're weeding,' Brian called, walking the tool back to the shed.

'Saves your back, ruins your ankles. Who's this coming across the lawn?' Geraldine said, shielding her eyes from the late-afternoon sun and getting to her feet. 'Maddie must have changed her mind.'

April looked at the pair of matching gift bags she'd brought, glad she'd gambled on Maddie being there too.

But when their cooking instructor returned, it was not with their tween cooking enthusiast. Instead, a tall, angular woman with soft blonde hair and wrists as fragile as the thin straps on her sundress tailed Geraldine.

'Phoebe!' Connor leaped to his feet.

Phoebe? April took a sharp breath and glanced at Connor, who looked as shocked as she felt. She willed herself to stay calm and stood, wincing as she slopped red wine from her glass onto her dress.

'Um . . . hi, Phoebe. Welcome to South Australia.'

As April walked across to greet Phoebe, Mishka bounded out of the garden shed, the tinsel on her collar flapping. Catching the dip in the grass where the cape weed had been just minutes earlier, the golden retriever cut behind her bare legs and Phoebe pitched sideways.

'Ooof!'

Mishka barked.

'I'm so, so sorry. Here,' April said, her face flushed red as she reached for Phoebe's hand to help her up. If she'd been sturdier looking, April mightn't have been so worried, but there was something fragile about the British girl—it felt like sheer luck that she had escaped broken bones, scrapes or at the very least, a whopping bruise.

'Brian and his bloody grubber,' said Geraldine, trying to assist April.

Mishka pranced between them, her canine concern hampering Phoebe's attempts to get off the ground.

Connor, who'd been frozen to the spot, suddenly kicked into action and grabbed the dog by the collar. Receiving a grateful but still mortified look from April, he hauled the licking, tail-wagging bundle of wriggly golden fur away.

'You right?' He gave the two women a harried look, then shook his head at Mishka, her chocolate eyes gazing at him with adoration. 'Phoebe, what brings you here?'

Before she had a chance to answer, Brian, who'd marched over from the garden shed with a bag of potting mix in his hand, cut in, 'Murphy's Law, isn't it? My apologies.'

Phoebe brushed the grass off her lilac dress, looking slightly flustered from the kerfuffle. She forced a bright smile at Brian.

'No harm done.' Then moved towards Connor. 'I think I might go,' she said.

'Please, don't go, honestly, I feel terrible,' said April.

'Stay, stay,' added Geraldine. 'There's way too much food. Please, I insist.'

April looked at Connor, who had remained quiet.

'I meant I might go to a hotel—I shouldn't have imposed,' Phoebe said, with a sigh that sounded like it came from the soles of her feet. 'I've packed my suitcase, I just need a lift into town.'

April watched Connor's eyes scanning Phoebe's drawn face, while Geraldine and Brian hurried off in search of another bottle of wine.

It was hard to watch the silent conversation going on between the two Brits and April felt a chill down her spine as she deliberated on what to do. Offer Phoebe a lift into town or a spare bed? Implore her to stay so she had an opportunity to get to know the woman who'd once been a big part of Connor's life? Or stay the hell out of it?

She opted for the latter, following Geraldine and Brian inside the farmhouse kitchen.

'Thank goodness she's not American or she'd probably sue us both,' Geraldine said to Brian, poking his arm. 'I've never had a student injured on the premises.'

April took a stool at the island bench, trying to avoid blatantly staring at the conversation going on outside.

Connor looked resigned, worlds away from the man who'd made her coffee in bed that morning, his cheeks turning a familiar shiraz-colour. She could see Phoebe's hands gesturing as she spoke.

Connor opened the glass door and gave them all a weary smile. 'Sorry about that,' he said. 'I don't know about Phoebe but I'll definitely take you up on that glass of wine, Brian.'

Phoebe followed him in. 'Yes, me too, thanks,' she said, crossing her arms. 'Only if you're sure you don't mind a gate-crasher?'

Geraldine nodded eagerly. 'Absolutely,' she said. 'As long as you promise to eat some of the food and forgive us for the uneven lawn.'

'And the boisterous dog,' added April.

Phoebe nodded and soon they were all outside again with food and more wine.

'I've heard great things about Lacewing Estate, April. You've got beautiful photos on your website and the reviews are amazing,' Phoebe said, beaming at her with those white, straight teeth.

April mustered up a smile in response. 'Thanks,' she said. 'It's a pretty special spot.'

'Special's an understatement,' said Brian. 'You should see how much effort's gone into the B & B renovation. We had a grand tour last month, you'd never know it was a storage shed this time last year.'

'And I have it on good authority the homemade muffins are a hit,' added Geraldine, her voice ringing with pride. 'They both took my cooking classes, you see. Improved in leaps and bounds with every weekend.'

'I'd love to see both,' said Phoebe, 'the winery *and* the cooking.' She soon had them laughing with a story about Connor's gritty attempt at scrambled eggs, and his initial success at camouflaging bits of shell with a generous helping of cracked black pepper, chilli flakes and salt flakes.

'Our tongues were burning after a few mouthfuls and little Nelly was drinking milk straight from the carton. Cooking isn't my thing, so I'm glad he finally sought skilled instruction from someone who knows what they're doing. I bet your guests love the homemade touch, April, and if you don't mind giving tours, I'd love to check it out.'

'I'm sure we can arrange that,' said April. 'Are you staying long?'

Please say no, please say no.

Phoebe wiggled her hand left and then right. 'My ticket's open-ended, so I'm playing it by ear.'

April nodded, sipping at her wine, ignoring the simmering unease in her stomach. *Maybe it's a good thing*, she told herself. Perhaps she and Phoebe would become friends. From the sounds of it, Connor and Phoebe needed to have a long, hard talk, and the sooner it happened, the better.

It wasn't even 8 pm but Connor felt bone tired and ready for bed. He felt April's fingers slide through his and he squeezed them back, grateful she'd taken their unexpected visitor in her stride. Phoebe might have had a misguided notion about rekindling things, but that didn't mean he had to play along.

Connor leaned closer, taking strength from April's familiar scent of wild plums and cherries, while Phoebe's words echoed in his ears.

I want to try again, Connor. I won't go back to England until you can tell me, without a hint of doubt, that you can't see a future for us.

It wasn't a conversation he'd wanted to have on Christmas Day in Geraldine's garden, with April and his new friends not far away, but he'd been quick to clarify things were well and truly over. He just hoped she'd accept it.

'Are you ready to call it a night?' he asked April softly.

She nodded, swatting away a mosquito.

'I am if you are,' she said. 'Shall we walk Phoebe back?'

He looked inside. Phoebe had insisted on helping Geraldine and Brian with the dishes and he'd been happy for the breathing space.

'She found her way here, she should be able to find her way back.'

April chuckled and rubbed his arm. 'She could be mobbed by a kangaroo or slip on a stray golf ball. Mishka's already given her a rough welcome. I think we can spare ten minutes to walk her home.'

April pulled him to his feet. They headed into the kitchen, where Phoebe was discussing her role at the hospital.

'There's never a dull moment in accident and emergency. I pretty much blink and the shift's over. Night shift's always hard but helping families through the tough times makes it worthwhile.'

Connor watched Phoebe hold court with a tea towel in one hand and cutlery in the other.

'Not to mention—' Phoebe grinned at him.

'All the chocolates.' He finished. She was a darn good nurse and there'd always been a steady stream of cards and sweets in their flat from appreciative patients. But it had made it harder for her when they'd lost Xavier, because she'd known the technical terms the doctors used and understood the gravity of the situation before he did—she was familiar with the carefully chosen words her colleagues favoured and was reminded of that painful loss every time she walked past the maternity ward.

'Anyone keen for a round of Celebrity Heads or Pictionary?' Geraldine asked, drying her hands.

Connor didn't miss Phoebe's knowing look. He'd never been a fan of board games, especially interactive ones. As he stood there, surrounded by his new Australian friends, he realised she was the only one who knew that about him.

'I think we'll be off, but thanks very much for the supper,' he said warmly.

'After all those glorious desserts, I could probably roll myself down the fairway,' April said, before turning to Phoebe. 'We'll walk you back.'

Phoebe nodded and Geraldine and Brian fussed over gathering up their belongings. *For someone who hadn't arranged anything official for the day, Geraldine had gone to quite a bit of effort,* Connor thought, accepting one of the gift bags she was passing out.

Connor reached for April's free hand. Being face to face with Phoebe for the first time in eighteen months was easier with April by his side.

When Phoebe kneeled down to adjust her sandal, he noticed a long fine silver chain dangling around her neck. She tucked it back into her dress as she straightened, but not before he saw what was on it. The engagement ring.

Connor exhaled slowly, hoping nobody else had seen it. Whatever Phoebe was playing at, April didn't deserve to get caught in the crossfire.

While Phoebe and April made small talk across the fairways, Connor felt like the short walk was painfully longer than usual, and he was relieved when the little rental came into view. Connor unlocked the door, then handed Phoebe his keys.

'The Camry and the house are yours for the week if you need,' he said. 'My housemate is back on New Year's Day, so you'll probably want to aim to head to Adelaide or Melbourne by then.'

April called goodbye and he held her hand as they retraced their steps to Geraldine's, collected the Hilux ute and headed for Lacewing Estate.

Connor looked out the window, silent as they drove through Penwarra. He'd told Phoebe they were over and he'd meant every word of it. There was no chance Phoebe could mistake the happiness between him and April when she saw it with her own eyes. But if she hadn't already, if it took her a week, it would be a week well spent.

19

Normally, the private gardens April managed felt like an oasis, with topiary hedges that she kept trimmed to perfection, a cascading jasmine arbour that brides posed beneath for their springtime weddings, and a stunning southern corner where clouds of blousy hydrangeas lapped up the shade.

But today, smack bang in the middle of the limbo week between Christmas and New Year, her mind was in turmoil. She tossed a discarded shawl, a toddler's sunhat and an empty confetti box into her wheelbarrow with a sigh, checked the watering system was running smoothly, and headed back to the shed. Lost property at the gardens was rarely claimed, unlike the chargers, pillows and jewellery guests left behind at Kookaburra Cottage. April had already been to the Penwarra post office several times to send items back to their forgetful owners.

If only it were that easy to dispatch unwanted ex-fiancées. The churlish thought was quickly replaced by a stab of guilt as April carried a bucket of flowers and her lunch box to her ute. She pondered the problem as she drove home. It would be so much easier to dislike Phoebe if she were nasty, or possessive, or blatantly out to steal Connor from under her nose, but so far there was nothing April could fault her on.

Apart from her very existence and her presence in Penwarra.

April had stripped the sheets and cleaned the B & B after yesterday's visitors checked out, so all that was left to do before the next couple arrived was arrange the hydrangeas in a vase, turn on the small split-system air conditioner so it was cool for the newcomers, and mix up a batch of muffins.

There was no sign of Connor, but Mishka was pleased to see her when she arrived back at the cottage. Happy to eat the snail-damaged strawberries, the dog stuck close to her as she collected a bowl of berries for the muffins, and when they got inside and she turned on her own air conditioner, the retriever flopped down in her basket.

'Sure is warm, hey Mish?' said April, noticing she'd had a touch too much sun herself today. Although she itched to change out of her work clothes and into a summer dress, she wanted to get the muffins in the oven first.

A memory of Geraldine's calm, wise voice was in her ear as she measured the flour, added the sugar and folded the berries through the mixture. After so many years of avoiding cooking, despising the burnt, inedible evidence of her incompetency, it was still surreal to know that if she followed the steps to a tee, double-checked the measurements and watched them carefully as they cooked, she could produce something beautiful.

And not just once, but again and again. *Cooking—once you knew how—really was its own brand of alchemy,* she thought.

But the satisfaction of turning out the muffins and the momentary calm as she taste-tested one evaporated when a knock and a cheery hello sounded from outside.

'Oh, Phoebe,' April said, answering the door with an oven mitt in her hands. She scooped her fringe away from her eyes—she probably looked like she'd been dragged through a hedge backwards. *Though anyone would*, she thought sadly, *standing beside this willowy blonde in the patterned dress.* 'I was just heading to the cottage to drop muffins off for today's guests.'

'Do you mind if I come? I've been dying for a look,' said Phoebe, with such enthusiasm that April had no option but to nod.

'It's absolutely adorable.' Phoebe's eyes widened as she stood in the B & B kitchen with the wooden chopping boards, tea chest and greenery against the subway tiles, her fingers trailing along the polished concrete benchtops. April sat the muffins in the centre of the bench, folded the tea towel until it was just right and picked an errant crumb off the gleaming counter. The room was cool and bright, and she knew that the warm baking would add a sweet scent for her guests' arrival.

'You're welcome to have a quick squiz, but Mr and Mrs Barber will be here shortly, and I can't meet them looking like this,' April said apologetically, gesturing to the grass stains on her knees and her sweat-stained gardening shirt. Phoebe looked at the staircase and then back at April.

'Do we have time?'

'Go on, it won't take a minute.' April nodded to the mezzanine.

Phoebe was effusive with her praise, noticing not just the soft furnishings and fittings, but the way the layout made the most of the small building.

'I especially love the way you used the old horseshoes for towel hooks and the leather straps holding up the bathroom shelves,' Phoebe said as they left the stables. 'Are they from the saddlery?'

April nodded, begrudgingly impressed. 'You're the first person to mention that. They used to be part of the ploughing harness, from my great-grandfather's era. He used horses to till the soil and cart the grapes. My dad remembers his father using the Clydesdales occasionally too.'

They arrived at the winemaker's cottage to find Archie heading in their direction.

'Hey Arch,' April called. 'This is Phoebe, she knows Connor—'

'Awesome, you're the lady who gave Con's sisters the tortoises, aren't you?'

Phoebe laughed, surprised. 'I had no idea they'd be such a talking point. But, yes, lovely to meet you.'

April left them chatting while she ducked into the shower, and when she got back from welcoming the Barbers and giving them the spiel about the district, the stables and the checkout time, Archie and Phoebe were crouched over his veggie patch.

'Shh,' said Archie, turning to her with a grin on his face and a finger over his lips. 'I'm trying to find Tiddalik.'

April wasn't sure how much Phoebe really liked amphibians, but she watched Archie carefully scoop up the small creature. He showed it off as if it were his pride and joy.

'He's heavier than he looks too, and he's nice and cold, not slimy at all,' Archie said. And before Phoebe could demur, she was holding the brown spotted frog and not even squealing when it piddled on her.

Archie collapsed in a fit of laughter. Phoebe looked mortified.

'I think Tiddalik's ready to return to the patch now,' April said, nestling the creature in a shady spot between the rhubarb stalks.

'Now there's a good story for Nell and Pippin,' Phoebe said, rinsing her hands under the tap April had indicated. 'They'll love that.'

And as they went inside for a proper wash-up and cool drink, April could just imagine Phoebe sitting around the Jamison's dining table upon her return, sharing stories with Connor's family. The thought was as vivid as it was infuriating.

Instead of the cruisy post-Christmas week he'd planned with April, Connor found his head in a whirl and soon there were only a few days left of the year. There was plenty to be done at Lacewing Estate, thankfully, and he welcomed the distraction.

With a coffee and piece of toast in each hand, he sat at the dining table and called Heidi as he ate.

'I bet you're missing this place,' she said from her living room, wiping her mouth with a serviette. 'I've just nipped out for a late-night chip butty and it's snowing. Slush up to my ankles and icy enough to make you consider every step. Tell me it's tanking down there, or at least it's so sweltering hot that you can't go outside?'

Connor laughed, peering out the window. 'Blue skies, heading for about twenty-eight degrees and sunny. I can't complain,' he said, turning his computer so she could see for herself. April had set the sprinklers before she'd left for Mount Gambier, keen to get the bulk of her horticulture tasks done before the heat set in. 'And if it's anything like last night, I think we'll head to the beach when April gets back. I do miss home, but it's hard to beat sundowners on the sand, cooling our feet in the ocean with a beer in hand,' he said.

'How's Phoebe liking it?'

Connor's smile faltered. Heidi knew about the conversation he and Phoebe had on Christmas day. 'I'm not terribly sure how she's liking it. I've been trying to steer clear of her, to be honest. I've given her my car and my house for a week and then, after I've driven her to the bus stop or airport, I'll be able to relax again.'

Heidi was silent for a moment, adding more HP sauce to her chip sandwich. 'So you're just avoiding her?'

'Sure am! I didn't ask Phoebe here.'

'Connor!' Heidi said sharply. 'You *were* perfect together, the golden couple. And everyone around here loves her. You know that. She's travelled a long way to see you, to talk to you.'

'Who goes around doing that type of stuff, though? I've made it clear I'm with April now,' Connor said, smearing a drop of coffee over the tabletop.

'And what does she think about it all?'

Connor raised both eyebrows. 'You think I'd tell April what Phoebe said? Are you bonkers? Phoebe's here another few days, then she leaves and we go back to normal.'

'I would have thought you'd at least hear Phoebe out, Con.'

Connor shook his head and changed the subject, but as he left the cottage later that morning, Heidi's words played on his mind. Was he just kicking the can further down the road by avoiding the issue rather than tackling it head on?

Connor found Lloyd in a chirpy mood in the barrel room.

'Now, tell me what you think of this one,' Lloyd said, pulling the wine thief from a barrel of cab sav.

'Not bad,' said Connor, swirling it in his mouth and listing the flavours as they came to him. He could see why Lloyd was pleased with the blend.

'And you'll be right with us going away for New Year's Eve? I've barely seen April this week, and I know she's just trying to put her stamp on the place, but I don't want to come home to any more surprises.' He tapped his chest. 'This old ticker can't handle too many more renovations and I've got a lotta living left to do.'

'No more surprises,' Connor promised wryly. Truth be told, he hadn't seen much of April this week either, but it didn't seem like something to mention to her father.

The conversation turned to the bed and breakfast, which Lloyd was pleased with, and then the food tourism, which he was ambivalent about.

'I'm still not in love with the idea, but the first three events we hosted went off without a hitch,' conceded Lloyd, moving to the next barrel and taking a sample. 'And April's worked her guts out to make it happen, so I can't get too stroppy about the whole thing.'

'And there's been quite the increase in traffic,' Connor added with a grin as tyres crunched on the gravel outside. 'Nothing like some new signs, a snazzy stone fence and some landscaping to make an impact.'

'Yeah, I'll give you that,' said Lloyd, a good-natured smile on his face. His mood was catching, but when Connor peered into the tasting room, rather than the tourist he'd expected, he found Phoebe chatting to Fran.

'I drove to Naracoorte today and saw the caves,' she was telling Fran. 'Imagine bumping into a two-metre-tall tree kangaroo on your morning walk, or a huge wombat.' She spotted Connor and smiled. 'Have you seen the megafauna displays there, Con?'

'I haven't had a chance yet,' he said, wiping his hands on his shorts. 'Everything okay at the house?'

'Yeah, it's fine, just a little tired of my own company, really. Oh, and there's some sheep on the loose near the B & B, are they supposed to be there?'

Archie's latest batch of lambs must have found the escape route. Connor met Fran's eye, knowing he'd better return them to the paddock before Lloyd discovered them. He pulled on a hat and beckoned to Phoebe. 'We'll herd them out, Fran. Back in a bit.'

They found the first lamb nibbling on the rosemary near the stables.

'Go back a bit, Phoebe, slowly now. Wait, back, back. Ergh!'

The lambs bolted around Phoebe, and she squealed as they whipped past her. The expression on her face made him burst out laughing.

'I'm rubbish at this,' she said, joining in with his laughter. Connor tried a few more times, but finally they gave up. 'We'll have to get Archie, he's got pellets that'll turn anyone into the Pied Piper.'

With a touch of sun on her face and enthusiasm in her voice as they walked across to the Winklins, Phoebe reminded him of the woman he'd met all those years ago.

'I've been thinking, maybe I should stay?'

Connor coughed. 'In Australia?'

'In Penwarra,' she said quickly. 'It's good for me here, the people are sweet. Geraldine said I was welcome anytime, April's nice, even the guy at the bakery offered me a job, which could come in handy while I'm waiting for something to come up at the hospital.'

Pausing at the gate, Connor shook his head. 'I'm not sure Penwarra's the best idea. Feel free to try your luck in a different country town, or over the border in Victoria, but not Penwarra.'

'It was just an idea,' she said, putting her hand on his. 'Have you thought any more about what I said? We were good together, Connor. We could *still* be good together. I really shouldn't have let you leave without me.'

Connor jammed his hands into his pockets, uncertainty swirling through his thoughts. Wasn't that exactly what he'd wanted to hear eighteen months ago? Hadn't he lain awake at night in the months before he flew to Australia, trying to think of ways to convince her he was wrong for breaking off their engagement, that they belonged together?

He stepped away, latching the gate behind them. 'A lot's happened in the last eighteen months, Phoebe. I know I was in two minds after our break-up, but I've settled in here, I've moved on.'

Connor tried to interpret the expression on her fine features. There was a vulnerability that he'd once been able to read like it was his own, but there was hope too, and right there, shrouded in a wary smile, was the admission that she'd never stopped loving him.

'It's too late, Phoebe,' he said, breaking it to her as gently as he could.

'I said it on Christmas Day, and I'll say it again. I'll never stop loving you, Con, even if it's not reciprocated.'

He took a steeling breath and continued to the Winklins' yard. He found Archie out the front, kicking a football to himself.

Connor explained the lamb situation. 'They're as naughty as last year's flock,' Archie said, his freckled nose wrinkling. He dropped the football immediately and spent the entire walk back to Lacewing explaining who the troublemakers had been amongst the various lambs he'd reared.

With Archie at the helm, they quickly got the lambs back into the paddock. The young boy didn't seem to notice Phoebe's pained expressed, and continued carrying the conversation, moving onto the New Year's Eve fireworks and carnival food.

Connor closed his eyes a beat, remembering his and Phoebe's last New Year's Eve together, how they'd rugged up against the polar blast, taking turns to warm Pippin and Nell's hands between their own and huddling together like penguins for the fireworks.

There was a fraction of truth in what Heidi had said; their loved-up couple bubble had been all-consuming. And what about the promise he'd made after losing Xavier? The promise that he'd never leave Phoebe. The promise that they'd forge a future together.

Connor kicked at the dusty limestone and exhaled slowly, trying to wash away the guilt and the sinking suspicion that after his role in the accident, he didn't deserve the love of one woman, let alone two.

April cruised through the vineyard later that week, her attention on the burgeoning clusters of fruit on the vines. There must be a god shining down on them from somewhere above, because not only were the vines laden with fruit, but the people who had spent Christmas in the barrel room had rebooked and spread the word among their wealthy farming networks, and now Lacewing Estate was taking bookings for Easter.

They were also hosting a fancy lunch on New Year's Day, with one of the DestinationSA team staying the night afterwards.

The only fly in the ointment was blonde, British and agonisingly nice.

April plucked a bunch of grapes off the vine, holding the tight green cluster up to the sun and twisting it in the light. They were still a few months away from ripening, but it always felt a little like a miracle in the making to appreciate the berries at each stage.

'Do they taste different to table grapes?'

April spun around at the familiar accent, a polite smile at the ready. Phoebe's black polo shirt fitted her like a glove, and her fair hair was swept back beneath a baseball cap.

'These ones have still got a few months left on the vine, so they're as hard as rocks right now,' April said. 'But when they're ripe, they've got a much bigger flavour profile than the grapes you buy at the supermarket.' She brushed aside the leafy canopy so Phoebe could see the immature bunches.

'They're teeny-tiny.'

'We don't want big grapes. The smaller the berry, the more intense the flavour,' April said. She put the pruners back into her pocket, quite sure Phoebe wasn't here for a Ted Talk on grapes. She noticed the white Camry in the winery car park. 'You out exploring?'

'Too nice to sit inside.' Phoebe played with the peak of her cap, moulding it between her palms. 'Connor said you might need a hand?'

April studied the tall blonde, wondering what else Connor had mentioned. Had he told Phoebe that he was falling for April, or was that just something he'd said in the heat of the moment? She wasn't sure what to make of his distance these last few days but an element of self-preservation had prompted her to keep her head down and channel the uncertainty into work. 'I'm just about to prep for the next guests,' she said, whistling for Mishka, who had spent the last half hour stalking butterflies.

'Sure, I can help with that,' she said, beaming at April and following her to the stables. Phoebe startled when raucous laughter came from the gum tree.

'What on earth was that?'

'Up there,' said April, pointing to the hollow where the family of kookaburras nested. 'Hence the name "Kookaburra Cottage".'

They stripped the bed in silence, and Phoebe worked her way around the building, unwinding windows and dusting as April fetched fresh linen.

'Sunshine and rest do the world of good, don't they?' Phoebe said, as if reading her mind. 'I can see why half of Britain spends a gap year Down Under. What are the facilities like in town? I've not explored it carefully yet.'

'It's just your regular country town, a couple of pubs and primary schools, a high school, a few shops, police, fire station and post office. Lots of wineries.'

'And a hospital?' Phoebe looked across at April as she asked the question, another of those bright smiles on her face while she waited for an answer. The neckline of April's shirt felt tight as she realised where Phoebe was heading. *Please don't tell me you want to settle in my town.*

'Yep, a tiny little hospital,' she said lightly, working hard to maintain a poker face.

Phoebe was the epitome of efficient, tucking the sheets with hospital corners so sharp they wouldn't dare come loose.

'Doesn't take long to clean,' Phoebe said, fluffing the linen cushions on the sofa and draping the Angora throw rug over the arm. 'And it really is a gorgeous spot to stay between the vines, I can see why you've got so many bookings.'

April accepted the praise with a silent nod. She swiped a damp mop across the floorboards, admiring the rich grain in the recycled timber and remembering the splinters and blood blisters that had come with laying the tongue-and-groove flooring.

'I nearly pulled out of the renovations at one stage.' She told Phoebe about the budget and timeline overrun, hoping to highlight the blood, sweat and tears that had gone into the project. 'But I'm glad we forged ahead. Really glad.'

Phoebe smiled, pulling Connor's car keys from her handbag. 'You just know when something's worth fighting for, don't you? When Connor and I got engaged, I wasn't really sure we'd weather all the storms, but sometimes those rocky bits make you a stronger person.'

April upended the mop bucket onto the lawn. She looked up and caught Phoebe staring towards the winery, her expression as transparent as the freshly washed windows.

Of course, she still loves him!

April steadied herself on the windowsill, the realisation sapping the strength from her body.

What did that mean for her and Connor?

Later, when Phoebe had gone and Lauren called for an update, she ran the conundrum past her best friend.

'If it were me, I'd be telling Phoebe she can go jump,' said Lauren.

'I'm tempted to,' April replied, 'but they've been through such tough times and like it or not, she represents everything about his life in the UK. What if I'm standing in the way of true love?'

April kneeled over her vegetable garden, phone jammed between her ear and her shoulder, tugging at little outliers of self-sown grass with more force than necessary.

'So what? You're willing to sacrifice your own happiness for Phoebe?' Lauren sounded unconvinced. 'People go through bad stuff all the time, April, but it doesn't mean a person with a traumatic background should take what they want, regardless of the impact on everyone else. He's *your* boyfriend, remember that first and foremost.'

'I know.' April paused. Connor had given her no reason to mistrust him ... but she'd been wrong about Justin, hadn't she?

She grabbed a handful of milk thistles, realising too late they were entwined with stinging nettles. Her hand smarted and eyes prickled as she tossed them into the bucket.

'But if his heart is tied up with Phoebe, it's fruitless for me to flog a dead horse, isn't it? Our relationship can't thrive if he's still even partly in love with her.'

Lauren had no more answers than she did, so when they hung up, April upended the weeds onto the compost pile and sagged against the bullbar of her ute, feeling a sudden urge to let down the tyres and go hooning up razorback sand dunes again. It felt like a safer bet than dwelling on the murky uncertainties of the heart.

While most of his students were away on holidays and had opted to pause their piano lessons until the new year, there were still three keen pianists to teach the day before New Year's Eve.

Between the scales and the set pieces, the Morley sisters were full of chatter about Christmas presents, beach trips and fireworks displays.

'Our dad said the fireworks will scare the crayfish right out of the craypots,' Ali said.

Her sister Grace chimed in, 'It's going to be the best night, are you going to Beachport or Mount Gambier?'

'Fireworks on the jetty at Beachport? Wouldn't miss it,' Connor answered, putting away their music folders. It was quiet in the club rooms after the girls left and with an hour before he was due in town for the final lesson of the day, he found himself reaching for the sheet music.

His shoulders relaxed the moment he sat down on the piano stool, and after the stop-start rhythm of the children's exercises, it was a joy to hear music flowing from his fingertips. He played the piece once, then ran through it again, faster this time. Then he closed his eyes, conjuring up the pieces he knew off by heart.

When he finished the final notes of 'Für Elise', a gentle clapping sounded from the doorway. He turned to see Phoebe silhouetted against the bright sunlight.

'It's been years since I heard you play,' she said softly, crossing the room. 'I'd forgotten how beautiful it sounds.'

Connor studied his hands, remembering the final performance in London, before the accident that had changed everything. It had been flawless—not a missed note. If he hadn't been so pleased with himself, if he'd used the wrong pedal or fumbled with the sheets, maybe he wouldn't have celebrated so hard, and maybe he could have driven, like he'd planned.

He grimaced, and Phoebe sat down beside him on the piano stool.

'It's not your fault, Con. You know that, right?' Phoebe said, as if she could read his thoughts. 'I didn't plan on getting into an accident, just like I didn't mean for everything to happen with Xavier, but I've forgiven myself for that. Can you say the same thing? We didn't know things would change forever that night, but they did and we're still here. Nobody else has been through what we have, that's why we're so good together. We've felt that pain, moved through that grief. We promised we'd never forget.'

Connor shook his head. 'I couldn't forget if I tried, and trust me, there was a while when I gave it my best shot, but I don't think that's what we should hang our hats on. We want different things, Phoebe. I'm happy here in Australia.'

The conversation fell into a lull.

'Do you love her?' she asked quietly.

He ran his fingers along the keys, not comfortable sharing that level of detail with Phoebe. 'We're taking things slowly but it feels right, you know? A fresh start. That's if she'll have me.'

'She'll be lucky to have you.' Phoebe sighed, resting her hands on the keys too. 'Do you know, when we found out we were having a boy, I would picture the two of you playing piano together, side by side on the stool.'

She tapped the keys cautiously, and he recognised the first few bars of 'Chopsticks', the only tune she remembered despite his many attempts to teach her others.

He reached across and adjusted her fingers. 'Try starting there,' he said gently, joining in at the far end of the piano.

It took a few attempts, but finally they got the tune right. Connor closed the lid and stepped out from the stool, giving Phoebe time to wipe her eyes.

She stood, her eyes welling again. 'So that's that then?'

Connor reached out and folded her into a hug, feeling her shoulders heaving against his chest. He nodded, blinking away the burning in his eyes. 'That's that,' he said softly.

20

A text buzzed in April's pocket and she pulled the phone out, hoping it was Connor. But instead, there was a photo of Fergus and Lauren pulling funny faces at the camera, with snorkelling gear and an azure beach in the background.

> Club Med brilliant. BTW Fergus says he'll be happy to stink out the rental with boiled haggis and leave the toilet seat up if need be when he gets home. #UnwantedGuestEvictionTricks101 xx Lauren

The message made April feel a little better but she was still frowning at the phone when Archie appeared at the edge of the driveway. 'I can't wait for the midnight fireworks tomorrow, April! All that music and the markets and the lollies. Does Connor like donuts or fairy floss best? Or maybe we'll just get both!'

Mishka jumped to her feet and bounded over to the young boy, who looked like he'd grown an inch since April had last seen him. Archie went straight to his veggie patch, inspecting the plants closely for signs of snail and slug damage, as he awaited her reply.

'Not sure, mate,' April said. Connor had told her he'd planned something for tomorrow night, but seeing as she hadn't heard from him all day, she wasn't sure exactly what it involved. Hopefully not another awkward catch up with Phoebe.

She wasn't sure if she mentioned it aloud, but she froze when Phoebe's name rolled off Archie's lips.

'What was that?' She kneeled down beside Archie. His hands were moving fast over the mulched soil, locating and removing weeds with a twist of his wrist.

'Phoebe said Connor loves fireworks. They never missed the New Year's Eve fireworks back in England. For five years they took Connor's little sisters and ate fairy floss and hot jam donuts and watched the fireworks lying on a picnic rug, blankets heaped over them—'

April was glad she was already kneeling, because Archie's snippet of information made her feel a little woozy, and his excited chatter about carnival food washed over her as she imagined trying to top five years of traditions. Five years of Connor and Phoebe huddled together on a picnic rug, marvelling at the fireworks. Five years of Christmas mornings, family jazz concerts, long weekend lie-ins and Easter egg hunts. She'd known Connor for almost a year, and they'd only been together for half that time. How could she possibly compete with five years? Of course Phoebe would win him back.

'You alright, April? You look a bit like Marty when the shearer slipped that little green ring around his knackers.' Archie grinned, then frowned, studying her nervously. 'You and Connor are both coming to the fireworks, right, or is that just something he does with Phoebe?' He scratched his head, leaving a smear of dirt on his freckled forehead. 'Or something he used to do with Phoebe? Do you think she'll be here for my birthday? Maybe she'll give me a tortoise too!'

April breathed out slowly. *Focus, April, focus.* She nodded mutely, then shook her head, blinking rapidly as she mustered up a bright smile for Archie.

'Hard to say, buddy. And speaking of animals, I think I saw the new lambs in the vineyard again. Can you be a gem and go and have a look for me?'

'Again?' Archie slapped a hand on his thigh, his brow furrowing. 'I thought they'd stopped escaping,' he said, getting to his feet quickly. 'I'll go and scout them out. The shiraz grapes or the chardonnay?'

'The chardonnay,' she whispered. It was the furthest away from the winemaker's cottage, which would give her plenty of time to pull herself together.

By the time Archie returned, looking bewildered about the missing sheep, she'd made a decision. 'I need to head off, mate,' she said, climbing into the Hilux and waving goodbye. She stopped a minute later at the winery.

'He's not here,' said Fran with a raised eyebrow. 'Doesn't he teach on Thursdays?'

Feeling like a scatterbrain, April drove to the golf club. There was music pouring through the club room windows when she parked and she sat still for a moment, letting the classical piece flow over her. Connor was private about his music, never playing more than a few bars in her presence, but in the hot, dusty car park, it was impossible to ignore how talented he was. The music stopped and April leaned forward, letting her head rest on the steering wheel as she ran over what she'd say; the questions she needed answered.

Was there a future for them? Was she enough to keep him in Australia long term or would he always be beholden to his past? And if Phoebe was to settle in Australia, as she'd inferred, how would that impact their relationship?

Right. You've got this.

The backs of April's sweaty legs felt stuck to the leather seat cover, and she was sure her work clothes were as dishevelled as her thoughts, but she was determined as she opened the car door and stepped into the dry, eucalyptus-scented heat.

A few hesitant notes rang through the air. April paused. There were no other cars in the car park, so it wasn't another student . . .

Laughter came next, and when she moved to the window, April could see Phoebe and Connor, shoulder to shoulder, playing a two-part tune. 'Chopsticks'. It wasn't complicated, nor was it beautiful, but there was something about the way they played it together that held such gravity.

With a thick throat and blurry vision, April ran back to the car.

※

Connor walked Phoebe back to the golf course house, glancing at his watch as he made her a cup of tea.

'I'm due in town in a minute, will you be alright by yourself?'

She nodded quietly, accepting the mug with both hands. 'I think so. I'll look at flights, see if I can book a few nights in Sydney or Melbourne before I head home.' She gave him a wry smile. 'I'd quietly hoped I'd be booking two seats for the return leg, but looks like it'll be just me.'

Connor unhooked his car keys from the rack by the back door. 'You're young and fit, Phoebs, you've got so much to look forward to. A handsome doctor might sweep you off your feet and you'll have your own tribe of little doctors and nurses before you know it.'

She shook her head. 'I can't put myself through that again,' she said. 'Not after last time.'

Connor had a job hiding his surprise. Losing Xavier was the hardest thing he'd ever endured, but he couldn't imagine not trying again. Every time he pictured his future, he imagined it filled with the chaos and comfort of family.

'I'm sorry, Phoebe. For everything,' he said softly, slipping out the door.

He headed into town for the final lesson of the night. Like Archie, young Selina Hughes had her own piano. Unlike Archie, she wasn't musically gifted, but what she lacked in talent, she made up for with enthusiasm.

Selina was just as excited about the New Year's Eve celebrations as the Morley sisters and Archie.

'There's the street party too, with markets and everything,' said Selina. 'I'm helping Nanna in her van. She doesn't let me use the coffee machine yet, but I'm good at taking the orders and giving change.'

Connor looked at the tween and then at her mother, Fiona, wondering how he'd overlooked the resemblance.

'I've been teaching you piano for six months now, and I completely missed this. Your nanna is match-making, coffee van Jean?'

Fiona laughed. 'I'm not sure there's another Jean quite like her,' she said, walking him to the door. 'You seem to have settled in well, I hear. Mum had bold plans for fixing you up with the new primary school teacher, but I'm not sure she was fast enough.'

He grinned. 'Speaking of which, I'd better get back before April sends out a search party. See you at the street party tomorrow.'

'Oh Connor, before you leave, how do I go about booking the B & B? My folks have a special wedding anniversary coming up, and after giving Mum a vacuum for Christmas, Dad's got some ground to make up.'

He fossicked around in the glovebox and handed her one of April's new flyers. 'I didn't realise there'd be such a market for anniversaries. The guests staying tomorrow night are celebrating their fortieth anniversary.'

Connor left town feeling a whole lot better than he had on the way in. As he drove, he hoped that if he were lucky enough to have a girl like April by his side in forty years' time, he'd be the type of bloke who was still thinking about ways to keep the romance alive.

※

April clutched the neck of her guitar, playing every song in her limited repertoire, but the distraction of strumming, singing and plucking at the strings was short-lived. The moment she returned the guitar to its stand, the grief for the life she'd imagined intensified.

This is like Justin all over again, only worse. I can't compete with their history or their connection.

April paced the small cottage that had always felt like a haven, wanting to banish everything that reminded her of Connor. But she knew there'd barely be anything left in the house if she did so. The monstera pot plants she'd grafted while Connor read a book on the couch beside her, the rug they'd sat cross-legged on while picking bindies from Mishka's coat, the coffee table they'd rested their feet on while they watched movies.

As much as she willed it to, a scented scorching-hot bath didn't offer the usual respite either. *How could I have been so wrong about Connor? Am I the only one who didn't realise he was making a fool of me with his ex, all over again?* The humiliation was just as painful as the loss of the future she'd imagined for the two them.

Mishka whined at the edge of the bath. 'I didn't want it to end this way, either, Mish,' she said, her eyes filling again. When it felt like she'd exhausted her supply of tears, April sank down into the water until her hair swirled around her, letting out slow breaths so she could focus on the bubbles forming.

A knocking from outside set off a fresh round of barking and when she surfaced, Mishka was racing between the front door and the bathroom door, her toenails clattering on the floorboards and sliding on the tiles.

'Mishka,' came Connor's deep voice. 'Did you miss me, girl?'

Go tell him it's over, you great big coward.

Fighting the urge to sink under the water and see how long she could hold her breath again, April hauled herself out of the tub, wrapped herself in a bathrobe and twirled her hair into a towel turban.

Would he be man enough to admit there was still something between him and Phoebe, or would he do what Justin had done and pretend it was all in her imagination? *I'm not falling for that again*, she told herself, dabbing her face with a cold flannel.

When she walked into the lounge, her resolve to tell him exactly what she'd seen at the golf club wavered.

'Hey, what's up?'

His concern was so convincing she almost fell for it. She yearned to lean into it and have him tell her it was all a misunderstanding. Closing her eyes, April conjured up the memory of Phoebe and Connor playing the piano side by side an hour earlier, purposely letting it wound her all over again.

Even if Connor and Phoebe weren't together now, their bond was like a ticking time bomb. It was just a matter of time and better if she got in first. The cleaner the break and the sooner it was done, the better.

'I made a mistake, Connor,' she said, walking to the door with as much dignity as she could muster. 'I should have known better than to confuse a fling for a real relationship. You probably weren't even planning to stay in Australia.' She saw him flinch at the word 'fling' and knew it had hit the intended target. He opened his mouth to reply but she cut over the top of him. 'In fact, that's probably beside the point.'

His confused expression reflected her own turbulent thoughts. A lock of wet hair had escaped from the towel and he swept it off her forehead before feeling her temperature. The tender gesture was almost her undoing.

'Are you coming down with something? We've got Daniel's pre-New Year's party tonight, and the Beachport fireworks tomorrow, but I'm not going if you're not.' He looked flustered now and April struggled to harden her heart against the pain. 'But I—'

'Stop. Please just stop.' April cut him off, knowing exactly how the excuses went. Justin had rolled them all out before he left.

But I didn't mean to hurt you . . .

But I can't help how I feel . . .

But I wouldn't have looked elsewhere if you hadn't . . .

'Clearly, we need to talk,' Connor said, reaching for her hand. She yanked it away like he'd stung her.

'Just go, Connor. Go to Daniel's party, go back to the golf club, go back to England if that's what you really want. I just need you gone right now.'

He gaped at her, equal parts hurt and shocked, then turned and walked away.

Shutting the door behind him, April sank to the ground. Sobs wracked her body. Mishka paced a semi-circle around her, whining uneasily and lapping at her tears before eventually flopping to the floor beside her.

'It'll be better tomorrow, Mish,' she sobbed, wishing she could convince herself of that.

When she finally dragged herself into bed, April numbly checked her emails, then logged two new bookings into her calendar and replied to a message from her incoming guest, Mr Henderson.

> No worries about your late arrival tomorrow, the keys will be in the key safe and I'll leave the air conditioning on so it's cool. Happy 40th wedding anniversary!

It was an effort to inject enthusiasm into the message. She switched off the light, silent tears running down her cheeks.

Connor drove to Daniel Winklin's house on autopilot, his eyes on the road ahead but his mind reeling from April's bombshell. The last week had been tough with Phoebe's unexpected arrival, and he thought he'd sheltered her from the worst of it but April hadn't even let him explain.

You didn't deserve April anyway, you already knew that.

He crested the hill, groaning at the sight of sheep spread across the road. *So much for my brilliant shortcut* ... A farmer on a quad bike zipped back and forth, waving a hat in the air as a pair of working dogs raced around, trying to muster the skittish livestock. Connor braked, unsure whether he was supposed to keeping driving or wait for them to go back into whatever paddock they'd escaped from.

He'd come across mobs like this before, grazing on the roadside or crossing from one property to the next. When it had happened previously, he'd been happy to take in the scenes of ridgy-didge Aussie farm life, but after the emotional conversation with Phoebe, and then April's rejection, he felt as scattered as the livestock.

Drawing to a stop, Connor lowered his window. A warm, sheep-scented breeze filtered in and he rested his forehead on the car's doorframe, feeling like his brain was in a slowly-tightening vice.

How could he have ruined things with April? Why didn't he notice things were terribly wrong before now? The quad bike rumbled towards him, with a border collie on the front and another behind the driver.

Pull yourself together, man. Connor swiped at his cheeks and blew out a deep breath.

'G'day mate, they're a bit skittish, so if you could take it slowly and stick to the left, that'd be gold.' The farmer flipped the visor of his helmet, spearing Connor with a sharp look. 'You right?'

Connor rubbed his chest like it would dislodge the pain and wash away the acid in his throat. 'Fine,' he lied, inching the car away.

A party was the last thing he felt like, but April had made it clear he wasn't welcome at the cottage, he didn't feel like returning to Phoebe at the golf course house either. At least at Daniel's there would be beer, or perhaps even something stronger, so he kept driving, eventually pulling up at a small property on the outskirts of town.

'Geez, I was worried nobody would show up,' said Daniel, clapping him on the shoulder when he walked inside. 'Bloody glad you could make it, come and meet my new partner.'

It wasn't until after he'd introduced Phil and a handful of uni graduates who'd arrived in the district that month that Dan realised Connor had come alone.

'Don't tell me April's crook too? Everyone's falling like flies,' Daniel said, showing Connor to the makeshift bar.

'Wine, beer or spirits, help yourself, and there's a swag and spare room in case anyone needs to kip here the night.'

Connor cracked a can of scotch and dry, the strongest thing on offer, and settled by the fire pit to drown his sorrows. The young winemakers were full of enthusiasm about their new careers and lifestyle, and Connor felt old and cynical listening to the animated discussion about their raucous New Year's plans.

'We'll ring it in with an all-nighter, for sure,' said one bloke, who looked too young for shaving, let alone recreational drugs. 'How about you, Connor? You getting on it?'

'Not sure. My girlfriend and I were planning on taking Daniel's little brother Archie to the fireworks in Beachport.'

He took another swig of his drink, not wanting to face the possibility that the new year and beyond mightn't involve April.

'Seriously? That's the raw end of the deal, getting stuck babysitting on New Year's Eve,' one of the girls replied. 'Danny's probably planned the trip to the city to avoid it. I know which night I'd prefer.'

Connor gave a dry laugh. It probably seemed dull from a twenty-year-old's perspective, but he'd been looking forward to it ever since Archie had asked. Seeing in the New Year with the woman he loved by his side, even in the company of their enthusiastic young neighbour, had sounded pretty perfect to him.

Daniel served salad and spit-roasted pork around the fire pit, and Connor quietly drank his way through most of Daniel's scotch cans and stumbled into the spare room early, much to the amusement of the young vintners.

'The night's still young,' Daniel cried, determined to keep the party alive.

Connor crawled into bed and tried April's number. There was no answer.

Connor splashed water on his face and downed a cup of coffee the next morning, hoping the greasy bacon and egg roll would help soak up the alcohol.

'Thanks for the bed, mate. I owe you a few cans, too.'

Daniel waved his offer away. 'You're doing me a favour tonight with those fireworks, Archie hasn't let up about it all week. Besides, I'm sure you and April will have us around for a barbie before the summer's out, now that you're on the cooking bandwagon.'

Connor looked at his phone. He'd tried April's number again first thing in the morning, before his pounding hangover had a chance to kick in. *Still no answer.*

Phil walked in at that moment, looking a little rough around the edges, and Connor was grateful for the interruption. He slipped away, taking the backroads to the winery. There was no sign of April at the cottage or the bed and breakfast, so he wandered through the vineyards, assessing the grapes for the very last time that year, before putting in a few hours inside the winery. It was quiet in there too, with Fran and Lloyd away, and he made strong progress on the paperwork he'd been putting off all week.

If he hadn't been looking for the post-it notes, he mightn't have noticed the report on Lloyd's desk, but as soon as he clapped eyes on it, he couldn't help but read it cover to cover.

A sad smile crossed Connor's lips. The winery was tracking better in this quarter than it had for the previous two years.

'April's hard work is paying off,' he murmured.

If she'd seen the report, she was keeping mighty quiet about it. Maybe she had planned to surprise him with the good news tonight, when they were watching the clock run down to midnight.

Connor's phone rang and he jumped to answer it.

'Phoebe?'

Last they'd spoken, she was going to text him her departure time so he could take her to the airport in the next day or two. 'Did you get an earlier flight?'

Her voice was just a whisper. 'Do you happen to have any headache tablets? I've a migraine.'

Connor hadn't forgotten how debilitating Phoebe's migraines were if they weren't nipped in the bud. And even though Phoebe's arrival had thrown everything into a spin, he couldn't ignore her plea for help. He wasn't sure which medication they had at the rental, but as he glanced at his watch, he knew there was a slim chance he could make the chemist before it shut. He leaped into the Camry and raced back to town.

Phoebe was curled up in bed with the curtains drawn when he arrived with a bag from the chemist.

'What can I do?'

She whimpered. 'Ear plugs. Eye mask. Painkillers.'

He gently doled out the supplies and fetched her a glass of water. She accepted them with a grateful grimace.

'I don't want to miss my flight, it's booked for late tomorrow afternoon.' Connor strained to hear her tiny voice. It was in his best interests that she caught that flight too, and he was going to do everything possible to smooth the path.

It's not like I've got anywhere else to be.

The thought sat like a stone in his guts as he closed the bedroom door and scanned the share house. If he was going to be there a while, keeping an eye on Phoebe, he may as well put the time to good use.

Connor swept and scrubbed surfaces as soundlessly as he could. Then he opened the freezer and pulled out the provisions he'd bought after one of Geraldine's cooking lessons. Rather than talking things over with April, maybe he could show her.

21

Beachport's street market was in full swing when April and Archie rolled into town on New Year's Eve. Knowing the main street would be blocked off, and that parking would be chaos in the town centre, April pulled up by the inlet drain and they followed the boardwalk into town.

Archie rattled off the names engraved on the bollards, his excited chatter a welcome distraction from the wrenching feeling that came over April whenever she thought about Connor. She wasn't sure if she was relieved or disappointed that he'd stayed away last night, but after months of his warmth and the soft snuffling noises he made in his sleep, the bed had felt cavernous and cold.

April hugged her arms around herself, pulling the sides of her knit cardigan taut, and reminded herself it was for the best.

A smarter woman would have stepped aside days ago. A smarter woman would have discussed long-term plans instead of worrying about rocking the boat.

She'd missed another call from Connor before they left and though she hadn't expected him to join them for New Year's, not after she'd pushed him away, it was still hard to read the follow-up text message saying he wouldn't make it.

'Chambers, Redden, Hales, McKenzie, Watson,' Archie said, pausing to read the faded lettering. 'Do you think there's a Winklin bollard too?'

April dragged her attention back to her young friend. 'Maybe,' she said, looking at the names more carefully as they walked, 'though most of these posts were bought by locals to help fundraise for this timber path. It wouldn't be here without the community's support.'

'Just like the Penwarra Show,' Archie said. 'Less than a hundred days to go now—I've asked Mum if I can enter more things this year. Only one kid entered the photography last time and he got invited to exhibit in the Royal Adelaide Show. Imagine that!'

They spent the rest of the walk discussing their entries, and April couldn't help but laugh when Archie declared he was determined to win a prize in every category.

'You can probably fill all the categories,' she said, 'as long as you remember it's about participating, not winning.'

The town was a hive of activity, slowing their progress through the market. There was a range of food options, from baked potatoes and dumplings to sausage sizzles and locally made kranskys. After a chilli and cheese kransky, an ice cream from the strawberry van, and not one but three lucky dips, Archie and April found themselves at the plant stall.

'Archie, this is Mr and Mrs Cooper,' she said, greeting the elderly couple sitting behind a sea of potted plants, veggie seedlings and homemade worm juice fertiliser.

'How's your garden, April? Are you expecting another clean sweep of the produce section come March?'

April shook her head. 'I was just telling Archie here about

the perils of expecting a ribbon on show day. Everyone's in with a shot.'

'Too right,' said Mr Cooper, nodding at Archie. 'Every show and every season is unique. I've been involved in more shows than you've had hot breakfasts, young man, and you never know how it's going to pan out. But we love seeing the younger crowd getting involved, and they're always looking for committee members and volunteers. How are you on a ladder?'

Archie looked between the three adults, trying to work out whether Mr Cooper was serious or not. 'I haven't had much to do with ladders, but I'm good at catching sheep.'

'He's also a whiz in the garden; his tomatoes were fruiting before mine this month,' April said.

'I'm sure the committee can find something for you if you're at a loose end in the holidays, Archie. The poultry pavilion needs work, not to mention the gardens around the hall. We want the place sparkling for the one hundredth anniversary,' said Mrs Cooper. 'A little birdie told me you've got a new beau, April, and from the look of that glorious stone entrance at your winery, he's good with his hands.'

Her stomach dropped, and April was struggling to think of a suitable reply when Archie piped up.

'Oh yeah, Connor's awesome at everything. He's a piano teacher, he makes wine, and you should see him working a drop saw. Mr Lacey says he's an all-rounder, and even though he's not great at catching sheep, he's getting better. He loves fireworks too, just like me, but he's not here tonight because he's looking after Phoebe,' Archie said. 'They were gonna get married ages ago, she's still got the ring and everything.'

That's how Connor was spending the night? With Phoebe? April wasn't sure which was worse, that news or the fact

Phoebe still had her engagement ring. Her voice came out gruffly. 'I'm not sure Mr and Mrs Cooper need that level of detail, Arch.'

She looked up to see the Coopers exchanging a meaningful glance. April grabbed Archie's shoulder and pointed him towards the coffee van, making a hasty retreat. 'You don't need to give everybody every piece of information you have, Archie,' she said, regretting her sharp tone when she saw his face fall. She joined the line and tried again, more gently this time. 'Connor's background isn't anyone else's business but his own, mate.'

'But he is really good at lots of things,' Archie insisted. 'If he was my age, we'd be best mates, I just know it.' April nodded, smoothing Archie's collar. Hers wouldn't be the only broken heart when Connor returned to England.

At the front of the line, April ordered a coffee for herself and a hot chocolate for Archie. 'Extra marshmallows, please Jean,' she said, hoping Archie would respond to the olive branch.

'No Connor tonight, then?' Jean asked.

April looked at Archie, willing him to stay silent. To his credit, Archie made a discreet zipping-his-lips gesture and stepped up to the counter.

'Hey Jean, look what I got from the lucky dip,' said Archie, twisting the Rubik's cube this way and that. Jean smiled at him, frothing the milk, then turned her curious gaze to April.

'Now you know I don't like meddling, April,' said Jean. April gritted her teeth, knowing those lines always preceded unwanted advice. 'But I've heard some whispers about an extra guest at the golf course house and I don't want you to be the last to know.'

If only I was bold enough to give Jean the same lecture I just gave Archie.

'It's fine, Jean, I'm well aware of the situation. It's all good.' April feigned a brightness she didn't feel.

'I've known you since you were in nappies, pet, and I'd hate to see you get hurt, that's all.'

Too late for that.

Jean handed over the coffee. 'Now, if you stick around a minute, I'll introduce you to my great-nephew, Jack. He's just moved back to town, lovely lad and he's easy on the eye too. A better fit than Connor, I suspect.'

April took the coffee and held out her hand for the hot chocolate. 'Sorry, we've got to dash.'

'Oh, there he is. Yoo-hoo, Jack.'

Eager to escape Jean's radar and slink away as quickly as possible, April mumbled an apologetic 'sorry' to the bloke striding towards Jean's coffee van with a crate full of milk and walked away as fast as she could. Going through the motions would only encourage Jean further. Besides, her heart was already in tatters.

'Wait, April,' said Archie, trotting to keep pace with her.

She slowed, but only a little, determined to find a fireworks vantage point without a Penwarra local within eyesight.

'Just me again, April . . .' Connor paused, the phone still at his ear as he looked at the ingredients spread across the kitchen bench in front of him. 'I guess you're on your way to Beachport now. Tell Archie to make a wish on the biggest firework for me. Sorry again, I really wish I was there with you both and I do want to talk. Anytime you're ready, I'll be here.'

He set down the phone, gave the bench one last spritz of antibacterial spray and set to work.

Nina Simone crooned in his headphones as he silently separated eggs, whisked milk and measured caster sugar until the custard was glop, glop, glopping on the stovetop. The cooking implements Fergus had acquired in the last few months, mostly from the church op shop that April was so fond of, weren't as fancy as the tools Geraldine kept in her commercial kitchen, nor were they all matching like the ones April had recently invested in, but they did the trick. The custard was almost at the Vaseline-like thickness Geraldine had told them to watch out for. He retrieved the puff pastry from the freezer, sandwiched the squares between sheets of baking paper and placed a second baking tray on top. He'd just slid the pastry into the oven when he smelled burning.

Connor turned back to the stove quickly, but when he lifted the wooden spoon, he saw the bottom of the custard was well and truly scorched.

'Sod it!' He looked at the mixture, then back at the pastry in the oven. 'Maybe I can salvage the top half of the custard, and the vanilla slice will just be smaller . . .' But a quick taste confirmed the scorched aroma that now filled the kitchen was infused through the custard too.

Taking the mess outside and scraping it onto the grass where the birds could eat it, Connor washed up and started again.

He watched the custard with an eagle eye this time, remembering to remove it from the heat once the consistency was perfect. He set it aside to cool and checked on Phoebe.

Even though she was asleep, she still looked unwell and her face was pale against the navy sheets. He returned to the kitchen and opened the windows, letting the breeze chase the burnt smell away, then checked the pastry. Just like Geraldine had told them, the weight of the top baking tray stopped the pastry from puffing up.

'Bang on,' he said to himself as he assembled the slice, then drizzled it with icing and started on the clean-up.

Finding a container of vanilla slice in her fridge with an apology note on top mightn't make up for upsetting April or missing their first New Year's together, but he hoped it would make her smile when she got home.

He was stopped for a breathalyser in the main street on his way through Penwarra.

'Big night tonight?' the young constable asked.

He gestured to the plastic container on the passenger seat. 'Never thought I'd say this, but I've spent the evening baking.'

'You're pulling my leg,' she laughed, hooting even louder when Connor lifted the lid to showcase the neat, glossy slices with their creamy filling. 'That's not something we see very often on New Year's, especially from your age demographic. Keep up the good work.'

The smile was still on Connor's face when he turned at Lacewing Estate, but it vanished when he realised there were more lights than normal on at Kookaburra Cottage. And not just lights, but people.

'What the hell?'

Not only was there a bonfire roaring in front of the stables where guests normally parked their cars, but there were dozens—no, maybe a hundred—people swarming around the cottage and through the vines.

🐨

'Wow! Look at that one,' said Archie, scrambling to his feet and nearly upending the picnic basket in the process. Even though he'd already snapped dozens of photos on Daniel's old iPhone, he pointed the camera to the sky once again and tried to capture the fireworks.

'There's got to be a show-winning shot in there, surely,' he said, collapsing back onto the rug with an indefatigable grin on his face. 'My phone's full now, so I guess it's too bad if I didn't get a good one.' He shuffled closer, resting his head on her shoulder. 'I thought fireworks made everyone happy, April. Don't you like them?'

She gestured at the fairy floss wrappers, crumpled donut bag and empty coffee cups. 'Sugar coma,' she said, hoping he'd buy the explanation.

Archie pulled back, studying her. 'If it makes you feel any better, I wish Connor was here too. I know I'm just a kid, but I think he likes you heaps better than Phoebe. For one thing, she squealed when the lambs came close, making them even more skittish, and she doesn't make him laugh like you do. I'm gonna tell him that next time I see him, too.'

April was touched by his comments. 'You're a trooper, Archie-boy. But don't you worry about all that stuff, okay mate? Hey, check out that one!'

He looked at the firework crackling and fizzing over the ocean, but she could see his mind was still churning over the issue. 'What do you say we get one more jam donut on the way out? And I'll get a photo of you with the fireworks in the background, so you can show your folks tomorrow.'

She pulled her phone out, her breath catching at the sight of more missed calls from Connor.

Tomorrow. I'll deal with it tomorrow, she told herself, minimising the notifications and opening her camera app.

'Who the hell's in charge around here?' Connor wanted a megaphone so he could yell over the horrid clash of music. He hadn't got any sense out of the first group he'd passed on the way in, but as he strode through the crowd towards the stables, three things were instantly, sickeningly clear.

Most of the kids were underage, their faces covered in acne and poorly-applied make-up; there was alcohol everywhere, and some of the kids were too drunk to even try to hide it; and finally, they were trashing the place.

There were countless clusters of teenagers, each little group with their own portable speaker, so it was like walking through a mosh pit. Some of the kids were as young as Pippin, many in clinches that could hardly be considered consenting given their age and inebriation, and those who weren't pashing or drinking were glued to phone screens.

I can deal with this, Connor told himself. *They're just kids, really, who need to be sent on their way.* He cringed at the sight of a throng of teenage boys standing in the middle of April's herb garden, with no regard for the rows of perfectly weeded and mulched plants underfoot as they watched a brawny lad chugging beer from his shoe.

'Shoey, shoey, shoey!' chanted the group, hollering with laughter as the lad finished and stumbled, his T-shirt catching on the roses.

'Serves you right, you bloody idiot,' Connor muttered as the young man got too close to the rose thorns. 'Get off the garden, you lot,' he said, flapping his hands. But the laughter petered out and when they turned, indignant that someone dare tell them what to do, Connor saw they were just as tall as he was. His skills in piano-playing, winemaking and baking were useless in the face of drunk, testosterone-heavy young men.

'Whaddaya say? *This* garden?' The tallest boy, who had a barrel chest and arms twice as thick as Connor's had ever been, lifted a foot and stomped on the coriander, then kicked at a tuft of parsley until it flew through the air.

Connor took a sharp breath and walked away. He pulled his phone from his pocket.

April's phone rang out and he looked over to the winery. More cars were pulling in off the highway. He needed to stop this, now.

He tried April again, then dialled Heidi's number. 'Heids, thank God.' He quickly explained the situation.

'Gatecrashers,' she said. 'Kids have a party, their friends see it on SnapMaps, and the gatecrashers start rolling in. Why did April rent it to an underage kid on New Year's Eve anyway?'

Connor explained how the New Year's booking had come through the moment the cottage accommodation site went live. 'April's not that daft. It was booked by an old couple, they had a milestone anniversary to celebrate, the husband was surprising his wife.' He surveyed the mass of people. 'Bollocks! Where are they in this crowd?'

Heidi gave a grim laugh. 'I bet you twenty quid it was a bogus booking. Happens all the time. You need to pull the power. And call the guards, obviously.'

'I don't know their number,' he said, 'I've never needed to call the Australian police until now.' Heidi searched for the number as Connor walked around the stables, trying to remember which side the meter box was on.

'Oh shit, they've started another fire,' said Connor, panic setting in as he spotted a small bonfire.

'Very original,' said Heidi. 'Wait, you'd best check inside first and warn them you're turning the power off.'

'Do they deserve warning?' Connor couldn't believe the suggestion. 'They're ruining the place by the second!'

'I know,' Heidi said, her calmness infuriating. 'But it's two storeys, right? If someone breaks their neck on the staircase in the dark, you'll have a lawsuit on your hands.'

Connor was grateful for her advice, feeling even more useless as a wave of teens walked towards the bonfire.

'No!'

One of the boys had an armful of garden fencing that April, Archie and Connor had spent hours making from twigs and vines, the other had the sawhorses that April had repurposed as the base of an outdoor table.

He called the police station, giving details to a polite but evidently busy officer. 'They've just packed up the breatho station and they're out at a car accident but I'm sure they'll be there as soon as they can. I've got your details, the complaint's lodged, just sit tight.'

Sit tight? Connor jogged to the front door, determined to clear out the B & B so he could lock the door and protect the building, if not the surrounds. Much longer and they'd probably start heaping stools and coffee tables onto the bonfire.

The sight inside didn't instil him with hope. 'Oh, Jesus.' Connor swore at the plastic cups, bottles of spirits, chips, backpacks and jackets strewn across the floorboards, the fug of cigarette smoke hovering around the group on the couch.

'You need to go home,' he said, pulling the television cord out at the wall. 'The police are on their way,' he said it as firmly but calmly as possible, when really he wanted to roar. The mention of the police had the desired effect, and it was only when they were off the couch that he saw a spray of bright red wine across the cream couch. A half-empty bottle sat beside the wood burner. The sparkling shiraz April left out for guests.

It'll break her heart to see this, he thought, his head spinning as he took the stairs two at a time, finding a couple in the bed.

'Get dressed and get out,' he yelled, throwing clothes in their direction and waiting at the bottom of the steps.

The young pair at least had the good grace to look sheepish as they scampered out of the room.

Whoever they were, Connor was pretty confident they weren't Mr and Mrs Henderson on their ruby wedding anniversary.

Connor closed his eyes a beat, resisting the urge to clean up, and did a quick check of the bathroom, finding cigarette butts in the sink, a pot plant upended in the bathtub and God knows what on the floor. With a silent prayer that they'd be able to get the stink out later, he locked the heavy oak doors behind him.

'Wait, what? I need to pee,' giggled a girl, knocking on the front door even though she'd just watched him lock it. 'Helloooo? Anyone inside? Can you open the door?'

Connor bit back a reply and strode to the side of the stables, gripping his phone torch between his teeth as he opened the fuse box and shut off the power. The outdoor lights spluttered out but the music continued.

If he hadn't been standing there, racking his brains for the next best course of action, Connor might have missed the low diesel hum over the noise pumping from the portable speakers. And in the dim night, it took him a while to understand what the slow hulking shape rumbling out of the lean-to was.

The sound suddenly made sense. Dread and anger circled in his stomach as the Lacey's little Fergie tractor puttered along the laneway.

Connor took off at a sprint. The drink driver ploughing into the winery or the vines was small fry compared to the potential damage they could do if they clipped someone in the crowd. And in the darkness, without headlights or seatbelts, he couldn't fathom them reaching the highway, especially since cars kept pausing and ejecting more and more teenagers.

'Stop the tractor! Get off,' Connor panted when he finally drew level with the driver. The lad had a John Deere hat on, which may have instilled a little bit of hope in Connor, had it not been for the fact he had a tinnie in one hand and a girl sitting on his lap.

'For fuck's sake. Pull UP!'

Connor looked ahead, trying not to panic, as another boy loped towards them, hooting with amusement. He kept pace with the tractor, and for a moment, Connor thought he was there to talk some sense into the driver. Instead, he ran in front and clumsily vaulted into the bucket.

'Legend!'

'Sick as, Simmo.'

Legend? One misstep and the kid would have been flat as a pancake, thought Connor, too gobsmacked to process the repercussions. By now, they had a parade of followers.

'Make him stop the bloody tractor,' Connor yelled, appealing to the girl on the driver's lap, who had started to look a little uncertain. 'If he's stupid enough to ruin his own life, tell him to go right ahead, but he'll kill three people at this rate.'

He felt desperate now as they neared the road, and when they reached the stone entrance, Connor found himself cut off. Short of jumping over the rock wall he'd built with April and Archie, he'd have to chase around it, and by then he'd be too late.

22

April's heartbeat sped up as they approached the winery. Why were there blue and red flashing lights and a convoy of cars crawling past Lacewing Estate at a snail's pace, everyone intent on rubbernecking despite the late hour?

'Oh no!' she murmured. Had someone veered off the highway and had an accident? A break-in at Lacewing Estate? Her first thought was for the guests celebrating their fortieth wedding anniversary tonight, and although she knew it was selfish, she hoped the misdemeanour hadn't disturbed the happy couple in Kookaburra Cottage.

Archie stirred in the backseat as she pulled up beside the police wagon.

'What's happened?' April asked, jumping out of the ute.

The officer turned his torch on her, and after clarifying she was the owner, gave a grimace. 'We've been trying to call you,' he said. April's mind flashed to the phone in the glove box, the battery dead from Archie filming the last of the fireworks. 'Were you aware of this party?'

April shook her head. 'The long lunch isn't until tomorrow and I wouldn't call it a party really, more fine dining.'

'There's been an underage party here,' the policeman clarified. 'At your B & B.'

Her eyes darted around the property. She'd been so fixated on the flashing lights that she hadn't noticed the beer cans and premix bottles littering the laneway.

The rock fence.

Behind the police car, she could see half the rocks were scattered around like discarded Lego blocks. Her hands flew to her mouth. 'What the . . .? But I have guests tonight. It's their wedding anniversary, they're not teenagers.'

'A false booking, we suspect. Underage gatecrashers, alcohol and the biggest night of the year.' He shook his head and handed her a business card. 'Bad combo, I'm afraid. It's lucky no one was seriously hurt. Get in touch with the station tomorrow, your insurance company will want a copy of our report.'

April rushed towards the stables. Was that a bonfire? A moan slipped from her mouth. She quickened her pace and was halfway there when the officer called her back.

'Miss, you've left a sleeping child in your car. I'd recommend getting him to bed and dealing with this later.'

Archie.

Fighting back tears, she nodded, swiping her fringe from her eyes with trembling hands and returning to the ute.

It was a struggle to drive past the glowing embers in the stables car park and continue on to the Winklins' house. Rousing Archie was like trying to wake the dead. She hadn't even checked if Felicity and Rupert were home or considered whether she was supposed to wait with Archie until they returned, when headlights flashed in the driveway.

'You had one hell of a party, by the looks of things,' Rupert laughed, stepping out of his car. 'I thought you and Archie were heading to Beachport?'

'We did,' April said weakly, then watched her neighbour's amusement turn to shock as she explained what had happened.

Felicity put her hand on April's arm. 'Oh, how terrible. How bad's the damage?'

April looked across the laneway, resisting the urge to bury her head in her hands. 'I don't know,' she said, 'but I'm about to find out.'

'I'll come with you,' said Rupert, his voice steely. 'Just in case anyone's left.'

A string of swear words erupted from April's mouth when she saw the trampled gardens, the snapped standard roses and the dining table chairs she'd sanded back and oiled to perfection lying haphazardly on the lawn. But it was nothing compared to the inside. April's knees buckled when she saw the damage and then Rupert's arm was around her waist, keeping her upright.

'Upsy-daisy, that's a girl, it'll be okay,' he said, pulling out a stool.

For some strange reason, she found herself laughing at the old-fashioned term, and as she surveyed the wine splatters on the couch and more on the walls, the broken glass in front of her, another laugh came, then another, before tears began pouring from her eyes.

'My cottage,' she said, sobs coming now in earnest.

'April!' Through her tears, April saw Connor in the doorway, dirtier and more rumpled than she'd ever seen him, and her body ached for the comfort of his arms.

The double whammy hit her then.

Connor and Phoebe together.

Her bed and breakfast ruined.

Was there anything more that could be taken from her tonight?

She sagged against the counter.

'I've been trying to call you,' he said, his face stricken. 'Are you okay?'

She shook her head, weeping silently now.

Connor swept a hand through his hair wearily. 'I'm so sorry. It was a nightmare here. I did what I could to help the police shut it down. And I've finally got onto Daniel, he said we could move tomorrow's long lunch to Winklins' instead if you think that'll work. Obviously, only if that's okay with you, Rupert?'

Rupert nodded. The breath left April's lungs in a rush. The New Year's Day event . . . How could she get everything in order for the long lunch? Not only that, how on earth was the executive from DestinationSA going to stay at the B & B when it looked like this?

Connor started towards April, wanting to comfort her, but despite the shock, despite the agony of seeing months of hard work sullied in several short hours, she turned away from him.

She doesn't want you. She can't even bear to look at you.

Just as much as he wanted to clear up the mess, he wanted to sweep her into his arms and reassure her they'd fix it, together—but she stiffened at his touch and strode away from him across the room.

'We can get it fixed, April,' Connor said. 'I've already been to your house and collected the cleaning stuff. That'll be the easy part after the effort it took to disperse the crowd.'

And it had been quite a task. Over a hundred teenagers intent on partying hadn't left quietly. Although the rock wall entrance to Lacewing Estate had been collateral, there had been an upside of the collision; when the joyriders clipped the stone wall with the corner of the tractor bucket, the cheering had turned to screaming. This, combined with the yelling from the idiot hitching a ride inside the bucket, had cut through the night and lured the mob away from the stables.

'I don't even know if we can fix this ...' April's voice cracked and Connor felt her pain as she swiped at her eyes. 'I appreciate you shutting the party down, Connor, and you coming across with me, Rupert, but this is my problem. I'll take care of it from here.' She gulped, tears streaming down her face, as she surveyed the damage.

'Or I'll just cancel everything in the morning,' she said, burying her head in her hands. And without a backwards glance, she pushed past Connor and slipped out into the night.

'April!'

An owl hooted from a gum tree and he heard the lambs across the laneway calling, but there was no response from April.

'Are you going to lock up? Suppose there's not much more damage that can be done,' said Rupert, with a wistful glance around the room.

Connor ducked outside to collect the cleaning supplies and shook his head. 'There's a chance we can fix this, and I'm not leaving until I've had a crack.'

And to his surprise, Rupert rolled up his white shirtsleeves and gave a nod. 'I'll give you a hand for a bit,' he said, taking the roll of garbage bags from Connor's hand.

Connor wasn't sure when Rupert switched the music on, but somewhere between scrubbing wine off the wall and stripping the bedsheets, the sound of Chopin's 'Piano Concerto No. 2 in F minor' floated up to the mezzanine.

'Been years since I've tried to get wine out of a couch—not my forte, I'm afraid,' said Rupert, tossing a scarlet-soaked rag in the bucket. He eyed the cracked picture frame Connor was carrying downstairs. 'Is that an old map of the region?'

'I gave it to April for Christmas,' Connor sighed, 'so it's spent less than a week hanging on the walls.'

'At least the print isn't damaged, just needs new glass,' said Rupert. He picked up his phone and wished Connor good luck, before heading home for the night. Connor sat the artwork by the oak doors and tried not to draw parallels between the shattered glass and the state of his relationship with April.

Ten minutes later, as Connor was continuing to right the bedroom, April returned to the stables wearing her gardening clothes, with an armful of extra supplies and two mugs of coffee.

He could deduce that April was still angry with him from the one-word answers, and her stout refusal to discuss their relationship, but there was something in the way she refused to look at him that made him fear she'd finally realised he wasn't worthy of her love.

If she won't let me tell her, I'll show her, thought Connor, scrubbing and cleaning into the wee hours.

The worst of the mess had been cleared by the time April collapsed onto the couch four hours later.

'That's it, I'm done,' she said, her voice husky with tiredness.

'You can barely keep your eyes open,' he said gently. 'You should sleep.'

She shook her head weakly, her eyelids fluttering closed before she snapped them open, fighting fiercely to stay awake. 'I've got to fix this, it's my B & B, I'll take care of it myself.'

Connor knew he was taking a gamble, but when he reached for her hands, this time she didn't push him away.

'I don't even have the strength to walk home,' she moaned, a yawn shuddering through her body. Up close, he could see how bloodshot her eyes were. He would have carried her there if she'd let him. 'I'll drive you to the cottage,' he said, talking over her protests. 'Have a power nap, I'll set an alarm and we can get back to work early.'

Common sense prevailed and she let him take her home. She stumbled as she kicked off her shoes at the cottage, but Connor caught her arm and gently righted her. She shuffled to the bedroom, then turned.

'Are you coming in?'

'I've got a little left in the tank, I'll keep going.'

'Don't forget to set the alarm,' she said, her voice thick with tiredness. 'And Connor?'

His breath caught in his chest. 'Yeah?'

'Thank you.'

Those two words kept Connor powering on until his eyes wouldn't stay open any longer. It felt like the entire Lord of the Dance troupe was tapdancing on his brain when he woke an hour or so later on the wine-stained couch. He blinked against a bright light, trying to establish why the ceiling light was strobing in his vision when he'd only sat down to rest for a moment.

Thankfully the teens had been too intent on their alcohol to fuss with coffee, and Connor heaped spoonfuls of coffee into a mug as the magpies heralded in the new day, and the new year.

The shrill ring of the phone came when he was draining his third cup of instant.

'Happy New Year's buddy, need anything from the Mount before we head back?'

Connor quickly filled Fergus in on the situation. Lauren jumped onto speaker phone with suggestions and when they ended the call, Connor felt a little better, knowing reinforcements were on their way.

The pot plant was soon back in its rightful spot in the window of the bathroom, and the tiles shone under the influence of a soapy mop.

At least one room is square again.

He looked out the window for signs of life at the winemaker's cottage, but the curtains were still drawn. April needed all the sleep she could get. Although he was tired, Connor was certain he could weather it better than April and silenced his alarm without waking her.

Another hour will do her the world of good.

'My twig fence!'

Connor heard Archie before he spotted him at the foot of the herb garden, a basket of linen in his arms, and went to greet him. The boy looked horrified by the trampled garden.

'I know, buddy, things got a bit out of hand here,' Connor said, taking the basket.

Archie fixed Connor with a doubtful look. 'You don't look so good either.'

Connor had caught a glimpse of his bloodshot eyes and dark circles when he'd washed his face earlier, and knew Archie's assessment was an understatement.

'I've had better days, but we could do with another set of muscles, and I reckon you fit the bill.'

Archie beamed.

'Nice jumper, by the way.'

The football guernsey almost came to Archie's knees, but it was a vast improvement on the faded red, blue and yellow singlet he normally wore.

'Thanks,' said Archie. 'Dad got it for me for Christmas, and he said I can use the old one for next year's scarecrow competition. I can have twin scarecrows!'

Connor smiled wearily. 'I can't wait to see them, mate.'

Rupert rounded the corner with a takeaway coffee and familiar brown bags from the Penwarra Bakery. Connor gratefully accepted the sustenance.

'Daniel's on his way back from the city,' said Rupert. 'And Felicity sends her apologies, she's a bit under the weather from the cocktail party last night. She's packed supplies, though—there're enough throw rugs in our house to sink a ship,' Rupert said, gesturing to Archie's basket. 'So there should be something in there to hide the wine stain. And she's got spare quilts and pillows on standby if needed.'

Connor wasn't quite sure how word had spread so quickly, but within the hour, a handful of locals had materialised to help whip the place into shape.

Jean set up her mobile coffee van behind the bed and breakfast. Daniel used the tractor to clear all traces of the bonfire. Archie worked alongside Rupert on the damaged entryway, showing his dad how to select just the right rocks for just the right spot, and Fergus and Lauren arrived at 10 am with Phoebe in tow.

'What can we do?' Fergus said.

Connor gave them instructions, barely able to contain a yawn. 'But only if you're sure you're okay? You guys have been flying all night, and Phoebe, are you sure you should be here?'

'By the looks of things, we got a lot more sleep than you, mate,' said Fergus, giving him a critical up and down. 'You should have a kip.'

'And I woke up fine, Con,' said Phoebe. 'Migraine all gone, thank God. I'll get started.' Phoebe followed Fergus to the overflowing rubbish bins.

Lauren looked over to the winemaker's cottage and then back to Connor. 'April still asleep? She'll be ropable if she knows we're all working and she's not.'

Connor ran his fingertips along his eyebrows, massaging his eyes. 'She's shattered,' he said eventually. 'I think I messed things up and I don't want to double down on it by pushing her.'

Lauren rested a hand on his arm, frowning. 'You love her though, right? No bullshit, no caveats or clauses?'

Caveats or clauses? Connor nodded, puzzled. 'I do.'

'I'm sure it's just a mix up, but last time we spoke she said something about Phoebe and chopsticks. Fergus has sworn black and blue you wouldn't, but if you're dicking her around, I want to know now, Connor. Before I march in there and talk some sense into my hard-headed friend.'

Chopsticks? Connor's stomach sank when he realised April must have seen him and Phoebe playing the piano together. 'But that wasn't . . .' Another yawn slipped out. It was getting harder and harder to string a sentence together. He shook his head, trying to unfog his sleep-deprived brain.

Lauren patted his arm. 'You know what, we're both going to the winemaker's cottage and you are going to get an hour's shut-eye, minimum. Whatever's going on with April, she's not going to want you trashing yourself.'

'But—'

Lauren cut him off. 'You've done an amazing job, Connor, look around you.'

He turned to see the rising sun casting long shadows across the grass, the place almost back to square and their friends working together.

'I don't know exactly how bad it was last night, but I can tell you've spent nearly every waking hour between now and then trying to fix it,' she added gently.

Connor looked at his watch. The event hire van would be pulling into the driveway in an hour and a half, the lunch guests were due at midday and he needed to be on the ball when they arrived. April, Lloyd, Fran and Lacewing were depending on him.

'Okay,' he conceded. 'Just one hour.'

April woke to Mishka's paw on the blankets, accompanied by a whine indicating she was overdue for the toilet. Memories of last night came rushing back, followed by a flood of heartache at Connor's betrayal.

All those months of hard work, all those years of dreaming about the B & B. And the loss of the future she'd been so excited about just a few days earlier.

'Oh, Mish, everything's ruined,' she moaned, dragging her broken heart out of bed.

Her hands hovered on the curtain cord, delaying the moment she'd have to face the music. She had to call the DestinationSA crew to cancel the event, or beg them to switch venues to Winklin Wines. It was harder to know which was worse—cancelling altogether or imposing on their neighbours at such late notice. Plus one look at the Winklins' shiny tasting room and they might never book another event at Lacewing Estate again . . .

What a horrid, horrid start to the new year.

April was staring at the lounge room curtains, gathering her courage, when there was a knock on the door. Lauren barged in before she had time to answer.

'Good, you're up,' Lauren said, a sympathetic look on her face as she drew April into a hug. 'Now get in that shower, we've got a long lunch to host.'

April shook her head. 'I can't, it's a wreck. Didn't you see it on the way in? The fence is ruined, the stables are trashed. It's a nightmare.' Ignoring the tears that sprang to her eyes, she swallowed the lump in her throat, gesturing to the phone plugged in on the kitchen bench. 'I need to call everyone and cancel.'

Lauren shook her head and stepped aside. April's heart flipped at the sight of Connor behind her, the ache turning to concern at the sight of him. He looked every bit as bad as she felt. Maybe even worse.

'Your fabulously talented Mr Fixit here has been working through the night and he's dead on his feet, so we need a change of guard. Hop in the shower and I'll find you clothes while this guy takes a power nap.'

Lauren marched into the bathroom and April could hear her turning on the shower, but she couldn't look away from Connor.

'Did you really—?'

'I'm sorry—'

They spoke at once, then stopped. Connor's sad smile was overtaken by a yawn, and even in his tired state, she felt the tiniest seed of hope sprout in her chest.

'It's not completely ruined?'

He shook his head and was about to say more when Lauren bustled back into the lounge room, steering April by the shoulders to the steamy bathroom. 'You in here and you in there, Connor,' she said, pointing to the bedroom. 'I've got a good feeling there'll be plenty of time for talking later. I'll see you back at Kookaburra Cottage in an hour.'

A soft snoring came from the bedroom when April emerged from the shower and she couldn't resist peering through the door. Connor hadn't even undressed or climbed under the covers before falling asleep.

Lying on her side of the bed, one hand curled under her pillow, the other holding a handful of blanket, he looked as handsome and vulnerable as ever. His fair hair was tousled, his clothes rumpled like her unmade bed, and she knew if she traced a fingertip along his jaw, the bristles would rasp against her skin. She pulled a knitted blanket over his body and let him sleep.

Had he really worked through the night? It felt like too much to hope that he'd really fixed the chaos, but stepping outside, she discovered he had indeed pulled off a small miracle.

Fergus was upending a mop bucket on the lawn, and Rupert and Archie were hard at work on the rock wall. Lauren had her hands around a rake, smoothing out new mulch from the look of things, and Phoebe ... even Phoebe was carting garbage bags of rubbish to Fergus's ute.

April felt more ashamed than ever. She'd thrown her hands into the air and given up, and everyone else had soldiered on in her absence.

Where do I start? she wondered. Adapting Fran's adage about tackling the hardest task first, she sought out Phoebe by Fergus's ute.

'Thanks for helping.'

'It's the least I can do,' Phoebe said. 'I'm useless when a migraine hits, like last night, but it's gone now, thankfully. Connor was an angel; I'd still be in the foetal position if he hadn't dropped around with supplies.'

Phoebe and Connor. Coming between them was like trying to defy gravity. April studied the rock wall in the distance, trying to find joy in the way the sunshine gave the paddock rock a honey tone.

At least I have my friends, the stables, the vines and my family. Somehow, I'll just have to make them enough.

She took a shaky breath, so desperate for coffee that she began to imagine the scent of it on the breeze. 'I'm sure you'll be happy with Connor's new-found cooking skills, too,' April said softly.

Phoebe stared at her for a long while, then turned to look towards the stables. 'I've booked my ticket home.'

April exhaled slowly. She'd accepted that she couldn't stand in their way any longer, but she hadn't prepared herself for Connor leaving already. Maybe it was better this way, like ripping off a Bandaid instead of a slow, painful goodbye.

Determined to cling to some dignity, April forced a smile. 'So when are you leaving?'

'Tonight, if you don't mind me stealing Connor for one last errand? I'll fly out from Mount Gambier.'

One last errand? 'But ...' April said carefully. 'When's Connor leaving?'

'He's not,' Phoebe said, puzzlement crossing her elegant features.

April looked at her in disbelief. 'He's staying and you're going?' She didn't care that she sounded like an imbecile, April was done with assumptions. 'Connor's staying in Penwarra?'

Phoebe nodded. 'As far as I know. He loves it here.' Her eyes returned to the ute-load of rubbish. 'I shouldn't have come. I knew he was falling for you and I panicked. I haven't seen him care about anyone as much as you. He loves you, April, and ...' She gulped, her words stiff. 'I knew that and I came anyway. I'm sorry.'

Could it really be true? It was too much to hope for, and yet ... April shook her head, still speechless. Phoebe didn't look like she was lying.

Mishka bounded around the corner, her wriggly excitement breaking the tension.

'I'm not really a dog person, but she's like sunshine with fur, isn't she?' said Phoebe, bending down to give Mishka a pat. 'I'd better keep going with these dustbins, Connor said you've got guests coming soon? The coffee van's just packing up, if you need caffeine.'

April gave Phoebe a stunned smile, then followed her nose around the back of the stables to find Jean's retro coffee van with its pink and white duco.

Jean unlocked the awning and opened it again when she saw April approaching. 'I thought I'd fed and watered everyone but you sure look like you could do with an extra strong one. Must have been a shock coming home to that last night?'

April nodded, still processing Phoebe's words. Jean studied her as she ground the coffee beans. 'And I think I owe you an apology.'

There was something unnerving about Jean offering an apology. In all the years April had known her, she'd thrown in her oar without waiting to be asked for advice, matched couples that didn't even know they were looking for love, and doled out well-intended but sometimes unsubtle hints with every cup of coffee she sold, just like last night.

'Righto . . .?'

'I may have been hasty about Connor. After seeing how that last bloke knocked your confidence, I thought someone outside the wine industry would be a safer bet. But when Connor called this morning at the crack of dawn and asked me to come down, I realised maybe he was the right one all along. I've been watching him work his little butt off for this place. He's no fly-by-nighter, that's for sure. And it turns out, sometimes I get things wrong.'

April took the coffee, willing the hot brew to clear her racing thoughts. Could it really be that simple?

The alarm felt like it had been set for five minutes, not sixty. Connor fumbled with his watch until it stopped chiming, then buried his head in the pillow a moment longer, taking in the familiar fragrance of cherries and wild plum.

When he opened his eyes, he noticed he was huddled on April's side of the bed, covered in the soft blanket that normally lived on the couch. The events of the last forty-eight hours came rushing back to him and Connor staggered to his feet. He needed coffee and food, fast, if he was going to make it through the rest of the day.

The vanilla slice was untouched in the fridge, exactly where he'd left it last night, and he ate a banana while making a coffee on April's espresso machine. After a splash of cold water on his face, a spray of deodorant and a quick once-over with his toothbrush, he felt a little more human.

He found everyone outside helping Rupert and Archie with the stone wall. They'd made great progress in the hour since he'd last seen it, but even with the extra helpers, he could see they wouldn't have it finished in time.

'Big job,' said Lauren, stopping for a swig of water. She passed the water bottle to Fergus, who took a long drink and then tipped the rest over his head.

'It took us weeks to build,' said Archie. 'We're never gonna have it fixed before the lunch guests get here.'

As if to prove the point, the event hire truck turned into the driveway. 'Where am I setting this up?' the driver asked through his open window. He was followed by a small grey Tesla, and Connor recognised the event planner, Luke.

Luke's jaw dropped as he climbed out of the car and looked around.

April dusted off her hands, and, sensing her hesitation, Connor walked across to join her. 'It'll be alright,' he said, reaching for her hand and feeling relieved when she took it. 'The B & B is back in order, we've almost got the exterior sorted, and if all else fails, I've got a backup plan. Can you trust me? Please?'

He gave her hand a gentle squeeze, and although her response was only a fraction more pressure, he took comfort in the fact she hadn't shied away from his touch like the previous night. He watched her give instructions to the delivery driver, noticing the way she'd pulled herself together in such a short space of time, and then explain the situation to the event planner.

'I think,' Connor said softly, when the truckie was busy unloading chairs and Luke went to fetch his supplies, 'we need to talk.'

April grimaced, her eyes searching his. 'We don't have enough time to cover all the ground we've hopped, skipped and jumped over in the last few days. I really appreciate everything you've done, Connor, and I've been doing a lot of thinking . . .'

She trailed off and he could hear the 'but' coming. If they'd still been holding hands, she would have felt his palms go clammy.

'I'm not sure we can make this work, Connor. You've got a whole life back in England, a family that will only miss you more as time goes on, and then there's Phoebe. It's been playing on my mind for a while now. We're kidding ourselves if we think we can gloss over that.'

Her words were so final, so thought out. And from the set of her jaw, he could see she hadn't made the decision lightly.

'C'mon you two, we could do with a hand over here,' called Fergus, frowning. And while he didn't miss the elbow in the ribs Fergus got from Lauren, Connor was somewhat relieved the Scotsman had saved him from embarrassing himself any further in front of them all.

April turned back to the delivery driver, and Connor kept his eyes on the dusty car park as he returned to the rock pile, woodenly passing the paddock rocks to Archie and Rupert.

'I hate to say it mate,' Fergus murmured under his breath. 'But you looked like a stunned mullet over there. Maybe get some more sleep before you go in for another deep and meaningful, or come up with a game plan in advance.'

'I'm all out of game plans,' Connor admitted, feeling at a loss for a way forward. He saw the winery windows winding open, one by one, as April moved around inside, airing the place out. From the depths of the cellar, he caught the strains of classical music and a kernel of a last-ditch attempt to help smooth things over came to mind.

'Archie, you're right about the stone fence. We're not going to get it done in time, but maybe we can divert the guests' attention instead.'

His words coming out in a rush, Connor explained his idea to Rupert, then headed towards Fergus's ute with Archie.

Phoebe caught up with them just before they left. 'Can I hitch a ride back to the golf course?' she asked, slipping into the backseat. 'I've got a bit of packing and cleaning to do before I go. Still okay for a lift later, Con?'

Connor nodded, though he had no idea how he'd stay awake for the drive to Mount Gambier.

'Are you going home for good, Phoebe?' Archie asked, turning in his seat as they drove along the Riddoch Highway.

She laughed. 'I think you'd get along just fine with Nell and Pippin, as subtle as a sledgehammer. But, yes, my time here is up. Too much sunshine around here anyway,' she said, catching Connor's eye in the rear-view mirror.

Connor smiled back tiredly. He wasn't sure what the future held with April, but he knew without a doubt that he'd turned the final page in this chapter with Phoebe.

He paused at the rental long enough to fish out his suit from the back of the wardrobe and with a quick wave to Phoebe, they headed up the highway to the Winklins', where Archie raced inside to find the electric piano.

'Hurry up, Con, we still need to set it all up,' Archie panted when they were back in the ute.

Fergus and Lauren had been busy in their absence, with the worst of the rock wall damage shielded by banners advertising

Lacewing Estate, Winklin Wines and the Beesley Brothers winery Fergus worked at.

'Where shall we put it, Arch?'

The young boy looked at the parking area he'd helped Connor and April revitalise, pointing to a spot on the new paving, between the rose garden and the dinner-plate dahlias. 'There,' Archie said, setting down the stool, dragging across an extension cord and helping Connor settle the instrument into just the right place.

Connor heard a car slowing on the highway and pressed the power button on the electric piano. He tapped the keys tentatively as the BMW rolled into the entryway.

Get it over and done with, he told himself. *The first few songs will be the hardest.*

Connor's mouth felt dry and he had to force his shoulders down and back.

He ran an unsteady hand down his white shirt. A lot of water had passed under the bridge between his last public performance and now, but he had the muscle memory, he had the skill, he just needed the confidence.

Let's do this.

The music felt jerky at first, the pressure growing as his audience increased.

'It's working, Con,' Archie whispered, turning the sheet music for Connor as he continued to the next piece. 'Keep going.'

And just as he'd hoped, the guests arriving for the long lunch gravitated to the piano instead of stopping to admire the rock wall and noticing its imperfections. Ladies in strappy dresses, shawls and heels, men in dark well-tailored suits, and even the head of DestinationSA stopped to sip wine by the piano on the way inside. When thoughts of the accident and Xavier arose, or the fear that his best efforts might not be enough to win April back, Connor closed his eyes, blocking out the worries along with the audience, and let the music flow through his fingers and onto the keyboard.

By the time the last guest had headed inside, the back of Connor's suit felt hot enough to fry an egg, the bare skin on his neck tingled with sunburn and his fingers were trembling from the exertion. Connor mightn't have been able to fix the rock wall in time, but the diversion had been worth every minute of his discomfort.

23

April looked from the ocean to Beachport's foreshore rotunda, where swimmers were towelling off after their morning dip, parents were laying out picnic rugs and bather-clad children were huddled in groups beside coloured flags and swimming instructors. The week since New Year's Eve had passed quickly.

'Lucky we're not in a hurry, those queues are out of control,' said Lauren, scanning the busy foreshore and the crowded jetty cafe. The small seaside village was bustling with holidaymakers cluttering the streets.

'I'll grab the donuts if you get the coffee?' April suggested. She watched Lauren dodging children on bicycles and pedestrians with fishing rods as she crossed the road.

Zipping up her jacket, April led Mishka towards the rotunda and the iconic Lions Club donut van. The line was peppered with tourists and locals alike, all eager for a bag of warm, sugary donuts on the chilly summer's day, and from the sound of the parents lining up beside her, the sweet treats were the bargaining tool of choice for reluctant swim students.

'This one's for your brother, but as soon as your lesson's done, Denise and Karen will cook you a fresh batch, okay?'

'Nope, just one kiddo. You'll turn into a donut if you eat more than one a day.'

'Remember to use your manners and bring me back the change!'

'The joy of swimming lessons, right?' April said, casting a sympathetic smile at the father standing beside her while she waited for her donuts to cook. He looked vaguely familiar and it wasn't until he lifted the small girl from his shoulders and stooped to hand her a ten dollar note that April recognised him.

Hadn't Jean mentioned a great-nephew? April had run away too quickly on New Year's Eve before the consummate match-maker could fully pitch her latest proposition but she was sure this was the bloke helping Jean with her coffee van.

'I'll never forget the freezing summers when we had to do swimming lessons—rain, hail or shine. I see the point in teaching kids to read the sea from a young age, but I'd be stuffed without bribery to sweeten the deal.'

'You're Jean's nephew, Jack? I'm April.'

He gave her a shrewd look. 'Nowhere to hide in a small town like Beachport, is there?'

April's laugh sounded foreign to herself after a miserable week moping around the winery, trying to get her head straight. 'Perhaps if your aunty wasn't Jean, you'd have a better chance at lying low. How old's this little one?'

Jack's smile softened. 'Harriet's five going on fifty. She's only been in the district a few weeks and she's already charming the socks off the locals.'

They both watched as the little girl returned with a bulging bag and change. 'Denise gave me an extra one,' she whispered with a toothy grin. 'Would you like it?' She turned her wide blue eyes on April, holding out the bag. Mishka snuffled forward, offering her services in dealing with excess donuts.

Pulling the retriever to her side, April shook her head. 'I've ordered my own, but thanks anyway,' she said, returning the girl's smile. 'Nice to meet you both.'

April watched them walking away, hand in hand, before her name was called to collect her order.

'See, I told you sugar, salt air and sunshine would be just the ticket. You're smiling more already,' Lauren said with satisfaction, handing her a takeaway cup of coffee and sitting down on the sand beside her.

April pointed out Jack and Harriet. 'I'm not sure why Jean thought I'd be ready for a package deal. I can barely control this Heffalump,' she said, patting Mishka's head, 'let alone a five-year-old.'

Lauren shaded her eyes and squinted in their direction. 'She was right on the handsome stakes, though. His kid's just as cute as him.'

April elbowed her gently. 'I'll tell Fergus that, will I?'

'Nothing wrong with looking, my friend, and I'm not sure Fergus and I are the perfect match after all.'

'What?' Her friend had stayed at the winemaker's cottage more nights than not since New Year's, but April had assumed it was to keep her company and lift her spirits. 'Was it something on your holidays? Do we hate him?' April bit her lip, mortified she'd completely missed this new development.

'We definitely *don't* hate him,' Lauren laughed. 'He's a nice bloke and I know he'll make someone happy with hordes of kilt-wearing, bagpipe-playing kids, but he's way too laid back and casual for me. I'll give it a few more weeks but I think we're better off as friends.'

'Why am I only hearing about this now?'

Lauren nudged her back good-naturedly. 'You've been a little preoccupied. Now, I know you said you didn't want to talk about it, but now you've got caffeine and sugar in your system, tell me what's happening with you and Connor. Fergus said he's as miserable as you, moping around the place with those big cow eyes. Phoebe's gone, he said he's only interested in you, and he even made you a vanilla slice, which is more than I can say for any man I've ever dated! What more do you need?'

Mishka's tail thumped on the sand as a family walked past, the children holding swirls of bright pink fairy floss on sticks. April's mind immediately leaped to Connor and Phoebe, and their wealth of New Year's Eve memories.

It had been two days since she'd received the last message from him. Six days since she'd watched him pour his heart out on the piano in the dusty winery car park under the blazing sun. The reviews had made special mention of Connor's impromptu performance, and she understood why—she hadn't been able to drag her eyes away from him either.

She had felt cowardly, watching him through the winery window and knowing the toll it must be taking on him to perform in front of an audience, and yet she'd felt too numb, too intent on keeping her carefully constructed walls in place, to acknowledge his effort. And a week later, it was taking everything she had to maintain those wavering walls that protected her heart.

'I don't know what I need,' April said truthfully. 'Surely it'll hurt less the longer I keep my head down?'

Lauren clicked her tongue, disagreeing, but before she could elaborate, a familiar towel-clad, wetsuited swimmer appeared in front of them.

'Geraldine, why doesn't it surprise me that you're one of the mad ones?' said Lauren.

Geraldine gave a cheerful laugh, reaching back to unzip her wetsuit. 'Given this sad attempt at sunshine it's probably warmer in the water than it is out,' she said, easing her shoulder from the suit. 'Hard to believe I used to be scared of the ocean.'

'I can't imagine you being scared of anything,' April said.

'I'll never be Lisa Curry-Kenny,' replied Geraldine, 'but it turns out I'm not the worst swimmer in the group and you only swim as far as you fancy, whether that's the entire length of the jetty or just to the pontoon. I suppose you're never too old to admit you were wrong, or to learn something new.'

Lauren gave April another nudge in the ribs. 'Much better than burying your head in the sand.'

'Ah, yes.' Geraldine's kind look made April's eyes prickle. 'How are you holding up? I've missed having you and Connor in the kitchen.'

April stretched out her legs on the sand, wondering if everyone on the foreshore could see that the mention of his name cut through her like a knife. She didn't miss the silent exchange between her two friends.

Lauren got to her feet, taking Mishka to the water's edge.

'I loved watching you renovate those stables, April, and I've seen how determined you were to learn how to cook once you'd got over the "I can't do this" stage, so it surprises me that you're pushing Connor away. You two were a great couple. I'd have thought that was worth fighting for.'

It wasn't anything Lauren hadn't already told her, but somehow the words held more weight coming from Geraldine.

'It's not so straightforward,' April said, looking down at the sand. 'He and Phoebe have so much history. Even though she's left, Phoebe still loves him and I've been cheated on before. I can't risk it happening again.'

'So you don't love him?'

April felt a sad smile cross her lips. 'I do,' she admitted. 'But I can't leave Lacewing Estate, and I can't ask Connor to give up his family—his entire life—on the off-chance that maybe we'll work out. It's better to treat it like a lovely fling than let myself get hurt again.'

'I find it hard to believe he'd have been unfaithful to you? You both seemed pretty invested to me?'

April kicked at a clump of seaweed, avoiding Geraldine's intent gaze. She didn't have a mixing bowl or an apron to hide behind here, nor did she have the tugging, wriggling distraction of Mishka to focus on. Connor had made it clear in his text messages that nothing had happened between him and Phoebe, but still . . .

'For what it's worth, April, I think you've got a lot to offer in a relationship, in a business and in our little community. I know Archie Winklin wouldn't have a fraction of the confidence in the garden without your guidance. You prefer the horticulture and events side of vineyard work, and Connor's a gun winemaker. Imagine the type of future you two could have with that pool of talent and resources. Sounds like a recipe for winery success, if you ask me.'

April closed her eyes. It wasn't that she hadn't seen that future too—the problem was that she had, in all its technicolour glory. She'd already pictured the sunsets they'd watch together at the ten-mile beach. In her head, she'd tasted the wine they'd make, heard their brood of unruly children playing tag between the rows of grapes, and felt the warmth of his arms around her as they surveyed their place in the vines.

With a shake of her head, April opened her eyes and focused on the waves lapping at the jetty pylons. There was no one to blame, and the quicker she accepted it, the quicker she could start getting over him.

'He'll always call England home and even if Connor wanted to stay, he mightn't be able to get residency. And he's already got recruiters in the UK after him,' April said. 'I can't offer that. I spend most of my working week gardening, not winemaking, and Dad's version of retirement is being carted out of the vineyards in a casket. It'll be years before I take over, and even then . . .' She trailed off.

Geraldine gave a gentle laugh as if she could see right through April's guff. 'Do you really think Connor would only have you if your winery was an implicit part of the deal?'

April lifted one shoulder. 'Some people would consider that an attractive prospect.'

Some people, but not Connor. She knew it, and Geraldine knew it, but instead of calling her out, the older woman simply studied the ocean with a peaceful expression on her face.

Lauren wandered back with Mishka. 'You two look like you're pondering the world's problems.'

'April's just getting my two cents' worth,' Geraldine chuckled. 'Sometimes you need to put yourself first and take a risk.'

April watched the fishing boats bobbing in the distance and the dozens of children following their instructors through the waves near the shoreline. Could she trust her own heart, when she'd been so badly let down before? And even if she took Geraldine's advice, had she left it too late?

※

'What do you say to a pub lunch, Connor? I still haven't thanked you for watching the winery while Fran and I were away, not to mention doing the hard yards with those ruddy gatecrashers,' Lloyd said, emerging from the cellar on a cool, mid-January day.

Connor shook his head, knowing that the pub's finest scotch fillet steak with mushroom sauce would probably taste like cardboard in his current state. He hadn't felt like eating much, or sleeping much, over the last fortnight and his body wasn't thrilled about the mistreatment.

'I'm all good, Lloyd, thanks anyway,' he said, mustering up a smile before turning back to his work.

'You look like you could do with feeding up. How about I bring you back a pizza from the Bushman's Inn? They do a mean woodfired mushy and rocket?' Connor knew that Lloyd felt bad about the chill that had settled between him and April but try as he might, there was nothing he or Lloyd or even Fran could do. The ball was completely in April's court and although he'd stopped glancing up every time the cellar door opened, or his phone buzzed, he still held out hope that maybe she could move past their tumultuous start to the year.

Despite Connor's assurances he wasn't hungry, when Lloyd returned half an hour later he came bearing pizza and news.

'The insurance company's approved an amount for the damages to the bed and breakfast, and we've got a formal apology from the kid who organised the party. His folks are making him volunteer at the wildlife sanctuary for the rest of the summer,' said Lloyd, reading aloud from the letter. 'So he'll be knee deep in wombat and kangaroo poo, washing pouches for the joeys and possums, and mixing up milk and medicine for injured and orphaned animals.'

'Sounds like a reward, not a punishment,' Connor said, taking a slice of the pizza from the box to satisfy Lloyd. He knew Nell would auction off the family's concert trophies and her eye teeth for undivided time at a wildlife shelter.

'Says here the little bugger didn't actually invite all those yahoos. He booked the stables under a false name, no doubting that, but apparently word got out through social media and it spread like a bushfire.'

'That gels with what Heidi said too.' Connor didn't have much sympathy for the kid after the carnage at Kookaburra Cottage, but still ... He knew a thing or two about best-laid plans.

When Connor arrived at the Winklins' house later that afternoon for Archie's piano lesson, his young student was in an upbeat mood and it took several attempts to divert the conversation from Lego, lambs, a new obsession with photography, football, and the burgeoning veggie patch before he settled enough to play.

'Try that piece again, Arch,' said Connor, flipping the sheet music back to the start. When he looked up next, Rupert was leaning against the doorframe.

'You're nailing it, mate,' Rupert said. Archie spun around, basking in the praise, and played it again, more confidently this time. *They've come a long way, these two,* Connor thought, pleased to see them more comfortable in one another's presence.

'Hey, Con?' Archie said when Rupert had gone back to his office. 'Wanna come see the lambs when we're done? They're all penned up for shearing. I can show you how the veggie patch is going too if you've got time?'

Connor was touched by the invitation. It would be better than rattling around the winery after dark or feeling like a third wheel at the golf course rental. Not that Fergus and Lauren ever made him feel unwelcome—they'd been more than understanding about his moping—but there was a funny vibe between them recently and the fishing shows Fergus was now obsessed with evoked too many memories of their trip to the ten-mile beach and his night in the dunes with April.

'Lead the way, Arch.'

They headed outside into the late afternoon, where the sun was trying its best to shine through the clouds. From the ants marching across the limestone gravel and the cockies shrieking in the trees, Archie deduced it would rain overnight.

'Mishka always knows when there's thunder on the way, too. The moment she scurries under the garden shed, you can tell there's a storm coming.'

Connor had only been to the Winklins' shearing shed once before, when lamb marking was underway, but he was pretty sure the fairy lights adorning the outside of the shed were a new addition.

'The shearing shed's all glammed up. Don't tell me your dad's onto the long lunches bandwagon?' He hated to think what that type of venue rivalry would mean for Lacewing Estate.

Archie's eyes darted to the fairy lights and then back to him. 'Um, it's a good distraction for the lambs when we're shearing and crutching.'

Connor laughed, only ninety per cent sure Archie was taking the mickey as he climbed the worn timber steps. It hadn't been a hot week but he could imagine how warm the shed would be inside with dozens of sheep and a team of shearers, wool classers and roustabouts.

A ute pulled up alongside the shearing shed just as they reached the heavy tin sliding door. Daniel leaned out the window. 'Jump in Archie, I need a hand for five minutes.'

'Just give the door a good pull, Con, I'll be back soon,' said Archie with a grin, ducking under Connor's arm. His boots clattered as he took the steps two at a time.

With a wave and a toot, Dan and Archie disappeared down the driveway, leaving a perplexed Connor standing outside the shearing shed door. With a shrug, he slid the door open, but instead of penned sheep and shearing prep, there was a tablecloth over the wool-classing table, set with candles and a feast.

'Wow!' Connor turned slowly to appreciate the rustic charm. Fairy lights hung from the dark timber beams, Duke Ellington played on a small stereo, and vases of gum leaves were dotted around the vast space.

'Do you like it?'

Looking over his shoulder, Connor was lost for words. April wore a red evening gown that dipped at the bust and flared at the knees, her long, dark hair pinned up on top of her head. And although high heels would have been the normal accompaniment for such a show-stopping gown, instead she wore a pair of R.M. Williams boots.

Connor dug his fingernails into his palm, certain he was imagining things. But when he looked down at the half-crescent marks in his hand, and then back up again, she was still there, looking as beautiful as ever, with the shearing shed looking like a scene from 'Farmer Wants a Wife' and the candlelight bringing out the caramel tones in her dark hair.

'I love every bit of it,' he said quietly. 'Especially the woman standing there in the R.M.s.'

She clasped her hands together and noticed they were shaking. 'I'm sorry it's taken me so long, Connor. It's been a lot to get my head around.'

Stepping closer, he nodded, aching for her to skip to the part he hoped was coming next.

'It doesn't matter,' he said. 'You're here, I'm here and I'm really hoping this all,' he lifted his hands, gesturing at the rustic shed around them, 'means we're going to be okay.'

Reaching for his hand, April slid her fingers between his. 'I came so close to losing everything that night, Connor. Kookaburra Cottage, the long lunch gig, our relationship. I know that, logically, the only reason everything didn't fall apart was because of you.' She managed a shaky breath, her eyes clouding with anguish. 'But I was scared, Con. I didn't mean to put my walls up again, especially after everything you did to convince me otherwise, but it felt like the safe choice.'

April paused. 'I need to know that you're not leaving Australia the minute your visa expires and that you're sure of how you feel, for me *and* for Phoebe. Can you see a long-term future for the two of us, here in the Limestone Coast?'

It was a question he'd considered many times in the last few months and he already knew the answer. 'I was hoping you'd ask me that,' he said, holding her eye. 'I love you, April, and I'd like that very, very much.'

A slow smile crossed her lips. She ducked her head, then looked back up at him. 'Then, if you'll still have me, I'm ready to jump in, boots and all.'

Things once again felt right in the world when April leaned into him, one hand on his chest while the other tugged him closer, nuzzling into his neck.

'I'm more than ready,' Connor replied, gently lifting her chin until their lips collided. His hands skimmed the silky fabric around her waist, reacquainting him with the curves of her body, and their tender kiss deepened.

A knock came at the sliding door and they reluctantly pulled apart.

'Delivery for Miss Lacey and Mr Jamison,' called Archie, sliding open the door and slipping an esky through the gap. 'Over and out.' His boots clattered down the steps again, followed by the sound of Daniel's ute leaving, and then it was just the two of them with the jazz playing softly.

'I roped in a few helpers,' April admitted. 'Though the cooking's all mine, and while I'm not sure the dessert can beat your amazing vanilla slice, it's made with love. Shall we?'

Still holding his hand, April carried the esky to the table. Inside, there was a mound of mixed berries and peaches on a bed of cream and a white crusty base.

'My very first pavlova, made under the extremely watchful eye of Geraldine. It was the most iconic Aussie dish I could think of,' she said, suddenly shy again. 'It might be terrible. But I can vouch for the quiches, sausage rolls and muffins.'

He looked at the table as she set down the pavlova, recognising their favourite dishes from the cooking classes. 'You'd best not tell Jean about all this; she'll throw in the towel if she realises people are capable of grand romantic gestures without her influence.'

April laughed, a sound he wanted to hear again and again and again until they were old and grey.

24

Three months later

April put a bookmark in her novel and turned her face up to the sun. After a quiet morning in the garden, and a quick cleaning session between guests, she had been happy to spend the afternoon in the hammock under the flowering gum trees with a book in hand, Mishka at her feet and Connor by her side.

And given the intensity of vintage, during which Connor's days and nights had been consumed with harvesting the grapes at just the right time, then wrangling the team of pickers and helping her father get everything into the tanks, it felt like a luxury to have a free weekend.

The hammock rocked as Connor reached for his water bottle. 'This is exactly what I needed today,' he said, taking a sip and passing it to her. 'I get the feeling next weekend will be a little different. How many entries have you got planned again?'

April stretched, feeling sated by sunshine, and rattled off the categories she was entering in next weekend's Penwarra Show.

'Everything that's growing nicely will make it onto the produce tables, of course,' she said, not missing his raised eyebrows.

'Of course,' he agreed with a grin, 'and how about the baking? Think we can top last year's shockers?'

'I know we can,' April said, snuggling into his side. The cooler weather had well and truly settled in and it wouldn't be long before they'd be lighting the wood fires inside the winemaker's cottage and Kookaburra Cottage. 'Fran's efforts to fill the tables seem to be going well this year. Last I heard, Fergus and Lauren were going head-to-head in the scone department. I don't envy Fergus; Lauren always plays to win. Did you see her latest Insta posts?'

Lauren had been given looser rein on the radio station's social media pages, profiling dozens of Penwarra Show devotees, from volunteers and committee members to entrants young and old. Between the radio promotions and word of mouth, all signs pointed towards an extraordinary weekend.

'Yep, and she's got Archie a spot on the breakfast show this Wednesday,' Connor said, swinging his legs over the side of the hammock and stretching. 'Speaking of which, he'll be here any minute to check on his pumpkin. It'll take three of us to lift the thing into the ute on show day, especially if it grows another five kilos like last week.'

Connor held out his hands to April. She took them, stealing a kiss before slipping her boots back on. They wandered hand in hand to the vegetable patch. Classical music was floating on the breeze, thanks to Archie, who was convinced it would help the giant pumpkin grow faster.

'Judging by the size of the thing, the music therapy's working,' said April, waving to their young neighbour as he trotted down the laneway. She left Connor and Archie to inspect the pumpkin, and went inside to set about making a batch of strawberry muffins.

The specks of strawberries and white chocolate chips—one of her new variations—looked picture perfect in the pink ceramic mixing bowl Fran had bought her for Christmas. April shuffled a pot plant beside the bowl and snapped a photo for her social media.

> Baking underway for tonight's guests at Kookaburra Cottage! Don't forget, the B & B is stocked with picnic supplies, so you can share a muffin and a glass of wine amongst the autumn colours in the vineyard with wallabies hopping past, or spread the rug out in the manicured cottage gardens with the scent of fresh herbs and blooms in the air. #livingthedream #winecountry #minibreak

Once the muffins were in the oven, and the post uploaded to Instagram, April glanced out the window. It was hard to believe that this time last year, Connor had only just moved to Penwarra, and she hadn't the foggiest idea of how to cook, let alone bake for guests at her very own bed and breakfast. She smiled as she watched him gardening with Archie, as if there was nowhere else they'd rather be on a Saturday afternoon. Connor looked up and caught her eye, giving her one of those winks that made her stomach flip-flop.

'Love you,' she said through the window, her smile deepening as he mouthed the words back to her. April turned the muffins out onto the cooling rack and glanced at the clock. The new guests were due in an hour, and apart from a Zoom call with Connor's family back home, they had the rest of the weekend free to potter around the property, perfect their show entries, and maybe even take a trip to the beach.

She lined a basket with a linen tea towel, loaded the baked goodies into it, and carried the tray with the three remaining muffins to the door.

'Any taste testers available?'

Archie scrambled to his feet, dusting the dirt from his hands and knees, then rushing to wash his hands under the tap while Connor leaned against the pergola. His eyes did a lazy sweep from her boots to her apron, meeting her gaze with an appreciative look.

'Ready and willing,' he said, his face breaking into a broad grin.

Connor shifted the laptop so both he and April could see the screen. The dial tone sounded, and before he knew it, he was gazing at his father's face.

'Hiya,' Connor said, looping an arm around April's shoulders. 'Have we missed Mam's cake?'

'We've just found the candles, haven't we girls?' said Jock.

The screen panned across to show Nell and Pippin in the kitchen, with Heidi rifling through the pantry behind them. 'Where on earth are the matches?' she asked.

Sharyn dashed down the corridor, waving as she steered Heidi in the right direction. It was a scene so familiar, so comforting, that he couldn't imagine it ever changing.

'We love the jumpers, Con,' Pippin called, twirling around so they could see the wombat-themed branding on the back of her hoodie.

'They're for a great cause,' Connor said, explaining they'd visited the wildlife sanctuary in Mount Gambier after an invitation from the New Year's Eve party-planner. The remorseful teenager had signed up to continue his volunteer role, and after apologising yet again for the mayhem he caused at April's property and giving them a tour of the facility, he'd made such a great sales pitch for the merchandise that they had purchased two jumpers for the girls, plus one for Archie.

April bent her head closer. 'Happy birthday, Sharyn. And did you like the earrings?'

Connor's mother leaned into the camera, nodding her head so the earrings flashed in the light. 'Absolutely brilliant, April. Nobody in Derby will have Australian sea glass earrings, I'd wager. We can't wait to see the coastline with our own eyes, though. September can't come fast enough. We're already looking at flights, did Connor tell you?'

Connor felt April nodding beside him. 'That's such great news, I'm looking forward to meeting you all properly.'

'Can we go to the wildlife shelter too, Con? I want to cuddle a baby joey,' Nell said.

'I'm pretty sure we can arrange that,' he replied. Heidi appeared onscreen with a candlelit cake in her hands, and April and Connor joined in for the chorus of happy birthday before signing off.

'They seem pretty excited about their trip,' April said, moving to the kitchen and flicking on the kettle for one last cup of tea before bed. 'Maybe we could move into Kookaburra Cottage for a week and they can all stay here?'

He looked up from the laptop and beamed at April across the room. 'That's a great idea.'

Connor's inbox pinged and he skimmed the email.

Dear Mr Jamison,

Re: Application for residency in Australia

Thank you for your query about our legal services regarding immigration. Congratulations on taking the first step in the journey. We pride ourselves in making this process as seamless as possible for our clients, so please see below the links to all the information you will need ahead of our initial meeting.

In response to your background, I can confirm that someone with your qualifications and experience is indeed a solid fit for the skilled migration program. We look forward to speaking with you in person soon.

Connor shut down the program with a single click, feeling more excited about the future than he could have ever imagined. A clever, funny and creative woman by his side, a community that had welcomed him with open arms, and a place in the vines. He was pretty sure it didn't get much better than that.

Acknowledgements

Writing this novel felt a lot like coming home. Although my first four books were set in the western districts of Victoria, where I've lived for much of my adult life, *Kookaburra Cottage* takes us to South Australia, my home state, and the beautiful Limestone Coast, where I grew up.

Throughout the story, you may notice I've used a mix of real place names and events, as well as fictional locations, characters and scenarios.

When I started brainstorming ideas for this novel, I knew I wanted to pay homage to the glorious local wineries, the hard-working grape-growing families and the beautiful terra rossa soil that produces some of Australia's finest wines. April Lacey first found her way onto the page, in the very first scene of the very first draft, one blustery day in 2021. I was nervous about spending my days with an entirely new leading lady (after four books with Diana, Lara, Penny and Angie McIntyre), but the moment April chased someone else's rubbish in the wind, I knew we'd be able to work together.

It's no secret, dear readers, that this writing gig is a nerve-wracking leap into the unknown. No matter how many novels I write, the first few chapters (and sometimes the first few drafts) of each book can feel like a dodgy blind date. I start with nothing but an idea, spend months at the keyboard trying to work out whether or not I like the settings, the characters, their occupations and their nicknames, and persist until the characters and I are firm friends. This book went in a gazillion different directions before I finally nailed it down. It taught me about patience and determination and the importance of telling stories that are close to the heart.

It was also a chance to shine a spotlight on country shows. Agricultural shows have always been part of my life, from entering the flower and handwriting categories as a little girl to the thrill of sideshow alley and fireworks as a teenager, and now as an enthusiastic baker and flower grower and mother of three keen show-goers. The local show has always been a highlight of the year for our family, and I'm endlessly grateful to the organisers, volunteers, stewards, committees and societies that keep these events running. Special mention must go to my lovely neighbour Heather, whose passion for keeping the baking tables stocked is an ongoing inspiration.

Those local to Penola and Coonawarra in South Australia will know I've taken liberties by shifting show day from spring to autumn, and I've modelled much of the action on the Tyrendarra Show, in Victoria—especially the beloved scarecrow competition. I've also let my imagination run wild with my fictional take on the Penola Golf Course, though I can picture quite clearly in my mind the bustling Friday nights and piano lessons at the club house, Fergus and Connor's little rental and Geraldine's neighbouring cooking school.

April's home is loosely based on a cottage set in the middle of a vineyard in Coonawarra. If you're driving along the Riddoch Highway and catch a glimpse of a quaint two-storey, paddock-rock cottage, then I hope you'll think of April, Connor and Mishka, and all the winemakers who may have lived there over the years. Archie and his Houdini-like lambs were inspired by several stints raising orphan lambs on our hobby farm, and I chose Derby, UK, as Connor's hometown to honour my mum's English heritage.

As I mention in every novel, my name is on the cover, but it wouldn't be possible without plenty of helping hands. Firstly, a huge thanks to my publisher Annette Barlow, editors Samantha Kent and Tessa Feggans, proofreader Megan Johnston, publicist Bella Breden, cover designer Nada Backovic and the entire team at Allen & Unwin for their support, commitment and shared vision. They are the cheerleaders, the invisible menders and the midwives at the birth of this book and I love working with them!

Big thanks to Victoria Leeke for letting me run through a bunch of winery scenarios and questions, Tracy Jenson for sharing her family's rent-a-row vineyard experience and the Wine Unearthed Podcast for a lot of great insights into wineries. While the podcast featured Margaret River businesses, the level of detail about vineyards, passionate producers and winery processes was super helpful. I also listened to The Wine Show podcast, with plenty of Coonawarra content. Thanks to Treloar Roses for information about British rose grafters working at local rose farms. This sub-plot didn't make it to the final draft, but I have filed it away for a future book!

Thanks to Ber Carroll and Petronella McGovern for sharing a tale about SnapMaps, Robyn Holcombe for helping me with golf lingo, Fiona Lowe for a snippet on piano terminology, Myra from Warrnambool Book Club for the quote 'old enough to know better and young enough to do it again,' my writing buddy Kaneana May for being a sounding board throughout the process, my Zoom writing buddies at

'Not So Solitary Scribes' for talking shop (and writing) on Friday mornings, and my dark o'clock walking buddy Karena Prevett, who always gives the best advice on everything.

To my family—I appreciate all the support, inspiration, suggestions, babysitting, promotion and problem-solving you offered when I was drafting, writing, editing, celebrating, touring and tearing my hair out (sometimes all on the very same day!). I will always be endlessly grateful for your love.

For Jase, my real-life hero. Thanks for believing in me (and April and Connor), especially when I didn't! I wouldn't be able to keep doing this author gig without your love, encouragement, cups of tea and problem-solving skills.

To my three not-so-little bookworms—Charles, Amelia and Elizabeth—I'm delighted that you're still happy being swept along in this publishing whirl, attending launch events, getting excited about covers and bookmarks and stepping up to the plate when I'm on deadline. I couldn't be any prouder. As I mentioned in the dedication, my daughters deserve extra-special mention for suggesting the book title and the tortoises, and helping me flesh out a difficult plot point. Their names will be on a cover soon, at this rate!

And finally to the readers, booksellers, podcasters, library staff, fellow authors, book clubs, journalists, bloggers, reviewers and media outlets who advocate for Australian authors. Thank you, thank you, thank you. I love hearing from you, seeing photos of you holding my novels and your word-of-mouth recommendations and reviews. Your willingness to invest in my writing and enthusiasm for my stories keep me returning to my desk day after day.

Love,

Maya

For a regular dose of country living, recipes, lamb spam, giveaways and author interviews, join Maya's newsletter community or find her online:

@maya.linnell.writes
@maya.linnell.writes
www.mayalinnell.com

I